SOLARIS
RISING

THE NEW SOLARIS BOOK
OF SCIENCE FICTION

EDITED BY
IAN WHATES

SOLARIS RISING

THE NEW SOLARIS BOOK OF SCIENCE FICTION

EDITED BY
IAN WHATES

INCLUDING STORIES BY

Ian McDonald

Dave Hutchinson

Paul di Filippo

Ken MacLeod

Tricia Sullivan

Stephen Baxter

Stephen Palmer

Adam Roberts

Lavie Tidhar

Jack Skillingstead

Mike Resnick and Laurie Tom

Steve Rasnic Tem

Ian Watson

Pat Cadigan

Richard Salter

Jaine Fenn

Keith Brooke and Eric Brown

Alastair Reynolds

Peter F. Hamilton

SOLARIS

First published 2011 by Solaris
an imprint of Rebellion Publishing Ltd,
Riverside House, Osney Mead,
Oxford, OX2 0ES, UK

www.solarisbooks.com

ISBN: 978 1 907992 09 4

Cover Art by Pye Parr

10 9 8 7 6 5 4 3 2 1

A CIP catalogue record for this book is available from the British Library.

Designed & typeset by Rebellion Publishing

Printed in the US

CONTENTS

INTRODUCTION

IAN WHATES

WHEN JONATHAN OLIVER approached me with the idea of reviving the *Solaris Book of New SF* series of anthologies, I was both flattered and thrilled. I still recall how excited I was when the very first in the series came out. The book, compiled and edited by George Mann, boasted a fabulous line-up of authors and proved to contain an equally impressive set of stories. I immediately resolved to try and have something of mine appear in a future volume (an ambition I realised in Vol 3). The opportunity to do justice to the tradition of quality established by George is a challenge that I've relished.

I love short stories, both to read and to write. A good short story provides a quick, sharp fix, almost instant gratification when compared to the slow burn of a novel, and its writing requires a skill in world-building and character development which is quite different from that demanded by the longer format, where the writer has so much more scope and time. I thought very carefully before sending out a call for submissions, approaching only authors I knew to be capable of delivering effective work within the strictures of the short story. This meant, inevitably, that I was approaching some of the busiest men and women in the industry. It came as no surprise, therefore, when not all of them were able to participate, which is why at the outset I contacted enough talented wordsmiths to fill two books. Thankfully, many responded with enthusiasm and were able to somehow squeeze the requisite writing time from their schedules. I ended up with enough high quality submissions that I've been forced to make a few tough choices, turning away some very good pieces by authors whose work I've long admired... But what a great situation for an editor to be in.

Something I should perhaps make clear; I've produced a number of themed anthologies in recent years, both through my own NewCon Press and in the Mammoth titles I've co-edited with Ian Watson. Just to say upfront that this isn't one of them. Those readers looking for a theme will, I fear, search in vain.

Science fiction is a very broad church – which perhaps goes some way to explaining why there are so many different interpretations of precisely what the conjunction of those two words means. SF touches on many other literary fields and contains any number of subgenres and tropes. A succinct definition guaranteed to satisfy everyone is nigh on impossible. *That* is what I wanted to represent with this book. Not highlight one flavour of SF but rather reflect its boundless variety, the energy and imagination that can carry science fiction in so many fascinating and entertaining directions. I don't claim for one moment that the selection here is definitive. Doubtless some will read *Solaris Rising* and note the absence of this type of SF or that, which just goes to show how diverse our genre is. No single volume could ever hope to encompass every nuance of the field. My ambition with *Solaris Rising* is rather to present a piquant tasting platter, a veritable smorgasbord representing some of the very best science fiction around at the moment. Both humour and darkness inhabit the collection, exotic environments cosy up to familiar elements imbued with a novel twist and the strange shadows the known; but above all you will find original thought and *story*.

Here it is then: *Solaris Rising*, the revival of *The Solaris Book of New Science Fiction* (now cunningly rejigged as *The New Solaris Book of Science Fiction*). I hope you enjoy.

Ian Whates
June 2011

A SMART WELL-MANNERED UPRISING OF THE DEAD

IAN MCDONALD

Ian McDonald lives just outside Belfast and sold his first story back in 1983. In his day job he works in development for Northern Ireland's largest independent television production company. His most recent book, The Dervish House *(Gollancz, Pyr), won the BSFA Award for best novel and the John W Campbell Memorial Award for 2011, as well as being nominated for the Arthur C Clarke Award and the Hugo. He's into the second volume of his YA(-ish) Everness series, and volume 1,* Planesrunner, *is out from Pyr in December 2011.*

I AM FELIX Cofie Addy and I am a dead man. I have been a dead man for three years, five months and twelve days. It was the cigarettes. Never start them, you young people. So I am dead, and I am aggrieved. Oh yes, mightily aggrieved. What for are you aggrieved, I hear you think. You're dead; grievances and aggravations are over for you. Pull the red earth over you, sleep. Do not trouble yourself. Why, what do you think we are, us dead men? You think we sit around on our stools all day waiting to become pure and clear as gin? I tell you, the first aggravation is being dead at all. That is the firm foundation on which the other aggravations rest, and they are many. What aggrieves me? FC Maamobi's atrocious last season. That defending would aggrieve anyone. The price of rice and flour and cooking oil at Maxmart. That aggrieves me. I have heard that children go hungry to school. How will they learn if they are hungry? They need brain food. We are not a hungry nation. We never have been. Yes, that aggrieves me much. The state of the potholes on the Kanda highway: it was more hole than highway even before I became a dead man. The price of diesel at the Shell Station on Nima Road. The fuel for the Maxmart trucks goes up, Maxmart puts its prices up, the City Council can't afford to fix the potholes. What for? We have oil. We are a wealthy country. We are proud and independent. But what aggrieves me most is you, Minister Raymond Kufuor. We have oil, we have wealth, we have independence and you are the man in charge of it, so tell me Mr Raymond Kufuor, why are there holes in our highways you could lose a pig in? Where is the money, Minister? Tell a dead man that.

YES YES YES, it's me, Felix Cofie Addy. Again. What for have you disturbed me from my death? I cannot sleep, my deep bed is full of spiders and on my stool my bones ache as if they are poking through my skin and I itch; the kind of itch you can never reach. Can you not see the wrong of this? I have worked moderately hard and attained some success. I have raised a family and I am content enough as a dead man. Can you then understand how annoying it is to find that I am still aggrieved? Things have not been done. Issues have not been addressed. Questions have not been answered. Just yesterday the Shell Station on Nima Road put five cedis on a litre of gasoline. I may be a dead man, but I know that Akron Kufuor who drives for Excelsior Taxis is having to work an extra two hours a shift to be able to pay for the price rise – and that is when he gets a fare at all. People are cutting back! Holes in the road, holes in the shoes, holes in the children's clothes. Rice and oil! Yet what do I see with my dead eye but Agriculture Minister Kofi Mensah entertaining the Chinese agricultural delegation at a reception at his own private villa? I would not begrudge a minister of the government of this great country his marble and his swimming pool because both are cooling and necessary in the heat. But a cousin of a cousin tells me that the contract for the catering went to Superb Chefs, owned by, who other than, yes, Minister Kofi Mensah. And cousin's cousin Abena should know. She works for Superb Chefs. Graft and corruption! See, I'm not afraid to accuse. We are the dead, you cannot touch us and there are many many of us, in our comfortable little houses, on our stools and chairs and at out our tables with the things we loved at our feet. We are many many voices. Yes yes yes.

SO, I'M BACK, and are you glad to see me? Are you? You know, a boy's got expectations. You come home after six months working up on the sun plants with those Algerians who think they're better than you a dozen different ways, no beer and less fun, and you expect, well, maybe not a parade, maybe not the whole street turning out with goats and chickens and kids on bikes and the soundsystem and all that, but some kind of welcome. Six months, every Saturday transferring money back here; I like the plasma screen, those are very smart smartphones, and how could I begrudge my own brother that funky little Chinese moped but, people, I am not a sorcerer. This is Azumah, come home from working away, so why do you think he's some kind of evil necromancer?

So, Dad has started speaking. I can see how that might cause alarm. In all the years he sat in that corner in his chair, smoking like a chimney, I only ever heard him speak three words and that was when FC Maamobi was relegated and those were not pretty words. In fact, on word count alone, he's said more dead than alive. But it's not me putting words in his mouth. It's not me making the dead speak. But it *is* me getting the looks on the street and down at the Maxmart, and the people leaning close to each other and whispering.

I may have been up on construction in Algeria for six months but I know what's going on here, I read the news, I keep in touch with family and friends, but you're the ones closest to it, you're the ones living it. You're the ones see the money walking, the funds drying up, the hospitals going unbuilt and the oil people slopping money around like fish in a bucket. I tell you this, it may be big Western companies building those solar plants out in the desert, but sun is never dirty like oil. Do you hear what I'm saying? I'm the least qualified to make Felix Cofie grumble about the state of the nation. And I'm disappointed that everyone thinks it's me being disrespectful to the dead. After all I've done. No, no, I'll get to the bottom of this. I'll redeem my good name. I'm no sorcerer, Azumah Addy is no necromancer.

But d'you know? I'm glad the old man's doing it.

I AM GRACE Ahulu and I too am dead. I also have a complaint. I have many complaints, a lot of which have no relevance here. Here's how I died: my heart stopped on the way to church and down I went in the street with my Bible going up in the air. The cardiac ambulance came but they could do nothing except take me away. It's a good way to go, it was quick and it only hurt for a moment and I was happy that I was on my way to church. I love it there very much, all my brothers and sisters in Christ.

Now, I can hear what you're thinking. How can you, a respectable lady washed in the blood and a one-time choir member as well, be with the Lord in heaven and in some terrible pagan Satanic house of demons and unbelievers? Well, if Pastor Nathaniel's Bible Study is true, we do not go straight to heaven, but only on the Day of Judgement when we are called from our graves and appear before Christ where we see our names written in the Book of Life. Then we are admitted to the realms of glory. Until then we sleep, and if we sleep, we dream – it is as obvious as day. And, if we dream, can we not dream usefully?

So: I am dead in the Lord, but I have a complaint, and it's this. Since when is it more important that we feed Chinese mouths than our own? Since when do Shanghai children come before our own children? Yet the government is signing over hundreds – no, thousands – of hectares of land, selling off our land, – your land, my land – to Chinese agriculture companies. And they guard these plantations with armed guards, and security cameras, and robot drones. And who are these guards, and who flies the drones, but our own men and boys. They're carrying guns against their own people! And who works this land, but the very people who were put off it by the big business! The very same land! Oh, I can't understand that. They work the land, for wages, to buy expensive food they could have grown in their own fields, and sold it, and made money. Where is the logic in that? I suppose the logic is that some Minister gets a kickback, and the money goes all the way down, hand to hand to hand. Shameful! Sinful. I tell you this, it's worth putting off the imminent hope of heaven to address such wrong on Earth!

(*Vision* magazine, Issue 27, May 2019)

The Ghost Machine

*Obo Quartey is the Maamobi man who built
a heaven – and made a million cedis.*

Welcome to the afterlife. Here the deceased live in personalised spirit-houses, each one built to their tastes and characters. They sit on stools, around their heads are photographs of the things they did in life, their work, their friends, their children and grandchildren, their cousins and loved ones, thousands of them. At their feet are the things they loved in life: clothes, bottles of beer, cars, make-up, pictures of footballers or fishing lines or books, guitars or dancing shoes. But most of all, there is money, spirit-money, billions in ghostly afterlife cash. It's not exactly how we think of heaven. But then it's not quite hell either. Teshie, the online afterlife where hundreds of thousands – soon to be millions, hopes Obo Quartey, the online afterlife's director – of memories of the dead are stored – is more like a noisy, overcrowded Unplanned Neighbourhood of a bustling city.

Obo Quartey is terrifyingly young and competent; dressed in the relaxed yet smart style of the modern digital entrepreneur – an open neck shirt, top label jeans, well-shined hand-made shoes. It's a very long way from Maamobi, the neighbourhood where he was born (he claims, with pride) in a thunderstorm on the first Friday of the 21st century. But, he insists, not so long. Teshie is still headquartered in the district, in the same area as the computer cafe where local people formed the computer co-operative that gave fourteen year-old Obo his first data-work. Maamobi's red dirt streets are the soil from which his online empire grew.

"Everyone goes on and on about Moore's Law." (This is a so-called 'law' of computing that every six months processor power doubles and the cost halves.) "What no one's thinking about is that the real revolution is in memory. You can get a flash drive the size of your thumb that's big enough to hold the entire University Library, for the price of a bag of rice. So, here's this kid tagging these photographs for this white woman in Ohio, but what he's really thinking is, I'm using one gig on this computer and a tiny corner of my brilliant brain, but down there at my feet is a terabyte of memory, just sitting there, doing nothing. Empty. Well, you know what this country's like, leave anything empty and someone will move into it."

Quartey's first micro-business was Lawbase, a data storage facility for digitising and archiving thirty years of court cases and legal documents. So how did he move from dry-as-dust legal archiving to an online afterlife?

"I got commissioned to design a simple website for Fantasy Coffins," Quartey says. "You know the sort of thing; Mercedes for businessmen, aeroplanes for travellers, hawks and eagles if you're a big man, computers if you're a geek. Beautiful things. They build them right sweet. Westerners put them in museums. It's a way of keeping the memory alive, by surrounding the dead with the things they loved in life; the things that defined them. And that got me to thinking, maybe there are other ways of keeping memories alive? More alive? What if there was a place, online, where you could put all the photographs, and all the videos you shot on your phone, and the press clippings and the phone messages and the recordings and all the things your family did, so that when they die, they don't fade away? They're all there in one place, and you can go and look at them, and remember them, and even add to them?"

It's become much more than that, with Quartey's company adding new features, like the ability to buy online gifts and offerings to the departed, and donations of Teshie-dollars – virtual cash, and most recently, the feature that allows subscribers to design fantasy houses for the deceased.

"What can I say? I'm a businessman. I'm led by the market. The market is eight hundred and fifty thousand Teshie subscribers and growing every day. Those subscribers are buying the spirit-houses, the Teshie-dollars. I tell you this, every day we get comments and emails and phone calls and, yes, sometimes even old fashioned letters, with new ideas."

In a rare display of inter-religious unity, both Christian pastors and Islamic imams have denounced Teshie as pagan and ungodly. Quartey is unimpressed.

"It's no different from keeping photographs on the shelf, or a box of newspaper cuttings under the bed," he says. "It's not an afterlife. It's a virtual environment. It's Facebook for the dead. All I've done is recognise something about us as people that the established religions haven't. We're a country that honours our ancestors. I've just given them a way to do it." He laughs. "But if that gets the clerics phoning each other, wait until they see what I want to do next." He waits a moment for effect. "What if I give them voices?"

WHAT? WHAT ARE you saying? This I cannot believe – and I will not accept. Who do you think you are, storming round here this time of night? Can't you see I've got work to do? Work that involves beer tins, and television? That's you; that always was you, you always think that because I'm a student I never do a stroke of work. We just sit around in the sun drinking beer and staring at television and watching the country go to hell in a handcart. Well, just you look over here. Tell me, what you see? Yeah. That's right. You don't get to be an economist drinking beer and staring at television, and as for the watching the country go to hell in a handcart, it's economists like me who're going to bring it back to the way it used to be, when everyone looked up to us. You're my brother but you make assumptions, Azumah, you make assumptions. I am not a parent abuser.

Moderate your tone. Calm down. Come out with me for coffee. There is a new place. It's good. There are lots of good looking women. Yes, they're students.

See, told you it was good. Now, let us be rational men here, brothers together. Listen to me. I am not putting words in our grandfather's mouth. Let me say that again so there can be no doubt. It is not me making Felix Cofie sound off on the Teshie-net. I'm glad he's doing it. I tell you this, things are bad if even the dead are complaining about them. You see, you don't know the half of it, up there in the Maghrib. You see those people down in Independence Square on the news and the police throwing tear gas and going in with the sticks and the shields and the helmets and you think, what's that about? I'll tell you what it's about. Corruption. That oil is ours, not Raymond Kufuor's. And he and his cronies are using that oil, that money – our money – to build a big shiny tower to take them right out of reach. A whole generation is being shut out of power.

Oh they're not so stupid as to close the whole internet down like those Arabs – the economy needs all those e-workers too much and it starts the Americans and the Europeans squawking like chickens – no, they're subtle. You let through a little grumble here, a little gossip there, a little complain and a little gripe, but you hide all the big stuff. That's the clever way to do it. I've been out, Azumah. I've been down to Independence Square. I've seen what it's like. I've been chased. The cops charged us, the bastards. They didn't beat me, thank the Lord, but they had this stuff they sprayed – no, it wasn't tear gas, it was like a powder, but it didn't burn like pepper spray. It got everywhere. We all looked like big white ghosts. I heard it's some new thing they got from China – millions of tiny electronic chips each the size of a dust grain. They can track you, they can identify you. No, they don't do anything like sling you in the back of the van. They're clever; they just shut down your credit, they blacklist your name so you never get a good job, you never get access to money, you never get a loan to start a business, you never get your head out of Maamobi. Azumah, that's much scarier. I've been showering. Twice a day, every day. I am the cleanest economist at Legon University.

And Dad's protesting? He's getting up on his stool and sounding off all these lamentations and lampoons? Hey hey. I wish it was me – that's the way to do it. They may try and silence us, but you can't threaten the dead. No, it's not me. But I think I have an idea who it might be, someone a little physically closer, you know what I mean?

YES YES YES. Again Felix Cofie finds it necessary to sit up and shake his stick. The impertinent dead? Is that what Justice Minister Kwame Charles Damoah called us? Mischief makers and anti-social elements? I will tell you who are the mischief-makers: Kwame Charles Damoah, Kofi Mensah, Raymond Kufuor, the men who each personally made a million cedis from the West Ga land sale. Our land, sold to the AMC-Shanghai Corporation. Food taken from the mouths of our own people so that the Chinese will have stable food prices. What about our own food prices? There. I have named you. I do not fear you. What will you do, take a dead man to court? And while I am at it, the holes of Kanda Highway must be fixed before the rains. These matters have not been attended to. Sort it out.

YES, IT'S ME, Grace Ahulu again. How can a woman's heart ache still, after she is dead? It aches because it sees rich men growing richer by selling all the things we have placed in their trust: our oil, our land – what will it be next, our people? Our future? Our children? I've seen how you treat our children, with your sticks and your dogs and your gas, like they are animals, or slaves.

Hah! So that is what it is to be. Sell our young people! That's an ache, that is. My aching heart killed me once, do not let it kill me again! Do you want to find out if ghosts have ghosts?

I NAME YOU, Kwame Charles Damoah. I name you Kofi Mensah. I name you before God and the whole congregation of the dead. I shame you, Raymond Kufuor. Shame on you, Development Minister James Anang.

I AM FAITH Anang, and I am dead, alas. Cancer the size of a football chewed out my bowel. We all die of something. But I am rising up my spirit house, and I am talking to you, James Anang, yes, you. I am talking to you from this grand and novelty spirit house with all its fine furniture and the French windows and the decking and infinity pool, which you bought for me. Tell me, where did this money come from? You can't defy me, you rascal, not your own grandmother. Yes, your own grandmother! I know you. Here, all you protestors and students: here's a thing only a grandmother would know. He's away on a trade mission to Ivory Coast – checking out all the money he has stashed there. You want to protest? You want to make him listen? You can march around Independence Square until you are dizzy, but if you really want to hurt him, listen to his grandmother. The account is in the Banque Nationale Cote D'Ivoire, sort code 987645, account number 1097856432, Ibann number: cdi109785. You're students, you know about computers. That is all I shall say.

(Television interview with Obo Quartey:
Ten O'clock News, May 27th, 2021)

John Tettey: Good Evening, Mr Quartey. The obvious question first: is the fact that you're giving this interview from Northern Mali not an indication that you feel threatened by the Fourth Republic?

Obo Quartey: Not at all, John, not at all. We've been working on moving our server farm to Mali for some time.

John Tettey; Well, I'm just saying how it might seem to the average viewer seeing the CEO of Teshie dot org, which has been threatened with closure by the government, opening up a new headquarters in another country.

Obo Quartey: Teshie dot org has been a major investor in Sahel Solar, which has brought prosperity and employment to what is undeniably a poor country. Mali offers us stable and cost-effective electricity. Oil prices are simply too volatile, and from Teshie's point of view, it's not just economically but environmentally and politically foolish to tie ourselves to local oil. It was local oil that started the problem in the first place. You can't sell off the sun.

John Tettey: Yes. So it is politically, environmentally and economically prudent, but is Teshie doing exactly what the protestors down in Independence Square accuse the government of doing, moving cash and assets out of the country?

Obo Quartey: John, our accounts are transparent. Anyone can go online to Companies House and look at them. It's cheap solar, first and foremost. But, if that cheap solar happens to remove us from the jurisdiction of a government that doesn't understand the nature of modern telecommunications and social media, that's a benefit, isn't it?

John Tettey: What do you say to Justice Minister Kwame Charles Damoah, who has called for the Mali Government to arrest and extradite you?

Obo Quartey: Well, I think he'll be a long time waiting for the Malian justice system to do anything, even lubricated with some of his oil money. But I'm not in hiding. I'm overseeing a transfer to a new server farm.

John Tettey: So, nothing to do with the fact that your company has refused to hand over the identities of people posting lampoons and critical messages masquerading as dead relatives?

Obo Quartey: Not so much refused to hand over, John, as *can't*. We don't collect those details, we don't have those details. We can't hand over what we don't have.

John Tettety: Oh come on, you expect me to believe that you don't record log-ins or keep records of ISPs?

Obo Quartey: The Spirit Chat Channel was originally a stripped down IM system for families to keep in touch. We wanted it to be as useful and ubiquitous as possible so it could be accessed from computers, Smartphones, dumbphones – it was designed to work with everything, from anywhere. So, it's become a vehicle for popular dissatisfaction with the government, but I'm not to blame them for that. If someone realised that speaking through the dead gives you anonymity, and also lends you a certain moral authority, yet again, I'm not responsible for that. If those same people start to think that maybe they should encrypt their postings on the Teshie network – we all need to improve our internet security these days – that's the kind of computer-literate, savvy country we are. Certainly not Teshie dot org's problem.

John Tettey: But the government is threatening to close you and freeze your assets.

Obo Quartey: Well, as you said, we are in a different jurisdiction here and we'll have to see what the legal position is. For the government to try and close down Teshie it would have to erect a firewall that would impact the entire digital economy, not just ours. And I truly believe that, morally, it would be a foolish government that would further antagonise popular opinion by cutting people off from their ancestors and their family history.

John Tettey: So the protests and lampoons will continue?

Obo Quartey: Don't ask me, ask the dead.

TEA? YES. HOW are you? You look tired, Azumah. Have they been working you too hard up in Algeria? Hard people. Very serious, I hear. What was it you were working on? Remind me again. Oh yes, the solar power. Yes, that is hard work in a dry place. Tired you look, but wealthy.

Sorry about the sugar, yes, I forgot. I can't take it without sugar. It doesn't taste of anything.

Thank you for the money. Did any of the others thank you for it? No, I didn't think so. You'll have to forgive Ayii, I don't think he even knows what you do, not really. Felix Cofie thanks you, the spirit house is looking lovely, it's so him, all the football mementos, and I've added a few things myself; little things he and I would know.

Yes it's me. You're surprised. What surprises you, Azumah? That I'm writing the posts for Felix Cofie, that I am one of those terrible dangerous people who want to bring down the Fourth Republic, or that I know how to write a post and work the Teshie system at all? That last is easy – it's the way these days. It's the future of the nation – look at that Obo Quartey boy in his smart suit and his Mercedes. He came from just up the street, you know. I learnt down at the community centre. They have special classes. All my friends go, it's the place to be. We type and have tea. I even have a little netbook, an old homeworker one. They sell them off very cheap.

Where do people get this idea that only the young care enough to change the world? I have eyes, I have ears, and when you get older, your skin grows thin and you can bear the suffering of others less. It scrapes you, rubs you raw. I saw the prices going up at Maxmart, I heard Akron Kufuor from Excelsior Taxis saying that more and more of his money was going on fuel. And I did some reading – we all did some reading, all the ladies in our little network, and we saw why the prices were going up and where the money was going to – who the money was going to – and we learned about what they call 'resource curse' and we thought, like a lot of other people, this is not our nation, this is not our people, this is not the way we are; we are better than this, we are better than oil. And it was an easy thing to do, to have this idea that I could pretend to be Felix Cofie, and give him a voice. We are full of stories of people being warned by spirits in the bush and ancestors in the special place in the house and I thought, now we can make this real. The dead really can warn and advise and nag.

And do you know, it's fun. It's fun to be your father. Because, do you know, I miss him. Can you believe that? I miss him every day. Oh, he would sit in his chair and say maybe three words a day and never pay attention to anything more interesting than how well or how badly FC Maamobi were doing, but I missed that. And I found I could give him a voice to say in death all the things he never could in life. And it made me remember why I loved him in the first place, what a big fine and loud man he once was, and how handsome. How good he was, how he cared. Life can drive that out of you.

Dangerous? No there is no danger. They will not come and break in my door with sticks. We would never stand for that around here. If they attack an old woman after they attack the dead, well, they are not far from a fall. And anyway, they won't find me. No no no. There is a new security patch for Teshie, some clever boy wrote it. No, there are more things Felix Cofie needs to say.

That tea must be cold. Would you like a little warm-up?

(Obo Quartey on *The Dead Net: Teshie.org,
social networking and social transformation.*
TED talk, concluding section)

...In themselves, the technologies don't effect social change. I don't even particularly believe that they enable social change. Teshie.org didn't offer anything radically new – none of the networking platforms do. There have only been two world-changing communications technologies. The first is the telegraph; the ability to send message by wire – and that's 19th century. Switching and networking. The other is the ability to put that in your pocket and carry it around. What Teshie did was offer us the most appropriate means, and by that I mean the most culturally appropriate. Our small, well-mannered uprising of the dead would not have worked anywhere else... and they weren't looking for revolution. Just some admission of wrong-doing, maybe a resignation. That we got a revolution – yet again, credit to us, a bloodless one – I think is a combination of unique factors: strong family ties, Teshie.org giving a shape and a structure to those family ties and turning them into a strong weapon of shame. There are guilt cultures and there are shame cultures, we a   e   w   n the Development   i   ot   says she is ashame c   e   that starts the land i   u   never have been mo   ov   ment hadn't threaten c   at   ou're going to cut me   d   mess with families.   it   s the strikes that brought down not just Raymond Kufuor but the entire Fourth Republic.

Six months on, what we have now in Teshie is a built-in subversion network. When the Government went to the courts to get an order for us to disclose our subscribers, that led directly to somebody – not us, some kid in a neighbourhood data centre somewhere

– writing a cheap, mobile compatible anonymizing app. Two hundred thousand downloads in forty-eight hours? I think that deserves some appreciation. Then when they tried to shut down the mobile networks, people built their own – and cheaper and better than the private ones. The micro-working companies are moving their servers off the big telecoms onto neighbourhood networks – they're cheaper, better, and it means people can home-work now. Anonymizing, encryption and open wifi – we are now the world leaders in popular, secure communications networks. The dead will never be silenced.

So, what for Teshie now? We're expanding, we're diversifying. We're much more than a social network company that grew out of a website for Fantasy Coffins. Our investments in Mali have convinced us that solar is the future. Leave the oil under the sea. Solar – particular micro-solar – is cheap, dependable and democratic. Every district can be a micro-solar power station. Open, local, distributed wireless and power networks – that's a strong economy and a strong society. But if there's one thing I want to leave you with, it's this: never underestimate a disgruntled ghost.

YES YES YES, so I am talking again, I am grumbling and complaining but do you expect me to go back to being quiet and well-behaved? Once we've been disturbed in our spirit houses, once we've been made uncomfortable on our stools, once we've remembered how good it is to talk and be listened to, do you think we'll go back to the silence? No: the country is quiet, prices are stable, we have good government and our good name in the eyes of the world back, and I hear someone is filling in the potholes on Kanda Highway. No, what I am aggrieved about is that Ike Okai Mensah is still Manager of FC Maamobi! Something must be done!

THE INCREDIBLE
EXPLODING MAN

DAVE HUTCHINSON

Dave Hutchinson is the author of one novel and five collections of short stories, and the editor of two anthologies. He's also the author of the BSFA-Award-nominated novella 'The Push', of which he is maniacally proud. Before being made redundant during the recent recession, Dave spent twenty-five years working as a journalist. He was born in Sheffield but lives in North London with his wife and assorted cats. One of the trickiest elements of this story was settling on the right title... He wanted it to have that Marvel Comics feel.

FROM A DISTANCE, the first thing you saw was the cloud.

It rose five thousand feet or more, a perfect vertical helix turning slowly in the sky above Point Zero. Winds high in the atmosphere smeared its very top into ribbons, but no matter how hard the winds blew at lower levels the main body kept its shape. A year ago, a tornado had tracked northwest across this part of Iowa and not disturbed the cloud at all. It looked eerie and frightening, but it was just an edge effect, harmless water vapour in the atmosphere gathered by what was going on below. The really scary stuff at Point Zero was invisible.

The young lieutenant sitting across from me looked tired and ill. They burned out quickly here on the Perimeter – the constant stress of keeping things from getting through the fence, the constant terror of what they would have to do if something did. A typical tour out here lasted less than six months, then they were rotated back to their units and replacements were brought in. I sometimes wondered why we were bothering to keep it secret; if we waited long enough the entire US Marine Corps would have spent time here.

I leaned forward, raised my voice over the sound of the engines and said to the lieutenant, "How old are you, son?"

The lieutenant just looked blankly at me. Beside him, I saw Former Corporal Fenwick roll his eyes.

"Just trying to make conversation," I said, sitting back. The lieutenant didn't respond. He didn't know who I was – or rather, he had been told I was a specialist, come to perform routine maintenance on the sensors installed all over the Site. There was no way to tell whether he believed that or not, or if he even cared. He was trying to maintain a veneer of professionalism, but when he thought nobody was looking he kept glancing at the windows. He wanted to look out, to check on his responsibilities on the ground. Was the Site still there? Was there a panic? Had a coyote got through?

It had been a coyote last time. At least, that was the general consensus of opinion – it was hard to be certain from the remains. The Board of Inquiry had found that the breach was due to gross negligence on the part of the officer in command. The officer in command, a colonel I had met a couple of times and rather liked, had saved Uncle Sam the cost of a court martial by dying, along with seventeen of his men, bringing down the thing the coyote had become. You could tell, just by looking at the lieutenant, that he had terrible nightmares.

The Black Hawk made another wide looping turn over Sioux Crossing, waiting for permission to land. Looking out, I thought I could see my old house. The city had been evacuated shortly after the Accident. It had taken weeks to clear the place out; even after dire stories of death and disaster, even with the cloud hanging over the Site, there were people who refused to leave. The fact that the skies by then were full of military helicopters, some of them black, hadn't helped. The government had handled the whole thing poorly, and there had been a couple of armed standoffs between householders and the military. Then a bunch of asshole militiamen had turned up from the wilds of Montana, vowing to oppose the Zionist World Government or the Bilderberg Group or whoever the hell they believed was running the world. I was glad I'd missed the whole thing.

Further out, I could see the buildings of the Collider in the distance. From here, all looked peaceful. Apart from the cloud, towering over everything, it was as if nothing had ever happened here.

The pilot eventually got permission to make final approach and we landed in a park on the edge of Sioux Crossing. The park was ringed by prefabricated buildings stacked four high, offices and barracks and mess halls and control rooms and armouries and garages surrounding a big white 'H' sprayed on the ground.

The lieutenant jumped down as soon as the door was opened, and the last I saw of him was his back as he strode away from us towards the control centre.

"Talkative fucker," Former Corporal Fenwick commented, hopping down from the helicopter beside me.

I sighed. A figure in fatigues was coming towards us from the control centre. The figure passed the lieutenant, and they snapped salutes at each other without breaking step.

"Welcoming committee," said Fenwick. "Nice. I approve."

"Shut up, Fenwick," I muttered.

The figure was the base commander, Colonel Newton J Kettering. He marched up to us and saluted. Fenwick returned the salute sloppily, as usual. I didn't bother.

"Sir," Kettering said, smartly. "Welcome to Camp Batavia."

"Well thank you kindly, Colonel," Fenwick said. "Looks like you're running a tight ship, here."

"Sir. Thank you, sir." Unlike the lieutenant, Kettering didn't look tired and ill. He looked alert and bright-eyed. He looked alert and bright-eyed to the point of madness. He was a veteran of Iraq and Afghanistan and he'd done three tours here, and I didn't want to spend a minute longer in his company than I had to.

I said to Fenwick, "I'd better supervise the unloading."

Fenwick gave me his big shit-eating grin. "I think that sounds like a fine idea, Mr Dolan." I wanted to punch him. "Perhaps Colonel Kettering could give me the guided tour while you're doing that thing."

"Sir, I was hoping you could join me in the Officers' Club," Kettering said. "We have a luncheon prepared."

Fenwick's grin widened. "Colonel, I would love to."

"We need to get onto the Site as soon as possible," I said to them both, but mainly to Fenwick. Kettering regarded me with a keen look of hostility. Fenwick pouted; he hated to miss a free meal. I said, "Colonel, it shouldn't take more than half an hour to unload my gear –"

"Hell," Fenwick put in amiably. "That's *plenty* of time for luncheon. Right, Colonel?"

"Sir. Yes, sir." Kettering gave me that hostile look again. I had already ruined his carefully-groomed routine; he wasn't about to let me ruin lunch too. Neither was Fenwick.

I looked at them both. "Half an hour," I said. "No longer."

Fenwick and Kettering exchanged a knowing glance. *Civilians.* Then Fenwick clapped Kettering on the back and said, "Lead the way, Colonel," and they walked off. A few yards away, Fenwick looked over his shoulder and called, "Would you like us to send a plate out for you, Mr Dolan?"

I shook my head. "No thank you, General, I'll be fine," I called back. Fenwick flipped me the bird surreptitiously and turned back to Kettering. The two of them, deep in conversation, walked towards the wall of prefabs.

I watched them go for a few moments, then went back to the helicopter, where, in the style of bored baggage handlers and cargo men the world over, half a dozen Marines were throwing my metal transport cases out onto the grass.

"Hey!" I shouted. "Careful with those things! They're delicate scientific instruments!"

Actually, the cases were full of old telephone directories, for weight, but I had to keep up the charade.

I HAD BEEN in a foul mood when I arrived for work that morning. I drove the short distance from home to the facility, stopped briefly at the gate to show my ID, then drove to the building housing the small control room Professor Delahaye and his team were using.

Most of them were already there ahead of me. Delahaye was over to one side of the room, conferring with half a dozen of his colleagues and grad students. Others were busily typing at consoles and peering at monitors. Nowhere, though, could I see the shock of white hair that I was looking for.

Delahaye spotted me and walked over. "What are you doing here, Dolan?" he asked. "Surely you've got enough material by now?"

The experiment's almost over, he doesn't need to be here. Is it important?

Is it important? No, maybe not to you, Professor. I said, "I just wanted a quick word, that's all."

Delahaye nodded irritably. "All right. But just –"

"Try not to get in the way. Yes, Professor, I know. I'll just stand over there in the corner." As if I was going to reach over and press some important big red button, or fall into a piece of machinery. Nothing I did here was going to make the slightest bit of difference to the enormous energies being generated, nanoseconds at a time, far below our feet in the tunnels of the Collider. And even if I did manage to screw something up, it wouldn't affect the experiment all that much; all the results were in, Delahaye was just using up his allotted time with a last couple of shots.

The Professor gave me a last admonitory glare and went back to the little group across the room. There was nothing world-shaking going on here; the Collider was brand new – the offices still smelled of fresh paint. Delahaye was just running warm-up tests, calibrating instruments, the high-energy physics equivalent of running-in a new car. I'd been there two months, working on an article about the new facility for *Time*. I thought the article was shaping up to be interesting and informative. The worst thing about the whole fucking business was that it had brought Larry into my life.

Andy Chen came over and we shook hands. "Been fun having you around, man," he said.

"Yes," I said. "Right."

"Nah, really," he insisted. "You piss old man Delahaye off mightily. It's been beautiful to watch."

Despite being beyond pissed off myself, I smiled. "You're welcome. What's for you now? Back to MIT?"

He shook his head. "Been offered a job at JPL."

"Hey, excellent, man. Congratulations."

"Ah, we'll see. It's not pure research, but at least it gets me away from that monstrous old fart." He looked over at Professor Delahaye, who was regaling some students with some tale or other. Andy snorted. "Brits," he said. "Who knows?" He looked over to where a small commotion had begun around the door. "Well, we can get the party started now."

I looked towards the door and saw Larry Day's leonine features over the heads of the others in the room, and I felt my heart thud in my chest. "Andy," I said, "I need to have a quick word with Larry." We shook hands again and I launched myself through the crowd. "Great news about JPL, man. Really."

Larry was drunk again. That much was obvious even before I got to him. He was wearing Bermuda shorts and a desert camouflage jacket and he was clutching a tattered sheaf of paper in one hand and a shrink-wrapped six pack of Dr Pepper in the other. His hair looked as if he had been dragged back and forth through a hedge a couple of times, and his eyes were hidden by mirrorshades with lenses the size of silver dollars.

"Larry," I said as I reached him.

mirrored lenses turned t ar 'He Alex
" There was a powerful a c Turl y an
cigars arou d him, and he ne at m
th were yellow and t nev
ing *Stone* had called a Ha king
win.' One o the most i ia cist of hi
tion, a legend at the c y-f r. O
, by that tim he had bee ro of H rvard
for an incident involving a home-made railgun, a frozen chicken, and his supervisor's vintage TransAm, but that was just part of his mystique, and pretty much every other university on Earth had offered him a place. His doctoral thesis was titled 'Why All Leptons Look Like Joey Ramone But Smell Like Lady GaGa', and it was generally agreed that it would have been embarrassing if

it *had* won him the Nobel Prize. Bad enough that it was shortlisted. His postdoc research had been a mixture of the mundane and the wildly exotic; he cherry-picked his way through some of the wilder outlands of quantum mechanics and nanotechnology, came up with a brand new theory of stellar evolution, published a paper which not only challenged the Big Bang but made it seem rather dull and simple-minded. Larry Day. Brilliant physicist. Brilliant drunk. Brilliant serial womaniser. He and I had visited all the bars in Sioux Crossing and been thrown out of most of them.

"I spoke with Ellie last night," I said, quietly.

He smiled down at me. "Hey," he said. "Outstanding."

I gritted my teeth. "She told me."

In the background, I could hear Delahaye saying something above the holiday atmosphere in the room, but I wasn't paying attention. All I could concentrate on was Larry's mouth, his lying lips as he said, "Ah. Okay."

"Is that all you can say?" I hissed. "'Ah. Okay'?"

He shrugged expansively and some of the papers in his hand escaped and fell to the floor. "What can I say, man? 'I'm sorry'?"

Delahaye seemed to be counting in a loud voice, but it was as if I heard him from a great echoing distance. I lunged at Larry, grabbed him by the front of the camouflage jacket, and drove him two steps back against the wall.

"... Three... two..." said Delahaye.

"You fucking *bastard!*" I screamed into Larry's face.

"... One!" said Delahaye, and the world filled with a sudden flash of something that was not blinding white light.

* * *

I HAD THE Humvee loaded by the time Fenwick and the Colonel returned from their lunch. In the end I'd told the Marines to go away, and I'd done it myself. Down the years I've noticed that Marines tend towards a certain disdain for people who are not themselves Marines. I was a *civilian specialist*. To most of them that was a euphemism for CIA, which was a direct invitation to dick around and try to get a rise out of me, but I wasn't going to play that game.

"How was your lunch, General?" I asked when Fenwick and Kettering arrived.

Fenwick looked at Kettering. "I think I can report that this camp is not lacking in creature comforts, Mr Dolan," he said, and Kettering smiled in relief.

I looked at my watch. "We really should be making a start, General," I said. "I'd like to be out of here before nightfall."

Fenwick snorted. "You and me both." He turned to Kettering. "Newt," he said, "if you're ever down at Bragg, I'll throw a party for you at the BOQ that'll make your head spin."

Kettering grinned. "Sir. Yes, sir." They shook hands and Kettering stood to attention while Fenwick and I got into the Hummer. I took the wheel.

I said, "I do hope you didn't breach any security protocols in there, Corporal."

Fenwick grinned and tapped the stars on his fatigues. "*General.*"

I put the Hummer in gear. "Oh, fuck off, Fenwick," I said. "You're no more a General than I am." And I drove the Humvee out of the gates of the camp and onto the road to the Site.

*   *   *

THERE WAS A place that was not a place. It was too small
and too large all at once, and it was either dark or it was
lit by something that wasn't light but came in from the
edge of vision like a hypnagogic nightmare. There was
an 'up' and a 'down.' Or maybe it was a 'down' and an
'up.' I screamed and I screamed and the noises I made
were not sounds. I was... I was...

It took me a long time to get my bearings. Or maybe
I never did, maybe it was all an accident. I walked.
Travelled, anyway. I couldn't understand what I was
seeing, couldn't be sure that I was seeing it. I wanted
to curl up and die, and I did in fact try that a couple of
times, but it was impossible. I couldn't even curl up, in
the sense that I understood it. I held my hands up and
looked at them. They were... they were...

At some point, maybe instantly, maybe it took a
hundred million years, I came upon a... structure. Too
small and too large to see, all at once. It looked like...
there's no way I can describe what it looked like, but
I *touched* it and I *reached down* and I *curled around*
it and the next thing I knew I was lying on my back
looking up at a starry sky and someone nearby was
screaming, "Don't move, you fucker! You stay right
where you are!"

I turned my head, astonished that I still remembered
how. A soldier was standing a few feet from me,
illuminated by moonlight, pointing an automatic
weapon at me.

"Who are you?" I asked, and almost choked myself
because I was still trying to speak as I might have when
I was *there*. I coughed and retched, and at some point

I realised I was naked and freezing cold. I said again, "Who are you?"

"Who are *you*?" shouted the soldier.

"Dolan," I said, and this time I managed to say it without strangling. "Alex Dolan. There's been some kind of accident."

There was a squawking noise and the soldier lifted a walkie-talkie to his lips. "Fenwick here, sir," he shouted into the radio. "I've got a civilian here. He claims there's been an accident."

AT GROUND LEVEL, fifteen years of abandonment were more obvious. There were Green Berets stationed at the gate, and they spent a good half-hour checking our documents and establishing our bona-fides before letting us through. As well as animals, the world's press were always trying to sneak through the fence. Nobody had made it yet. Nobody we knew about, anyway.

The buildings were weathered and dirty, th ass waist-high, despite regular helicopter inun ns of herbicides, and it was starting to encroach he cracked asphalt of the roadways.

I drove until we were a few hundred feet fr he control room building, directly under the ly-twisting spiral cloud. Unable to hush the cloud he government had admitted that there had been an accident at the Collider, explaining it as an electromagnetic effect. Scientists – government-sponsored and otherwise – were still arguing about this.

Fenwick looked up at the white helix and curled his lips. He was a man of many attributes, very few of them admirable, but he was not a coward. He had been told that there was no danger in him coming this close to Point Zero, and he believed that. It had never occurred to him that a significant fraction of the Defence Budget was devoted to stopping animals getting this close to Point Zero.

There had been much discussion about what to do about him after I appeared out of thin air in front of him. A quick look at his file suggested that appealing to his patriotic instincts would be pointless, and that giving him large amounts of money would be counterproductive and fruitless. A working-group of thirty very very bright men and women had been convened simply to study the problem of 'What To Do About Corporal Robert E Lee Fenwick', who one night while out on patrol at Fort Bragg had seen me appear from a direction that no one in the universe had ever seen before.

Their solution was elegant and, I thought, unusually humane. Corporal Fenwick was a simple organism, geared mainly to self-gratification, and his loyalty – and his silence – had been bought by the simple expedient of promoting him to the rank of three-star General. What fascinated me was that Fenwick never showed the slightest gratitude for this. It was as if the alternative never even occurred to him. He seemed totally oblivious to the concept that it would have been simpler, and far more cost-effective, to simply kill him.

"Here we are, then," Fenwick said.

"Yes," I said. "Here we are. I cannot argue with that." I looked at the cloud, looked at the buildings around us. Fenwick had surprised everyone by taking to his new rank like a duck to water. He was still *in* the army, but he was no longer *of* the army. He had no duties to speak of, apart from the duties that involved me. His General's pay had been backdated for a decade, and he had bought his parents a new house in West Virginia and his brother a new car, and he lived with his child bride Roselynne and their half-dozen squalling brats in a magnificent mansion in Alexandria, Virginia. The kids went to the best schools, and in moments of despair I hung onto that. The eldest girl, Bobbi-Sue, was starting at Princeton next year. Because of what had happened to me the Fenwick boys would not work all their lives in the local coal mines; the Fenwick girls would not marry the high school jock only to see him become a drunken wife-beater. They would be lawyers and doctors and Congressmen and Senators, and maybe even Presidents. In my darkest moments I looked at Former Corporal Fenwick, and I almost thought this was all worth it. Almost.

"How long do we have?" he asked. He always asked that.

shrugged. "Minutes?" a that, too. "Days?" I opened the doo g e Hummer. Fenwick got out too, an e loaded the transport cas . We carrie n f the other buildings a little way fr h room, and emptied them of their tel h en we put them back into the Humv n ny gear on the ground beside the vehicle.

Fenwick checked his watch. "Better be getting back," he said.

I nodded. In a couple of hours there would be an overflight. An unmarked black helicopter without an ID transponder would pass overhead, ignoring local traffic control until the last moment, when it would transmit a brief and curt series of digits that identified it as belonging to the NSA. It would dip down below the radar cover, hover for a few moments, and then lift up and fly off again. And that would be me, leaving. "This is stupid. Someone's going to work it out one day," I said.

Fenwick shrugged. "Not my problem." He put out his hand and I shook it. When I first met him he had been rangy and fidgety. Now he was calm and plump and sleek, and in my heart I couldn't grudge him that. "Happy trails, Alex," he said.

"You too, Bobby Lee. See you soon."

"Let's fucking hope, right?"

I smiled. "Yes. Let's."

Fenwick got back into the Hummer, gave me a wave, and drove off back towards the gate, where he would tell the Green Berets that the *civilian specialist* had arranged a separate means of departure. Which would, in its own way, be true.

I watched the Humvee disappear into the distance. When it was gone, I picked up my stuff and carried it into one of the nearby buildings. I dumped it in an empty office, unrolled my sleeping bag on the floor, wheeled a chair over to the window, and sat down.

THE ROOM WAS small and windowless and the only furniture in it was a table and a single folding plastic chair. The Captain was using the chair. I was standing on the other side of the table from him, flanked by two armed soldiers.

"Now, all I need to know, son, is your name and how you managed to get onto this base bare-ass naked without anybody seeing you," the Captain said. He'd said it a number of times.

"My name is Alexander Dolan," I said. "I'm a journalist. I was in the control room with Professor Delahaye's group. I think there's been an accident." I'd said this a number of times, too.

The Captain smiled and shook his head. He was base security, or maybe Intelligence, I didn't know. He was the image of reasonableness. We could, he seemed to be saying, keep doing this all day and all night until I told him what he wanted to know.

"Go and find Professor Delahaye," I said. "He'll vouch for me." I couldn't understand what the military were doing at the Collider; maybe the accident had been much worse than I thought. Which would make it truly world-shaking.

"I don't know any Professor Delahaye, son," the Captain said. "Did he help you break in here?"

I sighed and shook my head. "No. He's supervising the startup experiments. Look, if he was hurt, maybe one of the others can come here. Doctor Chen or Doctor Morley, maybe. Everyone knows me."

"I don't know any of these people, Mr Dolan," said the Captain. "What I want to know is who *you* are, and how in the name of blue blazes you managed to break into Fort Bragg without a stitch of clothing."

"Fort Bragg?"

The captain gave me a wry, long-suffering, don't-bullshit-me-son sort of look.

I looked around the room. There was only one door. It looked solid and it had big locks on it. But looking around the room again, I noticed that if I looked at it a certain *way*, it was not a locked room at all. It was just planes of mass that didn't even butt up against each other. It was actually wide open.

"I thought this was the Sioux Crossing Collider," I told the Captain.

He blinked. "The what?"

I said, "I don't like it here," and I *stepped* outside the room, went back *there*.

I HAD BROUGHT with me a gallon jug of water, a little solid-fuel camping stove, some basic camping cookware, and half a dozen MREs. I took the first package and opened it. Meals Ready to Eat. But only if you were desperate or not particularly fussy. The package contained beef ravioli in meat sauce, chipotle snack bread, a cookie, cheese spread, beef snacks, caffeine mints, candy, coffee, sugar, salt, gum, some dried fruit and some other bits and pieces. I'd heard that the French Army's MREs came with a pouch of red wine. If only the Accident had happened at CERN...

I BECAME AWARE of... something. If a solid object could have the equivalent of a negative image, this was it. A kind of *negative* tornado, turned inside-out. I *stepped* towards it...

And found myself standing at the SCC, outside the building where I had last seen Professor Delahaye and his team and Larry Day.

Above me towered a *colossal* sculptured pillar of cloud, rotating slowly in the sky. I tilted my head back and looked up at it, my mouth dropping open.

And all of a sudden I was writhing on the ground in agony, my muscles cramping and spasming. I tried to *step* away, but I was in too much pain to be able to focus.

And that was how they caught me the second time, lying in wait because they half-expected me to return to the Collider, and then tasering me half to death. Someone walked up to me and thumped his fist down on my thigh. When he took his hand away there was a thin plastic tube sticking out of my leg and then there was a wild roaring in my head and a wave of blackness broke over me and washed me away.

THEY TRIED THE same trick on the Captain and the two guards as they had on Former Corporal Fenwick. I was beginning to think that I was travelling across the world leaving generals in my wake. They showered them with money and promotions, and for some reason it didn't work with them the way it had worked with Fenwick. They blabbed their stories, and eventually the government had to make them all disappear. The officers were in solitary confinement in Leavenworth and the people they blabbed to were *sequestered* somewhere.

I finished my dinner and sat by the window drinking coffee and smoking a small cigar. The cigar was from a tin I'd found in my rucksack; a little gift from Fenwick. I'd heard the helicopter fly over while I was eating; it had dipped down momentarily a few hundred metres from Point Zero – which was actually an act of insane bravery on the part of its pilot in order to maintain what I considered the fatuous and transparent fiction of my 'departure' – and then lifted away again to the West. Now everything was quiet and night was falling.

I remembered when this whole place had been busy and bustling. All abandoned now, the surviving staff scattered to other facilities. I thought about Delahaye and Andy Chen and Caitlin Morley and all the others who had been in that room with me on the day of the Accident. Delahaye had been an uptight asshole and Larry had been having an affair with my wife, but I'd liked the others; they were good, calm, professional people and it had been good to know them.

I was resting my arm on the windowsill. As I looked at it, the hairs on my forearm began to stir slowly and stand up.

THIS TIME, IT was a General opposite me, and I was sitting down. To one side of the General were two middle-aged men in suits; on the other side was a youngish man with thinning hair and an eager expression.

"You tasered me and drugged me," I told them. "That wasn't very friendly."

"We apologise for that, Mr Dolan," said one of the middle-aged men. "We couldn't risk you... *leaving* again. Put yourself in our position."

I held up my hands. I was wearing manacles. The manacles were connected to a generator behind my chair; if I looked as if I was going to do something outrageous – or if I even sneezed a bit forcefully – the manacles would deliver a shock strong enough to stun me. I knew this because they'd demonstrated the process to me when I came round from the sedative.

"I would *love* to put myself in your position," I said. "So long as you could put yourself in mine."

"It's only a precaution, Mr Dolan," said the other

middle-aged man. "Until we can be sure you won't leave us again."

I looked at the manacles. From a certain point of view, they didn't go round my wrists at all. I lowered my hands and folded them in my lap. "Professor Delahaye," I said.

"We don't know," said the youngish man. "We don't dare go into the control room. We sent in bomb disposal robots with remote cameras and there's... something there, but no bodies, nothing alive."

"*Something?*" I asked.

He shook his head. "We don't know. The cameras won't image it. It's just a dead point in the middle of the room. Can you remember what happened?"

I was busy attacking Larry Day for having an affair with my wife. "They were doing the last shot of the series," I said. "Delahaye counted down and then there was..." I looked at them. "Sorry. I *won't image* it."

"Did anything seem out of the ordinary? Anything at all?"

Yes, I'd just found out Larry Day was having an affair with my wife. "No, everything seemed normal. But I'm not a physicist, I'm a journalist."

"Where do you... go?"

"I don't know. Somewhere. Nowhere. *Anywhere.*"

The four men exchanged glances. One of the middle-aged men said, "We think there may be another survivor."

I leaned forward.

"A day after your first, um, *appearance* there was an incident in Cairo," he went on. "Half the city centre was destroyed. There's no footage of what happened, but some of the survivors say they saw a *djinn* walking through the city, a human figure that walked through buildings and wrecked them."

A terrible thought occurred to me. "That might have been me."

The other middle-aged man shook his head. "We don't think so."

"Why?"

"Because it happened again yesterday in Nevada. While you were unconscious here. A small town called Spicerville was totally destroyed. Eight hundred people dead."

"We're calling it an explosion in a railcar full of chemicals," the General said. "The Egyptians say theirs was a meteorite strike. But we think it's... someone like you."

"Whatever happened at the SCC, it changed you," said the younger man, with what I thought was admirable understatement. "We think it changed this other person too, whoever they are. But where you seem to have found a way to... cope with your... situation, the other person has not."

"I haven't found a way to *cope* at all," I told them. I looked at the table between us. It was a rather cheap-looking conference table, the kind of thing the government bought in huge amounts from cut-rate office supply stores. It seemed that I had never looked at things properly before; now I could see how the table was constructed, from the subatomic level upward.

"Obviously this... person is dangerous," one of the middle-aged men said. "Any help you could give us would be very much appreciated."

I sighed. I took the table to pieces and put it back together in a shape that I found rather pleasing. Nobody else in the room found it pleasing at all, though, judging by the way they all jumped up and ran screaming for the door. I slipped away from the manacles and went back *there*.

I WENT OUTSIDE and stood in front of the building with my hands in my pockets. About seven hours ago I had been sitting in a briefing room in a White House basement with the President and about a dozen NSA and CIA staffers, watching a video.

The video had been taken by a Predator drone flying over Afghanistan. It was the spearpoint of a long-running operation to kill a Taliban warlord codenamed WATERSHED, who had been tracked down to a compound in Helmand. It was the usual combat video, not black and white but that weird mixture of shades of grey. The landscape tipped and dipped as the Predator's operator, thousands of miles away in the continental United States, steered the drone in on its target. Then a scatter of buildings popped up over a hill and the drone launched its missile, and as it did a human figure came walking around the corner of one of the buildings. The cross-hairs of the drone's camera danced around the centre of the screen for a few moments, then the building puffed smoke in all directions and disappeared.

And moments later, unaffected, seemingly not even having noticed the explosion, the figure calmly walked out of the smoke and carried on its way.

"Well," the President had said, when the video was over, "either the war in Afghanistan just took a *very* strange turn, or we're going to need your services, Mr Dolan."

I looked into the sky. The Moon was low down on the horizon and everything was bathed in a strange directionless silvery light that cast strange shadows from the buildings. There was an electrical *expectancy* in the air, a smell of ozone and burnt sugar, a breeze that blew from nowhere, and then he was there, standing a few yards from me, looking about him and making strange noises. I sighed.

"Larry," I called.

Larry looked round, saw me, and said, "Jesus, Alex. What the hell happened?"

Larry didn't remember the Accident, which was good. And he didn't remember what came after, which was even better. But he was surprisingly adaptable, and I couldn't afford to relax, even for a moment.

I walked over and stood looking at him. He looked like part of a comic strip illustration of a man blowing up. Here he was in Frame One, a solid, whole human being. Here he was, at the end of the strip, nothing more than a widely-distributed scattering of bone and meat and other tissue. And here he was, three or four frames in, the explosion just getting going, his body flying apart. And that was Larry, a man impossibly caught in the middle of detonating. His body looked repugnant and absurd all at the same time, an animated human-shaped cloud of meat and blood, about twice normal size.

"There was an accident," I said. "Something happened during the last shot, we still don't know exactly what."

Larry's voice issued from somewhere other than his exploding larynx. It seemed to be coming from a long distance away, like a radio tuned to a distant galaxy. He said, "What happened to your hair, Alex?"

I ran a hand over my head. "It's been a while, Larry. I got old."

"How long?" asked that eerie voice.

"Nearly twenty-five years."

Larry looked around him and made those strange noises again. "Delahaye…"

"All dead," I said. "Delahaye, Warren, Chen, Bright, Morley. The whole team. You and I are the only survivors."

Larry looked at his hands; it was impossible to read the expression on what passed for his face, but he made a noise that might, if one were psychotic enough, be mistaken for a laugh. "I don't seem to have survived very well, Alex." He looked at me. "*You* seem to be doing all right, though."

I shrugged. "As I said, we still don't know exactly what happened."

Larry emitted that awful laugh again. "My god," he said, "it's like something from a Marvel comic. You think maybe I've become a superhero, Alex?"

"That's an… unusual way of looking at it," I allowed warily.

Larry sighed. "You'd think I'd get X-ray vision or something. Not…" he waved his not-quite-hands at me, "… *this*."

"Larry," I said, "you need help."

Larry laughed. "Oh? You *think*? Jesus, Alex." He started to pace back and forth. Then he stopped. "Where was I? Before?"

"Afghanistan. We think you were just trying to find your way back here."

Larry shook his head, which was an awful thing to watch. "No. Before that. There was… everything was the wrong… *shape*…"

I took a step forward and said, "Larry..."

"And before that... I was *here*, and we were having this conversation..."

"It's just *déjà vu*," I told him. "It's hardly the worst of your worries."

Larry straightened up and his body seemed to gain coherence. "Alex," he said, "how many times have we done this before?"

I shook my head. "Too fucking many," I said, and I plunged my hands into the seething exploding mass of Larry Day's body and pulled us both back into Hell.

I STILL WASN'T sure why I went back after escaping the second time. Maybe I just wanted to know what had happened to me, and there was no way to find out on my own. Maybe I was afraid that if I spent too long *there* I would forget what it was like to be human.

The General and his three friends were unavailable. I later discovered that they had been in hospital ever since they saw what I turned the table into; one of them never recovered. In their place, I was assigned two more Generals – one from the Air Force and one from the Army – and an Admiral, and a team of eager young scientists, all looked after by quiet, efficient people from the CIA and the NSA.

I was questioned, over and over and over again, and the answers I was able to give them wouldn't have covered the back of a postage stamp. One of the scientists asked me, "What's it like there? How many dimensions does it have?" and all I could tell him was, "Not enough. Too many. I don't know."

We were unprepared. We knew too little, and that was why he nearly got me that first time. I knew that Point Zero was like a beacon *there*, a great solid negative tornado, and one of the few useful pieces of advice I was able to contribute was to keep a watch on the SCC for any manifestations. I went back to our old house in Sioux Crossing to wait, because I *knew*. I knew he was looking for a landmark, a reference point, because that was what *I* had done. When the manifestations began, I was bustled in great secrecy to the Site, and I saw him appear for the first time. Heard him speak for the first time. Thought, not for the last time, *Of course. It had to be Larry*.

He was confused, frightened, angry, but he recovered quickly. I told him what had happened – what we understood, anyway – and he seemed to pull his exploding form together a little. He looked about him and said, "This must be what God feels like," and my blood ran cold. And then I felt him try to take me apart and remake me, the way I had remade the table.

I did the first thing that crossed my mind. I grabbed him and went back *there* with him, and I let him go and came back *here*.

The second time he came back, it was the same thing. A few random manifestations, some baffling but relatively minor destruction. Then he found his way to Point Zero, confused, amnesiac. But he came to the same conclusion. *This must be what God feels like*. And I had to take him back *there*.

And again. And again. And again.

I WALKED AN unimaginable distance. It took me an impossible length of time. Nothing here meant anything or made any sense, but there were structures, colossal things that were almost too small to see: the remains of Professor Delahaye and the other victims of The Accident. There were also the remains of a specially-trained SEAL team, sent in here by the President – not the present one but her predecessor – when he thought he could create a group of all-American superheroes. I, and pretty much every scientist involved in investigating the Accident, argued against that, but when the President says jump you just ask what altitude he wants, so the SEALs remain. There is no life or death *there*, only existence, so Professor Delahaye and the others exist in a Schrödinger not-quite-state, trying to make sense of what and where they are. If they ever succeed, I'm going to be busy.

The scientists call this 'Calabi-Yau space,' or, if they're trying to be particularly mysterious, 'The Manifold.' Which it may or may not be, nobody knows. The String Theorists, overwhelmed with joy at having eyewitness evidence of another space, named it, even though I could give them little in the way of confirmatory testimony. Calabi-Yau space exists a tiny fraction of a nanometre away from what I used to think of as 'normal' space, but it would take more than the total energy output of the entire universe to force a single photon between them.

Travel between dimensions appears to be, however, more like judo than karate, more a manipulation of force than a direct application of it. Somehow, Delahaye's final shot manipulated those forces in just the wrong way, pitching everything within a radius of five metres into a terrible emptiness and leaving behind Point Zero, a pulsing, open wound between the worlds, a point that *won't be imaged*. Someone once told me that the odds of the Accident happening at all were billions and billions to one against. Like going into every casino on The Strip in Vegas and playing every slot machine and winning the jackpot on all of them, all in one evening. But here's the thing about odds and probability. You can talk about them as much as you want, do all the fancy math, but in the end there's only Either/Or. That's all that matters. Either you win all the jackpots on The Strip, or you don't. Either it will happen, or it won't. It did, and here I am. And here, somewhere, is Larry Day.

Existing in Calabi-Yau space, being able to step between dimensions, being able to use the insight this gives you to manipulate the 'real' world, really *is* like being a god. Unfortunately, it's like being one of the gods HP Lovecraft used to write about, immense and unfathomable and entirely without human scruple. So far, the human race is lucky that Larry seems unable to quite get the knack of godhood. None of us can work out why I acclimatised to it so easily, or why it's still so difficult for Larry, why returning him *there* screws him up all over again while I can cross back and forth at will, without harm. Larry is one of the biggest brains humanity ever produced, and he can't get the hang of The Manifold, while I, the world's most prosaic man, as my ex-wife liked to remind me, took it more or less in my stride. All I can tell them is that every time we meet – and we've done this particular little pantomime fifty-two times so far – he seems to recover more quickly. One day he's going to come out of it bright-eyed and bushy-tailed and I won't be able to take him back *there*. I'll have to fight him *here*, and it'll be like nothing Stan Lee ever imagined. Either/Or. Either the world will survive, or it won't.

Larry is not a nice man. He was a great man, before the Accident, and I liked him a lot, until I found out about him and my wife. But he's not a nice man. Of all the people in the world you'd want to get bitten by the radioactive spider, he'd probably come close to the bottom of the list.

And the wonderful, extravagant cosmic joke of it is that Larry is not even the Nightmare Scenario. The Nightmare Scenario is that Delahaye and Chen and Morley and the SEAL team and all the animals who got onto the Site despite the billion-dollar-per-annum containment operation somehow drop into a rest state at once, and find their way *here*. If that happens, it'll make the Twilight of the Gods look like a quiet morning in a roadside diner. I plan to be somewhere else on that day. I'm happy enough to present the appearance of humanity for the moment, but I don't owe these people anything.

Eventually, I came across a room. Although this wasn't a room in the sense that anyone *here* would recognise. It was all distributed planes of stress and knots of mass, open on all sides, too huge to measure. I stepped into the room and sat down in a comfortable chair.

Nobody screamed. Nobody ran away. They were expecting me, of course, and I had learned long ago how to clothe myself before I came *here*. People hate it when naked men appear out of nowhere in the Situation Room at the White House. Someone brought me coffee. The coffee here was always excellent.

"Mr Dolan," said the President.

"Madam President," I said. I sipped my coffee. "He's recovering more quickly."

"We noticed," said one of the scientists, a man named Sierpinski. "The others?"

"I saw some of them. They're still aestivating. I'm not sure I should be checking them out; won't observing them collapse them into one state or the other?"

Sierpinski shrugged. *We don't know*. Maybe we should make that our company song.

"You look tired," said the President.

"I look how I want to look," I snapped, and regretted it. She was not an unkind person, and I *was* tired. And anyway, it was ridiculous. Why would a godlike transdimensional superhero want to look like a tubby, balding, middle-aged man? If I wanted, I could look like Lady Gaga or Robert Downey Jr., or an enormous crystal eagle, but what I *really* want is to be ordinary again, and that, of all things, I cannot do.

I looked up at the expectant faces, all of them waiting to hear how I had saved the world again.

SWEET SPOTS

PAUL DI FILIPPO

Paul Di Filippo lives on Rhode Island and describes himself as a 'Willy Nilly Buddhist,' in that he adheres to the religion's spiritual underpinning without necessarily following all its dictates. He also happens to be an extraordinary writer. Paul is the author of more than twenty novels, novellas and collections. He has won a BSFA Award and France's Grand Prix de l'Imaginaire, and has been a finalist twice for the Nebula Award and once for the Philip K. Dick Award.

"Officials were trying to determine on Monday how a man who walked through the wrong door on Sunday afternoon turned the busiest terminal at Newark Liberty International Airport into a human traffic jam on one of the busiest travel days of the year."

– James Barron,
'Security Investigation Begins
at Newark Airport,'
The New York Times, January 4, 2010

THE WAY ARPAD Stroll discovered his unique ability to identify and utilize universal sweet spots involved the unlikely confluence of his unrequited love for Veronica Kingslake, Mrs. Christelli's physics class, the apelike antics of Willy Squidgeon, half a raisin bagel, an errant shaft of sunlight, a colored marker, a pair of cheap shoes, and a host of other unqualifiable factors, many of which were unknown to Arpad himself – at least on the conscious level.

Arpad's desk in Mrs. Christelli's class occupied the front row, and stood nearest the door. Thus the teen had, if he so chose, an unrestricted view of one of the corridors of Edward Lorenz High School through the wire-gridded glass panels of the classroom's exit door.

Now, generally speaking, Arp enjoyed Mrs. Christelli's physics lectures, and paid close attention. Science was cool, and offered a lot to occupy Arpad's ingenious, busy mind.

But on this grey, changeable, mostly overcast day, his mind was elsewhere. He had absorbed this section on entropy already, reading the textbook at home. The concepts of thermodynamics, intriguing as they were, held no mysteries for him.

So, slumped in his seat, he was daydreaming about Veronica Kingslake – her long glossy blonde hair, her lush shape, her hypnotic, ass-switching walk, her light-hearted laughter – in short, all the assorted physical and temperamental characteristics which, conjoined into one exotic package, made her so alluring to Arp and to practically every other straight male at the school. How, Arp wondered, could he ever vault to the front of the pack of Veronica's wannabe boyfriends—

At that very moment, as dumpling-shaped Mrs. Christelli lectured with her back to the class while scrawling equations on the whiteboard, Arp chanced to look to his right and spotted Veronica herself ambling down the corridor.

Arp straightened up magnetically, drawn to his beloved. If only he could escape this class and join her on whatever lone errand she pursued! Separated from the clique that normally accompanied Veronica everywhere, he might attain some new relationship with her that transcended mere indifferent tolerance.

But Mrs. Christelli handed out lavatory passes with a parsimony approaching zero tolerance, especially in these waning minutes of class. If he couldn't escape within the next few seconds, all was lost.

What inspired Arp's next move, he could not say, then or ever. There was no conscious thought, no deliberation or reasoned chain of logic. No calculating assessment of circumstances and possibilities and potentials. Whatever obscure engine of parsing and action that took command dwelled deep below even his subconscious, and transmitted its impulses directly to his muscles.

Arp turned his head back to the class and caught the eye of Willy Squidgeon, fidgeting and bored.

Willy was the class clown. It was a role he cherished and seemed positively born to. He resembled a good-natured, shaggy, red-haired Neanderthal with a face of malleable rubber. Once, Willy had legendarily climbed semi-naked to the top of the school's cupola on a dare, substituting his boxer shorts for the state flag.

Arp made the silent archetypical suite of chimp gestures – armpit scrabbling with curved hands, pop-eyed duckface hooting – and that was all it took.

This shorthand semiotic challenge invariably provoked a vivid display of imitation Cheetah behavior from Willy. There was no possibility he would decline a performance if triggered. Even in the midst of memorial services for car-crash senior-prom fatalities, Willy would respond.

Now he leaped to his feet, scrabbled atop his desk, and began to cavort noisily and exuberantly, with simian grace.

Everything else fell into place almost simultaneously.

Of course, the class went wild.

Mrs. Christelli turned away from the whiteboard, marker in hand, to chastise Willy.

At the back of the room, Ludmilla Duda instantly choked on the piece of bagel she was surreptitiously eating. Her frantic, panicky gasping for breath distracted the teacher's reprimand, causing Mrs. Christelli to pivot uncertainly between harmless Willy and the direly choking girl.

The clouds outside parted just then in a perfectly configured slit, and a blazing hot beam of sunlight, made all the more dazzling by the circumambient gloom, drove down from the heavens to strike square upon Mrs. Christelli's face. Momentarily blinded, the teacher shuffled awkwardly in place like a tango dancer encountering a banana skin while trying to partner a horse. One shoe of her cheap, overstressed pair of Payless pumps chose that moment to exhibit a structural weakness, and its heel snapped off.

The hefty Mrs. Christelli went down like a felled sequoia, but not before she launched the whiteboard marker in her hand directly at Arp.

The marker struck Arp weakly on the forehead, but without a moment's surprise or hesitation he spontaneously clapped both hands to his left eye, bellowed wordlessly, and dashed from the room, yelling, "Nurse Miller, Nurse Miller, help!"

Out in the corridor Arp slowed, lowered his arms, tugged his T-shirt into place, tried to assume a look of nonchalance, and caught up with Veronica.

"Hi, Ron, what's up?"

Veronica, in all her Abercrombie & Fitch finery, bestowed a look upon Arp which, under the most charitable interpretation, might be deemed one of charitably suppressed pity mingled with innate repugnance.

"Hey, Stroll. Going home early. Severe cramps and wicked PMS. See ya."

This intimate datum so disconcerted Arp, engendering a wild welter of stunning mental visuals, that he ground to a halt, mouth open like the bell of a tuba, and let Veronica depart.

Opportunity blown.

But – opportunity at least initially secured.

The stunning reality of his providential escape from Mrs. Christelli's class suddenly hit him.

How in hell had all that unlikely stuff come together so perfectly?

JASON WARDLAW, ARP'S best friend, enjoyed a curious pastime of his own invention, which he had dubbed "urbex skateboarding." Disdaining professional skateparks as lame, and even turning up his nose at forbidden, police-patrolled municipal venues such as plazas, staircases and promenades, Jason would employ his battered Toy Machine Devil Cat deck only in ruined and abandoned industrial facilities, where dangling wires, cables and chains; rotting planks, detritus-laden floors and roofs; as well as teetering girders, ramps and towers offered the largest challenges to his art.

Luckily, living in Detroit afforded Jay innumerable such sites.

This afternoon, Arp was watching Jay shred inside the old Fisher Body Plant Number 21 at Piquette and St. Antoine. As Arp sipped his Orange Mango frappuccino amidst the somber decay, Jay executed some truly sick moves involving several fifty-five-gallon drums, a handtruck, a seventy-foot-long conveyer belt, and a stack of empty doorframes.

Observing his friend's maneuvers, Arp, who had no skills whatsoever involving skateboards, became possessed of a curious yet adamant knowledge amounting to a certainty. If Jay were only to *twist* like so at this point, and *leap* like so at this other point, while *landing* just so at the finale, his generally dismal GPA would rise by some twenty-five per cent.

The absurd certitude of this unrequested intuition unsettled Arp, and recalled to him the weird sequence of events that had freed him from physics class yesterday. What could such sensations mean? Was he going crazy, having a brain meltdown? If his incitement of Willy had not led precisely to the desired yet utterly unforeseeable outcome, Arp would have been sure he was going nuts. He wished he could test this new skateboard-generated revelation by having Jay perform as he envisioned, and then wait till next report card. But the moment was already over, Jay having ground to a halt amidst a pile of metal shavings.

Arp noisily sucked down the dregs of his drink and walked over to his friend's side. At least he could share his experiences with Jay and perhaps get some reassurance.

"Jay, listen to what happened to me yesterday…"

Like a good pal, Jay paid attentive heed, even while he fussed with the trucks of his deck, picking out aluminum flinders. Arp finished his account with the epiphany that had just struck him.

Jay remained silent for an interval, and then said, "Follow me."

Arp trailed Jay over to a spot in the vast pillared space where a storage firm had stacked a giant mound of cartons before going bankrupt. Weather-beaten and decaying, the listing cartons contained hundreds of thousands of big rough glass marbles that served as feedstock in fiberglass production.

Jay stood by one corner of the mound and said, "Watch this." He surveyed the setup intently, and then, with both hands, peeled away the lower half of one shoddy carton.

Immediately, all the marbles began to avalanche noisily out of the ripped carton, spilling across the floor like frightened mice. As that carton deflated, the ones above it and around it began also to tip and burst, releasing their contents. Ultimately, a flood of marbles caused the boys to dance backward. The avalanche finally ceased of its own volition when a new equilibrium in the pile of cartons had been reached.

Jay gestured to the sea of marbles. "Okay, show me the moves you would make to get them all back to where they were."

Arp snorted. "That's impossible!"

"Of course it is. And you know why as well as I do. It's entropy. The whole universe is rigged for chaos. Mankind is fucked from the start. There are so many more crummy states of being than good ones, that the odds are stacked against us doing anything useful or desirable. Chances are that whatever move we make will result in a lousy outcome. That's how a single person can cause so much grief with so little effort. I don't care whether it's a pile of marbles or sand or snow, or some kind of human system, like a computer program or a democracy. Chances are, you stick your oar in, you just churn up a shitstorm. One little wrong twist of your car's steering wheel, and you've got a mile-long fatal pileup involving a hundred other people. Not some kind of spontaneous Shriners parade."

Arp nodded thoughtfully. "It's all true. Entropy rules, and that sucks. You and I have talked about this before. Murphy's Law is a bitch. But you don't understand exactly what I'm getting at. First off, we know that humans are negentropy agents. Even if only temporarily, we can push chaos back. But that's not even what I'm theorizing here. It's more like, more like --"

"Yeah, more like what? I'm waiting."

The perfect analogy from science struck Arp like a dodgeball taking out a nerd in the gymnasium of his mind. "It's like the Butterfly Effect!"

"Butterfly wags its wings in Brazil, you get a blizzard in Chicago?"

"Yes! By being in just the right place and doing just the right thing, a small action can launch a major result. It's called, um, sensible impedance --"

"'Sensitive dependence on initial conditions,' jerkface!" Jason pondered where the discussion was leading. "And you're saying you can suddenly see just what the butterfly has to do for something specific to happen?"

"Yeah, exactly! It's not something I can verbalize, and if I tried to pass on the knowledge to anyone else, the moment would have slipped away. And you obviously can't achieve every possible outcome from any given starting point in time and space. You'd be limited to the network of cause and effect radiating out from that particular moment in spacetime. But I can do it, I know! I did it in class!"

"How come all of a sudden?"

"How the hell do I know? My body's changing! Maybe I was bitten by a radioactive butterfly!"

Jason punched Arp in the shoulder. "Did it feel anything like that?"

Arp punched back, and the two tussled for a few seconds. Breaking out of a clinch, Jason ran a hand through his flyaway hair and said, "Arp, my buddy, we need to experiment with this new skill of yours. And I've got just the goal to shoot for."

ARP AND JASON meandered through the GM Ren Cen. On this Saturday, the mall was packed with families and packs of teens, squads of power-walking elderly and alert security guards.

"You seen any invisible hooks yet?" asked Jason.

"I don't think of them as hooks," said Arp. "That analogy just doesn't work somehow. It's not anything that reaches out and grabs me. It's more like –"

"Sweet spots! That's what you're seeing. The Nexus of All Realities, like where Man-Thing lives! Except there's millions of them everywhere! Millions of little nex-eyes!"

"Yeah, right. No, that's not exactly it either."

"Or maybe it's more like the universe's clit! Tickle it just right, and everything explodes. You should know, the way you always score with Ronnie K!"

"Shut the fuck up!"

Seething at his friend's crude yet cutting joke, Arp surged ahead, entering the food court on Level A. Jason caught up with him, genuinely apologetic.

"Aw, c'mon, did you forget I was a lowlife ballbuster? Look, I'll buy you a couple of dogs at Coney Town, okay?"

Mollified, yet feeling slightly bummed that he had not yet encountered the sweet spot he was searching for at Jason's behest, Arp agreed to the offer.

Seated at a table with their food, Arp and Jason ate and surveyed the passing scene.

In the middle of the food court, employees were setting up an inflatable bounce house for the enjoyment of the kiddies. The muted roar of the fan designed to keep the structure erect and bouncy suddenly sounded, as the blower underwent a test activation. Then the fan was shut off and disconnected from the flattened bounce house for examination of its workings.

And that was when Arp saw the desired sweet spot, pure and potent and invisible to anyone but him.

He only had time briefly to advise Jason – "Watch!" – before the moment demanded his action.

Arp threw his half-eaten hotdog at a nearby trashcan, deliberately undershooting so that the food waste landed on the floor.

One of the ever-circulating food court cleaning staff, armed with broom and dustpan, saw the defiantly messy gesture and spun around indignantly to confront and chastise Arp.

The handle of the guy's horizontally held, lance-like, fast-moving broom caught a geezer right in his stomach, causing him to *oof* and stumble against his geezer wife. The woman lurched forward, catapulting her many bursting bags of purchases directly under the feet of one particular passerby.

This important passerby, a brown-clad UPS delivery fellow, was pushing his heavily laden flatbed at top speed across the polished floor. He tripped over the strewn consumer goods and went down, releasing his grip on his cart, altering its vector and even imparting a slightly greater impetus to it.

The cart barrelled toward the kneeling bounce house worker inspecting the fan. He activated the blower just as the cart took him out and glancingly hit the fan.

The roaring untethered fan swivelled around on its wheels and caught a new group in its blast.

Entering the food court at that exact moment, the heretofore-unseen shoppers who became the target of the rogue blower consisted of a pack of insouciant and attitudinous Bad Girls. These adolescent Snooki-lookalikes wore crop tops emblazoned with legends such as FUTURE MILF and GUESS WHERE I'M PIERCED. They also sported incredibly abbreviated skirts over bare legs.

Whomped by the blast from the high-powered fan, the shrieking girls felt their fluttering minuscule skirts being blown skyward. They fought at first to tug down their garments, but then a pedestal table bearing a highly breakable sugar shaker crashed into the path of the whirlwind, and their eyes were filled with flying sucrose, forcing them to abandon decorum. Now their various styles of risqué undergarments, barely concealing a catalogue of tramp stamps, were on shameful display.

As various Good Samaritans and mall employees raced to the aid of the Bad Girls, Jason turned to Arp with awe suffusing his face.

Arp said coolly, "You asked me to provide...?"

"Girls in their underwear standing around in the mall. Sweet bleeding Jesus!"

THE NEXT SEVERAL days after the stirringly and reassuringly confirmational mall incident, Arp faced nearly continuous uncertainty about how to proceed with his new powers. The aching dilemma occupied his mind almost every minute. A pure case of 'new superhero' angst. The whole "With great power..." thing.

Should he proceed selfishly, as unconflicted Jason counselled, employing his gifts solely for personal satisfaction?

Or should he embark on a course of selfless altruism, seeking to right a worldful of wrongs?

Didn't he have an obligation to function as a counteragent to all the entropic fuckups accidentally sowing pain and disorder everywhere? Walking through airport security the wrong way and immobilizing thousands? Tapping into oil pipelines and causing massive conflagrations? Speeding down a freeway and racking up scores of crashed vehicles?

But on the other hand, how could he know just what goals would best reverberate to mankind's advantage?

Suppose he pushed at a sweet spot to force the discovery of a brand new mega-barrel oil field in the Gulf of Mexico? He had actually half-sensed just such a sweet spot lurking at the periphery of his consciousness. It was over in Chicago somewhere, a not unreasonable distance to cover, given the payoff. Sure, doing so would make a lot of rich people richer and even help some middle-class schlubs and the general economy. But what would the long-term effects be? More pollution, a swifter plummet into Greenhouse Earth? How could he, sixteen-year-old average teenager Arpad Stroll, make such decisions wisely? Wouldn't he be better off just going for little things that would mean a lot to him alone? But what a waste of his gifts!

The circular labyrinth of reasoning and worrying preoccupied Arp for a week during which, despite Jason's imploring, he did not employ his powers again. And, to add insult to injury, he had to deal with an old problem as well.

Blueberry Chefafa.

Blueberry Chefafa was in love with Arpad Stroll, and the feeling was not mutual. Just as he pined for Ronnie Kingslake, so Blue longed for him.

Really, there was no solid reason for Arp's lack of interest in the pretty girl. Granted, Blue was not a knockout like Veronica, but her distinctive looks, derived from a blend of African-American and Greco-American genes, attracted many a male glance. There was, admittedly, the matter of her, ah, somewhat robust build to contend with. No petite princess, Blue captained the female wrestling squad at Edward Lorenz High. To report that the team was undefeated was to convey something of Blueberry's possibly intimidating physicality. Arp knew from experience that she could beat him at arm-wrestling. But her muscles were packed along attractive curves, and she certainly sported a more impressive rack than slim and WASPy Ronnie. And Blue's academic record matched her sporting accomplishments: sharp and quick, she excelled in the classes she shared with Arp.

No, there was no reason not to have the hots for Blue, other than the sheer mysteries of the heart.

But would the girl give up in the face of Arp's deliberate cold shoulder? Never! She pestered Arp ceaselessly, doing him unrequested favors, finding reasons to be wherever he was, casting meaningful glances his way in crowds, getting her friends to go to bat for her. It was enough to give a guy the jitters.

The week of Arp's special befuddlement, Blueberry exhibited extra attentiveness toward the object of her affection, as if she could detect that something potent was troubling Arp. She even showed up at his house, ostensibly bringing news of a homework assignment she thought he had missed hearing about. It took him half an hour to ditch her.

And now here she was, in Mrs. Christelli's class, auditing it for extra credit during her study period, she claimed, and seated right next to Arp. Her foot had strayed more than once into his personal space, and she kept fluffing her abundant dark hair to waft the scents of her floral shampoo his way. What a pain in the ass!

Mrs. Christelli, fully recovered from her spill of a week past, finished cabling her laptop to the big flatscreen at the front of the room. "Today, class, we are going to watch the most recent episode of NOVA. The topic is earth-grazing asteroids, how to detect them and what might be done to stop one from impacting the planet. I'm sure you will all find it extremely interesting."

The lights went down, giving Blueberry a chance to inch closer, and the screen came alive with solar system vistas and the narrator's placid yet somehow alarmist voice.

"Always at risk for another celestial impact event such as the one during the Permian-Triassic era that killed ninety per cent of life on Earth, our planet dodges many near-misses each year. In fact, scientists at the University of Arizona's Spacewatch mission currently have their telescopes focused on one newly observed and fast-moving asteroid, dubbed Perses after the destructive Titan of Greek mythology. The experts are nearly certain that the hurtling rock will miss our world, but the projected clearance is the smallest ever recorded…"

Blueberry took that cue to utter a gasp of exaggerated fright and grab Arp's arm. That was when he lost it.

The two sweet spots which Arp had heretofore poked had resulted in a cascade of macroscopic events. But somehow, this time, he knew he was tapping into something more subtle.

Instead of casting off Blue's hand, as he wanted to, he took it in both of his own and squeezed. He could feel her pulse accelerate and a hot blood rush beneath her skin. Metabolic and cellular processes began to churn within the girl. At the same time, Arp put his head closer to hers, but then forced a sneeze out directly at her, spraying her with his personal blend of microbes.

"Oh, dude, sorry," Arp said unctuously.

Blueberry took no offense. "Don't worry," she whispered.

"Class, quiet, please!" Mrs Christelli admonished.

Arp continued to squeeze Blue's hand, even massaging a pressure point on the underside of her wrist. Blue practically purred. He listened for a rustling of paper. Sure enough, under cover of darkness Ludmilla Duda was unwrapping a sandwich. The odor of a highly spiced Middle Eastern shawarma filled the room.

Blue began to fidget. She withdrew her hand. "I – I don't feel so good. My stomach –" She began to retch and jumped awkwardly to her feet. Gagging wholeheartedly, she dashed from the room amidst unsympathetic laughter, and Arp sat back with a feeling of relief, accomplishment, and, if truth be told, a smidgen of guilt and remorse.

But overall, it felt sweet.

JASON AND ARP came to call the sequence of events triggered by poking a sweet spot 'okiegoes' or 'rubes,' after the elaborate Rube Goldberg device depicted in OK Go's video for 'This Too Shall Pass.' Witnessing the perfectly sequenced cascades of improbable events – at least the parts that fell under their remote point of view – began to assume an allure almost as great as obtaining the desired outcome.

Not that Arp turned his nose up getting things he wanted for almost no effort.

The incident with Blueberry Chefafa had tipped Arp's mind over into the 'for profit' side of the moral equation. After many months of trying to discourage Blue's unwanted attentions, he had disposed of her in ninety seconds. The aftermath of contracting a flukey and short-lived stomach virus, coincidental with Arp responding to her overtures, had weirded Blueberry out.

Although not actually repulsed by his presence when their paths crossed, Blue reacted like a startled fawn, jerking up short and leaping back an inch or so, while regarding Arp with puzzlement as to his intentions or exact nature. She seemed to regard him nowadays as something other than human.

Every time she jumped so, Arp winced a bit inside.

But on the whole, he was satisfied with what he had accomplished.

Rewarded instantly, his brain demanded more. Forgotten or buried were all thoughts of embarking on a do-gooder's career.

For nearly a month now, Arp had indulged his every idle wish. Or at least those for which local sweet spots availed themselves. None of his desires reeked of megalomania, cruelty or excessive greed. But they were all self-centered. Except for those which he activated for Jason's sake.

A partial catalogue of Arp's conquests – or, viewed another way, presents from the obliging universe – included: a thousand-dollar gift card at the Dearborn branch of Marshall Field's; the grade of A-plus on his latest civics paper, composed in half an hour with copious use of the internet; a promotion for his Mom in her job at the Detroit Metro Airport; the public humiliation of a crooked city councilman who had taken away a local park by eminent domain for his own profit; and the infusion of an unexpected federal grant into the cafeteria at Edward Lorenz High, ensuring that Arp's favorite lunch of steak tips, asparagus and French fries appeared on the menu with increased frequency.

As for buddy Jason, the cynical slacker now sported a sick new Bump-brand deck, a closet full of Neff

T-shirts and hats, and six new pairs of Vans kicks, all obtained at no cost to him, thanks to his unwarranted but uncontested inclusion on a list of professional skateboarders.

After tapping so many sweet spots, Arp had begun to understand them better and better on some deep, non-verbal level. He began to intuit where they could be found and what kind led where. He just hoped that his extra-normal senses were not developing along the lines experienced by the hyperacute hero of *The Man with the X-Ray Eyes*, a movie which had scared the pants off him a few years ago, when he had streamed it off his Mom's Netflix. But so far as he could tell, his sanity remained solid.

One thing Arp had learned: not every goal was obtainable in every location. In computer networking terms, Arp realized, sweet spots featured only a 'partially connected mesh topology.' Some sweet spots persisted, while others were highly evanescent. And some required more physical input on his part than others. For instance, to obtain the thousand-dollar gift card, he had been forced to wade out into the yucky River Route, with son acting as spotter and lookout, dive to the bottom and push a shopping cart exactly one foot deep into the muck. Not exactly easy.

But taken all in all, the employment of sweet spots for personal gain offered immense payoffs for very little input.

Having gained confidence in his new talents, Arp decided he could proceed with his ultimate goal: to get Veronica Kingslake to fall in love with him. After that, what more could he possibly ask for?

Arp would have preferred to poke one of the multiple relevant sweet spots when he was alone with Ronnie.

But since that never happened, he had to do it at school.

Under the lackadaisical and inattentive guidance of Mr. Mollusk, who as a former youthful track star had no real interest in any sporting activity other than sprints, mixed phys-ed classes generally devolved into groups of girls standing around gossiping and bunches of guys horsing around the equipment. Today was no different.

Arp was chilling with Jason and a few other dudes, while they shot baskets in a half-assed fashion. He participated with one eye on Ronnie where she stood across the gym with her friends, near an exterior wall. He hardly heard the banter of his pals until something Armando Zavala said made him take notice.

"Hey, who's ready to die?"

Arp got nervous. His formless intuition regarding the effects of the sweet spot he was about to employ revealed potential for some collateral danger. But he felt he had to risk it.

"Whatta ya mean?" Arp asked.

"Aren't you following news about that Percy asteroid? Seems like it might've hit something out in space and gotten aimed our way. The scientists aren't so sure it's gonna miss us anymore."

Jason commented dryly, "The margin for error in their predictions is plus or minus fifteen per cent. Not exactly betting odds."

Arp was going to reply, but then the basketball was passed to him, and his moment to poke the sweet spot had arrived.

Arp heaved the ball high and wide of the basket. It soared through the air and struck a small frosted window fifteen feet up the wall near where Veronica stood.

Held in place only loosely by an invisibly deteriorated seal, the glass popped outward. The rest of the okiegoes cascade was not immediately visible, but Arp heard the unmistakeable indignant yawp of a disturbed crow, the frantic cursing of what was presumably a passing pedestrian, and the screech of car tires. Even while everyone was laughing at him for his failed throw, he was running toward Veronica and the other girls.

With a tremendous crash, accompanied by female screams and shrieks, the forequarters of a huge SUV thrust through the wall, blasting bricks everywhere even as it lost momentum amidst the wreckage. Several girls, including Ronnie, had fallen to the floor, but no one seemed really hurt. Arp spared a microsecond to give thanks, but kept racing forward.

Once securely attached to the destroyed wall, an accordion-style folding room divider tall as the gym began to peel off and fall directly toward Ronnie. Waking, the made a scrabbling attempt to rise, but seemed to have forgotten how to work her limbs.

Almost without seeing it, Arp encountered the pommel horse he had been aiming for, braced his hands against the device and began to push. Only some hundred and twenty pounds, the device slid easily, especially under Arp's adrenaline-powered urgency.

The pommel horse stopped precisely alongside Ronnie, and Arp dropped down to further shield her fetally recumbent form just as the detached assemblage of aluminum and vinyl crashed down onto the sturdy support – and no further.

An eerie silence reigned for a moment, before shouts erupted. But Arp hardly heard anything.

Ronnie's beautiful tear-streaked face loomed inches from his, her lips parted invitingly, albeit unromantically slicked with snot, and a look of absolute adoration bloomed across her features, betokening her heart as forever his.

At his moment of triumph, doubt suddenly besieged Arp.

He sure hoped Veronica was worth it.

"Aw, C'MON, ARP, just one little rube, please! Winter'll be here soon, and I really need that new snowboard and a plane ticket to Aspen."

"No! I told you, no more sweet spots!"

This Saturday morning the two friends were hanging out on the old Thornhill Place Bridge, where Jason had been practicing his moves on the crumbling bridge railing, despite risking a fifteen-foot drop to the greenway below. Some three weeks had passed since Arp's staged heroics in the gym, and this was the first time he and Jason had been able to chill together.

Veronica had fallen for her factitious savior more deeply than Arp could have predicted. She was inseparable from him, and much of their time together was spent in lusty clinches that stopped just short of sex. (Ambitious Mom and Pop Kingslake had plans for Veronica that did not include any chances at teenage pregnancy, and she had internalized their goals completely.) Arp found himself chafing under his new role and responsibilities. He felt like a total fake. He had gotten precisely what he wanted, but it was proving less – or rather, more – than he had envisioned. In short, Ronnie was cramping his style and freedom, and making him feel continuously guilty of fraud.

And besides, the disturbing fallout from that last sweet spot still bothered him. People had gotten hurt! Several of the other girls had suffered contusions and even a fracture or three. All as the result of Arp's selfish actions. The thought of unintended consequences accompanying future use of sweet spots plagued him. Sure, he got what he wanted every time, but at what ancillary cost, seen or unseen?

And now douchebag Jason was bugging him for a frigging snowboard and plane ticket, of all things!

Arp got ready to tell his friend off, but Jason spoke first.

"Aw, fuck it! What's the point of pretending we'll ever even see another winter anyhow? This planet is totally doomed."

The two teens automatically cast their eyes heavenward, though of course no sign of the killer asteroid, dubbed Perses, showed in the bright daytime sky.

"You really figure it's gonna hit us, Jay?"

"I don't think anybody figures otherwise anymore. Even Glenn Beck and Bill O'Reilly caved in. But everybody's just too stunned to argue or give a fuck anymore."

Arp recognized this much to be true. Under the imminent threat of inescapable planetary catastrophe, the global population was proving remarkably calm. Maybe because no one could really envision the catastrophe. Oh, sure, there had been isolated riots and protests. The loss of the Taj Mahal, the Kremlin, the Vatican, and Lubbock, Texas, still stung. But on the whole, there had been no scenes of contagious mass hysteria. Something about the certitude of the non-human-engineered destruction and its mutual nature, as well as a tiny smidgen of hope, had forestalled utter panic. There was no place to run or hide, no one exempt or special. Everyone was in it together, and so a sense of ostrich-head-in-the-sand resignation and willful cognitive dissonance prevailed.

Arp had reacted much the same as everyone else. With one small difference.

He had a nagging, half-unadmitted intuition that he could save the world.

Being alone now with Jason for the first time in weeks, he finally felt compelled to spill his guts.

"Jay, what would you say if I told you I saw a sweet spot that could stop the asteroid?"

Jason grabbed Arp by both shoulders, his face beaming, and shook his friend. "I knew it! I knew it! I told Blueberry you could do it!"

Arp jerked away. "What! You told Blueberry! How does she even know anything about sweet spots?"

Jason had the grace to look sheepish for once. "Aw, Arp, you didn't have to see her and listen to her these past few weeks. You know I like to hang with Blue, but she was getting to be a royal pain. She was so bummed about you and Ronnie hooking up. But at the same time she was all like, 'Oh, what a hero he is! How could I have ever doubted him? He's so good and noble. Yada yada yada!' I just couldn't take it anymore. So I had to set her straight."

Arp pondered this development. "So now what does she think of me?"

"She thinks you're a total jerkwad, and she loves you more than ever." Jason snorted. "Girls!"

A strange, hot sensation suffused Arp. He knew that if Ronnie ever found out the truth about him, she would turn on him in an instant and despise him forever. As she probably well should. Yet Blueberry Chefafa knew the whole story, and still loved him.

Suddenly the world seemed to invert like an old sock, and Arp saw everything differently.

"Let's go find Blue and talk all this over with her."

"Righteous!"

The boys found Blueberry home alone, so they could discuss everything without pretense or secrecy.

"So it's like that," concluded Arp. "The sweet spot's somewhere in Chicago, but I can't pin it down at this distance. It seems to shift back and forth across a small area. Plus, it looks like it will involve some major input to trigger the rube. And it's the, um, densest one I've ever seen. Totally gnarly with connectivity. I don't really understand the complexity of it. Some of the links seem to go down to the subatomic level. All those factors are why I just didn't rush in and trigger it. Of course I want to save the planet. But who knows if I wouldn't be causing something even worse?"

Her gaze earnest and wise, Blue cut to the heart of the matter. "Exactly what could be worse, Arp? You'd urge the planet into the sun? Not likely, I say. No, you've got to take the chance."

Arp felt truly heroic at last. "All right, I will!" He instantly deflated. "But how can we get to Chicago?"

"Just look around," Jay said. "There's got to be a useful sweet spot right under your nose."

With Jason driving, it still took Arp two whole hours into the five-hour trip to Chicago to master all the dashboard controls of the stolen Lexus LX570, Blue offering helpful advice from the back seat. They didn't feel rushed or nervous – at least in terms of the police; the threat of Armageddon was another matter entirely – since the decisive suicide note found along with the car keys on the seat of the unlocked vehicle indicated that the owner would not be reporting the theft anytime soon.

Around hour four, as they got into the city proper, everyone quieted down to let Arp focus his powers. Eyes closed, he began to issue directions based on his sweet spot GPS, until finally he called, "Stop!"

Opening his eyes, Arp found himself at an iconic spot.

The street at the base of the Sears Tower, once the world's tallest building, and, coincident with its loss of that stature, redubbed the Willis Tower.

"Where now?" asked Jason.

"Up."

The car-owner's wallet afforded them the fifty dollars needed for three Skydeck passes. They rode to the 103rd floor in silence.

At the point of exiting the elevator, Blueberry suddenly balked, letting the other visitors stream past. Jason held the door open.

"No, Arpad, I don't feel good about this. Something tells me there's danger ahead. Let's turn back. It's ridiculous to think you can do anything here to change the fate of a whole planet."

Arp felt himself in the grip of dreamlike forces larger than himself. Vistas of luminous cosmic webs full of shining nodes of action swam before his eyes. "No, we've come this far. I have to try, now."

Arp exited the elevator, followed by Jason and Blue, and headed straight for one wall.

Attached to the wall at intervals, glass boxes projected outward a few feet, so that visitors could step inside and have the illusion of standing unsupported in midair. As a family of tourists emptied out of one, Arp and his friends crowded in. The whole panorama stretched away below them like a Lego cityscape.

"It's right out there," said Arp. "The sweet spot to deflect the asteroid and save the planet."

Jason squinted. "Where?"

"About five feet ahead at the level of my chest."

"How can you possibly use it, Arp?" Blue asked plaintively.

Arp pressed his face to the glass separating him from saving the planet. "I *know* I can trigger it if I can reach it. But reaching it –"

Arp suddenly paused. "Of course! I just need to use *this* rube right here. A sweet spot whose function is to give me access to the other sweet spot!"

At once Arp knew why Blue had to be present. "Give me your bag!"

Blue's bag in hand, he rummaged inside and found what he was looking for: Blue's pretty science-girl laser pointer.

He turned back to the window and shone the little intense laser out and up at a precisely limited angle.

Seconds later, a small plume of object appeared in the sky.

Information flooded Arp's brain, as if the sweet spot were talking to him.

The object consisted of a chunk of blue airplane toilet ice, discharged from a United Express flight. But more importantly, frozen in the middle of the chunk was a worker's forgotten steel alloy wrench.

Arp yelled, "Get back!" He shoved Jason and Blue away from the observation box.

The glass shattered into a million fragments and rained downward to the street and inside the Skydeck. Freed from its icy casing upon impact, the wrench bounced along the floor until it hit the elevator door, wedging itself between the panels so that the elevator could not be easily opened to permit the arrival of any interfering authorities.

Arp stepped forward to where cold clean air gusted in. He could sense the floating sweet spot even more vividly now, since access had become unimpeded. It called to him. He couldn't fathom the entire long and braided cascade of events connected with it, but he knew with a certainty that triggering the okiego would save the planet.

"What now?" said Blueberry.

"I jump!"

Jason was shedding atypical tears. "Do it, dude, do it! We believe!"

"Kiss me, Arp!"

Arp hesitated. His timing had to be perfect. Was a kiss allowed?

Intuition told him to go for it.

He hugged Blueberry and kissed her for what seemed forever. And at the same time, further illumination flooded his mind.

A few stories above the Skydeck, having duplicated the 1999 feat of daredevil Alain Robert, who had ascended the Sears Tower's exterior human-fly-style by hand and foot alone, an illegal BASE jumper named Burnett Kershaw, resting on a ledge, was preparing to leap off, ripcord of his chute firmly in hand.

The very last part of the first stage of the rube fell into place as a TV station's helicopter arrived.

Arp broke off his kiss, smiled, ran toward the empty window, and hurled himself into space, eyes tightly shut, praying wordlessly.

Something told him to tuck and roll.

He felt himself passing perfectly through the sweet spot, activating the rube.

He untucked at just at the right moment to intersect an extremely startled Burnett Kershaw in his descent. Arp clamped his arms around the guy's torso, then burst out laughing.

And a quarter of a million miles distant in space, an asteroid named Perses began to shiver.

THE BEST SCIENCE
FICTION OF THE
YEAR THREE

KEN MACLEOD

Ken MacLeod is the author of twelve novels, from The
Star Fraction *(1995) to* The Restoration Game *(2010).
In 2009 he was a Writer in Residence at the ESRC
Genomics Policy and Research Forum at Edinburgh
University. His forthcoming novel* Intrusion *(2012) is
'a democratic dystopia.' He has wanted to write a short
story called 'The Best Science Fiction of the Year Three'
ever since he saw an anthology of that title a scary
number of years ago. Ken's blog is:* The Early Days of a
Better Nation *at kenmacleod.blogspot.com.*

IN THE YEAR Three, *l'année trois* as it's called here,
there are three kinds of Americans living in Paris: the
old expats, the new émigrés, and the spooks. And then
there are the tourists, who've travelled via Dublin, their
passports unstamped at Shannon. You can find them all
at Shakespeare and Co.; or they can find you.

I was browsing the bargain boxes for SF paperbacks
when I noticed that the guy at my elbow wasn't going
away. At a sideways glance I identified him as a tourist –

something in the skin texture, the clothes, the expression. He looked back at me, and we both did a double take.

"Bob!" I said, sticking out my hand. "Haven't seen you since – when?"

"The London Worldcon," said Bob, shaking my hand. "God, that's... a long time."

"How are you doing?"

"Fine, fine. You know how it is."

I nodded. Yes, I knew how it was.

"What brings you here?" I asked.

"Business," said Bob. He smiled wryly. "Yet another SF anthology. The angle this time is that it features stories from American writers in exile. So I'm systematically approaching the ones I know, trying to track down those I don't have a contact for, and commissioning. The deal's already set up with Editions Jules Verne – the anthology will be published here, in English. In the US it'll be available on Amazon. That way, I can get around all the censorship problems. It's not so bad: you can't read what you like, but publishing what you like is more of a problem."

"So bad you had to come here just to contact the writers?"

"That's right. Trying to set this up online from outside the US might be... well. Let's just say I don't want to take the chance."

"Jeez," I said. "That bad."

I looked back down at the books and saw that my forefinger had landed, as if guided by an invisible hand, on the spine of a J. Neil Schulman paperback. I tugged out *Alongside Night*.

"Well," I said, "I've found what I'm looking for. You?"

Bob shrugged. "Just browsing," he said. "Fancy a coffee?"

"Sure."

I nipped inside, paid a euro for the book, and rejoined Bob outside in the chilly February afternoon. He stood gazing across the Seine at Notre-Dame.

"Hard to believe I'm actually looking at it," he said. He blinked and shook his head. "Where to?"

I indicated left. "Couple of hundred metres, nice traditional place."

The cafe was on the Quai des Grands Augustins. The bitter wind blew grit in our faces. Along the way, I noticed Bob looking askance at the flaring reds, yellows and blacks of the leftist, anarchist and *altermondialiste* posters plastered on walls and parapets.

"Must be kind of weird, seeing all that commie kipple everywhere," he said.

"You stop noticing," I said.

The doorway was easy to miss. Inside, the cafe seemed higher than it was wide, a little canyon of advertisement mirrors and verdegrised brass and smoke-stained woodwork. Two old guys eyed us and returned to their low-voiced conversation around a tiny handheld screen across which horses galloped. I ordered a couple of espressos and we took a table near the back under a Ricard poster that looked like it predated the Moon landings, if not the Wright brothers. We fiddled with envelopes of sugar and slivers of wood, and sipped for a few moments in silence.

"Well," Bob said at last, "I suppose I have to ask. What do you think of the Revolution?"

"It always reminds me," I said, "of something Marx

said about the French state: how all the revolutions have 'perfected this machine, instead of smashing it'."

Bob yelped with laughter. "Fuck, yeah! But trust you to come up with a Marx quote. You were always a bit of a wanker in that respect."

I laughed too, and we took some time to reminisce and catch up.

Bob was a science-fiction fan, an occasional SF editor, and an anarchist, but none of these paid his bills. He was an anthropology professor at a Catholic university deep in the Bible Belt. He spent very little time propagating the ideas of anarchism, even in the days when that had been safe – 'wanker' and 'hobbyist' were among his kinder terms for ideologues. Instead, he worked with trade union locals, small business forums, free software start-ups, and tribal guerrillas in Papua New Guinea. This was all anthropological research, or so he claimed. Such groups tended to be more effective after he'd worked with them.

I hadn't thought much about him over the ... be honest – we were never exactly close – but ... had, I'd wondered how he was doing under the ... in the United States. Not ... well, by the sour ... Still, it would probably have been worse ... I'd emailed to ask. This thought helped to qua... ... of guilt about not having kept in touch.

"Hey," Bob was saying, "wait a minute – you must know some of these writers!"

I nodded.

"Maybe you could give me some contact details?"

At that moment I began to suspect that we hadn't met by accident.

"I don't know if I can," I said.

I had the numbers of most of the writers Bob was looking for on my mobile. "But," I went on, "I do know where you can find them tomorrow morning. Every SF writer in Paris, I shouldn't wonder."

Bob looked puzzled for a moment.

"The ascent," I said.

He smacked his forehead with the heel of his hand. "Of course!"

Like he'd forgotten; like he hadn't timed his visit just for this. The date had been announced on New Year's Eve, in a special Presidential broadcast from the Elysée Palace.

We exchanged phone numbers and finished our coffees.

"Fancy a glass of wine?" Bob said.

I looked at my watch. "Sorry, I've got to go," I said. "But I'll see you tomorrow. Jardin de Luxembourg, main gate, 11 a.m."

'See you there,' Bob said.

I STROLLED ACROSS the Île de la Cité, pausing for a moment to soak in the glow of the low sun off the front of Notre-Dame. As always, it sent me down long passages of reminiscence and· meditation. Something about that complexity that fills your eyes, that you can take in at a single glance, lifts the spirit. It reminds me of the remaining frontage of the Library of Celsus in Ephesus, which many years ago I gazed at bedazzled, dusty, heat-struck, light-struck, dumb-struck. The pagan and the Christian architectural exuberance are in that respect alike.

And as always, as a sort of footnote as I turned and stepped away, came the thought of another building on that island, one as representative of our age, in its chill cement modernism, as the cathedral's gothic was of its. Embarrassing to admit: my response to the Memorial to the Deportation has always been shaped by a prior description, the one in Iain M. Banks's novella *The State of the Art*. My eyes, as always, pricked at the thought; the hairs of my chin and neck, as always, prickled. Seeing the memorial, for a moment, through the eyes of an imaginary alien communist: why should that move me so much? That is on top, you understand, of the import of the thing itself, of its monstrous synecdoche. Perhaps I'm just nostalgic for that alien communist view. These days, in the Year Three, the view's hard to conjure – but when was it not?

I took the Metro from Châtelet to Bastille and walked briskly up Richard Lenoir, turned left to buy a few expensive necessities – a baguette, a half-litre of table wine, a handful of vegetables, a jar of sauce – in the

a quotidian reality, a name on thousands of signboards for opticians, dentists, doctors. I hoped I had the opportunity to rub Bob's nose in this at some point.

As for my own work... it too is exhausting, but in a different way.

*   *   *

I BROUGHT MY wife coffee in bed at nine the following morning. She gave me a glare from under the cover.

"It's early."

"I thought you might want to come along."

"You must be joking. I'm knackered. If I'm awake I'll watch it on the telly."

"Okay," I said.

I kissed her forehead and left the coffee on the bedside table. I caught up with the news and online chatter over my own breakfast, and left the flat about ten-thirty. The sky was cloudless, the air cold and still. The low sun gilded the gold of the Bastille monument a few hundred metres down the road. Children whooped and yelled on the slides and swings in the little park along the centre of the boulevard. On a bench a homeless man slept, or lay very still, under rimed newspaper sheets. On the next bench, a young couple shared a joint and glanced furtively at the tramp. The market stalls had been up for hours, at this season selling preserves, knick-knacks, knock-offs, football shirts.

I'd intended to start the day with a brisk walk, but changed my mind when, after a hundred metres, my left knee played up. I turned back and limped down the entrance stairs of Richard Lenoir. The Metro was crowded and slow, stinking of Friday night. Things hadn't always been like this, I reminded myself.

Of course, we'd been ridiculously optimistic about meeting at the agreed place and time. That Saturday morning, a good hour before the ascent was scheduled, the exit from the Metro at Luxembourg was as crowded as the entrance to a football stadium on the night of a Cup Final; the Boulevard St-Michel looked as if – ha-ha – the revolution had started, or at least a rowdy *manif*. Cops, traffic, meeting someone: you could forget about all of those.

I did the sensible thing and found in the middle of the boulevard a bollard against which to brace myself in the throng. I switched on my earpiece, fired up my phone, and called Bob.

"Where are you?" I asked.

"Just inside the gate," he said. "Not going anywhere."

"I'm just outside," I said, "and likewise. Let's do this electronically."

Within a few minutes I had a conference call going with Bob and the half dozen American SF writers already scattered through the crowd. Jack, of course, and Nicole, and Catherine, and Seymour and good old Milton and Ali. I tuned out their eager catch-up gossip and flicked through news channels.

Nothing much was happening at the launch site in the middle of the park – the machine was still in its crate – so they were filling in with talking heads and shots of its arrival a couple of days earlier: the wide-load truck, the police outriders, the military escort vehicles, the faces and flags lining Rue de Vaugirard; the white gloves, the flashing lights, the gleaming rifle-barrels. Some comic relief as the convoy negotiated corners and the park gate. Then the crane, straining to lift the broad flat crate and lower it to the grass. The guard of honour around the hidden machine, and the real guard among the trees, armed and wired.

I thumbed over to the phone conversation.

" – *got* to be a fake," Jack was saying, in his usual confident bray. "You wait."

"We *are* waiting," said Nicole.

Laughter crackled across the phones.

"Why d'you think it's a fake?" Bob asked, a note of anxiety in his voice.

"Anti-gravity, come on!" said Jack. "Where's the theory?"

A babble of interruptions, shouted names of marginal physicists and outright cranks, was drowned out by a collective intake of breath, like a gust of wind in the still air. I left the phone channel open and flipped to the news. Four technicians in white coats had marched out onto the grass, towards the crate. They slid the top off – it looked like an aluminium roll-up door, which they duly rolled up – and, staggering slightly, lugged it like a log to lay it down a few metres away. Then they took up positions at the crate's corners. With a flourish, each reached for an edge, pressed some switch, and stepped well back.

The sides of the crate fell away, to reveal a silvery lens about fifteen metres across and just over three metres high in the centre.

A huge roar went up.

"My God," Milton said. "A goddam flying saucer."

He didn't sound impressed.

"If this is a stunt," said Catherine, "they're sure doing it very publicly."

"You know what this reminds me of?" said Nicole. "That scene in *Jefferson in Paris*, you know, the Nick Nolte thing? Where he's watching a Montgolfier ascent?"

"Too right," said Jack. "It's a fucking balloon! Just like at Roswell!"

The SF writers all laughed. I smiled to myself. They'd see.

Another roar erupted as the pilot walked out, helmet in the crook of his arm. He smiled around, gave a wave.

The news channels were beside themselves – the test pilot was Jean-Luc Jabril, an air force veteran in his thirties, something of a mascot for the Republic because of his origins: a son of Moroccans from the banlieues who'd made good, proving his French patriotism to the hilt in the fiery skies of North Africa. Everyone around me was looking at their phones, rapt. A few metres away in the crush, a girl in a hijab had tears on her cheeks.

Ceremoniously, Jabril put on his helmet, slid the visor down, took another wave for the cameras, and ducked under the machine's perimeter. A hatch in the underside swung open, forming a short ramp. He disappeared inside, and the hatch closed. White vapour puffed from vents on the rim.

And then, without fanfare, on the stroke of noon, the machine lifted into the air. It moved in a straight vertical, without a wobble or a yaw. The news channels' microphones caught and amplified a faint humming sound that rose to a whine as the disc ascended. I could see it directly now, rising above the wall and the tops of the trees. I stopped watching on the screen and raised my phone to record. Everyone around me did the same.

Up and up the machine rose, faster and faster, into the clear blue sky. A thousand feet, two thousand – I wasn't thinking in metres at this point. At three thousand feet the machine was a shining dot. I wished I'd thought to bring binoculars.

The flash was so bright that I felt sorry for those who had.

There was a sound as if half a million people had simultaneously been punched in the gut. A moment later, a sound like thunder. Then screams.

I was still blinking at purple after-images when I spotted a black dot drop from the fading flare. A parachute snapped open, perilously low. It floated downward for a few seconds and passed out of view. I'd tracked it with my camera, open-mouthed. I turned the phone over and looked at the news screen, just in time to catch a figure landing and rolling, then standing as the parachute collapsed beside him. Mobbed, Jibril had time to take his helmet off and deliver a shaky smile before the technicians and medics bundled him away.

"Jesus," I said. Nobody heard me. I could hardly hear myself above the yells and screams and cries of relief.

IT WAS TOWARDS the middle of that afternoon before we all met up, at a bistro in the Marais, not far from my own flat. I'd dropped by and picked up my wife, who was by now well awake and as shaken as everyone else who'd watched the ascent. We strolled around a few corners and joined the now somewhat larger group outside a bistro off Beaumarchais. They were outside because Jack had evidently insisted on smoking one of his Cuban cigars (a gesture somewhat redundant in the Year Three, but he'd acquired the taste in the old days). I bought our drinks and joined the huddle, introducing my wife to Bob and to two writers who hadn't met her before. She smiled politely and retreated to a table with Milton and Ali, over glasses of dry white and a saucer of black olives.

"But why," Bob was saying, "would they have their big show-off demonstration flight blow up like that? In front of everyone? If it was a fake, a *balloon* for fuck's sake, they'd have done much better just bringing it back down after a shorter flight."

"A double bluff," Jack said. He jabbed with his cigar. "Exactly so that everyone would think the way you're thinking."

The discussion went around and around, not getting anywhere.

"We'll know soon enough," Nicole pointed out. "With all those cameras and phones pointed at it, and no doubt all kinds of instruments – hell, there'll be a spectrograph analysis –"

"Wait a minute," said Jack. He dropped the butt of his cigar and crushed it out on the pavement, then reached into his jacket and pulled out his phone. He thumbed the screen.

"Knew I had the app," he said.

He poked about for a moment, then triumphantly held up his phone screen for all to see. I peered at a colour-coded histogram.

"What?" I said.

"Analysis of the light from my pics," he said. "Hydrogen and magnesium, mostly. No wonder the flash was so fucking bright!"

The sky had clouded over, the sun had set, rain began to spit. We headed indoors. After another round, of drinks and argument, we headed out. Across the boulevard and deeper into the Marais, wandering westward. It turned into one of those evenings. Standing outside a serving hatch in the drizzle, we dined on Breton pancakes out of waxed paper, reeled across the street, occupied a bar. Got into arguments, left, got turned away from a gay club that Milton and Ali had fancied they'd get us into, found another bistro. Bob bought more rounds than he drank. He worked his way around our tables, talking to each of the writers, and eventually squeezed in beside me and my wife.

"Done it!" he said. "Got everyone signed up."

"Good for you," I said.

"You're forgetting someone," my wife pointed out.

Bob mimed a double take. "Shit. *Pardon, madame.* Yes, of course." He looked me in the eye. "You up for a story?"

"I'm not American," I said.

"Hey, man, that's got nothing to do with it. You're one of the gang, even if you are a Brit."

"I appreciate the offer, Bob," I said. "But I think it would kind of... dilute the focus, know what I mean? And I don't have any problem getting published, even in English."

"Don't be so stupid," my wife said. "The Ozzies and Kiwis? They don't pay well, and it's not much of a market."

I smiled at her, then at Bob. "She guards my interests fiercely," I said. "Never lets me pass up a cent. But the fact is, I have a job that pays all right."

"Yeah, maintaining university admin legacy code in the Sorbonne basement," said Bob.

How had he known that? Maybe someone had mentioned it.

I shrugged. "It suits me fine. And like I said, it pays."

"Come on, you haven't sold a story in the US for years. And readers would like something from you, you know. It wouldn't narrow the anthology, it would broaden it out, having your name on the cover."

"Having your name as editor would do as much," I said.

"The offer's open," Bob said. He leaned forward and murmured: "For you – fifty cents a word."

I laughed. "What's a cent, these days?"

"I'm talking euros," Bob said. "Half a euro a word."

My wife heard that, and yelped. I must admit I sat up sharply myself.

"That's ridiculous," I said. "A few grand a story?"

"Not for every story," said Bob, ostentatiously glancing around to make sure no one had overheard. Not much chance of that – the bar was loud, and the conversation of the SF writers made it louder yet. "From you, I'll take ten-kay words. Five grand."

For the first time in weeks, I had a craving for a cigarette.

'I'll have to go outside and think about it,' I said.

I bummed a Gitane off Nicole, grinned at my wife's frown, and headed out. The rain had stopped. The street was dark, half the street-lamps out. My Zippo flared – I keep it topped up, for just these contingencies. After a minute, Bob joined me. He took a fresh pack from his pocket, peeled cellophane, and lit up.

"You too?" I said, surprised.

He shrugged. "Only when I'm travelling. Breaks the ice in some places."

"I'll bet," I said. I glared at him. "Fucking Yank."

"What?"

"Don't mess with my friends."

"What?"

"I know what you're up to," I said. "Checking them out, seeing who's all mouth and who's serious enough to be interested in one of your little schemes."

"Have you got *me* wrong," said Bob. "I'm not interested in them. I'm interested in you."

He spread his hands, flashed me a conspiratorial grin.

"Forget it," I said.

"Come on, you hate the bastards as much as I do."

"That's the trouble," I said. "You don't."

"What do you mean by that?" He sounded genuinely indignant, almost hurt. I knew that meant nothing. It was a tone I'd practiced often enough.

"You don't hate the revolution," I said. I waved a trail of smoke. "Civil war, terror, censorship, shortages, dictatorship – yeah, I'm sure you hate all that. But it's still the beginning of socialism. It's still *the revolution*, isn't it?"

"Not my revolution!"

"You were never a wanker," I said. "Don't mistake me for one, either."

He tossed his cigarette into the running gutter, and continued the arm movement in a wave.

"So why... all this?"

"We have perfected this machine," I said.

He gave me a long look.

"Ah," he said. "I see. Like that, is it?"

"Like that," I said.

I held the door open for him as we went back in. The telly over the bar was showing yet another clip of the disastrous flight. Bob laughed as the door swung shut behind us.

"You didn't perfect *that* machine!"

We picked our way through the patrons to the gang, who by now had shoved two tables together and were all in the same huddle of heads.

"Describe what happened," I said, as we re-joined them. "At the Jardin."

"Well," Bob began, looking puzzled, "we all saw what was *claimed* to be an anti-gravity flying machine rise in the air and blow up. And some of us think –"

"No," I said. I banged the table. "Listen up, all of you. Bob is going to tell us what he saw."

"What do you want me to say?" Bob demanded. "I saw the same as the rest of you. I was just inside the park, I saw it on my phone and when the thing cleared the treetops I saw it with my own eyes. The machine, or what we'd been told was a machine, rose up –"

"Not that," I said. "Start from when you got to the park."

Bob frowned. "The Place was crowded. I couldn't see what was happening around the crate. There were people in the way, trees..." He shrugged. "What's to say?"

"Describe the trees. Think back to looking up at them."

Bob sipped the dregs of the green drink in front of him, shaking his head.

"Bare branches, clear blue sky."

"Were the branches moving?"

"What's that got to do with anything?"

"Well, were they?"

"Of course not!" he said. "There wasn't a breath of wind."

"Bingo!" I said. "There was *a clear blue sky*. There *wasn't a breath of wind*."

"I don't get it."

Nor did anyone else, by the looks I was getting.

"The machine moved straight up," I said. "And we're all fairly sure it was some fake, right? An arrangement of balsa and mylar, hydrogen and magnesium."

I took out my Zippo, and flicked the lid and the wheel. "That's all it would have taken. Whoof!"

"Yeah," said Jack, looking interested. "So?"

"The ascent was announced a month and a half ago," I said. "New Year's Eve. Announced to the day, to the hour, the minute! Noon, Saturday fifteenth Feb."

"I don't get it."

"Imagine what today's little demonstration would have been like," I said, "if there had been... a breath of wind. Or low cloud. The fake would have been blatant." I held out my hand, fingers spread, and waggled it as I gestured drifting. "Like that."

Jack guffawed, and Bob joined in. Everyone else just frowned.

"You're saying the French have weather control?"

"No," I said. "I'm saying they have weather *prediction*. That's what they demonstrated today, not anti-gravity – and that's what is going to scare the shit out of the Americans and the Brits. Probably has already."

"It's impossible to predict the weather forty days in advance," said Catherine. "Chaos theory, butterfly effect, all that, you know?"

"Apparently not," I said. "A lot of mathematics research going on at the Sorbonne, you know." I turned to Bob. "Take that back to your revolution."

He stared at me for a long moment.

"Fuck you," he said. "And the horse you rode in on."

He stood up and stormed out.

None of us heard from him again. Editions Jules Verne, the publishing company, never heard from him either. They honoured the contracts, but nothing came of the anthology.

The ascent at the Jardin de Luxembourg is still the best science fiction of the Year Three.

THE ONE THAT GOT AWAY

TRICIA SULLIVAN

Tricia Sullivan is the author of seven SF novels including the Clarke-winning Dreaming in Smoke *and most recently* Lightborn, *which was shortlisted for the Clarke. Tricia works from home, cares for three children and studies fitfully with the Open University. She says of 'The One That Got Away' that this is one of those unusual stories that invent themselves without much authorial interference, so anybody wondering what it's trying to say please don't ask her... go ask the nearest fish.*

LATELY THERE AREN'T enough corpses to go around. The flies sell stories about how being a rag is a lost way of life. They interview the rags who have left the beach for good, taking their afflictions and overall stinky atmosphere with them. Sad birds, migrating. Some are bitter about the lack of death, about the fact that what there is gets monopolized by celebrities like Jacques Trachea. He doesn't even call himself a rag. No, he's a fucking *pilgrim*, he is.

As the sun goes down, Trachea's team are busy setting out extra receivers so that his cloud can float him for the big duel between Daw and Drake. Flies scramble the air, waiting for their Man.

Nobody interviews Gran. She couldn't speak if she wanted to, but it bothers me that nobody even tries. She's one of the last of the old school rags. She must know something. I find her... what's the word? I don't know how to put it.

It's like this. Of all of the rags, Gran is the one who has most reason to leave. She has family in the Meta. She could stay with my parents; they have money. Poverty may have forced Gran to take up the rag to start, but it's no longer an issue. Does she care? No. Gran won't go. Ever. She doesn't even care how sick she gets.

So what if she's never, ever found core? She won't – *can't?* – leave the beach. She's so much a fixture that she shows up on postcards and tourist videos. Rich people from faraway think she's poetic, or pathetic. Both.

Mysterious. That's the word. I find her mysterious. And mysterious works for me, especially because when I first came down here it was to hide. Get away from Karl and his friends and their fucked-up scams and schemes. Lick my wounds. Deal with the fact that all my education had done for me was turn me into a petty criminal. Gran's never judged me.

Actually, being around her cheers me up. By comparison with Gran's problems, mine look like a premenstrual zit or hangnail. She's totally fucked in this life, and it's only going to get worse. She needs my help. So I live in her tent that was designed as an emergency shelter for hurricane victims but has lasted her fifteen years because she's so careful with everything she does.

I live with her and try to convince her to walk away from the beach – because that's what you do, right? You say, "Come away from all this mess and suffering. You've done your best, but it's over. Come on up to the Meta, we'll have a barbeque and a few beers."

Even though you know every word dresses you in your hypocrite suit, you say it. Because it's hard to watch somebody slowly die.

I've thought about going straight. I might even do it, if she asked me. But she doesn't ask me. I get the feeling she doesn't care about anything but what's on this beach. Or – lately – what's not on it.

Tonight brings the world to this beach. Drake and Daw have bet on whether Daw's prediction dog Genji can pinpoint the location of core. They have wagered a case of Mountain Dew. Daw says his dog is a core-detecting algorithm. Drake says the nature of core is elusive, that the spirit of nature will not be tamed. Daw says the gods are already dead so being 'tamed' is a barn with no horse left in it.

Then he releases his dog. Genji runs up and down the beach, a blue searchlight strapped to his head like a miner's lamp. Flies zigzag in an effort to track the dog, their commentators talking faster and faster, like it's a hockey playoff and the game's gone into overtime. The commentators' little moustaches of anti-microbial ointment make them look like Charlie Chaplin or Hitler.

The smell won't reach the restaurants overlooking the beach. The Meta people can look out over the waves and the corpses and watch the rags work without ever scenting death. They have suction devices and air current regulators and a whole outfit of microbial helpers so that they won't have to smell anything but their

Lobster Thermidor. Up by the rock pools, closest to the promenade, spectacularly expensive microbial colonies are strewn across the beach like sand dollars, turning shit to sugar with modern efficiency. The brilliance from those colonies is a thousand times brighter than anything ever derived from all the core found by all the rags who ever lived, all put together.

Yet that old core built Meta. I know that because I have an expensive education. And we can all see where that got me.

GENJI TROTS ALONG the sand, snout to windward. His searchlight strokes the sky, core-seeking.

JACQUES TRACHEA'S CREW have set up a rack of power tools down near the water. He makes a point of hacking off tendrils, sawing ribs, gouging dead eyes and searching the rotting meat with the smart core-detectors his swanky pilgrim's contract affords him. I try not to look too closely but you can't miss the silver nimbus over his head where a representative sample of his followers display themselves: the grieving, the sick, the dying, the prisoners, the out-of-work, the bored, the lost. The battered believers with their deep-fried soul, they need Jacques to find core and he needs them to need him.

The other rags have weaker haloes. Each has a cam or two fleabagging them, and each cam represents several thousand people who have put their faith in that rag, like bettors backing a greyhound. Even a glimpse of core can sustain a person for years.

Her armpits permanently stained by the entrail-slime of dead gods, my grandmother displays no followers at all. In seventy-two years of cleaning she has processed and removed tons of dead godflesh from this beach. She has bent her back and ruined her knees and her eyes. Her voice is lost and some say so is her mind. But every day she's here, rags, bucket, spade. Hope.

I claim I'm here to help her but she knows I'm on the run from Karl and his friends. Sleight of hand is my game, and I'm good at it. I don't even feel guilty because in my experience people are asking to be fooled. But I don't like being used by assholes, and things came to a head. I work on my raft by night, hiding it in the dunes. It should have been done by now, but I find myself stalling. Gran vomits a little every morning. I don't know how long she can go on.

I'm stuck. Some people have grandparents they can go to for money when they're in trouble. My Gran's home is only useful as an aromatic deterrent to pursuers. Plus, no one would think to look for me here with the stupid old people, who believe in something.

And the thing is, as soon as I start thinking about how stupid she is and how annoying it is that she's not like a normal grandmother, it makes me feel guilty and kind of nasty. Which, let's face it, I am. Gran loves me. Gran has time for me, no matter what mess I've made. Mess doesn't phase Gran one single bit. And I love her, too, but I wish to fuck she'd find some core and retire.

She's the only rag on this beach without a single mote, let alone a cloud. I mean, in the world's lowliest vocation she's at absolute bottom.

Once, when she could still speak, she told me that clouds are a distraction. "No good rag needs followers," she said. "I've never wanted them, and I think they sense that and leave me alone. I can't work with someone looking over my shoulder."

Whatever you want to believe, Gran, I said to myself. The ways people console themselves for their failure. It's so sad. Not that I should talk.

"Jacques is successful," I tell her now. "He has over a hundred million followers and they don't stop him finding core. He has some kind of... I don't know, some kind of gift."

She shows me the wrinkled-tree-bark face. Maybe Mom is right. Gran must be in denial. It must burn her so bad that she's been here her whole life looking for core and has only found some tiny unauthorized gleams once or twice a decade. She has so little to offer any possible motes, while Jacques has only been on the beach a year and he's already a celebrity. From even the weakest, most decayed, wretched has-been of a corpse, Jacques can extract core of exquisite brilliance and meaning.

I have this problem with my mouth. I say the wrong thing. It's happening now.

"But Gran, you haven't found anything in a long time."

She shrugs.

"Do you hate him?"

She points to Jacques, and then to her throat. She makes a point of swallowing, then shakes her head.

"He doesn't swallow? Gran, really – don't tell me you *swallow*? You don't swallow their... flesh?"

Dordogne, another old-school cleaner, staggers past us. He's carrying two reeky buckets on a yoke around his neck like something out of the Dark Ages. He pauses, panting, and in his drainpipe voice asserts, "Some people don't swallow like some people don't inhale. You get what you pay for. Everybody got a right to search. Trachea got a right. Core be core. He find it, then bless him. He trying, then bless him anyway. He's an asshole, then bless his holy ass."

He wheezes away, shaking his head at his own humour.

GRAN HIKES UP her skirt and wades out. She wears no gloves. Claims she's immune to all the corpse bugs now, but I know that's not true. They took her voice. Mom and Aunt Shara don't come here because of that. Mom stopped me coming, too. Afraid for my fertility, sanity, mobility – you name it.

"I know you love Gran," Mom told me when I was eleven. "You lived on that beach when you were little and I was working. But things are different now. She's gone... too far. She's chosen to leave us behind. Not the other way around."

But the smell of dead gods is the smell of my childhood. The only waves I know are dirty and foul. When I go up to the garden district to visit my family, they talk about the beach and the shit and the death that Gran lives with. Like they own it. "Those were hard times," they say, munching barbecue beside their private pools.

Mom says Gran has invested so much searching for core that she can't stop. "It's an addiction," Mom says sadly.

"It's not an addiction," Gran told me when she could still talk. "It's common sense. The bodies of dead gods must be honored."

Gods take funny shapes. Octopi, whale sharks, clams, sea horses larger than land horses. Giant water spiders. Washed ashore below the glittering town, like tampons and cola bottles. From a distance, they are a tourist attraction. Artists come to be inspired (bringing nasal plugs).

Now Drake is talking about the failures of science. He waves his arms a lot, and his anti-microbial moustache makes his nose run. His followers will find him even more authentic for it. I stay away from the cams. Don't want Karl to find me.

Trachea waits until everyone's looking at Drake. He flips his hair, which smears a bit of blackish blood across his cheekbone, stylishly, just in time for the cams to swing back on him and show how real he is. The other rags scurry and hurry, eager to be spotlighted as Genji's searchlight passes over them.

Daw is answering the same questions Rogers always asks. Talking about how he has spent his career designing Genji's abilities. He didn't design the dog itself, of course, but he makes it sound like one day he'll probably whip one up in his spare time.

"Why are fewer gods appearing? Because they've rotted away to nothing, of course!" He pauses to chortle. "And that is because there is no more need for gods now that we have pinned down how to make life with such breathtaking specificity."

Breathtaking specificity? Really? I am stacking Gran's buckets and checking her nets for holes. I mean, holes apart from the ones that are supposed to be there. That's the funny thing about nets.

"Gods," says Daw, "were only ever thoughts in the minds of humans, not the other way round. So even as we use their core energies to light up our world" – and he sweeps an arm toward the Meta – "we can let the gods go."

GRAN'S TOENAILS HAVE been black ever since I can remember. I don't think she's left the beach in twenty years. My mother told me that every moment of her childhood, every hurt and triumph, was accompanied by the smell of death because Gran couldn't afford to live anywhere but here. Rags depended on handouts – like monks, only smellier. As Mom got older, she just couldn't stand it anymore. She went to live with her aunt, who soft-soaped the smell out of Mom until not a whiff of dead god could be detected on her skin. Both of them want to forget the beach exists, and they mostly succeed. Now Mom pays a contractor to clean her house and shield her from the brilliance of entropy.

Gran and I are up to our waists, near the rotting bones now. These usually collapse by the time a god comes to shore. Bioluminescence replaces structure as gods are broken down by tiny creatures that shit light. The smell is overpowering. I have vomited twice by the time Genji stops running up and down the beach.

Why is he stopping here? Squinting, I see his neck bristle. His tail goes stiff. He begins to bark. Then he points. While the flies swarm on Trachea, the telling beam of Genji's light has landed on Gran's ass where she bends down to drag a torn intestine from the lapping water. The end of the intestine coughs out globs of crap fitfully, like a dribbly hose. Behind her towers the half-melted rib cage of a foetid fish-god. The bones are becoming holey and translucent as they liquefy.

"Well, that's a surprise, Bettina! Dr Daw, is this the official prediction?"

Daw has a deeply unhappy expression on his face. Flies are abandoning Trachea and his fluffed-out hair for my grandmother and her stained mouth. She squints into the light but doesn't smile. I duck away.

"Madame?"

Gran tries to ignore the flies but they've got her surrounded. Trachea's halo abandons him and gathers around Gran's head. She swats at it in thinly-disguised annoyance. Her new followers won't go, though. They make a bright nimbus of suffering: young people on chemo, old people on respirators, newborns plugged in by overeager parents, etiolated women on a bad connection that blurs their empty, begging hands and pixelates the hollowness beneath their eyes. Children with no hands and their elders, all expectant, half-weeping with anticipation of the sight of core.

Drake looks pleased, starts rubbing his hands. *That prediction machine's a piece of shit*, you can hear him thinking. He's already tasting the sweet, sweet Mountain Dew.

Rogers intones, "And we're told Madame here has a track record of... zero for 40,104. Can this really be right, Bettina? Has this person really never found anything in all her years as a Cleaner?"

"Never," says Bettina. "The dedication of these Cleaners is truly remarkable. Madame lost her voice seven years ago in the infectious wave following the dismemberment of the Giant Goddess, but she continues to work here every day in all weathers. Despite the unconscionable smell."

"Probably she can't smell anything," quips Rogers. "Maybe that's why she stays."

"Of course she can smell." I snarl. "I can smell. We all can smell it. We're here anyway."

Bettina starts to ask Gran questions.

"She can't speak," I say. "Don't frighten her. She's old. Her voice is gone."

Flies begin aligning themselves to me, buzzing.

What's your name? Bucky.

Is that your real name? My name's Baksheesh. It means 'little gift'. My mother thought it was cute. Obviously it isn't.

How old is the Madame? 109.

Has she ever found core? Not to my knowledge.

Why doesn't she leave? God calls her.

But the gods are dead, or dying. She must honor them, I say. I say it out of duty to her, not because I believe it. Once they were alive, I say. Do they become less divine, in death?

"They can hardly qualify as gods if they die," Daw drawls. I can feel his blue, intelligent eyes picking a trail over my face. I can feel him dismissing me, too. "But Genji predicts that core will be found here, tonight, by your grandmother. So perhaps she will get her wish after all."

Yeah, and perhaps you'll give out lollipops after? I don't say it, but I think it.

Drake does nothing to take Daw down. Instead he launches into a description of his latest research proving that fairies and rainbows really are the same thing (or something) and I slip away from Bettina and Daw and the millions of tiny, distant eyes. Of course, just then Jacques Trachea would have to give a shout.

"Aha!" Drake cries, waving long arms. "It would appear that even Genji is not infallible!"

"The results aren't all in yet," Daw replies in a crabby voice, and the clouds swarm and re-form as followers change camps. Daw holds position behind Gran's bony butt. "We are close to pinpointing something quite extraordinary here. Please don't be distracted by the shiny things you may see in Mr. Trachea's camp."

Gran reaches her hand into the decaying body and licks her fingers, sucks them with her thin lips. I wince.

"Look at this!" It's Drake again. He's very excited. Trachea works his trapezoids attractively as he pulls' out cogs, wires, lights. From the sump he removes a long-flute-like thing that nobody quite recognizes. Then he pulls out an intact brass ship's bell. I'm not sure what it means, but there is a collective gasp of wonder.

"Eureka!" Jacques' teeth flash in the glow of his own halo. The bell rings wildly. Trachea's halo is so full of rapt souls it flickers like static, a field of insect-sparkles and dim suggested outlines, entities not well-received but trying hard to be here. Share in the glory. Everyone loves him, the core-finder, the salvager, our salvation. I find myself caught up in it.

Gran's mouth works. She vomits a little. She's up to her hips in fish guts. She gives a jerk and I see her hands fumbling, like she's trying to catch something that's falling out of a cupboard. She bends over furtively, hissing, desperate eyed.

Gagging, I reach her side. So do a cloud of flies. She's juggling something shimmery.

"Is that a fish?" Bettina squeaks, turning her attention back to Gran. "What fish could survive inside the body of a dead god? Or was it loose in the harbour? We need to see that better..."

"A fish isn't core!" Drake warns. "Core is inanimate and the product of abstract thought."

Daw frowns. The smell must be getting through to him, because he turns his head and spits.

Gran makes a throwing motion with her right hand, but her left side leans into me and she secretly passes something small and slippery and moving. Holding it in my fist, I find the cloud all around me. Tiny lights, glimmering. My lips peel back from my teeth.

"It was just a fish," I report, backing away. "She threw it back."

I POINT TO the lapping waves, and some of the cams go that way. Others follow me. They know what they saw. Most people do. But the thing is, in my line of work you quickly learn that people train themselves not to see what they see. They train themselves to be victims to people like me. I know how to play their expectations. It's how I work.

So I weave among the clouds to bend over the disorderly pile of nets and rags. I slide the fish into a wet rag, unseen. I don't know why Gran wants to keep it secret, but she does.

Drake is laughing and pontificating. "Stand down, everyone, it was just a fish!" he says. "Genji didn't predict fish, he predicted core. So, let's see where the core is tonight."

While they're distracted I slip away and put the fish into a cafeteria-sized baked bean tin that Gran uses to store her bits. It swims on its side in the dirty water. I leave it in the tent.

I can't find Gran. I search everywhere, and I'm beginning to worry that she's slipped and fallen in the murky shallows when I spot her.

Gran is walking up the beach without her rags. Bettina is walking alongside her. I run up there. Bettina is saying, "Your family will be so happy to have you home. Here, chew this gum. Your breath…"

Daw huffs up alongside Gran. He's trying to convince her to continue searching. She shakes her head. No moving Gran when she doesn't want to go.

I smile, and chewing Bettina's gum Gran turns and looks at me. I don't know what to say.

It seems a betrayal, but how can I argue when I know it's best for her?

"Are you really going?"

She nods. She blows me a kiss with her mucky fingers, and then she turns into Bettina's halo and walks away just like that. Daw throws up his hands.

I return to the shoreline to see Genji sitting on one of Gran's rags, whining. Daw tries to get him to make another prediction, but he refuses.

DRAKE IS DANCING because he has won a case of Mountain Dew, if not respect in the scientific community. He is dancing and almost singing. Daw scowls at his dog.

"WHAT YOU GOT there?"

It's two days later. I forgot how well Karl knows me. He is in the tent, pointing to the baked bean tin. I try to shrug, but I'm shaking.

"Your Gran pull that out god's ass? I heard something about that shit."

"Nah, we threw that away. This is just... you know. Just a regular fish."

His eyes are so big and dark and long at the edges. He blinks slow. If Karl were a woman people would call him a siren.

"Regular fish. You keeping it why?"

Another attempt at a shrug by me. "No reason."

He lunges past me, displacing the air so suddenly that the sides of the tent billow. Before I can move, he has the tin in his hands. The fish lies sideways in the water, still looking up with one eye.

"You got core in this fish. Don't lie to me, Bucky. I already know. You think I'm stupid? Genji the core dog pointed to your old Gran. Not Jack-off Trachea. Now I'm giving you a chance. You want to split the fish, you pay what you owe and keep the rest, then we go our separate ways."

Yeah, right. Pay what I owe? He wants the whole fish.

"You can't sell this fish, Karl. It isn't core. It isn't anything. It's just a fish."

"Bullshit. So core's usually some kind of man-made object. So what? A fish is a god-made object. What's the difference?"

"The difference is the gods are dead."

"Only if Daw's right. And if Daw's right, then his dog picked your Gran. So that's core."

"It's not core. Anyway, Drake won the bet."

"If Drake won the bet, then we *can't* understand nature. I'm not stupid, Bucky. I get how this works. So the gods can't all be dead after all. That fish is a symbol of hope."

"Karl, you're not making sense. They could both be wrong. Maybe we don't understand nature. But the gods are dead also. God being dead is a fact. Can't you smell it?'

He touches his nasal plugs, smiles.

"It has to be one or the other. Maybe Daw's dog made a mistake this one time, but he could improve the design."

All my conversations with Karl, always, are this discursive. Exactly this discursive, no more and no less.

"I thought we were arguing about who owns the fish."

"That fish is mine," says Karl, heatedly.

I FUCK HIM two or three times to get rid of him. Agree to meet him at the pricing outlet up in Koko-mart. He seems spooked by the fish, and leaves it with me when he goes away beating his hands on his thighs and chanting to the rage track in his ears.

LATER. WASHING KARL'S doomed little fishes out of my blowhole. Thinking, ha, die little fuckers. You not eat my sweet. I can't even imagine a world where every little pleasure could represent someone's whole lifetime, exploding out of me.

Gran trying all those years to serve the gods. Who knows what gods want anyway? It's not like they tell you. Not now, in death. Not ever. Probably.

On my way to Koko-mart with the fish I see something dark lying too close to a patch of city bugs, just at the edge of the beach. It's angular and shiny, and for a moment I think Trachea has left some of his equipment behind. Then I blink and recognise Dordogne. The bugs are onto him.

"It's over," he whispers. "New dawn. New day. I wasted my life. Can you take me to hospital?"

He's skinny, but it's hard getting him up and taking his weight. His muscles are like soup all the way up the beach to the train, but there's a stickiness to his skin. Maybe it's the bugs, but he feels like rubber.

"I stick to you," he sighs in my ear. "That what I do now. I stick to you.'

I keep him going all the way from the train to the hospital waiting room, where his eyes turn yellow in the artificial light. The last thing he says to me is, "You sell that fish, Bucks. Don't waste your chances. Fish gonna be big. Offspring of a god? Gonna be big. You get a piece of it. Don't be like me and your Gran. Bless you, Bucks, you gonna be alright."

ON MY WAY home I look up the numbers wagered at Koko's to try and get an idea of the possible value of this fish. The numbers, in theory, are big. The fish's existence is just a rumour and that makes it special, like it's glowing with some kind of potential energy. If I'm going to act, I need to do it soon, before people forget all about Drake and Daw and their bet.

Standing in the crowd outside Koko-mart, the fish and I observe each other extensively. There's something wrong with that one fin. It swims on its side, looking up at me out of its left eye.

Offspring of a god? Really? Hnh. I doubt it.

I should take that money. It would be great. But the thing is, in all of this whole thing, nobody ever asks the fish about its own plans. And that doesn't seem fair after all Gran went through, and after all the fish (presumably) went through.

Then again, Gran gave me the fish. It was all she had to give and now it's worth money. She turned out to be a proper money-giving Gran, in the end.

I'm a little surprised with myself when I say, 'What you want, fish?'

It doesn't answer me. It's not like Genji. Nobody has improved it. It's just a fish that swims slightly screwy.

So I have to guess. I have to guess at this, just like I have to guess at everything else.

THE UNFINISHED RAFT, I leave it behind. I'm a thief, remember. So I steal this boat. I go out by night, no motor, only a paddle.

When I loose the fish in the sea I don't say anything. I don't even think anything. If the fish is god, it knows what I'm thinking anyway.

When it's in the open water I look hopefully for a sign that something's changed. All it does differently is stop swimming on its side with only one fin working, stop looking up at me from the water. It straightens itself out and swims down and away into darkness.

After it's gone I feel quiet. I wish I could stay out here, never go back to land. Out here on the moving water with the bioluminescence starring my wet hands like I'm five years old playing with glitter. Galactic me.

Wish I could stay, but I'm not made for this place.

When finally I turn back, paddle in hand, I see the Meta gleaming on the shore. The bluffs on either side are dark and blurry, but the Meta is so sharp and bright that even from this distance my throat tightens and I catch my breath. The memory of Dordogne's skin sings against my palms. I know what I have to do. It doesn't even feel like a choice. I put the paddle down and kick off my shoes.

The whole world can't be like Meta. There must be other places, other shores or certainties, where the tide doesn't cast up toxic brilliance. I can swim for one of them. The water's fucking cold tonight, but I can swim.

ROCK DAY

STEPHEN BAXTER

Stephen Baxter has some 35 novels to his credit and has won the Philip K. Dick, the John W. Campbell, the BSFA, the Sidewise, and the Locus awards. Stephen's latest project has been the Northland trilogy: Stone Spring, Bronze Summer, *and* Iron Winter, *a saga of a different prehistory. He is involved with the international SETI (Search for Extraterrestrial Intelligence) programme, and a study to design a starship with the British Interplanetary Society, both of which activities fed into the inspiration behind the story in this volume.*

MATT WOKE THAT morning to the usual noises. The buzz of a lawn mower, probably Mister Bowden's a few doors down. The soft pad of a dog's paws outside his bedroom. That was Prince.

He rolled out of bed in his pyjamas, and walked barefoot to the door. But the door wouldn't open. He almost walked right into it. He took a step back and tried again. The door was straightforward promat, it should have broken up at his approach and folded back into its frame. It remained a stubborn blank panel.

Matt was eleven years old. He rubbed his face, greasy with sleep sweat. Maybe he wasn't quite awake yet.

Something smelled funny.

He looked around at his room. It seemed messy, the bed with the crumpled sheets, heavy cobwebs up on the ceiling, the smart-posters inert and peeling off the walls. He didn't remember the room being this bad. He wasn't that much of a slob. Dad would kill him, if he saw it.

And the Mist wasn't working. Everywhere he looked stuff should have been sparkling with messages sent and received, his projects and games, reminders about school. Nothing. Maybe Dad had grounded him, shut it off. But for what? He couldn't remember doing anything wrong, or at least no more wrong than usual.

He tried the door again. It still wouldn't open. But there was always a backup system, as Dad would say, in this case a handle and hinges. He turned the handle, the door was sticky in its frame, but it opened with a tug.

And there was Prince, waiting outside Matt's bedroom just like every morning. Prince was a blue roan cocker spaniel. He'd been lying there with his head between his paws. Now he got to his feet a bit heavily, as he was ten years old, and, tail wagging, jumped up for a tickle. Then he grabbed the toy he'd brought this morning, a chewed rubber bone, and Matt had to wrestle him for that for a bit. And then Prince curled up against the wall again and raised his front paw so Matt could stroke the soft hairs on his chest. The same every morning, just the way boy and dog liked it.

But the hallway light hadn't come on, and the floor here was dusty too. Maybe Matt really was the slob his Dad claimed he was, if he didn't even *notice* this stuff.

He walked down the short hallway, past his Dad's bedroom where the door was Closed, a sign that Dad was asleep or working and not to be disturbed. He found the bathroom door stuck on open, whereas his bedroom door had stayed closed. He went in to use the toilet.

But he found he didn't need to pee. He tried, but there was nothing there.

There was muck and mess in the bowl, however. He passed his hand over the flush panel, but it wouldn't work. Another stupid thing gone wrong. Matt decided he'd come back up later with a bucket of water to flush it through, if Dad didn't fix it first.

Prince was waiting, tail wagging, pink tongue lolling. "Come on, boy!" He ran down the stairs two at a time, and the dog tumbled at his feet.

IN THE DOWNSTAIRS hall there was more muck, he saw, and little pellets that looked like mouse droppings. Yecch! And the news panel by the full-length mirror near the door was frozen on a Liverpool EchoNet shoutline:

ROCK DAY!
4th JUNE 2087!
DOOM OR JOKE?
WE'LL KNOW BY 3pm –
OR NOT!
PAGING ALL ALIENS...

Was it Rock Day today? He felt confused, as if he'd forgotten something. He tried thumping the panel, but the wording wouldn't refresh.

He tried to let Prince out of the house, but the front door was another non-opener. He had to turn an emergency-exit handle and practically yank the door out of its frame.

Prince trotted out into bright morning sunshine, and began sniffing around the grass, choosing a spot for a luxurious leg-raise. Matt followed him out and, in his bare feet, stepped to the end of the path. He pushed through patches of overgrown mod-potato plants, their big black leaves heavy. Dad wouldn't be pleased they'd not been earthed up.

Luckily the gate was closed, Matt hadn't thought to check, but even if Prince had got out there was no traffic. Or at least nothing moving. There was a pod bus that had come off the road a little way down the avenue of neat identical houses, the bulbous passenger pods empty and tumbled against the side of the road.

This was Wavertree, an inner suburb of Liverpool, only a few kilometres east of the city centre and the docks. It should have been buzzing with activity, the noise from the city a dull roar. But this morning there was only silence, save for that mower a few doors away. And things looked – shabby. The houses were dark, the big solar-power panels on their roofs mucky and peeling, their gardens overgrown. One house down the road looked burned out, that was the Palleys', and he didn't remember that happening and you'd think he would, you didn't see a house burn down every day.

Mister Bowden came into view around the corner of his house, three along from Matt's. Of course Mister Bowden didn't need to be following his mower around the lawn, but he evidently liked the gentle stroll. Mister Bowden was a widower, about fifty. He'd always been friendly to Dad and Matt, especially after Mum had died, and it was as if he and Dad suddenly had something in common. Matt was less interested in him now he was growing up. He couldn't remember the last time he'd spoken to old Mister Bowden, in fact. But this was a funny morning.

On impulse Matt waved. "Mister Bowden!" His voice echoed off the blank faces of the houses.

Mister Bowden stopped dead, as the mower tooled on, and looked around. When he saw Matt he stared, as if he was surprised, or, oddly, as if he'd just woken up. "Matt? Are you all right?"

Yes. No. Nothing's *working*. Matt said none of these things. Suddenly he felt as if he'd acted like a little kid. He ran back into the house, Prince at his heels, and slammed the door.

Covering his embarrassment he went straight to the cupboard under the stairs and pulled out the vacuum cleaner. "You! If you're not cleaning the muck off the floor, go out and earth up the potatoes!"

The cleaner shuddered, gave a kind of burp, and lurched forward. After all that had happened this morning Matt was faintly surprised it responded at all. But it didn't head for the garden, and it didn't switch modes. It should have dissolved into a puddle of programmable-matter component parts, and then reassembled for its gardening function. Instead it lurched past Matt, heading back along the hall to a point on the wall where it began to bump its base against the skirting board. Matt saw what it was trying to do. There was a power outlet there, fed from the solar cells on the roof, but the wall wasn't opening up. Thump, thump, thump. Matt was reminded of his own attempts to open his bedroom door. The longer it went on the slower the cleaner got – thump... thump... thump...

Matt couldn't bear to watch any more.

He pushed on to the kitchen. But that was another disappointment.

This had always been the most Mist-dense, gadget-laden room in the whole house, where Mum and Dad used to have competitions cooking each other the fanciest meal, and Matt aged nine or eight or seven would be roped in to help one or the other, while the living room furniture noisily reassembled itself for dining. Since Mum had died Matt and Dad had enjoyed coming in here to work together, remembering her in a sweet and sour sort of way, as Dad expressed it.

Today the kitchen was dead. Every surface was flat, plain, inert. He couldn't even open the big fridge, which had none of its usual scrolling updates on the freshness of its contents. In most of the cupboards there was nothing but rot and damp and mould, and cardboard packets chewed by hungry little teeth. But when Matt checked the cupboard where they kept the dog food he found it stacked high with cans – plain, no label, that was funny – and a manual can-opener on the door that he didn't remember seeing before.

At least there was plenty of food for Prince, when it was his meal time later. But there was nothing at all in the kitchen for Matt to eat, or Dad, and it looked like there hadn't been for a long time. That just baffled him. What had he eaten yesterday, then? He couldn't remember.

He stood there. *Why* couldn't he remember? Strangeness upon strangeness. And on Rock Day too, if the Echo was up to date, "the day those idiots in space are playing out their game of cosmic chicken with God," as Dad described it, and the world ended or it didn't. Matt started to get a panicky, fluttery feeling in his stomach. What was going on?

But here was the dog, wagging his tail.

Prince's blue plastic water bowl was empty. That was one thing Matt could do. But nothing came out of the taps when he waved the bowl under them. He had to force open the back door, which was as inert as all the other doors, and he went out to the rain barrel and bent to fill the bowl at the tap.

"Hi again, Matt."

Here was Mister Bowden, looking in from the street, leaning on the fence.

"Mister Bowden." Matt felt oddly uncomfortable. He put down the dog's bowl. Prince lapped up the water.

Mister Bowden was a little on the portly side, but with a round, fleshy, open face, big eyes, and a wide grin. "Everything all right this morning?"

"Why shouldn't it be?"

"Well, I don't know. I don't mean anything by it." He looked faintly confused himself. He had a strong, coarse Knowsley accent. "It's just, you know... How was your breakfast this morning?"

"Breakfast?"

He nodded to the kitchen, through the open door. "What did you have, cereal, juice, toast, coffee? Water from the tap?"

"I..."

"What about your father? Is he around today?"

Suddenly Matt panicked again. "Prince, come." He grabbed the water bowl, spilling half of what was left.

"Matt, I think we should talk –"

Matt dashed through the door back into the kitchen, and as soon as the dog was inside he slammed the door shut. He could see Mister Bowden through the murky window, standing patiently, leaning on the fence, looking in. Then, with the gentlest shake of his head, Mister Bowden withdrew.

Matt stood there in the dark, stuffy, smelly kitchen, heart thumping, breathing hard. Something was wrong. *Everything* was wrong.

Prince looked up at him, eyes wide, wagging his tail. It was time for the fetching game they always played before his morning walk.

But Matt had to see Dad, Closed Door or not. He ran upstairs. Prince followed, thinking he was playing, wanting his walk.

Of course Dad's bedroom door didn't fold away. Matt took the handle, and hesitated. Once, long ago, he had been the one who found his mother dead, lying in bed, of a heart attack. You didn't forget a thing like that. Now he didn't know what to expect on the other side of *this* door. Buzzing flies?

He turned the handle, and shoved the sticky door.

The room was dark, the curtains drawn. He avoided looking at the bed and went straight to the curtains, and pulled them back to allow in the daylight. Then, holding his breath, he turned around.

There was nobody on the bed but Prince, who had jumped up. The duvet was pushed back, as if somebody had just got up – or you might have thought that if not for the thick layer of cobwebs that lay over everything, and the smell of mould.

No bones, no rotting corpse. On the other hand, no Dad. He had that feeling of panic again.

He had to get out of the house. Anyhow, Prince needed his walk.

He ran to his own room and found jeans and a shirt, he didn't recognise them but they were his size, and got dressed quickly. Then he went downstairs to the front door. "Prince! Walk!" The dog came running, jumping up at him the way he did at walk time. His lead was hanging by the front door, and Matt hooked it on his collar. He pushed open the front door, and out the two of them went. Matt shoved the door closed, but it wouldn't lock.

"Don't worry." That was Mister Bowden. He was back in his own garden now, with the mower inert at his side. "I'll keep an eye on the house."

"Thanks." Matt turned away and started walking, down the path and onto the road.

"If you need anything, Matt, just knock…"

Matt didn't look back. Half-running to get away from Mister Bowden, he headed west towards town, with Prince trotting at his heels.

EVERYTHING WAS WRONG, out here too.

There was nobody around. No people on the street, no traffic, nobody behind the blank windows of the houses and offices and shops. Not even any other dogs. Stuff was broken down, fences fallen, windows smashed, doors gaping open. In some places fires had taken out a house or two from the neat suburban streets, like gaps in a row of teeth. The pavements were in a bad way with the stones lifted and broken by tree roots. It was easier to walk on the tarmac of the road surface, but even that was potholed and cracked, broken up by weeds and roots, and he had to step carefully.

And none of it was smart any more. As he walked down these familiar roads there should have been icons crystallising out of the air all around him, as his buddies called, or he got updates from school on the day's schedule, or ads competed to grab his attention, everything a riot of colour and constant communication. This was the Mist, a blanket of smartness laid over the whole world, the product of tiny instruments embedded in every surface, his own clothing, his skin, suspended as minute particles in the air. Today there was none of that. Everything was plain and flat and dead, and it was all kind of old-fashioned, like he was in some museum recreation of the 1990s.

After a few hundred metres Prince paused and squatted. Matt had bags ready in his pocket. Expertly he wrapped a bag around his hand, picked up the waste and tied off the bag. There was a bin nearby, and he popped the bag in there. He ⬚⬚⬚⬚⬚⬚⬚⬚⬚⬚⬚⬚ y the bin, then sh⬚⬚⬚

With no t⬚⬚⬚⬚⬚⬚⬚⬚⬚⬚⬚⬚⬚⬚ ⬚ ⬚c off his lead⬚⬚⬚⬚⬚⬚⬚⬚⬚⬚ ⬚ a slabs. It was⬚⬚⬚⬚⬚⬚⬚⬚⬚⬚ ⬚t c a ruined gar⬚

Matt pass⬚⬚⬚⬚⬚⬚⬚⬚⬚⬚ a glas window fac⬚⬚⬚⬚⬚⬚⬚⬚ ⬚ wa

Matt had an impulse to lob a rock at that window. Now he supposed he could do it. Who was going to stop him? He thought about it for a full five seconds, before moving on. With nobody around it would have seemed an odd and sad thing to do.

He turned onto Wavertree Road, one of the main roads heading west into town, and came to Mount

Vernon. From this high point, the site of an open modern development, the ground fell away, and there was a view across the centre of the city all the way to the river, whose water pushed deeply into the heart of the city to lap at the feet of the buildings. Matt picked out the two cathedrals separated by no more than a kilometre or so, and the modern glass blocks of the shopping and business centre, and the tapering silver and green multi-storey city farms, and the older buildings of the docks. Had things changed? There was more green than he remembered, threading along the crumbling roadways and spilling out from the parks and public places. And many of the buildings were damaged. Some of the big glass blocks looked as if they had exploded, and the red sandstone mass of the Anglican cathedral was soot-smeared from fire.

Nothing moved, nothing but a flock of gulls flapping casually over the Pier Head. No sound but the rustle of the breeze in the trees. And no Mist, which from here should have been like a shining translucent dome hanging over the whole city.

Matt, feeling lost, sat on a wall. Prince wagged his tail and jumped up so his front paws were on Matt's knees. Matt tickled his ear absently. The sun was rising, it was going to be a warm day, and in a deep blue sky Matt thought he saw a glimmering lens shape, like a very long, very high cloud. Probably a Sunshield. And there was a spark, brilliant as a bit of the sun, slowly tracking the horizon. A plane? No, there was no contrail, no noise. A satellite, maybe.

"Matt Clancy, welcome to Liverpool!"

Matt's heart nearly stopped. He jumped up and whirled around. Prince backed off, barking ferociously.

The man was short, slender, in his twenties maybe, with a sad moustache. He wore a brilliant pink old-fashioned soldier's uniform, complete with peaked cap. He was standing to attention and smiling.

"You nearly – oh, hush, Prince – you nearly scared me to death."

"I'm Mister Mersey. Matt Clancy, welcome to Liverpool! Port of empire in the nineteenth century, hub of artistic creativity in the twentieth, as you can see," and he did a sort of twirl, showing off his costume, "and pioneer of eco-adaptation and climate resilience in the twenty-first twenty-first the twen-twen-twenty-first –" He froze and glitched, blocky pixels scarring his face.

Matt saw that he was tilting slightly away from the vertical, and that his feet hovered a few centimetres above the broken road surface. A bit of the Mist still working then, just.

It never occurred to him to wonder how this virtual tourist guide knew his name. The Mist knew everybody name.

Mister Mersey recovered. He even straightened a bit. "Matt Clancy, welcome to Liverpool! Ask anything!"

"What happened? Where are all the people?"

"Ask me anything!"

"Is this Rock Day? What happened on Rock Day?"

That seemed to trigger a new routine. The virtual blinked, and came back looking a little more sombre. "Vote!"

"What?"

"Your opinion counts. What do you think's going to happen today?"

"Today?"

"Rock Day! Is asteroid 2021 MN *really* going to strike the Earth? Do you *believe* the astronomers when they say we're safe? Are they lying to keep us all calm? Do you *believe* that Singles, Park and Rossi really aimed that rock so it would hit the planet? The City of Liverpool values your opinion!"

"Why? What difference does my opinion make?"

Blink. A different tone again. "Background. 2021 MN. A rock that was coming close to the Earth anyway, within a million kilometres. Harmless! We'd never have known it was there. Not until Singles, Park and Rossi went out and redirected it. If you believe that's what they did!"

Blink. Another voice. "Nearly half a century after the first manned mission to an asteroid, the encounter with asteroid 2021 MN was supposedly for scientific purposes, mineral evaluation and a test bed for asteroid deflection technology." He pointed to a non-existent visual in the air. "The four Orion T-23 spacecraft, with their solar panels like butterfly wings, were launched from –"

"I know this. Go on."

Blink. "The crew. Benjamin Singles. Passionate atheist, and believer that we are not alone in the universe. Jennifer Park, one of the first female Catholic bishops, but a fringe figure in the Church for her controversial views on *Silentium Dei* – the Silence of God. Mario Rossi, spacecraft engineer, who –"

"Go on!"

Blink. "Why deflect the rock at Earth? Singles believes there are aliens all around us, but they are hiding. 'They will come out to save us. They won't allow the rock to strike. It's the ultimate SETI experiment!' he claims."

Mister Mersey had shifted to the astronaut's own voice. "Jennifer Park." A woman's voice now. "'Ben and I make odd allies. I'm supporting his plan even though I'm expecting an entirely different outcome. God has been silent since the death of His only Son. We will welcome His return as an intervening deity, when He deflects this Wormwood from the sky.' Good luck with that, sister! Mario Rossi: 'So they locked me up in the cargo drone. If I'd known these assholes were planning this game of cosmic chicken I'd never have got on board this tub –'"

"Enough."

"Vote, vote, vote! The City of Liverpool values your opinion!" The virtual held out a hand. "Please step forward for alternative identity verification."

Matt had spent his whole life undergoing such processes. Automatically he held out his right hand.

Mister Mersey passed his own hand over Matt's, scanning for fingerprints and running a remote DNA test. Then he stepped back. "Identity not confirmed."

"What?"

"Identity not confirmed. Please step forward for alternative identity verification."

"But I –"

"Please step forward – please step step step –"

"I'm going."

"No! Please!" Mister Mersey suddenly looked directly at him. "Please. I am officially semi-sentient, Grade IV. But I'm only activated in the presence of a tourist. Otherwise –"

Matt, disturbed by his sudden desperation, backed away. "I can't help you."

"Otherwise otherwise I-I-I-I-" Blink. "The City of

Liverpool values your opinion! Matt Clancy, welcome to Liverpool! Wel-wel-wel –" There was a pop. Mister Mersey burst into a shower of random pixels, which faded and died.

Matt, left alone again, stood staring.

But here was Prince, wagging his tail and looking up at him. Matt found a stick to throw, at the foot of a young ash tree pushing through the pavement. Prince bounded after the stick, and went off to bury it in the rubble of a burned-out house.

Lots of strange ideas were whirling around in Matt's head. Scary ideas. But he knew where he had to go next.

THEY WALKED BRISKLY down the hill. Every so often Matt whistled for Prince, but he knew the dog would follow.

He cut through a complex of university buildings, as deserted as the rest, and then headed down Brownlow Hill to the Catholic cathedral, a great cone of concrete and glass set on the massive slab of its crypt. The cathedral seemed to have been spared the ruin of some of the city's monuments, even the huge cylindrical lantern tower of stained glass seemed intact, but green streaks from the copper roof stained the pale concrete walls. Matt walked down Mount Pleasant and climbed the concrete steps up to the cathedral's main entrance. The steps were littered with leaves and bird droppings. The doors were modern, they looked like wood but were surely promat, but they did not shift at his approach. When Matt tried a handle, one door creaked open.

"Wait."

"Go away, Mister Mersey."

"It's me, Matt. Bob Bowden."

Matt turned. Mister Bowden stood there a few steps below him. "What are you doing here?"

Mister Bowden still had that odd air of bafflement. "I'm not entirely sure."

"Did you follow me? All the way from home?"

"I thought it was best."

"That's kind of creepy."

"I'm sorry. I didn't want you to come to any harm."

"Well, I haven't."

"What are you doing here, Matt?"

"People come to churches, don't they? For sanctuary. When the world ends. You see it in games."

"So you think you're going to find people here? Or are you looking for sanctuary yourself?"

Matt just pulled back the door and strode into the cathedral.

Pigeons, disturbed, fluttered up into the stained-glass lantern tower over the vast circular space of the cathedral's main chamber. The grand altar on its platform at the centre of the floor still stood, but many of the rows of benches around it had been tipped over and smashed. Matt saw that there had been a fire in here, in one side chapel, but evidently it hadn't spread too far. And there were what looked like bloodstains on one of the great concrete supports. Maybe there had been trouble here. A riot. There was nobody here now. No bodies, even.

Prince, wandering, found a puddle on the floor from some leak in the roof. He lapped noisily.

Mister Bowden laid a hand on Matt's shoulder. Matt's instinct was to shake it off, but there was something comforting in its presence, its warm weight.

"Nothing alive in here but those pigeons," Mister Bowden said. "And not many of them. Maybe a few bats. But then the wild hasn't really taken Liverpool back, yet. Too close to the plume from Sellafield."

"Sellafield?"

"The nuclear plant. It went pop a few weeks after being untended. A few weeks after –"

"What?"

"After Rock Day."

"Isn't it Rock Day today?"

"No. That was some time ago. Some *years*. I know it's hard to understand. Matt, let me ask you a question. Prince is thirsty, right? Are you?"

He thought about that. "No."

"Have you felt thirsty all day? Do you feel like you'll ever be thirsty again?"

"No."

"Are you hungry? Have you been to the bathroom?"

"No. No!" Now Matt pulled away from him. He felt tears dangerously close to the surface.

Mister Bowden said gently, "What do you *think* is going on, Matt?"

The corners of Matt's head were full of lurid possibilities. "Maybe I'm a ghost. A zombie. Dead after everybody else has been killed."

Mister Bowden laughed. "I can assure you you're not a ghost or a zombie. Prince still comes to you, doesn't he? Would he come to a zombie?"

"I don't know."

"Come to that, neither do I. I don't know much about zombies."

"I think everybody's dead. I think the Rock fell. But if that's so –"

"Yes?"

"Why is the city still here? It should all be flattened."

"Good question. And why are *you* here?"

Matt had no answer.

Mister Bowden took a deep breath. "The thing is, Matt, you're *not* Matt. Not really."

That was so weird it wasn't even frightening. "I don't get it."

"You know, I'm not sure I do either. Come on. Let's sit down on one of these benches and try to work it out together."

He sat down. Slowly, reluctantly, Matt followed suit.

Prince, his thirst quenched, went sniffing around the floor of the cathedral, on the trail of rats or rabbits.

MISTER BOWDEN SIGHED and rubbed his face. "I tell you, I'm the wrong man for this job. Speaking to you, I mean. I always was a pompous old duffer, even before I was old. Never much use with kids, even my own. Or rather *his* own."

"His?"

"Me. The original Bob Bowden. *I'm* not *him* either! On top of that, I'm feeling a little groggy myself if you want the truth. I only woke up a few hours ago."

"Woke up?"

"That's not the right expression. A few hours ago I became fully aware of who I was and where I was and what I was supposed to do, for the very first time. It was more like being born than waking up. But not like either, really. That's the limitations of human language for you."

"What are you supposed to do?"

He smiled. "Why, isn't it obvious? I'm here to keep an eye on you, Matt. I'm a backup system. Like a, a –"

"A handle on a promat door."

"Exactly. That's exactly right."

"Why not my Dad? Why haven't I got my Dad?" He was having trouble controlling his voice.

Mister Bowden sighed. "Well, I'm not sure about that, son. I'm sorry. Maybe they thought that would be too difficult for you. Maybe it was too difficult for *them*. You're stuck with me, I'm afraid."

Prince trotted past them, a bit of wood in his mouth, intent on his own projects, utterly oblivious to the two of them.

"I always liked them, you know," Mr Bowden said. "Spaniels. Grew up with them. Working dogs. You have to keep them busy, don't you?"

Matt looked at his hand. He flexed his fingers. It looked like a hand, a human hand. Evidently it wasn't. And here was Mister Bowden talking about dogs. He shrugged, unable even to frame a sensible question.

Mister Bowden said, "You see, they were right."

"Who were?"

"Those astronauts, you know? Ben Singles, who wanted to make the aliens come out of hiding by throwing an asteroid at the Earth. And Jennifer Park, who wanted to call down God. They were both right – and both wrong. *They* did come. But *they* are neither ET nor Jesus." He shook his head. "Those are human categories. *They* don't fit any human category. Why should they? Any more than humans fit any category dreamed up by a chimp. And they don't have morals like humans, or chimps come to that."

"So they did save the world from the Rock."

"That they did. They turned the Rock away. Oh, you might see it in the sky. It's orbiting Earth now, like a space station. It was easy for them." He lifted his own hand. "As you might guide a moth away from a flame. Trivial, you see. But still a compassionate act."

"But the people –"

He said firmly, "They saved the world. They didn't save the people. They let them die, as they would have if the Rock had struck. Even though the Rock didn't fall. It's complicated. Well, actually it's not, not for them."

"Why didn't they save the people?"

"Because people brought this down on themselves. They threw an asteroid at their own planet! They would have destroyed themselves, *and* their world, *and* all the creatures they shared it with, and all for – what? Philosophical games? That's not to mention other close calls in the past, with nuclear weapons and the designer virus that got out in 2043 –"

"*Three* people did that. The Rock. Just three."

"Actually two. Rossi tried to stop them –"

"My Dad wasn't on that ship. I wasn't. We had no say in it. Nobody did! Why did they all have to die? Even little babies –" He felt those tears again, but he was determined not to give in to them. "Why did my Dad have to die?"

Mister Bowden seemed to be thinking of reaching out to him, but thought better of it, and folded his hands in his lap. "This is from *their* point of view, you understand. Look at it this way. I bet you have impulses to do stupid things, at times. I don't know – smash things up. Jump off cliffs."

"Break stained glass windows."

Mister Bowden looked at him sideways. "You're thinking of Saint James's, aren't you? I've always had my eye on that one. Like a great big target, begging for a rock. But you never did it, did you? Everybody has these impulses, and most of us control them.

"Well, intelligent races have their crazy elements too. Most races control them. Not us. *We* give them the power to do what they like, or anyhow we don't stop them from taking it."

"But *all* of them died. The ill, the old. The children too young to understand."

"You have to draw a boundary somewhere," Mister Bowden said. "And they drew it around humanity, around the whole species. I'm not saying I agree with it, myself. We had promise, I would have said. I think *they'd* say this was the most merciful way, in the long run.

"But they did save the rest of the ecology. All the other minds on this world who, even if they can't build rocket ships, are capable of feelings just as deep and meaningful as ours. *You* know that. You have Prince. You understand what's going on in his head, as well as anybody does. All those others didn't deserve extinction."

Matt nodded slowly. "So why am I here?"

"Because there were loose ends. Ragged boundaries. Look – the wild things will take back the Earth, and it won't take that long. But in the meantime –"

"Loose ends." He guessed, "Like Prince?"

"Like Prince. The world was full of creatures that had become utterly dependent on humans. In some cases on individual humans. All the domesticates – the cows needed to be milked –"

Matt started to see it. "And somebody would be there to milk them. Not somebody. Some *thing* like me."

"Well, you're not a *thing*. Yes. As long as it was needed. It won't be for long, the domesticates weren't encouraged to breed. Most of them have gone already. You're not likely to see anyone else. As for Prince —" Hearing his name, the dog came trotting over. "The rest of the world can go away. But Prince needs *you*."

"We grew up together."

"I know. I was there."

"And so I was given back to him."

"That's the idea. It's another trivial bit of kindness. Why not do it, if you can?"

Matt leaned forward and scratched Prince behind the ear, and then the back of his head where he liked it. Prince sat and closed his eyes, submitting to the touch. "I'm like Mister Mersey, then. *He* thinks he's real too." And, Matt thought, he'd backed away when Mister Mersey asked *him* for help.

"A bit like that."

"Something went wrong, though. I woke up. I came here."

"Yes. Matt, you're not a whole human. But there's just enough of Matt in you for the dog. You're supposed to go through the cycle of each day, with the dog, without you, umm, *noticing* that anything's missing, that anything's wrong. And then at the end of each day you are — reset. You retain just enough trace memory to look after the dog." He rubbed his face again. "Oh, this is coming out all wrong. It's more subtle than that. But anyhow —"

"My reset button broke."

"Yes. Yes, it did. You became aware, well, *too* aware. There are lots of categories of consciousness, degrees of awareness. Something like that. It's as if you woke from a dream. Look, it was a glitch. They were trying to do something pretty subtle if you think about it, and a long way from their own experience. But all with the best of intentions."

Matt grunted. "Very nice of them. So what now?"

"You've been fixed. But, given what you've been through and the distress it must have caused you – and will cause when it all sinks in – they've decided to give you a choice. You can have your, umm, reset button pressed."

"And go back to the dream."

"Yes."

"Or?"

"Or you can stay awake. Here, like this."

"With Prince."

"That's the point. But when Prince dies – well, that's it." He bent to stroke Prince's face with his finger. "He's not a young dog, is he?"

"He may have a couple of years."

"That's all they can offer you, Matt. That or the dreaming."

"Where I didn't even notice Dad was gone."

"Yes –"

"I'll stay awake. Tell them."

Mister Bowden smiled. "Well, they already know. Good choice, by the way." He stood and stretched. "I'd better get back. That lawn won't cut itself. Actually, it will, sort of, but you know what I mean."

"I'll see you around, Mister Bowden."

"That you will, Matt. Take care now." He walked away, his steps echoing.

Prince, still submitting to the stroking, was falling asleep, his head heavy, his eyes closing. With a last burst of energy he jumped onto Matt's lap, turned around a couple of times, and then slumped down, curled up, his head resting on Matt's arm.

Matt had just found out his father was dead. That *he* was dead. That he wasn't real, he was some kind of copy. Maybe he was in shock. It didn't seem to matter. After all, at least Prince was real. And there was always Mister Mersey to call in on.

He sat quietly, working out where the two of them could go for their long walk that afternoon. As the day wore on the rich light from the lantern tower shifted across the cathedral's deep, empty spaces.

ELUNA

STEPHEN PALMER

Stephen Palmer first came to the attention of the SF world in 1996 with his debut novel Memory Seed, *followed by its sequel* Glass, *both published by Orbit in the UK. Further novels followed, including the critically lauded* Muezzinland. *His most recent novel is* Urbis Morpheos, *the reading of which was described by one reviewer as "…the obtuse gift it is, to wallow in this utterly striking universe that Palmer has created… a supremely odd yet deeply rewarding experience." Stephen lives and works in Shropshire.*

"YOU ARE LOOKING at ancient laser sail starships circling a distant cloud of interstellar gas backlit by young, hot stars. Can you see how the cloud seems to be brown and green ink in water? Look more closely. The starships appear as tiny glittering dots."

"Are they what people call spiderwebs?" I asked.

"They used to. You can see them now?"

"There are about thirty. Do they orbit a common focus?"

"No. Don't forget, the objects you see now are not what left the solar system. The starships have evolved over many centuries. Every now and again they come together to mate, pass on their artificial genes, then give birth to new starships."

"But we're seeing them as they were a few centuries ago. Anything could have happened in that time."

"Indeed! A good point, child. But this is always the problem with self-replicating machines. Ancient records suggest that many of the starships have left the region of interstellar space you are observing. We cannot say where they are. You observe today those that remain."

"And you don't know how many new spiderwebs have been born, do you?"

"No."

After a pause I said, "Why are they attracted to the clouds of gas?"

"They need raw materials and energy to survive – and to evolve. They circle it like marsh-crows circling a kill."

I shuddered. "But there aren't any spiderwebs any more, are there?"

"We use more advanced techniques now, aided by the alien races."

"In Eluna!"

"Yes, child."

"I'd like to work at the starport. It sounds interesting."

"Your family will help, of course. You know they will. But at the moment you are naught but a student. In a hundred years or so, when you grow up…"

"Then?"

"Perhaps."

*   *   *

THE EXNOO WAS the size of a cat, the shape of a wart and the colour of coffee, and its keening voice began to worry Freosanrai. Her alien companion was forbidden in the swamps of Eluna. And her father was about to arrive.

Freosanrai glanced around the cubicle in which she had set up her workshop. With the flick of a hand she made opaque the plexi-wall, dropping the exnoo into an aluminium bin.

"No, no, not darkness!" came the whine of the alien.

"Shush! Just while my father is here, then we'll leave. I told you before, you're not allowed here."

"Darkness..."

"Quiet, now!"

Freosanrai stood straight and checked her appearance in a roll-on mirror: short blue hair, large dark eyes, thin mouth. Clothes of wispy silk and plastic knee boots. There came the sound of footsteps outside, a tap on the cubicle door, and then her father walked in.

As usual, he frowned. "What are you doing here?"

Freosanrai was for a moment perplexed by the question. "I'm meant to be here –"

"Oh, yes... the chemtree recreating the xmech mining ship, isn't it?"

Freosanrai nodded. Her father must have much on his mind to make such a simple mistake.

Osanagai muttered, "You placed this cubicle too far from the chemtrees. I've told you before about that."

He opened the door and looked out. The music of the Elunan swamp became audible, and Freosanrai detected its methanous smell. She saw dozens of chemtrees, their grey trunks like elephant skin, roots sunk in black water, their leaves red and purple, the size of blankets;

the ends of their branches suspending pale flowers like wet papers.

Without looking at his daughter, Osanagai said, "This time I shan't tell Zebenunai. But please learn from your mistake. Too far from the chemtrees and you will miss the development of the seed. Too close and you will interfere with the pollination. Get it just right. You are a member of the Artisans now, and you have to get it right."

Freosanrai glanced at her father and murmured, "Yes."

Osanagai frowned. "Is there no work that you can apply yourself to?"

"I am working. Here."

Osanagai took a few steps out of the cubicle. He turned and said, "Will you stay here tonight?"

Freosanrai nodded. "I think a multifigur will come tonight to pollinate the xmech mining ship flower. I saw one the last two nights, a big one like a silver dragonfly, but the flower wasn't fully developed. Anyway, the fruit should be ripe this time tomorrow if the flower is pollinated tonight."

"Make sure you eat it immediately."

"Yes, father..."

"Then bury your excrement to a depth of ten centimetres. That allows the seed to develop into the ship –"

"Without hindrance or delay, yet without exposing the undeveloped machine to danger."

Osanagai shook his head. "I suppose you think you know it all because you are no longer a student."

Freosanrai shrugged. "I know the basics, which is what you were just telling me."

"*Don't* fail on this one like you have before. The xmech are unable to forget a mistake. Zebenunai will lose respect if the mining ship is not delivered to the Ruby Faction – he has known them for three centuries or more."

Freosanrai raised her eyebrows. "The who?"

"Oh... the Ruby Faction – one of the sections of the xmech populace. Zebenunai has been trying to trace their origin by extrapolating from the positions of stars they transmit data from. Nothing you need to know about. Goodbye."

Osanagai walked away, his cloak leaving a trail in the damp grass of the chemtree clearing. Freosanrai sighed as she walked out of the cubicle. Around her the dense chemtrees of Eluna moaned as the wind gusted over them. She glanced up to see the outer barrier of Luna translucent white, like the cirrus clouds of the original Earth; below that barrier, more than a kilometre above her, a column of butterflies flew, their myriad wings reflecting sunlight like a cloud of tinsel.

"Get me out of here. I want to be inside your backpack again."

Freosanrai entered the cubicle and pulled the exnoo from the bin, putting it inside her rucksack and letting the flap fall over the leathery face of the alien. "Is that too dark for you?"

"No, I am comfortable. Have I assisted you enough here? Can we leave?"

Freosanrai hesitated. She only had an hour before evening fell over Ministrator – not enough time to return the exnoo to its hide in the Marshy Sector and then return. But her private task was done, using the exnoo to memorise chemtree types in preparation for later examinations. Yet if the exnoo were discovered she would be expelled from the Artisans, to the eternal shame of her father, and of his father.

"I'm going to keep you here until tomorrow," she decided. "I can't risk missing the multifigur."

"It will come tonight?"

"I'm sure the xmech flower is ready."

Decision made, Freosanrai lifted the rucksack and carried it across the clearing to the nearest chemtrees, which she clambered across, slipping on their moss-covered roots, until she found a hole in the ground. Into this she placed the rucksack. She glanced around. This part of Eluna, close to the Marshy Sector and Mount Black, was little used. She could see only one hologram marking the position of a growing seed, a golden spiral fifty metres away. The rucksack would be safe.

"Goodbye," she said. "Tomorrow I'll return to pick you up."

"Very well."

Freosanrai returned to the cubicle, checked the monitor computers, then settled into a yoga position the grass outside.

Gloom fell over Eluna. Many of the chemtre relaxed, their boles creaking, their branches droopir Evening multifigur flitted between the chemtre catching final beams of light as the sun descended, b as time passed Freosanrai began to worry that the silver dragonfly would not reappear. This hour was the usual time for scent-directed pollinations to occur. She put on her image enhancing spectacles. Nothing.

Night fell, and still nothing. Freosanrai began to fret.

*　　*　　*

THE MERCANTILE SECTOR, positioned between the Marshy Sector and the edge of the sector upon which Ministrator is built, is usually quiet at night. An intricate collection of shops and businesses spread out over fifty square kilometres, it is required by law to shut down when the sun sets. But the border with the Olive Sector is leaky, unpatrolled, and the hedonists of that region will on occasion use its broad streets as their lavatories, bordellos and drug dens.

Tonight, a man totters along Point Zero Street, a thoroughfare close to the edge of Eluna. Though he is drunk he can hear the whirrs, screeches and bellows of Elunan technology, incomprehensible to him – a commoner, a voter – yet recognisable, and somehow comforting. He knows where he is. He stops, injects another few millilitres into his veins, and stumbles on.

The stars are invisible beyond the great Lunan barrier, the sphere that is tonight dark and swirling. Alien computers control with precision the amount of solar energy reaching the environment within. Today they increased Luna's albedo by a fraction of a per cent, responding to innumerable data sent by botanic sensors.

The man leans into a dark doorway. Behind the plexi at his side he sees goods from lower sectors: gene therapy kits, portable microbe generators, auxiliary eyes. At his feet a number of black automechs work, digging miniature trenches so that optical cables can be laid. He is tempted to kick them aside, but even in his inebriated state he will not ignore the taboo.

He staggers out into the street. Something shiny and as large as a child flies towards him. He stops.

He has never seen anything like it. Though it is silver metal, reflective as a new mirror, it is shaped like an insect. It hovers a few metres away from him, its wings creating pseudo-patterns from reflected light. There is a chittering noise. Then it strikes.

The insect's face clamps to his own and tries to mould itself to that form. Blood spurts out from the wounds created. The man tries to scream, but the insect is suffocating him in its effort to replicate the form of his face, and his cries cannot be heard. He falls to the ground. His eyes burst. Still the insect tries to copy. But now it is confused. This is not how it is supposed to be. This is something *other*, something with a face that is mobile, plastic, weak.

It flies off. Perplexed, it tries to locate its resting branch. It cannot. There is something inside its head that is stopping it from thinking straight. An itch that it cannot scratch. So it finds an emergency shelter beneath a series of stone blocks. It must wait. It must become calm. It must decide what to do.

The man is dead, his face crushed and bloody. He lies in a red pool.

FREOSANRAI REALISED THAT something had gone wrong with the pollination. There would be no xmech mining ship. Frightened of what her father would say, she considered her options.

The obvious thing to do was to ask for help. But she could not; it was essential that she display her skills whenever possible. Besides, she was not naturally inclined to ask for assistance. That left the option of a private investigation.

It was easy for her to check the overnight monitors, and soon she spotted something unusual, a multifigur that had missed its trajectory and departed Eluna. She sat alone by a chemtree and considered the implications of this. Eluna and the multifigur were a symbiotic system, so there was nothing for a multifigur outside the starport. Why, then, had this happened?

In moments she was adjusting the motion track record so that the multifigur error was lost to the Artisan system: a simple deception. Then she grabbed the exnoo and headed for the gateway.

"Where are we going?" came a plaintive voice from the rucksack on her back.

"Returning to Ministrator. You'll like that."

"Yes! Luna. Interesting people and no horrid trees."

"I told you before, they're not trees."

"You'll tell me again, you will!" chanted the exnoo.

"*Quiet.* I'll need your help out there on the streets. Away from Eluna I'm like an oyster out of its shell."

"I know. I've seen you. But you said you are allowed out."

"I'm allowed out… but the Artisans don't like it. We're supposed to live apart from the populace."

"I will be quiet now, you're approaching the gateway."

The gateway was a solid mass of rock with a tunnel through it. Realising that technological fixes would generate technological opponents, the Artisans had decided to use the most rudimentary force possible to keep Eluna secure: brute force. This plan had worked for over a millennium. Freosanrai ducked as she entered the tunnel, the sound of her soft boots echoing in a series of reverberated thuds.

A dozen green-clad women sat beside a plastic table at the outer end of the tunnel. One stood up and said, "Where are you going?"

"Into Ministrator."

"For what reason?"

"Private business."

The woman hesitated for just long enough to indicate that she thought Freosanrai was lying, then let her pass. Freosanrai did not care. Records were kept of Artisan movements but they were almost never checked, an advantage to living in so exclusive a hierarchy.

She found herself in a dark street. Though it was day, the height of the buildings to either side of her blocked out what little sunlight penetrated the outer sphere, today as white as snow. She was in Show, the administrative heart of Ministrator. She hurried on.

"Where should I go?" she asked the exnoo.

"Don't run," came the reply. "You will stand out if you appear anxious. Walk slowly. Don't stare at people and buildings like an outsider. Now, what exactly needs to be done?"

"We need to find traces of the multifigur. I can't imagine what it was doing out here. What was it thinking?"

"What type of trace are we looking for?"

"Anything unusual that happened last night."

"That will be a wide search," said the exnoo. "Ministrator is well over a thousand square kilometres. Please narrow it down."

Freosanrai began to feel frustration creeping over her. "How can I? No multifigur has ever escaped before, how should I know what to look for?"

The exnoo said nothing. Freosanrai sat in a shadowed doorway and took it out of her rucksack, placing it on her lap as if it were a babe. The creased, leathery face peered up at her: saucer eyes, hairy mouth, black external gills like whiskers.

"Haven't you got any ideas?" she asked. "You were human imprinted, you must have *some* idea where to begin."

"I'm thinking," said the exnoo.

It shut its eyes and began whimpering to itself. Freosanrai waited.

"The chemtree that you hoped would create the xmech vehicle fruit, that was on the Mercantile Sector side of Eluna, wasn't it?"

Freosanrai shrugged. "Closer to the Olive Sector, I think."

"We should go there. The border between the two sectors is insecure. We could check the overnight records of the Mercantile cameras."

"Cameras?"

"Merchants don't like drunkards and junkies spoiling their territory," said the exnoo. "You've got detectors that will locate the multifigur metal?"

"A kit, yes."

"Then we need transport. An airship, an airship!"

Freosanrai muttered, "Just tell me where to go."

Guided by the exnoo's memorised map Freosanrai walked two kilometres deeper into Show, until she arrived at an airfield, where sat a number of indigo-coloured airships. Downloading timetables into her handset, she chose the ship that would soonest reach the Olivean border, a journey of fifteen kilometres. From her pocket she took her faked docu-card. She paid, then walked into the airfield.

The airship rose fifteen minutes later. Freosanrai sat in the extended basket beneath the dirigible, relaxing in a window-seat. As the airship rose she saw the Xiix Sector, which lay beneath her like a vast pincushion;

then she was floating over Mount Black and the Marshy Sector. The sky shimmered as the two-mol boundary containing Ministrator's air split asunder, grew and reformed under the pressure of external weather.

At the border of the Mercantile and Olive Sectors the exnoo directed Freosanrai to a camera battery. It was easy to use her docu-card to access overnight records.

Six merchants group together to form anti-muzik society. Muzik users form opposing society. Talks to broker peace expected by nightfall.

Nooling threads choke stream, cause floods. Automechs brought in to redirect stream – nooling threads all safe.

Raids made on Olivean choke-dens. Six kilogrammes of choke confiscated.

Man killed by having face ground off. Unknown assailant thought to be hiding nearby. Investigators reviewing local information.

Miles Fayne nominated leader of mercantile forum currency group. Says, "Major change to occur."

Freosanrai shrugged. "Is this of any use?" she asked the exnoo.

The exnoo remained silent for a few moments before saying, "We can discount the first, third and fifth reports, as they're about ongoing events. Expand the fourth report."

Freosanrai did as she was told.

A man was last night killed by an unknown assailant in Point Zero Street –

"Where's that?" Freosanrai asked.

"Close to the Elunan border."

"Ah!"

– when during an apparently motiveless attack his face was ground off by an unknown device. Found dead at the scene, he has been taken to the Reusing Sector, where his family have said goodbye. Investigators from the Mercantile Lobby are analysing local infos in the hope that a picture of the assailant can be created. An investigator said, "There was a faint blood trail, but it was impossible to follow further than Zil Square. We are preparing noses, which we hope will be able to detect blood molecules further afield."

"Would the multifigur have killed a man?" asked the exnoo.

"It's as likely to do that as it is to write poetry," Freosanrai grumbled. "Can we get along to Zil Square?"

Soon Freosanrai was studying Zil Square, a paved area surrounded by low buildings. Mercantile investigators, distinguished by their grey hats, walked around the further reaches of the square.

"We had better wait until they leave," said the exnoo. "If they suspect you are from the Artisans they might get suspicious."

"Why should they? I've got my docu-card. They've no reason to suspect me."

"Experienced investigators make intuitive guesses. You are foolish to think you cannot be touched! A man may guess where you come from by your speech."

"Be quiet. People might hear you. Besides, I've had an idea."

The exnoo did not ask what the idea was. Two hours passed. Freosanrai sat outside a vin-shop and waited for the investigators to depart. The square was quiet, more of an administrative centre than a place of mercantilism, with the hum of computers audible amidst the chatter of distant children. At length the investigators departed and Freosanrai was free to act.

First, she walked around the square. With no idea what had happened during the night she let her mind remain open to any clue, however subtle, however strange. After a few minutes she noticed a new crack in a paving slab.

"What is it?" said the exnoo.

Freosanrai said nothing as from her rucksack she pulled out a detection kit. From it she extracted a box of magnetic ants. Opening the lid, she stood back, then dispersed the ants in a sweeping arc, so that they were strewn over the slabs in their thousands. She leaped back, defocusing her eyes a little so that she could see patterns of movement as the ants went into defence mode and tried to locate their home. But they had no home here, their motion was random, and because of that she could see a shape emerging as a multitude of ant lanes were guided by met neath the bs.

A winged shape. H r guess been corre .

"It's hiding, or i active,' e said. S glanced around the square. few p had seen er throw the ants, but nobody pproac he. This w s as good a time as any to perf rm the pture. In s onds she had grabbed the bro en corr f the slab arest the concealed multifigur nd lifte to see a s gle silver leg. She grabbed it and pulled. Like mirrored cellophane the defunct multifigur emerged, and Freosanrai was able to drop it into a bag, then into her rucksack.

"Will it hurt me?" asked the exnoo.

"No. It's not dead, but it isn't going to move until it's reactivated."

"What next?"

"Strange... there's bamboo here, beneath the slabs. Fresh bamboo. I wonder..."

FROM HER PODIUM Suzan Cnasis gazed out over the rustling greenery of Bambooine. Far to the north she saw the grey silhouette of the Siggurat, stepped and pyramidic in form, with pale blue mist floating around its flat summit. Its base was lost in a billowing mass of bamboo.

She turned back to the archaeological dig that lay around her. The dig team had removed two hundred square metres of bamboo, revealing chocolate brown topsoil peppered with stones. She checked her fingerwatch. Lackshmi Devatasive, her colleague, was late for work. Again.

Suzan sighed.

An hour later she heard a familiar belch, then voices amidst the rustle of the bamboo, then the sound of metal shod boots clacking on a board path. Moments later Lackshmi stood beside her on the podium.

Lackshmi smiled. "You're early, Su!"

Suzan ignored the remark.

Lackshmi stretched like a cat emerging from deep sleep. "Weather's looking bad. The forecast was for storms."

Suzan glanced at the sky, pale with *faux*-cirrus. "Perhaps," she said. Glancing at Lackshmi's long white hair she said, "What's that stuck in your...?"

Lackshmi pulled what appeared to be a lump of toffee from her hair. "Oh, just some stuff. We were at Moosha's place in Olivea last night, drinking muzik."

"Drinking... what?"

"Muzik. I don't suppose you've ever heard of it. A new drug synthesized by kids in Vin. It leaves your sight alone but gives you *amazing* sonic hallucinations." She laughed, then stretched again. "I could get addicted to it, easy!"

Suzan turned away. She had heard enough.

"To work," said Lackshmi. She glanced over the revealed earth, then pointed to the northern corner. "What's that?"

"What's what?"

Lackshmi pointed again. "That dark patch in the corner."

Suzan was annoyed to discover Lackshmi had spotted a feature that she had missed. "I don't know," she said. But before she could tell her colleague about the pre-dig survey Lackshmi had jumped off the podium and was running over the earth.

Suzan followed. Together, they studied the earth in the corner. "That might be new," Suzan said.

"Yeah, I agree. But this place hasn't been touched for decades. Centuries, I'm guessing."

Suzan bent down to check the surface of the earth. "You don't know for certain that it hasn't been touched for decades," she said. "Call the dig."

A few minutes later a bot-mole dig arrived. Suzan downloaded their logs into her handset and studied what they had done, but was disappointed to find a set of normal statistics. She took a trowel and began scratching at the dark patch of earth. It led directly into the uncut topsoil at the edge of the new site.

"Are you going to be long?" Lackshmi said.

"This needs to be done layer by layer," Suzan replied. "I think this is very recent. There's no archaeology here, this is the edge of a new pit, and it goes on beneath the bamboo."

Lackshmi shrugged. "Pull up a few more metres of bamboo."

Suzan considered this suggestion. The borders of the site were undefined. Bot-moles were on hand. "Very well," she said. "Just a few more square metres."

Lackshmi drank O-lime tonic water while the bot-moles dug. Suzan dragged her hand through her bobbed black hair and watched. She was nervous. Nerves struck her every time a new site opened. From her flask she sipped rose tea.

After half an hour they stood facing the top of a fresh pit. "It's no more than five years old," said Lackshmi. "Five months, even."

"We do not know that yet," Suzan replied. "It will be difficult to date –"

"Get digging. This is just building work or something, we need to get it out of the way and reach the interesting stuff."

"But there has been no building work here for a century. You said so yourself."

"Oh, give it a rest! It's obviously new. Dig an exploratory trench and find out what's in there. I'm getting bored with this already."

Suzan cleaned her spectacles while the bot-moles removed layers of earth, their multiple legs a blur.

Then, "Stop!"

Lackshmi had yelled. She spat green water.

"*All* stop." The bot-moles froze.

"What's the matter?" asked Suzan.

Lackshmi did not answer. Like a gymnast she bounded over the bot-moles, to kneel down in the earth and with her bare hands pull clods away. Then she sat up. "Su, come look!"

There in the earth lay the top of a metal box.

Lackshmi dug more. Suzan bit her lip. This was unorthodox.

Within a minute Lackshmi had revealed a steel box, less than a metre long on each side. "I told you it was new," she said. "Somebody buried this recently." She glanced at the bamboo surrounding her. "They chose this spot because it was quiet and out of the way, even for this quarter." Then she shivered. "I wonder if there's a body in there?"

"Must be a small one if there is. A child. Shall I call Show –"

"No! We'll just open it ourselves. It's probably nothing."

Suzan recognised the signs – Lackshmi was unstoppable in this mood. It had on previous occasions led to bitter struggles: the artist versus the scientist. Yet they both needed the other.

The bot-moles were not suited to intricate work, so Suzan summoned a sentient. It arrived, brown and hairy with twenty eyes, and like a gothic clockmaker it fiddled with the edges of the seal, the ticking and tapping of its mechanisms contrasting with the nearby voices of the human dig team. After ten minutes it stopped, paused, adjusted its position, then used its front leg to force open the lid in one sudden motion. It scuttled away, leaving Suzan and Lackshmi to peer into the box.

A chaotic jumble: computer memory, data disks, electromagnetic equipment, ancient paper. Even books, real books, like the ones Suzan had seen in museums.

"Oh, my," said Lackshmi. "Oh... no!"

"What?"

"You know what this is, don't you?"

Astonished, then annoyed, Suzan stared at her colleague. "No, I do not know what this is," she said.

"It's an information burial."

None the wiser, Suzan frowned and looked again into the box.

"This box was buried by xmech," said Lackshmi. "This is information, knowledge, pertaining to somebody or something."

"I don't know what you mean."

"The complete obliteration of facts. If it was deliberate, it's the equivalent of murder. We need to locate a bounty hunter."

"A what?"

"Hah! *I* studied the xmech decades ago, when I was an archaeology student in the Philosophers' Sector."

"The xmech?" asked Suzan. This was news to her. "Why not human?"

"An ex-lover got me interested. Human archaeology isn't everything."

Suzan nodded. "Yes, I understand that, but –"

"Anyway, I know something of their ways. Not much, of course, they're impossible to deconstruct because of the way they interact."

Suzan shrugged.

"There's a fixed number of xmech personalities. Lots of jostling to get the best identities, which are always the oldest – the wisest, you see. Xmech individuals are recreations of past public identities. They change, ever so slowly, as the years pass."

"What has this to do with our information burial?"

"Well, with the xmech being entirely artificial, and alien, they don't see information the way we do. Su, I've *seen* reconstructions of information burials before. What puzzles me though is why xmech would bury information in the human zone... normally they'd only bury in their own territory."

A thought struck Suzan at once. "Perhaps a human asked xmech to arrange and perform the burial."

Lackshmi stared at her. "Of course!" Clapping her on the shoulder she said, "Well done! Yes, somebody wanted an obliteration of facts. Now, I wonder who? And why?"

THE WEATHER TURNED as the sun set. Rain began to patter over the Lunan sectors, reducing visibility, soaking everything. As evening fell, Lackshmi returned with a young woman at her side.

"This is Freosanrai," said Lackshmi. "She's going to analyse the burial."

Freosanrai nodded. "Pleased to meet you," she said. "Where's the box?"

Suzan hesitated. The voice came from the rucksack on the woman's back.

Indicating the rucksack, Freosanrai said, "No vocal cords – pulled out by muzik assassins. I speak through a leather machine."

Suzan had instructed one of the diggers to carry the box to the rear of the makeshift tent, where it lay concealed by chitin scales. Freosanrai pulled off the cover, carried the box to the table and set it down. Then she opened it and began taking out the contents one by one. Each object she studied for a few seconds, sniffing on occasion, once shaking a tube, riffling through the books, then investigating more. After half an hour she was done. Over a hundred objects lay scattered around the box.

"There does not seem enough here to guarantee information death," Suzan observed.

Lackshmi nodded. To Freosanrai she said, "Suzan thinks a human requested this to be done."

Suzan smiled. Generosity was one of Lackshmi's many faults.

Freosanrai drawled, "The lady's right. The mechoes, they never bury outside their zones unless for another race. A guy did this, probably one who lives in this sector."

"A man or a woman," Suzan remarked.

Freosanrai shook her head. "No, 'twas a guy. I know. I sense the pattern of male friendship here. You realise there's religion in this box?"

"How do you know?"

"I know the way mechoes view our stuff. See, they have their own view, that we don't understand. But they see us distinctly, which I recognise. I see clues here. Check out the books. Old. I can tell you what all this is about. Me, I think it was a small fact that was excised and buried – you were right, lady. With computers everywhere we live in a big big network. It's not easy to untangle information. But a small fact... that you can untangle and excise."

"Is this what you would call an information murder?" asked Lackshmi.

"Depends on the context. I'll tell you more after you pay me."

Suzan handed over an e-note.

Pocketing the note, Freosanrai said, "This burial was made recently. I'm able to tease out the threads of information that the mechoes had to cut. See, they do that good. They cut and cut and cut, until a network is isolated. Very clever. And a network, it can be any shape, see? Not just a circle or a square. Can be looped in three-dee space. But the mechoes are able to isolate everything pertaining to a fact, and bury. This what we have here. The burial of just one thing." She nodded and smiled, as if pleased with her analysis.

"But what is the fact?" Suzan asked.

"That I can't tell you, not exactly, not yet."

"What?"

"Shush," Lackshmi said. "There's more Su, if you'll listen."

"As I suspected," Freosanrai continued, "this is to do with religion. You know the Jules guy?"

"The who?" Suzan asked.

"Jules Aonnarron," Lackshmi said, "the cultist at the Temple of Stela."

Suzan had heard this name. "Yes," she said, "his reputation is bad."

"I think he's the man that buried this information," said Freosanrai. "With these finds I'll go to the Temple of Stela and interrogate Jules Aonnarron. Reckon he deliberately buried an idea. Then I'll come back."

"You'd better go now," said Suzan. "Download your report into my handset before you leave."

FREOSANRAI TOOK THE retrieved information away as fast as she could. She congratulated the exnoo on its mimicry. "You spoke well," she said.

"Once we knew the burial was real," the exnoo replied, "it was easy. But now you have to discover from Jules Aonnarron why he buried the xmech idea."

"Let me make a guess," Freosanrai replied. "There is no such person as Jules Aonnarron. It will be one of the Artisans – somebody is trying to frame me. Somebody is trying to force me out of Eluna, but I'm *not* going to let them succeed. I have one advantage. I found the multifigur."

"Without it you'd have no evidence," agreed the exnoo. "But the might of the Artisans opposes you, and you are just one woman –"

"I'll succeed! Back into the rucksack, quickly. I want this over with."

The Temple of Stela was a tall, dark building made of stone. Ivy grew over its upper half, while the lower half was covered with damp, brown moss. Freosanrai opened the main door and walked into a long, narrow chamber whose ceiling was so high she could not see it.

"The xmech will take over Luna," said a voice.

"Grandfather!" Freosanrai gasped.

Zebenunai walked out of the shadows to her side. "But do you have evidence?" he asked.

Freosanrai frowned. "Evidence?"

"Come, child!"

"Oh… you mean the multifigur. Er, yes, I found it. And of course I recognised your handwriting on the objects in the box you had the xmech bury."

"This is a great shame. I would have succeeded, otherwise."

"Succeeded?"

Zebenunai nodded. "The xmech mining ship is not an xmech mining ship. It is the first of the spiderwebs returned to Sol – the vanguard of the coming colonisation. But, you see, the Earth is not alive anymore. Many things are not as they were millennia ago when the spiderwebs departed. And so the spiderwebs are jostling for knowledge of us, of Luna, of Eluna."

"Then that's why the multifigur didn't pollinate –"

"I assumed it would remain within Eluna. There, I made a mistake. Then events developed beyond my control. And now I will have you kill you."

"Me? No! Why?"

"You know too much. You have asserted your freedom from the Artisans by uncovering knowledge – you have effectively become a commoner. And no commoner can know what you now know."

"But… grandfather, no! You can't kill me!"

Zebenunai hesitated. "There is one way out," he said.

Freosanrai trembled. "What?"

Zebenunai walked over to Freosanrai and took her rucksack, lifting it up and shaking it so that the exnoo fell out. He stamped on it, squashing it with the heel of his boot. Freosanrai stared, too shocked to cry.

"That is the first part," Zebenunai said. "And now for you –"

"But you said you wouldn't –"

"I'm not going to kill you! I'm going to properly make you part of the family. The family of Artisans. Unfortunately, in becoming part of the family you will lose your freedom. But you are almost an adult now, and I think the time is right. Do you know what we are?"

"The rulers of Luna. The elite, the long-lived. The marsh people of Eluna."

"We are not exactly human, child. But our makers were. Have you not wondered why we alone live and work in Eluna? It is because we are symbiotic with the chemtrees. Once, they were human. But such distinctions are no longer relevant. Life has become smudged now it is off the Earth. Alas that I had to tell you this so early in your life."

"I don't understand what you mean."

Zebenunai replied, "My mistake means the time has come for you to assume a new identity. I am not just Jules Aonnarron, I am many others in Luna. Come to me, child. Let me show you who else you will be."

Freosanrai nodded. "You don't want me to be independent, do you? You framed me –"

"To *teach* you." Zebenunai shook his head. "I am sorry it had to be this way. But the family is more important than the individual. This, you have learned."

Freosanrai nodded again. She had been crushed, she had been moulded. With a sinking heart she realised her fate. There was no escape. She would no longer be Freosanrai.

SHALL I TELL YOU THE PROBLEM WITH TIME TRAVEL?

ADAM ROBERTS

Adam Roberts was born in the year 3,061,965 and has time-travelled back to London, England, to the early years of the extraordinarily backward and primitive 21st century, in order to convey a message of the utmost importance to humankind. That message is hidden somewhere in one of his dozen SF novels or several dozen SF short stories. You have to read them all to find it.

Zero

THIS IS NO simulation. The friction-screaming fills the sky. An iceberg as big as the sun is up there, and then it is bigger than the sun, getting huger with terrifying rapidity. This is happening to a world that had, up to this moment, known no noise at all save the swishing of insects through tropical air; or the snoring of surf on the beach. But *this*, *now*, is the biggest shout ever heard. Apocalyptic panic. And the asteroid falls further, superheating the atmosphere around it, the outer layer of ice subliming away in a glorious windsock of red and orange and black, down and down, until this world ends.

But – stop. Wait a minute. This hasn't anything to do with anything. Disregard this. There's no asteroid, and there never was. He doesn't know whether he is going on or coming back. Which is it, forward or backward? Let's go to

One

A CITY. A pleasant, well-ordered city, houses and factories and hospitals, built on a delta through which seven rivers flow to the sea. The megalosaurs have long gone, and the swamps have long since dried up, and the mega-forests have sunk underground, the massive trunks taller than ships' masts, sinking slowly under the surface and through the sticky medium, down, to be transformed into something rich and strange, to blacks and purples, to settle as coal brittle as coral. The world that the asteroid ended is stone now: stone bones and stone shells, scattered through the earth's crust. Imagine a capricious god playing at an enormous game of Easter-egg-hunt, hiding the treasures in the bizarrest places. Except there is no god, it is chance that scattered the petrified confetti under the soil in this manner.

So, yes, here we are – in a city. It is a splendid morning in August, the sky as clear as a healthy cornea, bright as fresh ice, hot as baked bread. Sunlight is flashing up in sheets from the sea.

The city is several miles across, from the foothills, from the suburbs inland and the factories to the sea into which the seven rivers flare and empty. The seven rivers all branch from one great stream that rushes down from the northern mountains. The city abuts the sea to the south, docks and warehouses fringing the coastline, and beyond it the island-rich Inland Sea. The mountains run round the three remaining sides of the delta, iced with snow at their peaks, really lovely-looking. Really beautiful. To stand in the central area, where most of the shops are, and look over the low-roofs to the horizon, and note the way the light touches the mountains – it makes the soul feel clean. This is Japan and it is 1945.

Two

MOVE ALONG, MOVE on, and so, to another city; and this one very different. This city stretches sixty miles across, from the two-dozen spacious estates and the clusters of large houses in the east, nearer the sea, to the more closely-packed blocks, dorms, factories of the west. The city is threaded through with many freeways, tarmac the colour of moondust, all alive with traffic and curving and broad as Saturn's wings. Sweep further west, drive through the bulk of the town, to where the buildings lose height and spaces open up between them, and away further into the sand-coloured waste, and here – a mountain. And at its base a perfectly sheared and cut block of green. This is the lawn, maintained by automated systems. The style of the white marble buildings is utopian; for this is the closest we come to utopia in this sublunary world – a spacious and well-funded research facility. This is the Bonneville Particle Acceleration Laboratory. Let's step inside this temple of science. Through the roof (it presents us with no obstacle), down from the height to the polished floor, and the shoes of Professor Hermann Bradley clakclaking along that surface.

He steps through into a room and his beaming, grinning, smiling, happy-o jolly-o face shouts to the world: "We've done it, we've cracked it – *thirteen seconds*!"

The room is full of people, and they all rise up as one at this news, cheering and whooping. And there is *much* rejoicing. People are leaping up from their seats and knocking over their cups of cold coffee, spilling the inky stuff all over their papers, and they don't care. Thirteen seconds!

Three

SO, HERE, CLEARLY, this narrative is in the business of *zipping rapidly forward* through time. That much is obvious. Some stories are like that: the skipping stone kisses the surface of the water and reels away again, touches the sea and leaps, and so on until momentum is all bled away by the friction. That's the kind of tale we're dealing with. So another little skip, through time, not far this time – three small years, in fact. Hardly a hop. And here's our old friend Professor Bradley, a little thinner, a little less well-supplied with head hair. There's a meeting going on, and the whole of Professor Bradley's career is in the balance.

Four people, two men and two women, are sitting in chairs, arranged in a U shape. Bradley is sitting in the middle. One of the women has just said, "three years, and *trillions of dollars* in funding…" but now she has let the sentence trail away in an accusing tone.

The mood of this meeting is sombre. Whatever happened to '*thirteen seconds*'? Whatever happened to the celebration *that* single datum occasioned?

Bradley says: "Shall I tell you the problem with Time Travel?"

"No need for you to patronise us, Professor," says one of the others.

"It's the metaphor," says Bradley, quickly, not wanting to be interrupted, "of *travel*. Time is not space. You can't wander around in it like a landscape."

"There are five people in this room," says one of the women. "Must I tell you how many *PhDs* there are in this room? It's a prime number larger than five."

"That's just dindy-dandy!" says Bradley, aggressively.

"If you think the point of your being here is to gloss over your experimental failings…"

"OK!" barks Bradley. "Alright! OK! Alright!"

You can tell from this that the mood of the meeting is hostile. You can imagine why: *trillions of dollars*!

"Last month you reported *seventeen* seconds."

"That's right," says Bradley. "And let's not underestimate the real achievement in the…"

"Three years ago you came to us with *thirteen* seconds. You have worked *three years* to find those four seconds – and you're still at least fifteen seconds short! How am I to see this as an improvement?"

"We have," says Bradley, "*cracked* it. I am *convinced* that we have cracked it. I'm more than convinced. I'm certain, absolutely certain. One more test will prove the matter. One more!"

"You have *run out* of test slots, Professor. Run out! This means *there are no more test slots*. Do you understand? You have conducted over *two thousand* tests so far! You have conducted *so many experiments* that you have literally run out of slots –"

"Shall I tell you the problem," says one of the men, waggishly, "with using up all your test slots?"

Bradley hasn't got time for this. Urgently, he says: "The Tungayika…"

"Let us not," interrupts one of the men, "let us not rehearse all the reasons why Tungayika would be – a terrible idea."

"A *terrible* idea!" repeats one of the women.

"Terrible," agrees the third.

"But of all the remaining possibilities," urges Bradley, "it's the best we have. Entertain this idea, I ask you. Please: *entertain the idea*. What if I really am only *one more trial away* from perfecting the technology?"

"Tungayika is a good half century further back than any test you've conducted."

"It's not the distance," says Bradley, rubbing his eyes, as if he's been over this a million times. Million, billion, trillion: these numbers are all friends of his. "It's not a question of *distance*. Time isn't like space. That's what I'm saying. It's an energy sine."

"It *is* the distance," retorted one of the men. "Not in terms of reaching the target, maybe not, but *definitely* in controlling the experiment via such a long temporal lag. And quite apart from anything else, nobody really knows what *happened* at Tungayika…"

Bradley seizes on this. You know what? He thinks this is his trump card. "That's right!" he says, leaping up, actually bouncing up from his chair. He's an energetic and impetuous fellow, is Bradley. "That's the *best* reason why you should authorise the drop! Think of the *metrics* we'll get back! We're guaranteed *at least* seventeen seconds there. But in fact I'm certain we've finally got the containment right; we'll be there right up to the proper moment. And that means ... we'll be able to *see* what it was that created such a big bang, back there in 1908. Solving that mystery is, well, icing on the... icing on the..."

"You're playing with real things here, Brad," says one of the men. "This is no game. Real people, real lives."

Professor Bradley nods, and lowers his gaze, but this could be the problem – right there. Because you know what? Professor Bradley doesn't *really think* he is playing with real things. Many years and scores of drops have reinforced his belief that reality can't be played with. History is as it is; time paradoxes are harder to generate than kai-chi muons. Tungayika in Siberia in 1908 is further away from his conscience than anything imaginable. It was such a *sparsely* populated area! And anyway, the asteroid wiped it out! And anyway, that event has already happened. The board is worried about killing people, but all the people he might kill *are all already long dead*! None of what he does is real.

That's the crucial one, really. That last one.

"It's *one more* drop," says Bradley. "Just that. Just one more! Then we'll be able to go back to Capitol Hill with a *fully-working* time travel insertion protocol! Think of it!"

"Brad..."

"This one chance to turn all the frustration around to victory – the chance to get a return on all that money!"

"But Professor Notkin says that..."

At this much-hated name Professor Bradley positively arches his back. Like a cat! Really – like a furious, hissing feline! "Come *on* Rosie," he cries. "Don't *bait* me, Rosie!"

"Brad, now, listen, Notkin is..."

"– after my bloody *job*," cried Professor Bradley, rolling his hands in an agitated dumb-show. "She's after my Lab. She *can't* have it. If I didn't have to keep pouring my energies into combating her *conspiracies* against me –"

"Oh," says Rosie, in a disappointed voice.

"Conspiracies is too *strong*," agrees another.

"Some might consider it actionable," opines a third.

"Agh!" yells Bradley, in the sheerest of sheer annoyance.

There is an embarrassed pause.

"Come now," says Rosie, in a placating tone. "Notkin is a good scientist. There's no need to get so worked-up about office politics. You can't blame Notkin for being ambitious. Being ambitious is not a *crime*."

"She has been undermining me for eighteen months now. She sells you on this pipe dream of remote viewing..."

"At least it doesn't involve shit being blown up," snaps one of the men.

And once again there is an awkward silence.

"Give me a break," growls Bradley. "Patrick, you of all people –"

"I'm not kidding, Brad,' says Patrick. 'The bandwidth may be small, but with Notkin's system..."

"... which she *stole* from my work..."

"... we get *real data*, and – and –*and* nothing *blows up*."

Everybody falls silent. After a short while, Rosie says: "Look, Brad, we're not out to get you. We're really not. We're not trying to replace you with Notkin. But you have to give us something to work with. Give us a result that's more than seventeen seconds."

"Then give me Tunguska," says Bradley.

Four

WE'VE COME A long way, from the asteroid that killed the dinosaurs to Japan in 1945, and then via diminishing leaps to the present. From that heated meeting we need to use the magic time-travel machine called 'story' to step forward only two more months. Hardly any time at all. And here we are, right now.

Bradley is in a corridor inside his own lab and trying to get in, but his way is being blocked by three people. One of them is a policeman. The policeman looks kind-of embarrassed, but he's there, and he's resting his palm on the back of the grip of his holstered gun. Of the other two people one is Professor Notkin, aforementioned; and the other is Rosie – Roseanna Chan, senior liaison, perhaps the most objectively powerful person (in terms of political power) anywhere on the mountain.

Bradley says: "Crimes against humanity?" He says this several times. "Crimes against *humanity*? *Crimes* against humanity?" Then, "I thought that was a joke. Rosie," he says, turning to her. "You're going to let Notkin hand me to the police for *crimes against humanity*?"

"I'm afraid my hands are tied," says Rosie, looking blank. Blank is her version of looking uncomfortable.

"Maybe if Tunguska had –"

"She *sabotaged* Tunguska!" cries Brad, pointing a finger at Notkin. "She sabotaged it to get my job, to take my *lab*, to…"

"Calm yourself," advises the policeman.

"There's no need for a scene," Notkin agrees, blandly.

"It does you no good," says Rosie.

"C'mon, Rosie! You know how she's been plotting for years to unseat me! I taught her everything she knows, and this is how she repays me?"

"You've taught me a lot, Brad," says Professor Notkin. "I'll always be grateful."

Brad's eyes do that bulgy-outy thing, as if they are filled with a metallic gel and Notkin is a massively powerful electromagnet. Words temporarily fail him.

"Time to come away, sir," says the policeman. "Leave these people to do their work."

"It's not their work!" Bradley complains. "It's *my* work!"

"You are under arrest," the policeman reminds him.

"Ah!" says Brad, as if the idea has just occurred to him. "And what about the statute of limitations, eh? There *is* such a thing as a statute of limitations, even on murder."

"But not," said Rosie, as gently as she can, "for crimes against humanity. That's why I'm afraid the officer here has got to take you in. But I'm certain it's a temporary thing. It'll only be a few days in jail until we find a judge prepared to bail you."

"Bail me on a charge of *crimes against humanity*?" boggles Brad.

"It is an unusual case, yes," says Rosie. "We all realise that."

"Too right it is. These people were all dead already! These people were *all* long dead already! How you can murder somebody who's already dead? Try and peg me with the guilt of these people when they're already…"

"Dead, yes, and long ago," says Notkin. "But dead because of *you*." And for the first time there is, as the phrase goes, steel in her voice. You see now how she might have moved herself in only four years from grad student to Head of the Bonneville Particle Acceleration Laboratory.

Bradley is blustery, and he can do no better than repeat himself. He's lost. It's over for him. "They died before I was even born!"

"It'll be interesting to see what the court makes of that defence," Notkin notes, "*Hey! Don't punish me! The people I killed are already dead!*"

"I am not a murderer," says Brad.

"Let's not –" says the policeman.

"This is bull," says Brad. "I flat don't *believe* this."

"I'm afraid that Professor Notkin's hunch has been proved," says Rosie. "Do you think we'd be acting like this otherwise? I'm afraid it's been looked into. There have been literally – literally – hundreds of federal agents and specialists looking into it. And it's fair to say that there have been… ructions. Oh, some pre-tty major ructions. At the highest levels."

"Just because a bunch of dead people are dead?"

"Not that! Well, *obviously*, that" says Rosie, "But the White House is more worried by the thought that – oh, come on Brad!" All one word: *cmnbrad*! uttered with the force of exasperation. "Our national defence is still predicated on nuclear deterrence, after all. We've still got thousands of missiles with nuclear warheads. It's a shock to discover that firing them at a target would have no more effect than…" and she searches for an analogy, before falling back (she is a scientist, after all) on the literal truth "… no more effect than dropping eight tons of inert metal. There's some high-level *rushing around* on that account, I don't mind telling you. There are some chickens deprived of their heads in the corridors of power, I *don't* mind telling you."

"All that nuclear physics, all the stuff I learned as a student – the basis of nuclear power stations," Brad splutters. "I refuse to believe it's wrong."

"It's not wholly wrong, of course. But it turns out – wrong in one important regard."

"Crazy!"

"Simply not *explosive*," says Rosie. "Nuclear tech will fuse of course, and go fissionable of course, but only slowly. It'll work in a nuclear pile. It just won't *explode* over Hiroshima. It's a tough lump to swallow, but swallow it you'd better. It's the truth. The defence chiefs of staff are having to swallow that none of our nuclear warheads are *actually* explosive. That's a big swallow for them. Those early bombs sent our physics a bit skewy. It might even be, you know, comical, if it weren't so serious. If the implications weren't so serious. Look, I'll send the research work to your phone. I'm sure they'll let you keep your phone in jail. You can read up on it. In actual fact, you know what? They took a regular warhead up to the Mojave last week and tried to explode it, and nothing happened."

"One damp squib," said Brad. But he sounded tired. Maybe the fight was finally going out of him.

"I'm afraid not. I'm afraid it's true of all our warheads. None of them work, which is to say; none of them will explode. The same is true of the Chinese nukes, and the Russian ones, and the Indonesian ones – turns out the technology just doesn't work. I mean, you can't blame those last-century scientists. They did their chalkboard calculations, and they figured the bomb *would* blow, and when the bomb really *did* blow it seemed to confirm their calculations. So they didn't worry too much about the more abstruse implications of the equations."

"And how easy it is," says Notkin, "to get one's calculations wrong. Wouldn't you say, Professor?" She may be forgiven this snide interjection. She's suffered under Bradley's cyclotropic eccentricities and incompetence for many years. And it's her facility now.

"And when Hiroshima, and Nagasaki, and the subsequent nuclear tests seemed to confirm…" Rosie says. "But the horrible truth is that although those military leaders thought they were dropping those bombs and killing those people, they didn't. *You* did it. You didn't realise that this was what you were doing, but it was. The responsibility is yours. And since…:"

And, suddenly, Brad is running. He is running as fast as his lanky legs will propel him, and the policeman is shouting "Stop or I'll shoot!" He has finally unholstered his pistol. But Rosie stops him. "There's no need to shoot," she says. "There's no way out of here. It's a closed facility."

Is she right, though? It is a closed facility, yes. But is there no way out?

What do *you* think?

Bradley runs, and runs. It's been his facility for many years, and there are things about which not even the ambitious Professor Notkin knows.

Like what?

Like this capsule, in this room, wired up with the full power the facility can provide.

Previous drops have propelled a capsule no larger than a human thumb, wrapped about in shielding and cladding designed to protect it. But size isn't actually a constraint, since time (it turns out) is not topographic in the way space is. It preserves angles, and an analogue of velocity; but not mass, or dimension, or, and to quote the great Algerian theoretical temporicist El-Dur *les êtres de l'hyperespace sont susceptibles de définitions précises comme ceux de l'espace ordinaire, et si nous ne pouvons les réprésenter nous pouvons les concevoir et...* – well, anyway. The point is that there's no reason, given enough energy, why a larger capsule might not be sent back. No reason at all. And you must understand this about Professor Bradley: he really *really* believes he's cracked the containment field problem. He thinks the Tunguska mess-up was deliberate sabotage by the envious, ambitious, scheming Professor Notkin. He's sure that he'll be able to shoot himself back – and *stabilize* – and *polarise* – and get *away*. And what's the alternative? Prison is the alternative. Crimes against humanity? – execution, like a Nuremberg villain? Ignominy, and a destroyed reputation, and his beloved technology thrown on the scrapheap? Or (this is what he is thinking) or: one final throw of the dice, one eucatastrophic twist in the story to turn failure into triumph, to vindicate everything he has done. A personal one way mission, backwards in time, simultaneously freeing him from captivity *and* proving the worth of his invention!

It's no choice at all, really, for Professor Bradley. It's exactly consonant with his impetuous personality; his *ressentiment*, his chafing restlessness. His fundamental incaution. He's in the room, and he fits a metal chairback snugly under the door handle.

His phone comes to life in his breast pocket. The ringtone is 'Rain' by The Beatles. A fumble with a trembling thumb, and the device is turned off.

Professor Bradley powers up the generators, and climbs into the padded innards of his own experimental capsule, and he pulls the lid down on top of him.

Crimes against humanity? Or? Maybe *beat* the rap with one flick of this –

Three

AND WE'RE OFF!

There's almost nothing to see from the tiny porthole in the capsule. There's not even really a seat to sit down on, just a little shelf to rest his narrow buttocks. But once the switch is flicked there's a whomp and a whoosh and Brad's head cracks against the ceiling of the capsule. A painful collision. Before he knows it he's back resting on the little shelf, trying to peer out of the fogged up porthole and rubbing his head. Why did he bounce upwards when he accelerated backwards? He ought not to have moved at all; time, after all, is not space. But there *is* a trembling thrum to the capsule, as if time travel involves *some* kind of friction, or something. He can't think. But it hardly matters. It hardly matters now. The switch has been thrown.

The view outside the capsule is not of a smooth backward-running movie. It's a strobey series of discontinuities, frozen moments that hold for second, or sometimes more, of subjective time and then jerk into a prior arrangement. Very strange. It hurts Bradley's eyes to watch.

The capsule is three months back. This is the time of his meeting with the suits, before the Tunguska debacle. It was at this time that Gupta, who worked directly for Notkin, came to his boss and said: "I've been looking at the underlining metrics from the drops, and something real screwy is going on with the numbers." ·

It was at this time that Notkin (by no means a fool) began to wonder: *but if the physics for the A-bomb was so misguided, then where did all that energy* come *from to flatten the city*? And *All those nuclear tests – that explosive energy must have come from somewhere!* And *what if the delta fold-up function that Brad included in his equations in fact follows an exponential rather than a sequential logic*?

So many people killed! Of course that had never been Brad's intent. Don't you think he should be judged on his *intentions*? He had the *best* of intentions. He personally wouldn't so much as pull a puppy's tail, consciously. He's a considerate and –

Too late! We've gone back past that moment.

Two

WHEN NOW? WE'VE jarred backwards a number of years before. This was the time of the first successful test: the probe lasting thirteen seconds of shielded life in the earlier time frame before exploding so violently. It was a frabjous day when that news was broached. On that day Brad drank two thirds of a bottle of champagne and, unused to the excess of such a gesture, was sick in a waste bin. You see, it *was* possible to shield the probe, even if only for a temporary period, when it –

No, we're earlier than that now. Hurtling backwards the whole time.

This was when Brad was giving his introductory lecture to the new recruits. These were all brilliant minds, but all of them ignorant of the business of time travel. The whole discipline was classified. The basic *equations* were classified. The government would hardly spend so many billions on a project and leave it flapping vulnerable in the public breeze. So the students sit expectantly. Notkin is there, looking much younger and plumper and with eager eyes; all twelve of them have eager eyes.

Bradley says: "Shall I tell you the problem with Time Travel?"

And they listen.

"You need to stop thinking of it as *travel*," says Bradley. "It's not like wandering around a landscape. When you put an object from our time into another time frame, it's like bringing matter and anti-matter together. It's actually very much like that; the matter of your probe" (he holds up the thumb-sized plasmetal object) "is of a radically temporally distinct sort to the matter of your surrounding environment – the air, the ground on which it finds itself, the water in the atmosphere. They mutually annihilate and release energy. Boom!"

The students are wide-eyed and attentive.

"That would be bad news for the chrononaut," says Brad, walking round to the front of the desk and leaning himself, rakishly, up against it. He is half-distracted – or no, a third-distracted, no more – by the eyes of that plump graduate student there, in the front row. Very striking. Attractive. He was not a man with a wide experience of women, but something about her gaze appealed to him. "Our chrononaut would step out of the door of his time machine into the world of 1850 and, *boom*! In fact he wouldn't even get the chance to open the door. The material out of which his time capsule was made would react as soon as it appeared. Boom! How big a boom?"

So he calls up the white board, and as a group they go through the numbers, with Brad leading them, to show how big a boom. And it is big. It's high explosive big. And as they do this, as he nudges their naïf misunderstandings in the right direction, and pushes the correct equations through the mass of variables, Brad thinks: *she's bright as well as pretty*. He starts to daydream, idly, about whether this young new-PhD might be interested in –

"So how do we solve it, professor?" asks one of the other students.

Snap out of it, Brad! "That's what *you* are all here to work on," he booms. "We know what we need to do. We need to *shield* the probe," and he holds up the probe again, "so that, once it's inserted in the previous time slot it lasts longer than a microsecond. And then we need to develop the means of temporally polarising its matter. Given a long enough period – thirty seconds should do it – we ought, theoretically, be able to align the matter of the probe with the local grain of time travel. And once we've done that it can slot into the new environment *non*-explosively. Once we've cracked that problem... then actual, real time travel becomes a possibility."

He grins; they grin. The world is all before them.

"One problem," he tells them, "is in finding places to test our probe. You see, the early probes are likely to fail; we have to factor that in. And *when* they fail they're going to go big boom-boom." He simpers, and pushes his glasses back up the bridge of his nose. "The past is a different country, and we don't want to go dropping random dynamite bombs on it hither and yon."

"Because of the sanctity of the time lines, professor?" asks one of the students.

"Because of the risk of killing people. But there's a way to avoid that danger."

What way?

No, we're slinking back further and further.

One

The 1940s. This is the moment of Hiroshima. What better place to hide an exploding device from the future than *inside a nuclear blast*? The time-locals are hardly going to notice it there, are they? Drop it at that place, at precisely that time. You'll recover metrics that let you know how well the shielding is holding up, how long it would have lasted for – and then, bang: vaporised. No chance of futuristic technology falling into 1940s hands. No chance of being noticed. No grandfather paradox. Oh it's an *ideal* solution.

One of the first things the team learn is that their theory is wrong. The device explodes not with high-explosive force, but with a more concentrated and devastating power. But it's still small beer compared with the force of ten thousand suns that the atomic bombs unleash.

They test, and probe. They drop their devices into Hiroshima and Nagasaki. There were 477 nuclear tests in the period from 1945-1970, and they can camouflage their work inside any one of them. Each time they inch a little closer to perfecting the technology, drawing out the power of the shielding, giving more time for the polarisation to take effect.

Eventually, of course, they're going to run out of nuclear explosions in which to hide their experiments. But by then they'll have perfected the technology. By then. And if they have not, then they'll have to find *other* historical explosions. That asteroid strike in Siberia in 1908 – you know the one. That's always a fall-back.

It'll be a long time before Notkin realises that the delta fold-up function that Professor Bradley included in his equations in fact follows an exponential rather than a sequential logic. Before she realises that the brown-paper-and-vinegar science of the Manhattan project, stuck with 1940s technology and assumptions, was simply not in the position to develop a working nuclear device. That the exponential factor in the equations, multiplied by the length of time through which the device travels, rubbing up a potent form of energetic friction, will produce an explosion of... precisely A-bomb dimensions. And that the later tests, with more sophisticated shields, would yield precisely the larger megatonnage of the test explosions into which they were dropped. That, in fact...

Missed it. Brad has shot backwards. He's now earlier than Hiroshima, and is getting more *before* by the minute.

Frankly, he's lost control. His grasp of the math has been wrong from an early stage, and he's massively overestimated the amount of energy he needs to place this much larger device back to the right time. (He was thinking the 1970s). There's an inverse scale on increasing math; but a straightforward exponential on the amount of energy you accumulate as you –

There he goes

Gone.

Before gone.

Zero

THE DEEPER IN time you sink, the more temporal static you build up. On the other hand, imagine an asteroid capable of causing mass extinction. That would have to be a *whopper*. But there never was such a large irregular polygon of ice and rock falling out of the highest high. You don't believe me? Fair enough. I tell you how we can solve it: go back there and see for ourselves. Imagine the time traveller, his capsule popping out and crashing into the foliage. It lands on its back, tumbles on its top, rolls on its back, and the chrononaut can see out through his porthole. He wipes the condensation away with his arm. There are weird contortions of green and black, and he recognises them straight away for foliage. He can see two things. Past the leaves, out in the wetland a grazing diplodocus raises its head, its long neck straightening upwards like a pointing arm. The other, of course, is the number seventeen on his inner display turning, second by second, into sixteen, and so into fifteen, and – well, I daresay you know how to count backwards just as well as you know how to count forwards.

THE LIVES AND DEATHS OF CHE GUEVARA

LAVIE TIDHAR

Lavie Tidhar is the author of steampunk novels The Bookman, Camera Obscura *and* The Great Game, *weird-lit novel* Osama, *linked story collection* HebrewPunk, *several novellas and many, many more short stories. During a recent two month visit to Jakarta, Lavie was dragged to watch* The Hands of Che Guevara, *a documentary film by Dutch director Peter de Kock. The film's theme gelled with a couple of ideas he had been mulling over for a while and this story emerged as a result.*

PART ONE: VALLEGRANDE

"This morning we are about 99% sure that 'Che' Guevara is dead."

– Walt W. Rostow to Lyndon Johnson,
October 11, 1967

1

ON THE NIGHT of October 10, 1967, the residents of Vallegrande woke up uneasily with their mouths watering and the smell of pork crackling wafting through the air. It was a rare delicacy in the small Bolivian town, and children and adults as one went out into the quiet street to look for the source of the smell.

It is a small, pretty colonial town, Vallegrande, about 125 kilometres away from Santa Cruz. It has a church and a town square, an airstrip and a bakery and a school.

And the smell was coming out of the bakery.

IT HAD BEEN an exciting day in the life of Vallegrande. Only on October 9, just one day before, a military helicopter had landed on the small strip and the lifeless body of Ernesto 'Che' Guevara was brought out. He had been shot nine times.

The following day two doctors, Moisés Abraham Baptista and José Martínez Cazo, performed the autopsy on the corpse and pronounced Che Guevara dead at the Hospital Knights of Malta, Vallegrande.

There were soldiers outside the bakery, the citizens noticed as they approached, with the smell of cooked meat filling their nostrils.

"Don't come near!"

The soldiers looked agitated.

"Why not?"

"Military operation in progress."

You didn't question the military, and so the parents and their disappointed children returned home, and to bed, where they lay for a long time without sleeping, still tantalised by the smell.

Inside the bakery the wood was burning in the oven and the flames licked the naked body of Che Guevara. The smell of roasting human flesh and the smell of pork crackling are surprisingly similar, and impact in the same fashion on the human olfactory sense.

But you cannot cremate a man in a bakery oven, as the soldiers found out, and finally they pulled out the corpse (one of them had thrown up by the sink, just missing it) and drove the cooling body to the airstrip, where it was buried.

If they noticed the corpse was missing both hands, they never said so.

2

THE DOCTOR DID not see himself as old, at 56, but he *was* frightened. While his one-time colleague, Klaus Barbie, now known as Klaus Altmann and with an Argentinean rather than German identity, had been helping the CIA in devising the plan for the capture and execution of Che Guevara, the doctor had so far managed to avoid attracting notice, or, indeed, capture.

He was just a German emigrant in a small town, working at the clinic, and if his methodology was occasionally odd and his interest in births – particularly of twins – sometimes disturbing, nevertheless he was a doctor, and as such was both respected and valued by the local community.

The men who were currently standing over him with guns in their hands, however, valued him for a different reason, and respected him not at all.

"We've been watching you, *Herr Doktor*, for a good long while," the one on the left said. He was dark skinned and bearded, and wore loose army fatigues that bore no insignia. "We know what goes on in the lab in the forest, and we know what happens to the babies who don't make it. And to the ones who do…"

"I am an innocent…" the doctor began, but the man cut him off. The one on the right, not speaking, slapped him. He wore thick rings on his hand, and the back-handed blow drew blood.

"You are innocent of nothing," he said. "Now. Let us go. Work, after all, makes us free, does it not, doctor?"

Arbeit macht frei. It was the sign that hung on the gates of the camp that he had worked in. But that had been during the war.

"Work for us, and we will let you live," the bearded man said.

The doctor shrugged, and got up, and wiped the blood from his mouth. He had not survived this long, first in Germany and then in the post-war years, without knowing when to follow an order.

"I am at your service," he said, and smiled ironically. "Comrade."

3

THE HANDS WERE gruesome things, cut off at the wrists – he couldn't see what had prompted anyone to do it. The job had been done professionally, but messily, by a local doctor in a town called Vallegrande. It had taken the man several tries before he had severed the hands clean off from the rest of the body.

They had taken a jeep and driven deep into the forest. He was no longer surprised. They knew where his second, secret, lab was. They knew everything. South America was crawling with these Marxist terrorists, but then it had enough of everything else, too, including his kind. More than one former colleague had made his way to South America after the war with new papers and sometimes a new face. So he shrugged and got on with it.

They stopped and he got out. The hands were stored in a glass jar filled with Formaldehyde.

"It would have been best if you'd kept the material fresh," he said. But he took the jar when it was given him.

"This was not our work."

The other one, he noticed, never spoke. Just watched him, like a hungry cat watching a rat he wasn't allowed to eat. The doctor liked cats, generally. But he did not like this man.

They went inside the building. From outside it was camouflaged, painted a dark green – the colour of the forest – and looked abandoned. Inside, the doctor switched on the lights and fan blades began to move overhead, making the light flicker.

His machines, his notebooks lined up on a heavy oak bookshelf, his desk and his operating table and, underneath the ground, deep below the lab, the waiting vats...

"What do you want me to do?" he said, though he thought he already knew.

The bearded man merely smiled, and the doctor sighed, inwardly and, giving up the pretence as futile, said, "How many?"

4

WHICH HAD BEEN the correct question to ask, as it turned out.

And so he got down to work.

The answer had been: "All of them."

He had thirty-two vats, and five weren't operational.

So the first batch was for twenty-seven.

Of which two didn't last the first three months, and one clocked out at seven and a half.

But that still made twenty-four, that first time.

There were over two hundred by the time it was finished.

PART TWO: DISCO YEARS

"Why did they think that by killing him, he would cease to exist as a fighter?... Today he is in every place, wherever there is a just cause to defend."

- Fidel Castro

1

BY THE TIME they were five they looked and acted ten. Accelerated growth had been a part of the doctor's process. How he came to perfect it – how many had died for these to be born – the bearded man didn't want to know, or ask.

By the time they were nine they had the bodies and minds of eighteen year old boys.

By the time the CIA had located the camp and sent a small army to investigate, helicopters swooping down with hardened Vietnam veterans manning the machines, they discovered nothing but a 10-mile radius of burned forest and a small crater where a building may once have stood.

In the centre of the crater they found a single corpse. It was burned beyond recognition. There were two bullet holes neatly drilled in the back of what was left of the skull.

Welcome to the seventies, *hombre*.

Party like it's 1976.

THE BAR WAS small and there were Xs on the windows in brown tape and sand bags outside but there was cold beer, and a generator and a small turntable was cranking out Abba's 'I Do, I Do, I Do, I Do, I Do'. It was very hot outside. This was Angola and he'd been fighting on the MPLA side for many weeks, running a bloody guerrilla campaign against the UNITA forces.

The battle was bigger than him, he knew. Bigger than all of them. Cuba and Moscow supplied the MPLA. The CIA and South Africa supplied UNITA.

"Socialism will always win," he said out loud, to no one in particular. He went and got himself a drink. "Even if the terms of the fight are unequal."

They had liberated the bar only two hours before. The place came with an airstrip but there were no planes. MPLA soldiers were settling down outside, ready to protect the newly-acquired landing strip. He took a sip of beer.

It was hot and dusty and he had been on the go for a long time. He missed home, for just a moment. Then it passed.

He heard the drone of an aircraft in the distance, growing closer. Putting the beer down he ran outside.

"They are coming back, Che!"

"Take cover! Man the guns!"

It didn't take much to bring down a plane, as he had found out. One well-placed bullet could do the trick, if the shooter was good enough and the plane low enough...

And then the sound of more engines filled the air, and suddenly the airfield was awash with flames, and the smell of burning, and blood, and a boy who couldn't have been more than sixteen staggered and fell into his arms. It took him a moment to realise that the boy's brain had been blasted out of his skull and now covered the front of his shirt. He lowered the boy gently to the ground.

"It was an ambush, Che!"

"If we die here today, others will take our place!"

His soldiers spoke little. Their perimeter of defence was already set up. They returned fire –

But now the planes were coming down low and they were dropping explosives. He heard a scream and dust blinded him momentarily. More explosions. And now there was confusion in the ranks.

"God damn it!" he said, and pulled out his gun, and fired into the air. He followed the sound of the engines, aimed. Going by sound.

THE PILOT OF the Cessna Skyhawk 172, Willem Botha, had been trained in South Africa and volunteered when the Angola opportunity presented itself. They had to show those kaffirs what was what, he knew, and stop the nationalistic aspirations – let alone communist degeneracy – of their brethren outside South Africa, who were fermenting unrest in the Motherland. It was almost funny, watching them run, scared and confused – the landing strip had proven too much of a temptation for them and the trap worked brilliantly.

He was pleased with himself. In many ways he was a lucky man, dying – when the single bullet entered his head from underneath, through the jawbone, breaking his teeth and turning his brain into slush – with no concept of his death, and with a joy that had no time to turn into confusion.

Losing control of his bowels and the plane at the same instant, the corpse sat at the controls as the plane plunged to the ground –

CHE, THE PLANE, the war. Smoke rising in slow motion, cries drifting in lower-tone bass. Brain on his shirt. The smell of petrol and machine gun oil. He fired again, uselessly. Then the plane was on him and the world became a ball of searing flame. Then all was quiet.

2

IT WAS QUIET in the jungle, and he was waiting for the boys from Vietnam to show up.

"We are very concerned," they told him, their first meeting. "*Very* concerned."

They were patriots, heroes, revolutionaries. All of the above. They had beaten the Americans after years in the bush, and were just trying to run their country.

Which didn't stop them watching over the border, and seeing what their brothers were doing. And getting concerned.

"Brother Number One," they told him. "He is a threat to the revolution."

"How so?"

"He is… unstable."

His name was Saloth Sar but he called himself Pol Pot. He had been educated in Paris and was the leader of the communist movement in the Kingdom of Cambodia, the red Khmers, as they were called. He was a revolutionary and commanded respect.

The Vietnamese wanted to kill him.

Now he waited, at the agreed spot. Finally they came – there were three of them, in khakis and no insignias. They paused when they saw him. "Che."

"Comrades."

Pol Pot's revolution had been successful. The year before he had become the prime minister of his country, which had been renamed Democratic Kampuchea. He had declared that year as Year Zero.

"He is killing his own people." the most senior of the three Vietnamese said. "He must be stopped."

"He is a hero of the revolution."

Uncertain smiles. They did not know how to take him, this symbol of resistance who should not be here, had no business being alive. "He must be terminated… with extreme prejudice."

The last was said in English. A strange expression, he thought… "You want him killed."

"Yes."

"Then say so!" he snapped.

"We want him dead and buried, and we believe you could do it."

"What about your own people?" he said, already knowing the answer.

"We have sent several trained comrades," the senior member told him. "None of them survived."

"He is executing thousands, hundreds of thousands!"

"And Vietnam would like control of its less stable neighbour?"

"You are cynical."

"A realist."

The senior member shrugged. "Would you do it?"

He never got a chance to answer. Shadows moving in the jungle – movement caught his eyes. He dropped to the ground even as the men were hit. Three shots, no more. Professionals, and they had been waiting.

The Vietnamese must have had a mole, he thought. Someone was reporting back to Pol Pot.

The fourth shot hit him in the leg. They were firing low. Then they were on him. A face looked down, apologetically. "It is a sad day," it said, in French, "for us all."

"There will be others," Che whispered. He held his leg in his hands. It was broken, and bleeding.

"And I shall be here," the figure above him said. "And I shall be waiting."

The man held a gun. He lowered it. The barrel pointed at the man on the ground.

The man with the gun pulled the trigger.

3

HE WAS IN bed with Christina when the knock on the door came. They had met in the hills around Londonderry, fighting the British. She was quick with a gun and with a knife and with a kiss. Her passion for the revolution equalled his own.

When the knock came they both tensed. Not speaking, they both grabbed hold of their guns. They were both semi-clothed, still, in preparation for just such a moment. They pulled on the clothes in silence, one-handed, listening, waiting.

But all was still.

Then the quiet was shattered by glass breaking – the window of the loft exploding into fragments – and a small metal oval shape came flying to land amidst the hay.

"Grenade!" Christina said.

Che picked it up and calmly threw it back out of the window. There was the sound of an explosion, curses in English, and then the gunfire started.

They both cowered on the floor while hay floated everywhere and bullet holes punctured the wooden walls. "Hold me," she said. "Please…"

Her mouth was close to his ear. He could feel the warmth of her breath. "I didn't tell you," she said. "I'm –"

Then she was limp in his arms, and her blood was as warm as her breath.

He got up, still unharmed. "You will die," he said. "Every single one of you, until Ireland is free. Until Christina is avenged. You will die for what you did today."

THE SOLDIERS WERE startled almost into immobility when the bearded, half-naked figure came flying out from the second level of the loft, seemingly-impervious to the hail of bullets, and landed in their midst.

The man wore only socks on his feet and had a gun in each hand and he was firing, his face a mask of mute anger. Several men were down before the company began to take cover and fire back, but though he was hurt several times he just kept coming, like a demon or a ghost, never speaking, covered in blood. In the confusion several soldiers died of friendly fire and several others, crossing themselves, ran away into the night and were later declared deserters.

When his guns were empty he snatched a machine gun from the hands of a young, dead soldier and continued to fire, until at last it was a single soldier, Grant Stone who, wounded earlier, rose up, confused, his empty gun still in his hand, and buried the bayonet deep into the demon's belly.

Later, he never spoke of that moment to anyone. The look in the demon's eyes as he died was something Grant Stone never found words to describe. When at last he shuddered on the blade his eyes had remained open, gateways into a vast, great soul.

4

THE PROTESTERS CARRIED plaques that said: *Down with Afrikaans* and *If we must do Afrikaans, Vorster must do Zulu*. They were young, and black, and rightfully angry. They were living under Apartheid, and the white government had just passed the Afrikaans Medium Decree, forcing all black schools to be taught in a mixture of Afrikaans and English. The protest was peaceful, thousands of young men and women marching from their schools towards Orlando Stadium.

There were few white people amongst them, and one young man in khaki and a beard who mostly seemed to blend into the crowd.

It was not clear what happened next.

Accounts agree that Colonel Kleingeld pulled out a handgun and fired a shot in the air.

Students panicked.

In the fear and confusion people began trying to escape. The police opened fire.

The man in khaki had tried to organise the protesters but, not being one of them, was nearly killed himself. Twenty-three people died that first day, two of them white. One of them, an opponent of Apartheid, was found stoned to death, left with a sign around his neck: *Beware Afrikaaners*.

The man in khaki had retreated with the others towards Soweto. He had been there for some time, quietly, organizing a resistance movement to operate outside of the city.

The bodies of dead and mutilated children lay in the street.

"It is a war," the man in khaki told his comrades. "The revolution is not an apple that falls when it is ripe. You have to make it fall."

Fifteen hundred armed police officers stormed Soweto the next day. The man in khaki and his comrades were waiting, though they knew the fight was doomed. Helicopters circled above the township. Armoured tanks drove through the streets.

The man in khaki was armed and dangerous. He killed three police officers close-up, with a handgun. He disabled one tank with a home-made grenade.

He was wounded in the arm as he carried a seven-year-old child, himself wounded, through a backyard demolished by heavy artillery. He rolled, still holding the boy, and fired back.

But there were too many of them coming after him, white men in riot gear, firing at him and the child both. He jumped over a broken wall and almost dropped the boy, but didn't. He made it to the safe house but the house was no longer safe.

"Look after him," he told the nurse. She nodded her head quickly, took the boy from him and ducked inside. "Go with God," she told him, and then she was gone.

"I do not believe in God," he told her; his tone was almost apologetic.

He was hit again by then, in the shoulder.

The man in khaki smiled. His smile was that of a lean, hungry wolf. He let the gun drop from his hand and walked towards the officers. They watched him come.

The third shot hit him in the stomach. His smile was no longer a smile but a grimace of pain, though he did not cry out. He crawled towards them. They began to laugh.

"Finish the kaffir-lover off," their leader said. The man in khaki heard guns cocking. They were taking their time. He tried to smile through the pain.

They shot him in the head, a confirmed kill. His hand rolled to the side, lifeless. His thumb came off the dead-man's-switch, opening the circuit he had been holding back, and a tiny current of electricity rushed along a new path, reaching the explosives wired to the dead man's chest.

The resultant explosion killed five of the seven officers. Of the other two, one lost both legs and the other only lost his arm.

The noise of the explosion went unnoticed amidst the screams and the gunfire.

PART THREE: FEAR AND LOATHING

"I am not Christ or a philanthropist, old lady, I am all the contrary of a Christ... I fight for the things I believe in, with all the weapons at my disposal, and try to leave the other man dead so that I don't get nailed to a cross or any other place."

– Che Guevara

WE WERE SOMEWHERE around West Beirut on the edge of the city when the drugs began to take hold. I remember saying something like "I feel a bit lightheaded; maybe you should drive..." And suddenly there was a terrible roar all around us and the sky was full of what looked like huge bats.

They were Israeli fighter planes.

They were pounding the shit out of Beirut.

Then it was quiet again. Che had taken his shirt off and was pouring beer on his chest, to facilitate the tanning process. "What the hell are you yelling about?" he muttered, staring up at the sun with his eyes closed and covered with wraparound Spanish sunglasses. "Never mind," I said. "It's your turn to drive."

Che was in Beirut to fight for the revolution. I was in Beirut for Rolling Stone. They had tracked me down at the Polo Lounge. I'd been sitting there for many hours with my attorney, drinking Singapore Slings with mescal on the side and beer chasers. And when the call came, I was ready.

The Dwarf approached our table cautiously, as I recall, and when he handed me the pink telephone I said nothing, merely listened. And then I hung up, turning to face my attorney. "That was headquarters," I said. "They want me to go to Beirut at once, and make contact with an Argentinean revolutionary named Che. All I have to do is check into my suite and he'll seek me out."

"I thought Guevara was dead," my attorney said. "Also, they don't have hotel suites in Beirut any more."

I should have listened to my attorney. Instead, here I was in Beirut with six sides all shooting at each other while I was shooting up…

– Extract from 'Fear and Loathing in Beirut' by Hunter S. Thompson, published 1982 in *Rolling Stone Magazine*

THEY CAME FROM all over to be witness to the gradual destruction of Beirut. Hunter S. Thompson was recently here, P.J. O'Rourke is currently writing a tourist guide to the capital and jokes of 'unspellables killing the unpronouncables'. The journalists meet at the Commodore Hotel. Shelling commences every night. There are several factions fighting in Lebanon, Shi'ites, Christians, Druze, the PLO,

Israel, Syria... the list goes on. The journalists – cynical, hard-bitten, hard-drinking and hard-done-by, watch it all unfold.

But the man everyone wants to see is a ghost; a shadow; a Dracula risen from the grave, a Frankenstein monster animated by who-knows what strange passions. His name is on the lips of militia fighters and busboys, of Syrian spies and Shi'ite commanders.

That name is Che.

For the past decade he has made his appearance wherever evil and injustice rear their ugly heads. Which is to say, he's been sighted everywhere.

Where has he come from? Where is he going? Tales abound of the cigar-smoking, bearded hero of the revolution, from Soweto to Phnom Penh.

And now he is here. As a series of mysterious assassinations rock the once-grand capital of Lebanon, leaders of all sides being taken down with military precision by an unknown killer, many speculate Che is, single-handedly, attempting to end the bitter civil war.

But where is he? Does he truly exist? Thompson claims to have met him, to have spoken with him, but his story shifts and changes with each telling. O'Rourke claims to have caught traces of him on a recent jaunt South, near the Israeli border.

Syria claims to have him in prison. So does Israel. At least one militia claims to have executed a man fitting Che's description.

Could all those stories be true at once? Or are none true at all?

"Che?" the hotel's busboy told me earlier tonight. "He stays here, at the Commodore. Room four-oh-one."

Everybody, it is said, comes to the Commodore. When I went up to investigate I found the room bare, the bed made, the sink cleaned. Could he have been there? Is he here at all?

> – Extract from *Strange Passions: A Memoir of the Civil War in Lebanon*, by Carl Bernstein, published 1985 by Random House, Inc.

THE ON-GOING civil war in Lebanon has officially ended today with the dissolution of the various militias (with the sole exception of Hezbollah) and the election of a new parliament. Lebanon now faces the long road to rebuilding a torn country and a city once described as "The Venice of the Orient" [...]

When asked about the whereabouts of Ernesto 'Che' Guevara, new president Elias Hrawi said, "I don't know to whom you are referring."

Mystery continues to surround –

> – Extract from *End of Civil War in Lebanon*, by Jeremy Levin, Associated Press, 1991.

Part Four: Destinations

"Why do we say Che is alive? Because of his grandeur, his transcendence. For us, Che is here, very much alive, in everything we say."

– Osvaldo 'Chato' Peredo

THERE WERE SEVEN of them who met at the Mojave Desert airfield. Seven dusty men with olive skin and haunted eyes. They had arrived separately. Outside, on the tarmac runway, a futuristic vehicle sat waiting, *SpaceShipOne* written in bold black typeface on its sides. One of the men lit up a cigar, coughed, and said, "I remember reading about these things in those American magazines we used to get sometimes."

"Science fiction," one of the others said. "I always thought such literature was ideological aspect."

"The world has changed," a third said. They moved inside, into the hangar. The place was theirs alone. "So few of us remain..."

The seven examined each other in silence. The pain in their eyes was visible.

"The world changes," said the first one, after a moment of reflection, "yet people don't..."

"Soon they will go to the stars," said one. "The Chinese already are talking of Mars, and the moon again..."

"Malaysia wants to explore commercial opportunities in the asteroid belt."

"In Equatorial Africa they are speaking of building something called a space elevator."

"Enough!" the first one said. "Where there is commerce there is exploitation. Miners once dug for coal. So now they would dig for precious metals on rocks in space, while others will grow rich from their labour. The world changes. We won't."

They all nodded. Veterans of endless conflicts, of the Balkans and Afghanistan, Gaza and Tibet, Timor and Argentina and the Western Sahara, they were weary but unbent, tired but not defeated.

"They put our face on undergarments now," said one of them. "They put them on T-shirts and bandanas."

"Rampant capitalism will seek to subjugate its opponents by commercialising their own image," another said. They all nodded.

It was quiet in the hangar. A giant model of a ship, half-completed, filled up the space. They avoided looking at it.

"Out there," said the first of them, his hand sweeping across the desert, the runway, the spaceship outside – "out there is not the future. But it is *a* future. One of many."

"So many of us are gone…" one said.

"Yet we remain."

They nodded. "Do you think we made any difference at all?" one asked.

"We cannot be the judges of that," the first said. "Only history can judge us."

He looked at them. The tip of his cigar glowed red. "And history is a thing to be shaped and remade."

None of them spoke after that. Outside, the sun beat down on the tarmac, and the desert, like the future, stretched far away and disappeared beyond the horizon.

STEEL LAKE

JACK SKILLINGSTEAD

*Jack Skillingstead lives in Seattle with his wife, Nancy
Kress, whom he's noticed seems to write a lot more than
he does. 'Steel Lake' marks his thirtieth professional
short story sale since 2002; the first twenty-six of which
are gathered in his Golden Gryphon collection,* Are You
There and Other Stories. *In 'Steel Lake', Jack wanted to
write about a father and son with parallel issues and that
slippery region that lies between dreams, imagination
and so-called reality. The piece proved a particularly
troublesome one to get right. Jack's 2009 debut novel,*
Harbinger, *prompted* The New York Review of Science
Fiction *to dub him 'The matador of our field.' The
author is quite proud of this, reckoning it has a nice ring
– as long as you don't ask him to explain what it means.*

"WHY ARE YOU doing this?" Brian Kerr asked his son.

"I'm an addict."

"Yeah, I *know* that. But why now?"

They sat at a table in an institutionally grim room.
The flat glare of fluorescent light made Brian's eyes

ache. His shirt clung to his body in dark patches of sweat. A big school-style clock counted the seconds in tiny jerks of a black needle.

"I took something that scared me," David said.

"According to the checklist we just went through, you've taken every damn drug known to man."

"This one wasn't on the list."

"Great. What was it?"

"It isn't even on the *street* yet. This guy, he stole it out of a UW lab, he said. Like he was a volunteer for this test?"

"Okay. But what *was* it?"

"I don't know."

"Jesus Christ."

David shrugged, looking away. His over-sized white T-shirt hung loose on his shoulders – the way it would on a coat hanger. Green spray paint speckled the shirt. Graffiti blow-back.

"You just took it. Without even knowing what it was?"

"Yeah, I guess."

"*Why?*"

"It was there so I took it, is all. You don't really get it, Dad."

"No, I don't. What scared you about this drug? I mean, what's scarier than –" He picked up the checklist, the unbelievable, terrifying checklist. "– heroin, for instance?"

"It turned my head inside out."

"What's that mean, turned your –"

The door opened and two men entered. The older man, Ray, was in charge – he handled the late shift intakes. About forty, lean and muscled, he looked like a penitentiary cliché. Tattooed thorns vined around his muscled forearms and a pack of smokes bulged in his short rolled up sleeve. Rehab wasn't jail, but so far it shared a similar flavor. Or so Brian imagined. The younger man was actually a kid David's age, eighteen or so, pale and blooming with acne.

"Nick's going to check your bag for contraband," Ray said.

Nick, all business, opened David's hastily-packed suitcase and began pawing through it. He tossed aside a paperback novel. Brian had packed the book for David, thinking it would help him get through the next month.

"Why can't he have that?"

Ray picked up the novel and handed it to Brian. "The only book allowed in here is The Big Book."

"That's –"

"Dad, it's okay. I don't care about it."

"What your son needs, he has to keep his mind on recovery."

"Yeah, I get that."

Ray pushed the insurance papers across the table and held out a Bic pen. Brian sighed and started on the forms. Until it was time to say goodbye, David did not speak another word.

Business as usual.

FOR A WEEK David had been living in his car, a black 1993 beat-to-shit Honda Civic. Turning the ignition key produced a rapid series of dead clicks. When Brian picked him up, they left the Honda parked on a residential street in a south Seattle working class neighbourhood. Sooner or later somebody would call the city to get it towed. Before that, Brian decided to strip out whatever 'contraband' he could find.

A Mag-Lite in his left hand, he popped the glove box. Registration papers, parking tickets, a dead cell phone, half a dozen disposable syringes, and a pipe that looked like it was hand-tooled out of plumbing parts. Brian sniffed the bowl, winced at the burnt smell.

He dropped the syringes and pipe into a plastic Safeway bag then swept the Mag-Lite around the foot wells. Among the crumpled cigarette packs and Taco Time wrappers, colonies of little Ziploc baggies gleamed in the moving light. Some were empty and some contained a faint residue of white powder. Brian scooped them all up and added them to the Safeway bag.

He found the miniature aspirin tin under the cup holder insert, shook it, flicked the lid up with his thumbnail. Five chalky blue tablets, each printed with the same Greek l[...] u[...] A car turned onto the s[...] headlights swinging through t[...] Brian froze but his shadow tilt[...] s[...] ducking out of sight. The c[...] wi[...]g.

Brian let his brea[...] in checked the backseat and th[...] kl[...] back to his own car. He d[...] a garbage dumpster behind a Korean restaurant.

BY MIDNIGHT HE was drunk, holding down a stool in The Sitting Room, a quiet lamp-lit bar two blocks from his apartment. Even on the best of nights, the studio apartment felt like a divorce tomb. This was not the best of nights. Murphy's Irish whiskey and pints of Stella failed to erase various realities, the tomb-apartment being one of them.

He fumbled his cell phone out and thumbed a garbled text. Immediately, he regretted it. But when Trish failed to reply, he regretted that even more. He ordered another drink and nursed it along until closing time.

Halfway up the hill, stumbling towards his apartment, the phone vibrated in his pocket. He squinted at the display window.

One word, from Trish: 'Okay.'

"YOU'RE A MESS," she said when she opened the door to her condo. She wore a Seahawks jersey and nothing else. Her hair was messed up, like she'd been asleep.

"Bad day," he said. "Look, I shouldn't have texted you."

"I know that."

"Oh –"

"And I shouldn't have invited you over. So we're both stupid."

In the bathroom he toed his shoes off, dumped the contents of his pockets on the towel rack. He rinsed his mouth in the sink, the tap water cold and metallic.

Trish was sitting up in bed, waiting for him. "I'd offer you a drink, but that would be like offering kerosene to a burning man."

"Yeah." He collapsed on the bed beside her.

"So what happened?"

"David called and I checked him into Lakeside."

"I'm so sorry, Brian." She held his hand, picking up where they left off – where Brian left, actually. The Man

Who Couldn't Stay. "But it's kind of good, too," Trish said. "I mean, maybe it'll straighten him out this time."

"There's always that chance. At least I'll know where he is for the next six weeks." Brian covered his eyes with his free hand. "I really am an idiot. My head's going to hurt so bad tomorrow."

"Wait a minute." She scooted off the bed, returning shortly with a tall glass of water. "Stick your tongue out."

He did, and she placed two bitter-tasting tablets on it.

"Aspirin. Swallow – and drink that whole glass. Plus the next one I'm going to bring you. It'll undercut the hangover."

BRIAN CAME AWAKE at some dead hour of the morning.

He had been dreaming about playing catch with his son. In the dream they stood on a grassy slope in S████ L██k█ ███ ne███ the ███ neighbo███ ████ David █ ██ ██oul██ ██ ag███ 1. T██ baseball ██ed ██wee█ t██ g██ove██ ██ the ███od ██orld, the l█ ██ w██l█, wa█ r██ ██red. T██ ██me██ ██ng ██ke Brian a██ it ██ over h██ ██r wa██ – a██ f D██ █ had step██ █ o██ ██ of the██ d██ ██n and ██ ██sou██ of ██ ██ passage ██ a ██kened B██ ██, like ██ ██son ██ ██vir██ he bedroo█ ██an█ ██lling t██ ██o██r s███

The good years, right. Not long after Brian taught his son to catch a baseball, a man was murdered in that same park, knifed repeatedly. Some gang thing, the opening event of the neighborhood's long, steep slide. The victim's blood stained Brian's good memories, like sour wine spilled across a holiday table cloth.

Trish's bedside clock read 4:17AM. Brian was *wide* awake. Sharply, almost painfully, wide awake. He did not feel drunk or hung-over. Trish slept on her side, turned away from him.

In the bathroom his haggard face regarded him from the mirror. He rubbed his sandpaper cheek. His mouth tasted like rust. He stuck his tongue out, almost expecting to see it coated with iron oxide. His wallet and keys were on the towel rack over the hamper. Brian stuffed them into his pockets.

In the living room he grabbed his empty water glass and carried it into the kitchen. A little tin of aspirin sat on the counter next to the microwave. Brian stared at it. He set his glass down, wiped his lips with the back of his hand. The tin rattled when he shook it. He pried it open. Three chalky blue tablets with Greek letters. When he found the tin in David's car it had contained five.

"Trish?" He shook her gently until she woke up.

"Huh? God, what are you doing awake, it's –"

"Five. Never mind that. Last night you gave me aspirin. Where did you get them?"

Lying on her back, she held the clock up and squinted at it. "My God, it *is* five."

"Trish, the aspirin. It's important."

"I was out but there were some with your wallet and keys in the bathroom. What's wrong?"

"Shit. *Shit*."

She sat up. "What's wrong, what's happening?"

"Nothing's wrong, except those weren't aspirin."

"Oh, God, Brian, what were they? Is it something David had?"

"Yeah."

She took the tin out of his hand. "What are they?"

"I don't know," he said, thinking: *Like father like son*.

"What's this symbol? Damn it, I'm sorry, Brian. I should have looked more closely. But I was half-asleep and –"

"It's not your fault."

"Let me hold on to one of the pills. I'll show it to a lab rat I know at the hospital. Maybe she can figure it out."

"You don't have to do that."

"Are you on any other medication? There might be something reactive –" Trish suddenly inhabiting her full-on RN mode.

"I'm not taking anything. Don't worry about it, okay?"

"Excuse me for trying to help."

"I'm sorry. Look, tell your rat they might be part of some kind of drug trial at the UW. David said that's where they came from. And I appreciate it, I really do."

"Okay." She looked closely at him. "Are you feeling anything… weird?"

"Just really wide awake."

"Maybe they're some kind of stimulant. That wouldn't be too bad."

"No, that wouldn't be bad."

IT WAS BAD.

A week later, Brain still hadn't slept. He no longer felt sharply awake, but he didn't feel sleepy, either. Or he felt he *was* asleep, walking through a dream. But he knew that wasn't true. Reality did not bend the way it did in dreams. At least, it hadn't so far.

Three north bound lanes of Interstate 5 were shut down for resurfacing, and even at ten-thirty PM traffic was slow, rolling into Seattle. Brian slouched behind the wheel of his Ford Focus, windows cranked down. He was wrung out after nine hours on the night shift, stringing wires in the fuselage of a 737. A big industrial fan circulated air through the hatch but it didn't help much; the air was thick and hot, stinking of human sweat and machine oil. The fan blades scraped the safety cage – like a blade scoring the inside of Brian's skull.

The lights at Safeco Field blazed over the twelfth inning of an interminable tie game between the Mariners and Toronto. A play-by-play broadcast chattered from the radio speakers, which was a lucky break, considering the radio hadn't worked in two weeks.

The last game he had taken David to had been four years ago. They sat in the sun, Brian with his seven dollar Budweiser and David with his four dollar Coke (all Brian could afford, after paying for the tickets and parking). The plastic cups sweating in their hands, they watched the Mariners take their lumps against the Oakland A's. The Mariners were *always* taking their lumps. David sipped his Coke and crunched ice with his teeth, speaking only when he had to respond to something Brian said.

In the traffic crawl, Dave Niehouse, the Mariners' venerable color commentator, was in the middle of calling a pop fly to right centre field, when the broadcast washed out in a tide of static. Brian reached for the knob to turn the volume down but hesitated when another voice, low and intense, began speaking. "I hate you, you fucker. You think you got away with it, but you didn't."

Despite the heat, a cold breath prickled the hairs on the back of Brian's neck. The voice was familiar but Brian couldn't quite identify it. He adjusted the volume up but there were no more words, just the usual static that had been hissing out of the speakers for weeks. After another moment, he punched the radio off. Then Brian remembered something, and it wasn't a good something.

Dave Niehouse was dead.

A heart attack had nailed the commentator over a year ago. So, what did that mean? Was Niehouse some kind of auditory hallucination? Was it starting, whatever 'it' was? David's 'inside-out' head?

A dog loped out of nowhere, head down, sniffing the hot, grated surface of the road. It appeared oblivious of the packed traffic. Brian gripped the steering wheel and hunched forward. A golden retriever, the dog favored its left hind leg, and Brian recognized her immediately. This was Gypsy, the family dog – back when Brian had a family.

Gypsy was as dead as Dave Niehouse.

The muscles tightened in Brian's chest. Behind him, somebody laid on a horn, and he jumped half out of his seat. A pair of truck lights glared in his rear-view mirror before swerving around and passing on the right. In the thick traffic the manoeuvre was impossible – but the truck managed it, anyway, as if there *were* no traffic. Or maybe it was the truck and dog that weren't really there. That seemed more likely, given what Brian now saw.

Cancerous rust had eaten holes in the Suburban's left front wheel hub. The driver's arm hung out the open window with a cigarette. The big, ramshackle SUV cut back in, almost clipping the Ford's bumper. Brian tapped the brakes. An old California plate, orange numbers on a black background, hung crookedly by a single screw from the Suburban's bumper.

It was the same truck that had killed Gypsy seven years ago.

Even before Brian could process that idea, the Suburban struck the resurrected dog. Brian almost felt the dull thud of impact reverberate in his bones. The dog yelped in pain.

"Asshole!"

The truck moved off, at times occupying the same space as other vehicles, overlaying them like an optical trick.

Brian pulled into the narrow break-down lane, parked, switched on his hazard flashers. The dog lay smashed against the jersey barrier, where the impact had landed her. Nobody but Brian seemed to notice. The tortured, squeaking yelps of pain drilled into Brian's mind – just as they had seven years ago. He had been having a rare, loud argument with Sheila. She had just discovered his first affair. David hadn't come home from school yet – except he had, and neither one of them knew it.

The boy stood by the open front door, listening to the whole thing. Gypsy, always in heedless puppy-behaviour mode, had streaked out the door. David shouted after her. Brian and Sheila stopped yelling at each other. A moment later tires screeched, and Brian bolted out of the house after his son. He got a good look at the Suburban.

Now Brian plugged his ears with his fingers but that didn't dampen the sound at all. It was as if Gypsy's heart-breaking whimpering was inside his head. Brian clenched his teeth. Gradually, the yelps and squeals of the dog faded. In his mind, close up, he saw Gypsy's heaving flank and the blood pumping out of her mouth – his memory like a dream awake in the world. He blinked back tears. When he looked again, the dog was gone. Thank Christ.

What was so scary...? It turned my head inside out.

Brian turned off his hazard flashers and re-entered the traffic flow. His hands were shaking. Just past the Convention Centre he moved into the exit lane and found himself behind the Suburban with its ancient orange-on-black plate hanging by a screw.

A young boy, maybe six-years-old, stared at him out the back window, his face white in Brian's headlights. David's face. Brian's heart pounded. The window was dirty, like looking at the boy through a sheet of crusted brown ice.

David at six years old – the good years.

Brian had pissed all over those years. Oh, he had his excuses lined up, but they all boiled down to his own weakness. The first affair had provided him temporary, selfish relief from an estranged marriage. At least he could pretend that first one was love. Subsequent affairs were just a bad habit.

You thought you got away with it, you fucker...

The voice on the radio, so familiar, had been his own voice. The relentless accuser.

The line of cars started to move. The Suburban pulled away, magically passing through the slower cars, oily blue exhaust belching from its jiggling tailpipe. The David hallucination or whatever it was raised his hand to the window. A shadow loomed behind the boy and yanked him roughly back. Brian made a small, trapped sound in his throat. He goosed the accelerator but could not get around the intervening traffic. The SUV melted away, like a lost opportunity.

ON THE PHONE, Trish said, "How are you feeling?"

"Still haven't slept."

"Jesus. You're up to nine days. Okay, I've got a number for you. A Dr. Weinstein. That Greek letter on the pills? It identifies them by experimental lot-trial. I made some calls."

"Thanks. What's the number?"

She told him and he wrote it down.

"Brian? Maybe you should come over, not be alone."

"I'm all right."

"Then maybe you should come over so *I* don't have to be alone. I'm just saying."

"I'll call you."

"I doubt it."

He knew he shouldn't say anything else, but he did: "What's wrong?"

"A lot of things."

"Trish, you know I never said –"

"Here's what it is. I don't hear from you for like a month, sometimes even longer. Then you have a crisis, and you want one of two things. The first is a mother. The mother's the one that listens patiently, commiserates, tells you it's all better, even takes you to bed, for God's sake."

"All right."

"The other is a child. When it's the child, you get to take care of me, fix stuff. Convey wisdom about things you know and I don't know, whatever. Be a comfort.

Be a man. Here's what's sad. I used to mistake both of these for the wrong thing. Love."

"I love you," he mumbled, like a guy coasting into a four-way intersection without conviction, just begging for a bus to T-bone him. And it did.

"You've learned to say it, but I think you're sketchy on the concept."

"Come on, you don't even –"

"Don't get all dramatic. All I'm saying, what I mean is… that I can't really do it anymore. I can't alternate between mother and child. Because you know what? I'm not either of those things. If you ever think you're over yourself, then call."

"Trish, I have to go."

"Big surprise."

"How many did you take?" Dr. Weinstein asked.

"Two."

"Since you won't come to my office, I strongly urge you to see your own physician as soon as possible."

"Won't the effect just wear off?"

"Eventually, of course. But there is an interim danger. The visions you describe are not, strictly speaking, hallucinations."

"Then what are they?"

"Dreams. Dreams of a very special type. The drug eliminates your body's need to sleep but it does not eliminate your mind's need to dream. I'm afraid we don't understand very much about this process, Mr. Kerr. But we've discovered that a mind deprived of REM sleep will begin to manifest the unconscious in the form of waking dreams."

"I don't see what the danger is."

"I suppose you're familiar with the adage, 'You can't die in a dream?'"

"Sure. You're falling, or drowning. Whatever. But you always wake up first. Because if you died in a dream you'd really die. Like your mind would just stop your heart. I never believed it."

"Let me just say, Mr. Kerr, we are now in possession of evidence that lends powerful credence to this particular wives' tale. These visions are dreams, but you are already wide awake. Do you understand what I'm saying?"

THREE NO-SLEEP pills remained in the aspirin tin. In his little kitchen nook at three o'clock in the morning, Brian dropped the pills into the palm of his left hand, his right hand loose around a glass of water. Time passed. He would never have this chance again – this chance to dream awake. Dream of the good time and see it before his eyes as if it were real. He clapped his hand to his mouth and chased the pills down with water.

See his son again, his little boy.

THIRTEEN DAYS.

David was eighteen and could do what he wanted. But because it was Brian's insurance paying for rehab, he received a call when David disappeared.

"How can that happen?" Brian said.

"Your son wasn't sent here on a court order, Mr. Kerr. There's nothing we can do if a patient decides to leave. Of course, we counsel against it. In this case, David left in the night. Nobody saw him go."

BRIAN CALLED HIS ex to let her know. Talking to Sheila was like talking to his own cranky reflection – the one that constantly blamed him for everything that had gone wrong. Well, she and it had a point. "I know," she said, when he told her David had checked himself out of rehab.

"Who told you?"

"Nobody. Evidentially I'm out of the loop around here. But I saw Kevin at the drugstore, and he said David was sleeping in Steel Lake Park. He'd talked to him. So I can figure it out from there, that David checked out of rehab."

"You're not out of the loop. I'm making this call, right? And who's Kevin?"

"Of course you wouldn't know. Kevin was David's best friend. Honest to God, how can you *not* know so much? Did you even live here, when you lived here?"

AFTER MIDNIGHT, BRIAN left his car in a church parking lot, walked to Steel Lake, and scaled the chain link fence. The grass appeared blue in the moonlight. It was still hot as a sauna. He stood on a grassy slope and turned slowly, searching for movement. David could be lying in the darkness under the trees right now, and Brian would have to step on him to know it.

A baseball smacked solidly into a leather glove.

Brian turned. The figure of a boy stood in the moon shadows. He was no more than a silhouette, his arms hanging slack at his sides, a baseball glove on his left hand. Brian's breath went shallow. This had been the good place, the good time. It would have continued if only Brian had allowed it. But you didn't get a second chance.

Except in dreams.

He started across the blue grass towards David.

A car door slammed.

Brian stopped. A vehicle had appeared, mixing dreams and nightmares. A big ramshackle Suburban with California plates. A man, faceless in the dark, strode across the grass, seized the boy and began to drag him towards the truck.

"Davy!" Brian ran towards them. At the last moment, the man released the boy and raised his hand – a knife in his fist. Brian threw himself at the man, driving him off his feet. They rolled down the slope.

"Davy, run, run!"

Thinking: *It's not real*. But he was on his back, struggling with the man's knife hand, fighting with himself. And dreams always felt real when you were in the middle of one.

So did nightmares.

The strength began to drain out of Brian's arm. The point of the knife descended inexorably.

His fault all the way, the dead marriage, his boy lost to drugs.

Brian stopped resisting.

The knife plunged. He arched his back, heaving into the thrust. A great piercing grief flooded up in his chest.

The killer leaned back, his face finally revealed in moonlight.

It was Brian's own face.

The nightmare-Brian stood and grabbed Davy's thin little-boy's-arm and dragged him to the waiting Suburban. Brian rolled onto his side, reached out, as if he could retrieve every mistake. The engine rumbled up and the headlamps came on like baleful amber eyes.

Brian's heart jerked and clenched.

"Dad?"

The Suburban started to roll, bouncing across the field, taking it all away.

"*Dad?*"

The Suburban dimmed back into his mind, and Brian looked up. "David."

The boy stood over him, a backpack slung from one shoulder. "What are you doing here, Dad?"

"I came to find you but I was too late. Fifteen years too late." Speaking was difficult. He couldn't seem to draw enough air into his lungs.

David laughed uncertainly. "I'm right here."

"Yeah, so I see." Somehow this lanky, dishevelled kid was less real than the dream-boy. Maybe that was the problem. Brian sat up, grimaced, placed his hand flat over his chest. His shirt was sopped with blood only he could see. The grief-wound.

"What's wrong, is there something wrong with your heart?" David dropped his backpack, hunkered beside him.

"No. Listen, I found those pills in your car. The ones from the UW. I took them."

"How many?"

"All of them."

"Dad, that wasn't such a great idea."

"No kidding."

"Are you… seeing things?"

Brian nodded. "You bugged out of rehab. Are you using again?"

"No," David said. "I just needed to get out of that place. I mean, like I didn't think I could be there. I might go back, though. Hey, you really don't look good. Is something happening?"

"Seeing things."

"Pretty bad?"

"Yeah." His breathing labored. *If you ever died in a dream...* "You remember we used to come here? I taught you to play catch."

"I remember."

The next words stuck in Brian's throat a couple of times before he could get them out, but he did get them out. "I'm really sorry about screwing everything up for you. I know it's mostly my fault."

"What are you talking about?"

"The way things turned out. If I'd been a better father, maybe –"

"Dad, it doesn't have anything to do with you. I'm an addict. Even before I started using, I was an addict. I'll always be one. I wish you'd quit blaming yourself for everything. It's my life, not yours. How long have you been awake, anyway?"

"Two weeks."

"Whoa."

"When you were a little kid, we used to have a great time."

"I'm not a little kid anymore."

"Right, I get that."

"You *really* don't look so good."

Brian lay back on the blue grass and closed his eyes. "I'll be okay in a couple of minutes."

"Let me see your phone."

"David –"

"Come on. I don't have mine."

Brian reluctantly slipped the phone out of his pocket. David grabbed it and flipped it open.

"Hey, slow down. I don't need any –"

David ignored him. He punched three numbers and moments later said, "Yeah, I think my Dad's having a heart attack or something."

IN THE AMBULANCE the paramedic immediately rigged an I.V. drip, something to compensate for Brian's inexplicably low blood pressure. Of course, the medic did not see what Brian saw: the front of his shirt saturated with blood.

Brian turned his head on the flat, Clorox-smelling pillow. David slouched on the other bench seat, hands shoved in his pockets, affecting indifference. But he was there. Brian studied his face. The eyes were all that was left of that six-year-old.

After a while, David said, "What?"

"Just looking."

"Okay."

At the hospital they wheeled him into Emergency. Brian craned his head around. David, backpack slung from one shoulder, stood talking to the admitting nurse. The nurse wrote on a clipboard.

Behind a curtain, in a brightly-lit room, a young doctor asked Brian questions.

"I'll be all right if I can get over myself," Brian said.

"Please try to focus on what I'm asking you, Mr. Kerr."

"Okay.

Staring at the white acoustical ceiling tiles, Brian felt himself slipping away. Don't get all dramatic, Trish had told him. Maybe *Brian* was the six-year-old around here. If you died in a dream, you really died. But Brian didn't want to die.

He interrupted the doctor. "I want to see my son."

"Where is he?"

"He was talking to the admitting nurse, I think. I really want to see him, if he hasn't already left."

"Why would I leave?" David said, in his usual half-belligerent tone, as he stepped around the curtain.

"No reason, son."

Brian opened his hand and moved it toward David. After a moment's hesitation, David took it – and the dream dissolved. The hand, however, was still there.

MOONCAKES

MIKE RESNICK AND LAURIE TOM

Mike Resnick is a long-established and highly-respected science fiction author, whose work has been entertaining readers for decades, whereas Laurie Tom's promising career has only just begun. The two met when Laurie won the 2010 Writers of the Future Award with her story 'Living Rooms'. Mike was one of the judges. Awards are something Mike knows a fair bit about, having been nominated for a Hugo some thirty-five times, which, he feels confident, makes him the greatest ever Hugo loser. Along the way, of course, he's also picked up a whole hatful of awards, including a Hugo and five Nebulas. In fact, as of 2011, Mike occupies 1st place in the Locus list of all-time award winners for short fiction. Mike is the author of 64 novels, over 250 short stories and two screen plays, and his work has been translated into 25 languages. Laurie has loved fantasy and science fiction for as long as she can remember. There came a point where other people's worlds simply weren't enough for her, so she determined to create her own. "Mooncakes" represents Laurie and Mike's first collaboration.

Rachel Wang lifted her phone to read the blunt, concise message left on the glowing screen. *Sorry. No go,* it said. *Seeing Nick.*

With a sigh, she shoved her cell back in her pocket and looked out the double glass doors at the slick pavement outside. Though it had stopped raining an hour ago, the sky was still cloudy and dim. The atmosphere was supposed to clear by tomorrow morning, in which case she would be flying up to the station. She needed to be on board the *Ark* for its final run of checks. As Earth's first colony ship, the launch of the *Ark* would be a moment for the history books.

The journey was set to take decades, and the captaincy would be a heavy responsibility, probably lasting as long as the captain lived. There had been hundreds of candidates from across the globe, and the commission had finally settled on her. She and her crew would be sailing into deep space, farther than humanity had ever gone – and they would not be coming back. Rachel had said all her good-byes to family and friends... all except for Kelly, her sister.

"Were you waiting for someone?"

It was David Silver, the supervising doctor of the colony ship. He was in his thirties, like most of the command team. The commission had deemed it desirable to find exceptional staff who would be able to remain at their posts for decades to come and pass on their specialized knowledge to the next generation. The lower-ranking members of the crew were allowed a greater spread in age, so that turnover due to retirement did not cripple the crew all at once.

"Not anymore," said Rachel, with a disgruntled shake of her head. She would have thought her only sister could have made room in her evening for her. It wasn't as if they could meet again next week, next month, or even twenty years from now.

"Hey, David?" she said suddenly. "I never asked, but is your family coming along on the *Ark*?"

He grinned and nodded. "Wife, kids, even parents. They won't be heading up for a couple more weeks, but they'll all be there. What about yours?"

Rachel shook her head, and tried to hide her disappointment with a smile. "My parents are pleased for me, but they're happy right here. And I'm still single, so..." She shrugged.

"Not to worry," he said, stepping up to the sliding door. "There are going to be plenty of single men on the *Ark*. I'm sure a good-looking captain will have her pick of them."

She fell into step alongside him. They took the shuttle to the apartment complex where most of the crew had lived ever since being selected for the program. Now that she had accepted Kelly wasn't meeting her, there was no reason to wait in the command center.

"I'm sure it won't be that easy," she said lightly. "After all, who's going to want to date" – she wrinkled her nose – "an officer?"

"Why not? Are you going to throw them in the brig for expressing interest?"

She laughed and let the subject drop.

Though a myriad of cultures would be represented on the *Ark*, she knew they wouldn't all remain intact during the ship's long journey to their destination. For the moment they were one great pot of heterogeneity, but give it a generation, maybe two, and eventually their cultures would almost certainly melt together, forming something entirely new for their new home. And she didn't like to think that her descendants would forget their past, their heritage.

Like Kelly.

"Weren't you going on about some sort of Chinese holiday this week?" asked David. "Is that over now?"

"It's actually later this week, but we're going to be in space by then. If you were thinking of picking up some mooncake, you can still do that. Buying mooncake for the Mooncake Festival's like buying eggnog for Christmas. You can always do it a couple weeks early."

David smiled. "Only if it tastes like gefilte fish."

She made a face. "Do you really like that?"

"Not really," he admitted.

"Then why --?"

"Because if my wife and I don't make it, our children and their children will never taste gefilte fish, and even if they don't like it any better than I do, that's part of who we are."

"We may become   h   d
the voyage," said Ra   l.

"That's okay. We   n   a
what we came from,   id   s
matter whether I be   e   o
I'm a Jew. They've   en   fo
thousand years. You   in   ve
fooled because my grandfather changed his name from Silverstein to Silver?" He smiled in embarrassment. "I'm sorry. I didn't mean to run on like that."

"It's all right," said Rachel. "I have a culture and heritage that I don't want to lose or forget either."

She and Kelly had fought as children over the mooncake. The flaky crusts of the mooncake covered a paste of black bean or lotus seed, and inside the paste would be a delicious salted egg yolk. But the yolk would never be in the exact middle, so when their father cut the little cake into quarters for each member of the family someone would always get more yolk than the rest.

Rachel frowned. Kelly probably wasn't even eating mooncake this year. Some second generation immigrants followed dutifully in their parents cultural footsteps. Others couldn't wait to go mainstream. Kelly was the latter; dating an endless string of white boyfriends, even forgetting how to write her own name in Chinese. One had to assimilate, Rachel knew that – but like David, not like Kelly, who wouldn't even be seeing her older sister off on a voyage that would take a lifetime.

"As for the mooncake," Rachel said to David, "I should be able to bring some up to the station for everyone." It would probably be the last time she was able to eat mooncake. She was fairly certain the *Ark* would not be bringing along the ingredients she'd need to make it herself. There were other staff members of Asian descent, but she wasn't sure how many of them were Chinese in particular. And even if they were, she couldn't know if they were what she thought of as Kelly Chinese or Rachel Chinese.

Rachel knew her parents wanted a Chinese grandchild, but she couldn't be sure that she could give them that aboard the ship. But she would damned well be the daughter they were proud of. She was going into space on the colony ship. She would be remembered, her name recorded on the pages of history.

"Great!" said David. "I'd like to try one. I'm sure Moses will forgive me." He suddenly smiled. "Golda Meier I have my doubts about."

She smiled in return. The cakes were meant to be eaten with friends and family. It probably would be a good start to share them with the people she'd be spending the rest of her life with.

"You know," she said. "They're supposed to be eaten under the light of the full moon. I think we'll have a good view up there."

Suddenly Rachel found herself wondering if mooncake would have any meaning in deep space where there would no longer be any moon.

HER APARTMENT WAS all packed up. The furniture belonged to the commission, and all her personal belongings fit into two large suitcases and a backpack. The accumulations of a lifetime suddenly seemed so small and unimpressive. The only unplanned item was the bag containing three tins of mooncake that she had purchased the night before. One had already been opened. She'd been unable to help herself last night, being alone for her last night on Earth. The cake had been good: Lotus seed. Her favorite.

She told herself that even if the *Ark* sailed light years away and the few Chinese on board forgot their heritage, here on Earth there were still billions of Chinese who remembered the old ways. It wasn't as though the culture was going to disappear.

But still... when (or if) she had children, she wanted to pass on what little she knew to them, as she was sure David passed *his* heritage on, as the Irish and Brazilian and Kenyan members did as well. Maybe it would only be a few broken words in their ancestral tongue, but she had to pass on *something*. She didn't want her family's heritage to die out with her, the way it would with Kelly.

Her cell beeped. *Open the door already.*

Kelly? It was her ID.

Rachel walked out of her bedroom and over to the front door. She opened it to find her sister standing outside, a shopping bag in either arm and her cell phone wedged in one hand. Kelly's hair was bleached blond, but there was no getting rid of the almond eyes and rounded face.

"I didn't think I'd see you," said Rachel.

Kelly rolled her eyes as she stepped inside. "You're leaving later today, aren't you?" She dropped one bag on the floor by the door. It was full of clothing with the pricetags still attached. The other she held up in front of her, the Chinese characters of the supermarket plainly marked on the bag. "You're still my only sister and I know mooncake season is important for you, God knows why... so I thought I'd bring some. You know, to say good-bye."

"I'm not sure I have the time," said Rachel. "I already packed most of my stuff. Pick-up's in a few hours."

"Isn't the silverware part of the apartment?" It was.

How can I say no to my own sister's peace offering? "I'll get it," said Rachel with a sigh. "I don't have any tea, though. I already used it up."

"Water's fine." Kelly reached in the bag and pulled out a square tin. There was Chinese lettering all over the box, but also a white sticker listing the contents in English. Rachel was reasonably certain that if it hadn't been there her sister would have had no idea what flavor she was buying.

Kelly followed her into the kitchen and set the tin on the counter. "I picked this one carefully," she said. "I know we've fought a lot, and I wanted to make sure you left on a good note. I want your last memory of me to be a happy one. This mooncake's special. I got the one with double moons."

Rachel glanced at the box, reading its contents for the first time. There were two eggs in each cake. It was probably the most expensive box in the store.

"So we don't have to fight," said Kelly.

Rachel allowed herself a smile and pulled her into a hug. "We'll always be different, but you're still my sister, and I love you."

"I know I haven't always been very Chinese, but I never forget mooncake day."

"No, you don't," agreed Rachel, remembering their childhood fights. She pulled out a couple of plates and a knife. "Let's open that up and eat a cake."

Maybe Kelly would never be as Chinese as she hoped, but even so she hadn't forgotten everything. Maybe, if Rachel had children on the *Ark* one day, they wouldn't either.

RACHEL BOARDED SHIP a few hours later, and found herself sitting next to David.

"May I ask you a personal question?" she said. "It has to do with what we were discussing earlier."

"Sure," he said. "If I can reserve the right not to answer it."

"Do you have any members of your family who ignore or even deny their heritage?" she asked.

"I think every family does," he said.

"What do you do about it?"

He smiled. "You love them for what they are, and forgive them for what they're not."

She leaned back, smiled, and closed her eyes, having reached the same conclusion herself upon saying goodbye to Kelly for the very last time.

AT PLAY IN
THE FIELDS

STEVE RASNIC TEM

Award-winning author Steve Rasnic Tem is perhaps best known for his horror and dark fantasy, but along the way he has also established a reputation for writing high quality SF. Steve says he is always glad of the opportunity to write science fiction, claiming that the stories often take longer but the experience is invariably a rewarding one. Steve's latest novel, Deadfall Hotel, *chronicling what happens when nightmares seek a place of sanctuary, will be released Spring 2012 from Solaris Books.*

AFTER YEARS OF repetition, waking up in some altered state had become the expected outcome of long, uninterrupted slumber. Since childhood, Tom had come to think of sleep as practically a means of transportation. If ill or depressed he'd take to his bed for that healing power of sleep, reviving at some point forward in time, in a better place, a healthier frame of mind.

So when he regained consciousness this time in a brilliant haze of light he was not extremely concerned, even when he saw an enormous plant maybe eight feet tall – some sort of succulent bromeliad, he believed – moving about in the room, its long fleshy leaves touching tables and racks, picking up bottles and tools, its flexible stamen waving. Near the top of the plant the leaves had widened into shoulders, where some sort of brightly-lit chandelier was mounted.

Clearly he should have screamed, or been overwhelmed by anxiety, and in some compartment of his mind he was. But the trauma was muted, the terror inaccessible.

The plant waved a cluster of long filaments in Tom's direction, emitting a high-pitched, scraping sound. Now feeling the beginnings of concern, he attempted to escape. But he appeared to be paralyzed, his limbs oblivious to urgent commands. He wasn't strong enough to even cover his ears.

The scraping ceased. "I apologize," said a voice inside his head. "I had not activated your implant."

Tom managed to twist his neck slightly in order to find the source of the voice, whether a presence or some visible speaker grille. He found nothing, but noticed that the handles on the tools, the vessels on the tables, were distorted, as if melted. He was hallucinating, then. Maybe he'd eaten something toxic.

The plant moved with unbelievable rapidity, as an octopus had moved across the ocean floor in a nature documentary he'd seen recently, and now leaned over him. "I will help you into a sitting position," it – the voice inside his head – said.

The leaves were cool and firm against his skin. One curled its tip around his shoulder and pulled, while another supported his back, and yet another pressed against his forehead as if to prevent his skull from flopping forward, which seemed unnecessary until he was actually upright and felt the heaviness. He noticed among the fleshy leaves numerous strands of wire or cable of varying thickness, some lit with flickering arrays, some ribbed, some featureless. Whatever they were, these additional appendages were not organic.

Now Tom *was* unsettled. But something was obviously working in his system to suppress the panic.

"Please maintain a state of calm. I will ask you questions. There are no right or wrong answers. I will help you make a safe transition into your next phase. You are feeling some anxiety. For your safety we treated your systems to decrease your level of anxiety. These treatments did not affect your cognitive abilities in any way."

Tom was now very clear about one thing – the voice was coming from inside this gigantic plant. "I will begin. What is the last thing you remember before you..." There was a pause, and a little bit of that scraping noise bled through. "Before you entered your sleep phase."

Tom used to exercise to help him sleep. Sometimes he tried heated milk, medications. But not the last time. The last time he'd been lying on a bed before surgery. "I was hooked up to an IV. They were going to do something with my inner ear. The right, no, the left side. I had been losing my balance for a very long time. That last month it had gotten much, much worse – just sitting up made me ill. The surgery was supposed to be... um." He swallowed. His mouth was like a cloth pocket containing a dried-out, forgotten tongue. The plant inserted a long straw into his mouth. He searched apprehensively for the other end of the straw, but could not find it. His mouth filled with cool liquid. "The surgery was supposed to be a simple procedure. Later, I woke up, but I didn't really wake up. Everything was so hazy, and the room seemed to be full of people – at least I could hear their... distorted echoes – but I couldn't see anyone." He could feel that distant fear approaching. It would arrive very soon now.

"We have repaired... your condition," it said. "I will answer those questions I have answers for. But please answer these first."

Tom took a deep breath and looked around. The room appeared sterile, and there were recognizable tubes, containers, liquids, instruments – with handles and other attachments distorted and unlike anything he'd ever seen before. But they made a kind of sense, given the nature of the creature before him, who gave an impression of floating on a mop of fine roots. He understood now that this plant-thing was in constant, subtle movement – its leaves, stems – gently flowing, changing shape in a way that emphasized this impression of floating. He also saw that a thin layer of greenish liquid coated the floor, streaked and shiny like some sort of lubricant.

There were objects on tables around the room. Tom thought he recognized the shell of an old toaster, some random auto parts, maybe a radio, what might have been a fragment of toilet bowl – all so stained and rusty, so worn that they might have been dredged out of the ocean mud.

"You were *suspended*."

"What? What do you mean?"

"You were placed in a state... cannot translate... cannot translate. You were placed in a condition of suspended animation. The technology was primitive then, but there have been... cannot translate. There have been survivors. Cannot translate. Did they make promises to you concerning the eventual outcome?"

"What? No... I told you. It was just supposed to be a simple procedure. No one said anything about suspended animation or anything like that. I didn't agree to anything but my ear operation!"

There was a very long pause. Tom felt increasingly uncomfortable, but periodic waves of cold moving through his body calmed him. Finally the plant spoke again. "Many of the records from this facility... cannot translate. Incomplete. Your record is incomplete. But they indicate that a mishap occurred. An anomalous event. An error was made during surgery. You could not be revived. Subsequently an agreement was reached."

"An agreement with whom? I told you I didn't agree to anything."

Another long, uncomfortable silence. "The agreement was signed by a Richard Johnston."

"My dad. He was my next of kin."

"He was told, according to the fragment remaining, that your life might not end. Your body would be suspended, until your condition could be rectified."

"He always believed in that sort of thing. They probably offered him all kinds of money, but he asked for this instead. He couldn't fix me, so he had them send me into the future. That's the way he thought about things."

"Are you stating that you would not have chosen this for yourself?"

"No, never. I am, was, a fatalist. There were so many diseases then. If it hadn't been a botched surgery, it would have probably been some terrible plague. Dying in your sleep would be so much better. Those last forty years, epidemics killed so many. And maybe that was actually a blessing."

"A blessing?"

"I know that sounds harsh, but sometimes you have to step back, view history with a bit of perspective. That's what I used to do – I taught high school history. There were too many people, and with the droughts, the infestations, many crops were lost. People came up from Latin America looking for food – Mexico was just a rest stop. Refugees were pouring out of Asia into Europe, away from flooded coastal cities everywhere. No way could all those people be fed. The fields were empty, and then the fields were filled with bodies. They deserved better. My father would have agreed with that much. People deserve better."

"Your father thought you deserved better. So he sent you forward –"

"To where?" Anxiety was beginning to fill him. "To when? *When* is this?"

"Cannot translate. Cannot translate," the plant's heavy leaves rose and fell, rhythmic and graceful as some deep jungle ballerina. "To here. To now."

IT WAS EASIER just to imagine yourself a new person than to attempt to adjust, carrying around the old self's vague memories, as if you'd read them in a book. "Therapy has been performed," according to the implanted translator, but details were untranslatable, answered instead by a series of random sounds. It bothered him, certainly, to have been tampered with, and to wake up owing someone for his revival. But it was all the life he had.

Loss and displacement aside, the most difficult thing that first year was coping with the apparent limits of the translator. Although the quality improved, there were always gaps where a lengthy period of attempted communication resulted in a disappointingly blunt "cannot translate," or worse, absolute silence.

Despite his plant-like appearance, it soon became apparent that the alien was not botanical in nature, nor bird, reptile, fish, or mammal or anything else he could compare it to on Earth. Obviously there was a cybernetic component, whether attached or integrated Tom couldn't say.

Of more practical concern was that Tom had nothing to call him – and he didn't want to use some disrespectful coinage or 'pet' name. Nor could he determine where the alien was from, or even the name of the van-like contraption they used to travel around together on the surface of a transformed Earth.

Tom understood that he was still in St. Louis, Missouri, but nothing was recognizable. Quakes and floods had distorted the town's profile, and the fact that the suspension facility where he'd been found had been relatively intact was, in the translator's terms, "an unlikely reality." The alien said the area was "architecture in recombination with landscape," a complexly ridged, sculptural field of debris and trash split by a narrow stream that was a vastly diminished and relocated Mississippi River.

The Gateway Arch was gone as well, and the companion had acquired a video so that Tom could watch in awe as the keystone failed and dropped out, the disconnected legs twisting away and falling in opposite directions, the translator narrating the analysis in an annoyingly detached, analytical monotone.

But at least Tom was finally allowed to drive the van. He stood before the segmented dashboard, his hands on the sections as the companion had demonstrated, maneuvering over the broken landscape. Despite having fewer appendages than the controls had been designed for, he was still able to make turns and stops, in most directions, just more slowly. Each day they returned to a predetermined location the companion picked via some untranslatable criteria.

As they came over the final rise from the lab, the clean, geometric lines of the excavation fields were clearly distinguishable from the muddle of destruction. It looked like a typical archaeological dig, he supposed, not having ever been on one during his own lifetime. (He'd have to stop thinking that way – it wasn't as if he'd died.)

Eight or nine aliens travelled their particular areas of the field, trailed by assistants like himself intent on the debris at their feet—picking things up, examining them, recording the scene, stealing glances at the others, but keeping on task. He supposed a lucky alien might unfreeze an actual archaeologist to assist him. Otherwise he had to settle for, say, a high school history teacher.

The natives – the people indigenous to this time, smaller than Tom and the other assistants who'd been suspended – looked like children playing in the fields of debris. They climbed up and down the rubble, scrambling frantically over each other in their search for objects for survival or trade. At first he thought they were scavenging for food, but after having sifted through tons of debris himself he discovered there was almost nothing organic left in the ruins of the city.

A swollen version of the alien vans sped rapidly into the center of the dig. The natives surrounded it in an eye blink. A panel slid aside disgorging dozens of green and brown packages. A swarm of natives hauled the parcels away like hungry insects. The aliens were feeding them.

From the patch directly in front of him, he picked up a small metallic jar and was looking at it when broad hands attached to skinny arms snatched it away. He had an impulse to chase after the native, who was now scrambling up a ridge, but thought better of it.

Angrily, he looked over at his companion for some help. A group of natives circled the alien as if he were some giant corn plant (extinct since Tom's own era) and they worshippers anticipating his moves, interpreting what he considered worthy of his attentions.

No alien ever made a move to stop the natives, or even alter their path. Other than supplying food, the aliens ignored them. And Tom had to concede the natives deserved every liberty they could take. Manners had become a luxury.

He went back to work, picked up a piece of hammer, a bowl, a cupboard door, a jar rattling with something mummified inside. He catalogued, reported, added some objects to the stack they would take back to the lab. He still didn't really know what they were looking for – the companion's criteria had been untranslatable, so everything seemed of potential interest. Back at the lab he would study the recordings, flagging anything different from what they had seen before.

He found a telescoping handle with a bowl-like end closed with some sort of shutter. A visual record sent to the van came back as audio from his implant: "a device used for the capture and inspection of rat corpses.

Decontaminated and safe to collect." It was dated from after his time. The function of most unfamiliar objects he found was easier to guess – these were things made by human beings for human use, after all. People used tools, ate, bathed, and relieved themselves with generally recognizable equipment.

When he found an old plastic pull-toy, he began to speak of toys his father had made for him. Every day he made more of these sometimes stressful but highly addictive recorded narratives.

A rhythmic crunching noise surprised him. One of his fellow assistants was jogging across the debris field toward him. "The name's Franklin!" the man shouted. "So, how long were you under?"

Tom's companion swivelled toward the noise, but made no attempt to discourage this meeting. Franklin looked like an old man – like Tom did, he knew, suspension being less the fountain of youth than had probably been promised. Franklin was all skin and bone, but he moved with easy, un-self-conscious energy.

"Do you know *when* this is?" Tom asked eagerly.

Franklin laughed. "Sorry. No, I don't think any of us do. 'Cannot translate,' which is what they say if there's something they don't want you to know."

"I don't think my companion would lie – I don't think he even *can*."

"But he can leave out the details, or say nothing at all. Surely he's like all the other flowers in this petunia patch, and you get these long, silent, brooding spells?"

"Well, yes. But there's no way for us to know what that silence actually means, or how it functions for them. They're not plants, by the way."

Franklin made a dismissive gesture with his hands. Or Tom thought it was dismissive – it had been a very long time since he'd actually witnessed a non-verbal human gesture. "Oh, I know. But you have to call them *something*, and they certainly look like plants. They look, well, they're identical, aren't they?"

Tom looked around and saw that his companion was now standing with Franklin's. They were as motionless as... as houseplants. Perhaps they were watching, but Tom sensed it was more complicated than that. "Mine is bluer around the base above the filaments, and slightly less symmetrical. He feels – I don't know – older than some of the others. They're not identical at all – you just have to study them to recognize the differences."

"I gather you call yours 'the companion.'"

"That's the way I *think* about him – it's better than 'the alien.' But I don't call him anything, at least when I speak to him. I just pretend I'm speaking to myself out loud."

"I call mine *Audrey*. It makes the conversation go more easily, to have an actual name."

"Audrey?"

"*The Little Shop of Horrors?* 'Feed me!'? That giant man-eating plant? Did you ever see it? There was a revival, very popular when I died, if you'll excuse the expression."

"That must have been after my time. When I – died – the refugees were just crossing into Arizona, Texas."

"They'd made it to St. Louis by the time I passed. By that time it made no difference – if they were from California, Arizona, Mexico or Latin American – they were all refugees. Starving, desperate, disease-ridden human beings. What were the rest of us supposed to do?"

Tom had no answer, and did not want to know what Franklin might have participated in. They both stood quietly looking around at the natives, as if anything but silence would be somehow disrespectful, and it occurred to Tom that this might offer another explanation for the aliens' long non-responsive silences. An alien drifted slowly by, several natives trailing excitedly. Franklin gazed after them, looking troubled.

"Have you tried to talk with one of them?" Tom asked. "A native?"

"Only at first. How much do you know about them?"

"Very little – they hardly ever speak, and when they do I can't understand them. But they're what's left of us."

"No, *we're* what's left of us – the ones from another time, the ones that were suspended. That's who we are, the survivors from that time. These people, they're from *this* time, and this, my friend, is a whole other world. You know they hate us, don't you? At least the ones who understand enough."

"No, I don't," Tom said firmly. "Why would they hate us?"

"Because we got to miss the worst of it. They don't look like much, but they're not dumb – it takes some smarts to survive this long in this environment. And we got to skip what they went through, and what their fathers and mothers went through, and who knows how many generations back, and now we're helping their invaders."

"They're hardly invaders, Franklin."

Franklin looked at Tom for a moment as if he felt sorry for him. "Then tell me, Tom. Who's in charge here?"

* * *

DURING THE NEXT few months Tom became obsessed with the complexities of reconstituting a vanished world from its pieces – his world, and that world which had evolved into being while he slept. A thick but feather weight oval so transparent it might be invisible proved to be a lamp. Nearby he found a piece of rainbow – he held the iridescent fragment against the sun and it began to vibrate with colors that filled the air. Alarmed, he dropped it, and heard a nearby laugh. When his eyes readjusted he saw Franklin a few yards away, scraping busily at the ground but sparing a glimpse Tom's way.

"Happened to me, too. It's a piece of something they were developing for energy storage. A lot of innovation was going on during my time, desperate attempts to save us all. I doubt that thing, or that lamp you found earlier, were ever finished. Least I never saw them. We were so *clever*, you know? Hard to understand how we failed so catastrophically."

Perhaps it was this, or Tom's growing fatigue over the futility of attempting to reclaim a lost world while not really living in *this* one, that made the day feel endless. Tom looked at his companion with growing suspicion. The creature's silences, his awful impenetrability. His invasion of Tom's life. The alien *was* in charge of him – he set the pace and the daily priorities.

And yet Tom would have no purpose at all if they had not brought him back from the darkness. They might be occupiers, but they kept him occupied.

At the end of that long day Franklin came to Tom and dropped a battered coin into his hand. It was inscribed *The Day of the Triffids*. "Just scan it with the lab recorder," he said. "It'll start playing on the monitor. It's a classic – and you may find it amusing."

As Tom watched the movie back at the lab he decided it was clumsy, but when an actor told an actress, "Keep behind me. There's no sense in getting killed by a plant," he laughed out loud.

"This amuses you," the companion said, behind him. Tom jumped up, alarmed.

"Some of the lines, yes, they made me laugh." Then, "but it's just a silly movie," he said unnecessarily.

"Cannot translate." Then a bit later, "You are uncomfortable."

"Yes. Just a bit. I didn't know you were there."

"You may always ask questions if you are uncomfortable."

"Yes, I know." Tom hesitated. "I wanted to ask you if you had considered that – that we might not welcome your help here?"

Again the awkward silence. And a few "Cannot translate" statements followed by a series of untranslatable sounds before the companion began to speak. "I – apologize. You have been – influenced – so you will not harm us. There has been – debate."

"You mean whatever you've done to us wouldn't let us try."

"Cannot translate. It would not. Cannot translate."

It made Tom uncomfortable that he'd never known where to look when he spoke to the companion. He didn't know where the eyes – or whatever the alien used for visual input – were located. He'd looked in numerous places for them. Today he simply looked away. "It is our world."

"You look out at the world, the sky, and you think that you see yourselves," the companion replied.

"You do not. Cannot translate. You witness our silences, our – soft – pauses between the efforts to communicate with you, and you think that they are about you. Cannot translate. They are not."

THERE WAS SOMETHING different about the companion. He moved more slowly across the ragged ridge, pausing now and then with his filaments trembling. Sometimes he stood for half an hour or more, fully exposed to the hot afternoon sun. The group of natives who normally followed the companion avoided him.

Tom discovered the door lying flat on the hillside under a thin layer of broken concrete. The companion paused but passed quickly. It was just a door, and they had examined many doors. Tom pried it up and verified that it was attached to nothing, like opening a door in the ground to more ground.

He lingered over it, brushing at it, touching it with his palms. The paint was worn, but still apparent. Blue. It was a sky-blue door. After a lengthy brushing, the scratches on its surface became legible:

The Collier family lived here 200 years. It sheltered & nourished us. God bless our home.

TOM LOADED THE door into their van to take back to the lab. He'd started back to the fields when Franklin ran up to him.

"Audrey died!"

"I –" He didn't know what to say. "I imagined they had a very long lifespan. Was there an accident?"

"No. I'd noticed some color changes, some fading, and the tips of the appendages? I'd been seeing some transparency there the past few months. Then one evening last week Audrey was silent and still for a very long time, and the next morning I found him in that same position, as if he'd just been switched off."

Tom saw some aliens off in the distance, their filaments floating gently back and forth, pushed by the breeze, natives running between them like children playing among trees. "I'm sorry, Franklin. What did you do?"

"I couldn't even get out of the lab – all the security was keyed to Audrey. But the next morning a group of them arrived with Audrey's replacement. You know, I've been noticing the differences since I first met you. Audrey's coloring was a little different, a little more orange. This new one acts differently, moves differently, I don't know, I'm thinking I may not like this one as much."

"Maybe they're more complex than you thought."

Franklin nodded, a bit wide-eyed, but Tom wasn't convinced he was actually listening. "Hey, have you seen the hands?"

"The hands?"

"Well, obviously you haven't. The natives built them, fairly recently, I think."

Tom followed Franklin down the slope and through labyrinthine mounds of debris until they reached a small clearing on the edge of the dig. A few natives working on something scattered as the two men approached.

He couldn't quite tell what he was looking at until he shifted angles. In the middle of the clearing it appeared the natives had built several tall, narrow mounds of refuse. But as he moved sideways the constructions became clear: eight or nine giant hands rising out of these fields of destruction.

Tom and Franklin approached as closely as they dared. It was obvious that whatever held these sculptures together was nothing more than a complex interlocking and placement of parts. They were meant to be temporary, and might dissolve at any moment into the rubble field they'd come from.

"Look at the way the palms are curved," Tom said. "There's no tension in them – no matter how tightly they were put together, those palms are relaxed, ready to accept whatever might fall into them. These aren't the desperate hands of someone needing rescue, or begging. They're just hands that have been raised, hands that are showing themselves."

"Do they make you feel guilty?" Franklin asked nervously. "These hands make me feel guilty. Not so much for surviving – these people survived. But for missing the worst of it. I don't know what to do about that."

Tom nodded. "I think you just do your work, continue to piece things back together. Sometimes the best thing is just doing the only thing that's left."

Franklin was silent for quite some time, then said, "They told me Audrey had lived a very long time. They said that most of the ones who come here to explore what's been left of us were at the very end of those long lives. They won't be seeing their homes again, Tom. They're spending their final days with us."

THE COMPANION HAD not taken him out to the St. Louis fields in several weeks. Tom was glad to be able to catch up on his research, his endless cataloging, but he was worried.

The companion had been standing beside him for days, as if unable to leave his side. Had he moved at all? When he could detect even the slightest of movements he would return to his labor, satisfied. There was increased transparency in the leaves, the filaments, even the mechanical threads, even in that chandelier-looking device whose function Tom had never determined. The companion had remained silent. Even a "cannot translate" would have been welcomed.

The transparent tips of the leaves were frayed, and their ragged failure seemed like movement, but Tom doubted it really was. They looked like jewelry in the hazy bright light of the lab.

Tom propped the blue door up against the lab wall to get a good view of it. The companion would be able to see it also, if the companion was seeing anything now. Then Tom began to speak, adding to the hundreds of hours of testimony he'd already made.

"My father believed every human being deserved two things – meaningful work and a home to live in or come back to when the world felt unsafe. My mother tended to agree but her practical nature told her that not everyone got what they deserved, and when survival was at stake self-fulfillment was a luxury.

"The fact that they never managed to own their own home caused my father great shame. He was a smart man but not formally educated. He read in libraries and watched educational shows and devoured the newspaper.

"He worked a lot of jobs and some were more interesting than others but he never found one that brought him joy. Mother always said his standards were too high and there wasn't a job invented that would make him happy.

"But he was determined that one day we would have a house of our own and toward that end he found what he thought was the perfect front door. On a demolition job he discovered this thick door with carved panels and an elaborate brass doorknob. He took it home to our little rented duplex, leaned it against the wall and announced to the family that we were going to have a great house someday and that this would be the front door.

"The next morning he replaced the door to the duplex with this new one. It didn't quite fit and he had to trim it and make some adjustments to the frame. He had an extra key made and gave it to the owner because, of course, it was actually *his* house. The owner wasn't very happy but my dad could be pretty charming.

"From then on, wherever we moved my father carried that door. Sometimes he had to cut it to fit a smaller opening and sometimes he had to add lumber to one end to widen it or make it taller. After a few years with all those alterations it didn't look so elegant, but it was still strong, and it was *our* door. I'm sure we were evicted more than once because of it, but he was stubborn. I think the uglier it became, the more he liked it.

"Dad used to tell me stories about early civilizations, about the night watch, and how people would lock themselves in at night behind a good door to protect themselves from wild animals and thieves. I think those stories are one reason I became a history teacher. He said the world wasn't like that anymore, that you didn't have to be so afraid. But by the time I was an adult it was obvious those times of the nightly lock in had come again.

"My father desperately wanted to make his mark but didn't know how. He said we should leave behind more than a few scattered bones in a field, that we all deserved better. He thought you should feel that your limited time here mattered. That you had opened doors.

"For me the worst thing about those last few years of my old life was that mattering didn't seem possible anymore. It appeared to be too late to make a difference. Has that changed? Can you tell me that?"

For a long time Tom waited there by that beautiful, unknowable alien thing. The answer finally came, faintly, as if across some vast distance.

Cannot translate.

HOW WE CAME BACK FROM MARS (A STORY THAT CANNOT BE TOLD)

IAN WATSON

Ian Watson has more than 40 published books to his credit, the most recent being The Beloved of My Beloved, *transgressively funny stories in collaboration with Italian surrealist Roberto Quaglia, one tale from which won the BSFA Award for short fiction in 2010, and the erotic satire* Orgasmachine, *finally published in English after almost 40 years; both from NewCon Press. His* Whores of Babylon *was a Clarke Award finalist ages ago; its recent reissue led to Russian, Latvian, and Spanish editions. Ian is perhaps best known for writing the screen story for Steven Spielberg's* A.I. Artificial Intelligence, *based on almost a year's work with Stanley Kubrick.*

OUR ASCENT ENGINE had failed, marooning the five of us on Mars. In ten years' time the Chinese might land on the red planet near our Birdie and diagnose what went wrong.

Neither our own efforts nor suggestions from Earth made any difference. We were stuck. Enough air, food and water with us for ten more days, our safety margin in case something unexpected such as a dust storm delayed our departure. Up in orbit were the bulk of the consumables we'd need for the long journey home.

At no point did we panic. Us Mars astronauts were chosen for our equanimity. Three married men and two married women confined in close proximity for a total mission profile of almost two years needed to have mild personalities. In actuality, for assorted reasons, all five of us were planning to leave our spouses some time after we returned to Earth, but for public relations reasons it was important that us five spacefarers should all be seen as contentedly wedded to spouses back home. A requirement for the mission. Likewise, that we had no children yet, which had narrowed the field of hopefuls. We'd all gone through·the ritual of storing sperm or ova.

We could have spun out the food and water, but not the air. So our final day came. We sent our last messages to supposedly loved ones, then the 'heroic statement' for public release. This was *not* scripted by NASA – we really worked on that, together.

Then static disrupted our radio contact. Consequently we couldn't report that a craft, several times the size of our own lander, floated down beside us. I refuse to use the term 'flying saucer' even though that's appropriate for a fat grey disc without any visible windows or nozzle exits.

Distorted and unnatural sounding, an English-speaking voice broke through the static. I couldn't say if we were hearing the synthesized speech of a machine intelligence, a program translating the language of some alien, or a human voice disguised electronically.

We were invited on board. We'd be returned to Earth alive. This was being done to honour our bravery. A hatch opened from the lower part of the disc, becoming a ribbed ramp. We should board right now, or else our window of opportunity would close. So we had no time to record any message for delayed transmission when the disruption cleared.

In our Mars suits we transferred, our cameras and datapads zipped in the pockets.

The suits bore a close resemblance to those in Kubrick's *2001* because that was such a good design. A NASA specialist had advised on those.

After mounting the ramp, we found ourselves in an oval chamber, softly lit and windowless, which swiftly pressurised. We took off our helmets and breathed clean warm air.

Five padded couches were around the walls. Evidently belts or harnesses were unnecessary. A toilet opened up, then a shower cubicle, and finally a cupboard containing plastic bottles of water and sandwiches wrapped in clingfilm. *Sandwiches!*

I opened one and devoured most of it: cheese and ham in a Kaiser roll with some sauerkraut and German-tasting mustard. A bit of the roll I kept, to wrap in the clingfilm and put in a pocket for, well, later analysis by NASA. Where on Earth did ET go shopping for sandwiches?

"We have left Mars," the voice told us very soon, though we'd felt nothing unusual. "We shall land on Earth in three hours."

Not even weeks, but *hours*! How this mocked our seven-month journey to the Red Planet. The technology involved couldn't be human.

"Who are you?" Juno asked.

"*What* are you?" asked Chuck.

"That is not for you to know," was the answer. And it *never* was for us to know; it never was.

We gladly used the facilities. No sense of motion accompanied our journey, yet after a while I began to feel heavier. So did we all. Our weight was increasing from Martian towards terrestrial, to adapt us somewhat. From time to time we tried to engage our invisible rescuer in conversation.

That is not for you to know.

Finally the voice said, "Put on your helmets again to contain any contamination."

I'd almost forgotten about the ten days of mandatory isolation scheduled for us after our return to Earth. We rose, feeling heavy. Obediently we refitted our helmets. Why did the voice remind us about the quarantine aspect? Ah, this implied we'd be landing somewhere close to a NASA facility; and also ensured that we'd look fully like proper astronauts, newly returned...

Presently the ramp opened in the wall and sunlight flooded in brightly. For a few dazzled moments the scenery looked like Mars, except that hereabouts sparse vegetation was growing in the dirty-looking desert. And the sun was bigger. Were we in Arizona? Nevada? New Mexico? Texas?

"You will leave now."

"Thank you so much for saving us," said Juno. "God bless you." The rest of us chorused our gratitude.

Rutted hills of dirt. The height of the sun suggested early to mid morning – unless the time was mid to late afternoon, but an instinct said morning. We all had about two hours of EVA air left in our suits.

I completely understood that a 'flying saucer' mightn't wish to land in full view at Houston or Vandenberg. So: choose a deserted area nearby. From which presumably we could now walk to a nearby highway where someone must drive by soon enough even if no one was paying attention to our suit radio frequency. I presumed the flying saucer had used some sort of stealth.

How would most people react to our heroic last words on Mars being followed a few hours later by us 'miraculously' turning up in New Mexico or Arizona? "We were brought back by a flying saucer." "Oh *really*?" I was very conscious of this.

We climbed a shallow rise. Some way downhill in the distance were wooden buildings exactly like those of a town in the old Wild West.

Over the suit radio I said, "So we've been brought home alive – but *to the past*? We've been saved, yet everybody in our own time will still believe we died on Mars?"

"The past?" echoed Juno, doubtfully.

"If that's so," said Jim, "maybe we ought to bury our cameras and datapads deep, so we don't disturb history. Heck, our suits too."

"Using what to dig?" asked Chuck. "Our helmets?"

"Then we walk into town out of the blue in our underwear?" queried Juno. "*Hey guys, Indians robbed us. Buddy, can you spare us some blankets?* We can't start a new life that way. I'm not dancing in a saloon. Black Beauty, the Belle of Bonanza, Nevada. What'll you do for a living, Jim? Shovel horseshit?" The situation was making Juno a bit outspoken, but I saw her point. And to prevent what kind of contamination were we still wearing our helmets, when obviously we would need to take them off fairly soon?

Evidently we'd been spotted, because a cowboy on horseback was heading our way, galloping up the slope.

Boots, white trousers, baggy white shirt, leather vest unbuttoned, red neckerchief. Hanging from his belt, a six-gun in a holster. A pocked moon of a face, long greasy-looking black hair. He reined in, gaping at us. Then he addressed us in throaty Spanish, which I understood -ish. Immediately I snapped back from the Wild West to the present day, and opened my visor. Quarantine could go hang. Hot air wafted in.

I told the others: "He just asked *Who we with?* He doesn't know of a *Sci-Fi commercial* shooting. Do you speak English?" I asked the presumed Mexican.

"I speak, Señor. Classes. Yeah."

"To become a citizen?"

He looked blank, then said, "I am Pablo."

"Where are we, Pablo?"

"Lost in desierto? Hey, you seem how those guys on Mars! Great costume!"

"We *are* those guys," said Jim. "We've been brought back."

"Where are we *exactly*?" I asked again.

"Here is Texas Hollywood."

"Hollywood isn't in Texas," protested Juno.

"Texas Hollywood *Spain*," said Pablo to our black co-astronaut. "Is near Almería."

That rang a bell. "Where they made the spaghetti westerns?"

"Many commercials now. Here and Mini Hollywood and Fort Bravo. Amigos, you need drink. You tell," with a boisterous laugh, "why you look Mars!"

This was all bad news. The spacecraft had put us down right by a movie set. *Capricorn One*, anyone? This could not be a coincidence.

In that movie, instead of blasting off for Mars three astronauts are suddenly whisked away to a desert base where their journey and their explorations will be simulated. That's because at the last moment the life-support system on their ship is found to be faulty. For reasons of national prestige, the mission must still be seen to go ahead. Two years later, the returning empty re-entry module – supposedly with the astronauts on board – burns up in Earth's atmosphere, posing a big problem. What's to be done with the astronauts who are actually alive in that desert base?

We weren't in America, where our return could perhaps be hushed up – along with new identities for us similar to the witness protection program, so that we could disappear to avoid major national embarrassment. *But also where we couldn't be snuffed out and buried in unmarked graves.* Had our alien rescuer been aware of that aspect? Did his 'people' watch Sci-Fi movies? Maybe, if they bought German deli-style sandwiches.

As Pablo led us down the gritty slope, I said quietly, "Guys, we'd better be careful what we tell people."

WE ENTERED THE Wild West town by way of its picket-fenced cemetery, low wooden crosses askew. Nearby on a raised platform stood a gallows, a stool waiting underneath a dangling noose. Several Hispanic cowboys who were feeding horses stared as Pablo led us along the sandy main street. We passed a bank built of adobe, then the red brick and barred windows of a

Sheriff's Office. Opposite, a clapboard-sided barber's and an undertaker's, so said the weathered signs.

Just then the undertaker's door opened and out stepped a tubby man sporting a Stetson and sunglasses, camera slung round his neck, accompanied by a tubby woman in a long pink-striped dress and baseball cap. The man promptly began taking photos of us while the woman called back inside, "May, will you come and see this!" A moment later May appeared, cameraphone in hand, visibly the woman's sister.

The undertaker's must be a mini-hotel where tourists could stay Western-style, authentically as it were. Other buildings along the street might be likewise.

Led by Pablo, we tramped through batwing doors into a big saloon in our Kubricky spacesuits. What looked like an unkempt outlaw in a long duster coat lounged against the bar, cradling a rifle, his blond hair long and tangled. Beside a stage a quartet of young women dressed as cancan dancers were chatting and giggling. The outlaw glared at us menacingly, acting in character I supposed. The cancan girls advanced on us, as though they were the local talent bent on relieving Jim, Chuck and me of our hard-earned silver dollars. Stairs led up to a balcony running around three sides of the saloon. Could it be, when the saloon got into full swing, that a cancan girl might take a guest up to a private room? No: two kids kitted out as junior cowboys came romping downstairs, firing blanks at each other, before gawping at us. Family entertainment here.

We took off our helmets and placed those in a row on the bar as if we were bikers, almost.

"You want drinks?" asked the thin-faced barman in English, an unlit cheroot in his mouth, silver armbands on his shirt sleeves like a croupier.

"I'm sorry," said Juno, "but we don't have any money."

Pablo laughed. "They not take dollars to Mars. Drinks for them obsequio de la casa. On the house."

"We'd better have Coca Colas," Juno said.

"Me, I'm for a beer," Chuck said.

"Count me in," agreed Jim.

"But it's only morning," I pointed out, as mission commander. "And it'll be your first alcohol in over a year. Surely it's wiser to stick to Coke or juice."

"We just escaped *death*," said Chuck. "Champagne might be the order of the day."

"I got good cold champán," said the barman.

Compared with the likely effects of champagne, beer seemed safer if Chuck and Jim insisted, so I pointed at the beer tap. "Two of those. Coke for me."

"Yeah," said Juno.

"Me too," from Barbara.

"Hey mister, hey mister," clamoured one of the kids, unmistakably American, "are you actors in a space movie?"

"No, we are *not* actors," Barbara said.

"You look actors," piped up a cancan girl.

At that point up bustled a plump, tanned, beaming middle-aged woman in jeans and a billowy yellow blouse.

"Boys, go and play in the street," she instructed. "Chicas," to the cancan dancers, "help with the drinks, las bebidas okay? Pablo ¿qué pasa?"

Pablo spoke rather quickly in Spanish, the woman nodding and saying *Si* from time to time.

"I have to sit down." Juno headed for a big round empty table, us four others following gladly.

Joining us at the table, the woman told us in a British accent, "I'm the wardrobe mistress of Texas Hollywood. My name's Rachel. Where *did* you get those spacesuits? They're so authentic looking. Is there a commercial I don't know about?"

"It's pretty hot in these," complained Juno.

"They from planet Mars," Pablo told her. "Hace muy frio... makes very cold on Mars."

A couple of the cancan girls brought our drinks, then Rachel shooed them away.

"Look now," Rachel said in a motherly way, "if you'll just step over the street I can fit you all out in something much more comfortable. Your spacesuits will be perfectly safe over there. May as well take your helmets with you too."

Chuck drained his chilled beer in one go. "I guess we oughta borrow someone's mobile... You know, phone the US embassy. That'll be in Lisbon, I guess. No, Madrid."

"Why would you want to do that?" asked Rachel. "Phone your director, your producer."

"We don't have those," said Chuck. Was his voice slurring already? "We have Mission Control."

"They say they brought back from Mars, not say how."

"Oh God, it's so awful," said Rachel quickly. "I watched on TV. I'm so sorry for your countrymen, those brave astronauts."

"We *are* those astronauts," said Chuck. "This is real. A flying saucer –"

"No," I hissed.

"– a flying saucer brought us back in – *three hours*, can you believe it?"

"I think he has heatstroke," I said. "In these suits. Or maybe it's the beer."

Rachel rose. "Come on, all of you. Over the street." She herded us.

WITHIN TWENTY MINUTES we were arrayed for the Wild West, the gals in ankle-length sleeveless striped dresses, me as a corporal in the US Cavalry in blue uniform, yellow neckerchief and chevrons. Chuck was a Marshall with pointy silver badge, Jim an ordinary cowpoke. Necessarily we'd abandoned our thermal long-johns cum long-sleeved vest combos, so we lacked underwear, which the wardrobe room didn't stock. On impulse I transferred the clingfilm with its bit of evidence to my new uniform.

Back to the table we went with Rachel, Chuck taking his Mars camera along as though he too had become a tourist. More beers and Cokes appeared.

Juno aired herself, and smiled at Rachel. "Sure feels a lot better."

"So, hombre," our cowboy said to Chuck, "not spaceman now, feel different?"

Chuck drank then yawned. "We still gotta phone."

"Phone American embassy, they believe you? Send black helicopters?"

I shook my head. "They'll be unlikely to believe us at first."

"So we phone Houston," said Chuck. "They know our voices."

"You have the number on you?"

Chuck looked frustrated. "Look, we don't have money, passports, anything of the sort. Just our suits. And cameras, datapads. I can show you us on Mars," he said to Rachel. So that was why he'd brought the camera. "Look, look," presenting images on the camera's screen, of us in a stony reddish desert, the big landing module standing there, a metal cabin on legs that looked like a model.

Without our noticing, more tourists had arrived in the saloon, mostly distinguishable from authentic pretend cowboys by cameras and pallid or lobster-red faces. One silvery-bearded crewcut fellow, who'd been here already, was shifting his chair ever closer to our table.

"Excuse me for butting in," he said. "You seen that conspiracy movie about how the Apollo 11 Moon landing was simulated? The White House was worried there mightn't be live TV from Apollo 11 on account of technical problems, so to be on the safe side they got Stanley Kubrick to simulate the video secretly on the set of *2001*. Flew over to England with moon suits and a spare lunar exploration module that Armstrong and Aldrin had practised with. Allegedly.

"There's footage of Kissinger and other White House big-wigs authorising the plan – *except* if you pay close attention they're merely talking about *a* plan, unspecified. It's the voiceover that says this is about Apollo 11. And there's an interview with Kubrick's widow Christiane, and her brother, what's his name, Harlan, Jan Harlan, that's it, talking about how impressed Kissinger was – Christiane mentions Kissinger by name, but again it's the voiceover that says this is about Kubrick shooting a simulated Apollo-on-the Moon in England. England, of course, because Kubrick lived near London and wouldn't fly. Clever bit of editing, that film! I'm a connoisseur of conspiracy theories. And *do* I seem to be in on the ground floor here and now!"

"But *look*." Chuck displayed more images for him. "These are *real* photos."

"They're real electronic photos, there's no denying. Kubrick's genius was in making *2001* look real with the technology of the late Sixties. Boy, have we moved on from there!"

Chuck put the camera on the table and slumped.

Our busybody went on: "I couldn't help overhearing you saying about having no documents or money, only those spacesuits and, before you went off to get changed, I'm sure I heard *flying saucer*. That's a beautiful touch, if I'm reading this correctly. So who's your director?"

"There ain't no director," I told him.

"You mean it's an amateur production, like *Indiana Jones* reshot in a garage? Just you five guys on your own?"

"Mister, it's *real*. What kind of movie has no cameraman?"

The bearded fellow winked. "Who needs a cameraman? Soon as you came into town, folks would be uploading vids of those spacesuits to YouTube. Those vids will go viral, so you don't even *need* to make a movie yourselves – very astute. Tell you what – I'm Mike Appleton, by the way – those suits looked worth three grand apiece."

"More like a hundred K each," Juno said hotly. NASA hadn't stinted on our Mars environment gear.

Appleton stroked his chin. "That sounds a bit greedy, but I'd go to twenty-five K for the complete set. Me being, as I say, keen on conspiracy theory movies and associated paraphernalia, and you do keep insisting you need money. Unless," and he darted a wary glance at Rachel, "there's a higher offer on the table."

Rachel was indignant. "Five supposed astronauts walk into a bar and tell a tall tale to a naïve wardrobe mistress. Then a total stranger, who happens to be conveniently present, pipes up, 'Wow, what great Sci-fi Costumes! I'll pay you tens of thousands of Euros.' I wasn't born yesterday!"

"That was dollars," corrected Mike Appleton.

"So the silly wardrobe mistress promptly says, 'I'll raise you five thousand,' and she empties her bank account. Away walk five happy actors with their accomplice."

"Rachel," I said gently, "we are *not* acquaintances of this gentleman. *Mister Appleton*, you are spoiling our hitherto cordial relationship with this good lady who has been kind enough to help us out."

"And isn't it a bit of a coincidence," persisted Rachel, "your Mr Appleton being so knowledgeable about that hoax film by Kubrick?"

"Alleged hoax," said Appleton. "That's the beauty of it. My offer stands."

Chuck seemed to have gone to sleep, and Jim was looking half-canned. The beer, and the fact that about five hours ago we'd been destined to die on Mars.

"Mister," said Barbara, "if we sell you our suits, at a ridiculous garage sale price, what do we do next? Use our five thousand dollars each – that would have to be cash, by the way, in the circumstances – to fund a new life in Spain with no ID? Fuck!" she cried. "I'm forgetting all about our families, who must be going through hell at this moment believing that we're gonna die!"

"That," I pointed out, "is because our spouses aren't exactly in the forefront of our minds."

Appleton seemed like an accomplice of whatever had returned us to Earth so near to this film-set theme-park where he happened to be staying, his intervention pushing us towards a route and a way of thinking that not long before I'd have regarded as absurd. Appleton was the mechanism by which a major part of our physical proof might be removed from us while we were in a disoriented state of mind!

"Five K each could get us back to America," went on Barbara, "but we can't board any plane without ID. We'd have to smuggle ourselves by boat to Mexico, sneak over the border like illegals, catch a Greyhound and turn up on our own doorsteps at midnight…"

Appleton clapped his hands. "I assume you watched *Capricorn One* a lot."

I could have groaned. Ten years on, if the Chinese land on Mars, since the USA mightn't risk another failure, it would become clear that our bodies had vanished. But meanwhile…

"We have a clear and urgent duty," announced Jim of a sudden, reviving, "not just to our grief-stricken spouses but to NASA and to our government and to the people. Yet here we are, cooling our heels in a bar."

"Hey, did you forget about you and Becky separating?" asked Barbara.

A commotion and gunfire somewhere in the street drew most of the tourists outside. A buckboard clattered by, bearing a coffin, and the bartender called to the few remaining tourists, "Gentlemen and ladies, outlaw will hang soon for murder!"

Chuck was snoring noticeably. Astronaut selection procedures had eliminated noisy snorers, although purring was acceptable, as NASA used to joke. Juno had been quite a purrer. Spanish air and the beer had started Chuck rumbling.

"A duty," said Appleton, "to alert everyone about *UFOs*? After all the previous official denials? Is that what this is all about, then – UFO revelations? That could be seen as bad taste, capitalising upon the deaths on Mars, even if you *do* resemble those brave guys quite closely. In fact, it can't be coincidence that you're spitting images of the Marsonauts. So this must have been cooked up months ago – as if knowing *in advance* that the lander wouldn't be able to take off. That's as good as saying that NASA is a party to this, and – yes! – they set this up ahead of time in case of any tragedy in order to minimise that. Maybe NASA never completely trusted the lander's engines. I guess your spouses will be able to tell the difference, so they need to be sworn to secrecy. Hey, but you guys need to be available for a media tour around the world! So you need to know astronaut talk and be wise about Mars, same as the real crew. Unless the UFO revelation distracts everybody…"

Appleton's brain was working overtime. Me, I was starting to feel unreal, as if I'd merely been hypnotised to imagine I'd been on Mars.

"So they'd set all this up in case of a national tragedy," Appleton continued, "at the cost of endorsing flying saucers and aliens! Wow, that's one giant step for the space agency, you might say. If you must tell a lie, tell it big."

"We never saw any aliens. We only heard a voice."

"In your heads?"

"On our radio."

"We oughta phone," repeated Jim.

"I'm serious about buying the suits. I'll go to thirty-five K – K for Kubrick, hey? – for the set including your cameras. That's cash. Euros'll be more use to you, so let's say forty K Euros. You come along to Almería with me so I can visit a bank. I'll throw in overnight at a decent hotel. My hire car'll hold three of you. Ma'am," he addressed Rachel, "may I hire one of your vehicles and someone to drive it? For the other two guys and the suits."

"I drive," said Pablo, doubtless in expectation of money.

"I really don't know," said Rachel.

"Two hundred Euros for vehicle and driver, how's that? Better than a taxi fare."

"We don't have authority to sell our suits," Juno said, as though selling them was even a plausible proposition. The trouble was, we weren't highly assertive, any of us. That's how we got to Mars in harmony.

"Supposing," said Appleton, "you'd come down in Amazonia or the Gobi Desert, you'd need to improvise to survive. Might have meant bartering your suits to Jivaros or Mongolians... Hey, see how I'm talking as if you really are astronauts! For this prank to work properly, those suits ought to disappear, leaving only the photos and video clips taken here uploaded and viral. The suits will vanish into a private collection."

"You're planning to sell them on!" Rachel accused Appleton. "You could easily ask a million each from rich obsessives. Or Russian billionaires."

"Ma'am, you have the option any time soon to make a bid of your own. Except that you think this is a hustle and that I'm in cahoots with these good gentlemen and ladies."

"You did choose a convenient time to visit Texas Hollywood."

"Look, lady, the supposed flying saucer dumps them here because movies made here *pretend* to be made in America. Part of Spain pretending to be the Wild West. Me, I'm fascinated by movies about pretences, or which are pretences themselves. 9/11 conspiracy stuff, or those allegedly faked Moon landings. So of course this is a place I always wanted to visit – but I might just as easily have come here last week or last month and missed all this. My presence is pure luck! What's going on here with these actor-astronauts is what you might call a meta-pretence because the genius is that *no movie even needs to be made*. The internet will make the movie spontaneously."

Hadn't it occurred to Appleton that Rachel and Pablo might be in cahoots with the five of us? That Rachel *the wardrobe mistress* might have kitted us out in our Kubrick suits, knowing that Mike Appleton was booked for a couple of days, and having cleverly hacked into his finances beforehand? Which would mean that they routinely did likewise with other tourists too, awaiting their chance... and now Rachel had upped the ante considerably with her accusation about Russian billionaire collectors...

"I've been trying," said Juno, "to remember my home phone number. It's in my mobile's memory. But not in my brain."

Nor could I remember mine clearly! Digits danced in my mind's eye like on some slot machine in Vegas, with a very wide window, but no jackpot lined up. This wasn't too amazing. Since when had I needed to recite my own phone number?

"So what's it to be?" said Appleton. "Sell the suits, or is there a Plan B?" He chuckled. "You must have a Plan B from outer space. B for back-up. I mean, some colleague's vehicle had to bring you here all suited up." He still wasn't suspecting Rachel!

"It was a *space* vehicle of unknown design," I insisted.

"Sure, sure, piloted by aliens fond of movie sets. *How* would they know where this place is?"

"By Googling?" I suggested. "Obviously they're familiar with Earth. They laid on German-style deli sandwiches for us."

"Aha!" exclaimed Appleton. "Here's the Nazi version! Hitler's scientists go to Antarctica by submarine and build a base underground, or under the ice, to make flying saucers designed in the Reich. Decades later the base is still operating, the source of every UFO sighting since 1947. Plus there's a big Aryan breeding programme. By now the Swastika flies inside the caverns of Phoebus, which explains how rescue was close at hand for you. Maybe the Nazi ufonauts are in cahoots with rightwing billionaires allied to the Illuminati or whoever, since why should NASA build big chemical rockets if antigravity is available to the US government? Look, you can't have both versions at the same time – aliens *and* Nazis."

"I never said *anything* about Nazis!" I protested.

"You mentioned sandwiches made in Deutschland."

"I'm just telling you what happened."

"Hmm, a Nazi sandwich… Symbolic none the less. Did your aliens buy sandwiches in Germany as disinformation? To throw people off the scent of aliens?

This is more devious than I thought. Are there any other surprise details you'd like to add?"

"Yes! Why aren't you wondering if Rachel and the management of Texas Hollywood set this up, *in league with us* supposing we're actors, in order to con you out of forty K Euros? And whether *that's* why Rachel accused *you* of setting this up to con *her*, so as to inoculate you against suspicion of a money sting!"

How could I have been drawn into such a weird way of thinking?

Appleton shrugged. "I know illegal things happen here all the time. Gypsies, drugs, property swindles. And this country's awash with illegal immigrants. But that's a bit imaginative."

Rachel burst out laughing. "I ought to resent what you just said, Jack," she told me. "But I can see where you're coming from. I still think Mr Appleton plans to sell your suits on at a huge profit."

Appleton looked momentarily disconcerted, but he rallied with the vigour of someone whose favourite ice cream might suddenly be snatched away.

"Great dialogue," he told me. "You really are covering all the bases. So should I say your suits look worth a lot *more*, and then the price goes up; or that most likely they were ordered on the net from a fancy-dress factory in China? By the way, before I finally commit myself I need a closer look at those suits. How's their air-conditioning?"

"We were heating up horribly in them!" insisted Juno. "Those were made for sub-zero Mars, not Spain."

Rachel rose. "Be my guest," she said to Appleton. "Let's go and inspect the goods right now. Pablo," she called, "ven conmigo! Will you come too?" she asked Jim. "They're your suits, so you know the workings."

The three of them were across the road for a while, during which we heard applause, doubtless due to the hangman doing his job and the outlaw pretending to perish in a non-tightening noose. Although mightn't that cause him whiplash? Maybe the outlaw trained his neck muscles. I was wasting my time even thinking about the matter, yet my brain seemed fixed on trivia. I had to snap out of this.

Our suits were *goods*. It was as if Rachel herself was selling them on our behalf. Somehow we had to empower ourselves, but I felt dozy.

I actually nodded off, recovering to hear Appleton say, "... classy enough to fool me if they're fakes..."

"So they'll fool the billionaires too?" Rachel and Appleton now sounded to be in conspiracy.

"Alternatively, NASA sent genuine spares over here just in case, ahead of the take-off from Mars. Or five rejects."

The pair of them, and Jim, resumed their seats.

"I want to go home," said Juno.

"That's unwise, supposing you're telling the truth. Think *Capricorn One*. How can you trust a government, or rogue secret agencies, that just might – I say *might* – have destroyed the Twin Towers, killing three thousand Americans – and some foreigners too – so as to authenticate the threat of Al Qaeda and Osama as the Santa Claus of Evil, and thus validate invading Iraq for oil motives, and then Afghanistan for consistency, huh?" Appleton held up his hand to avoid being interrupted. "Look, the CIA created and armed the Taliban in the first place to take on the Russians during the Cold War. Saddam wasn't a nice guy at all, but he sure kept the lid on Islamic militants, not to mention advancing the cause of women, so why rip the lid off Pandora's box? Who pulls the strings? Some powerful group stands to gain. Unless recent history is sheer stupidity. You five could be innocent patsies in all of this."

What a jolt back to wakefulness, which was nevertheless still dreamy, or pre-dreamy – I felt I'd been about to dream.

"All of *what*?" I protested. "You're making my head ache. This is paranoia."

"I'm merely mentioning possible aspects. I don't necessarily endorse any. Look, I own a company. I won't say what we do, but we have interests in several nations in Africa. You'd be better off in Africa, the five of you. I could fix you up with jobs, identities. You'd be safe. You can let some time roll by."

"That," said Rachel, "seems a much more substantial offer than forty K Euros."

"It's do-able. I've been costing things in my head. And maybe this'll all work better with rumours that the dead astronauts are alive and well somewhere or other in great big Africa. I can hear rumours spreading already. You, Rachel, you'll be able to say: *The weirdest thing happened at work the other day*... And Pancho here – "

"My name is Pablo," said the cowboy.

Appleton grinned. "Almost got it right, didn't I? My mother was a bit psychic. Pablo will gossip too, in Spanish, almost the second language of the USA. At last I shall actually have *assisted* in a conspiracy theory. That'll make me a happy man."

Juno yawned. "I'm so tired. It's so heavy here."

Chuck seemed to have fallen asleep again.

"A phone call," muttered Jim.

"You don't make major decisions when you're worn out. Let's get you all to a hotel in Almería. Sleep on it."

"I suppose," allowed Juno, "that couldn't do any *harm*. We'd be able to watch CNN. See how America is reacting."

"If the pics and vids go viral," opined Appleton, "there'll likely be patriotic outcries to shut any sites hosting the pics unless those pics are all taken down right away, on account of them being in bad taste. That's excellent for conspiracy pics. So Uncle Sam heeds a grief-stricken nation because nobody knows the flying saucer angle – *not as yet*. Thereafter, how can NASA plausibly deny its denials, even if investigators head out here in secret? And as regards investigative journalists, boy, just roll out that UFO…"

A black helicopter landed in the street outside, billowing dust. Masked special forces leapt out, snubby weapons pointing at the swing doors of the Saloon. I was nodding off again in micro-sleeps.

"Pablo," I heard Appleton say, "is there somewhere on the way we can buy them proper clothes easily?"

"Al Campo shopping centre is good."

Two special forces guys burst through the swing doors, gaped at the cancan girls dancing on stage, and the gunslinger fired at them. No, that didn't happen.

"I've a better idea," said Rachel. "Getting them out of Spain, new identities in Africa: that's going to cost you a lot and things might go wrong. You're being too ambitious. It's the *suits* you want, not the wearers. How about you pay me some of the money *to look after these guys here*? Sort of an advance on wages – since we can't afford much more than pocket money on top of their keep. I'm guessing they'll be able to act the Wild West part, help out generally, play poker, talk mysteriously to tourists when they get tipsy. After a while people might come here specially to spot the ghost astronauts, once it's decent to do so. The Magnificent Five! Remarkable resemblances! We need extra attractions."

"Seems to me," said Appleton, "with forty K in their pockets they can pay their own keep here for quite a while, I'd say."

Rachel beamed. "Oh of course, silly me. Well, call my little cut a finder's fee. Or an advance on their board and lodging."

Appleton nodded, sat back and thought.

"Excuse me," I said to Rachel, "but don't we get a say in the matter?"

"Good heavens, I'm offering you *sanctuary*."

"Sounds like a town in the Wild West, Sanctuary," said Jim. "Next stop, Salvation. Or Tombstone."

"We want to avoid the Tombstone outcome, don't we?" said Appleton. "The UFO in its wisdom brought you here as the best way to protect you. By pretending to be what you really are. Which of course you aren't. Unless you are."

Chuck woke up with a shudder and said, "I'm hungry."

"Of course you are," said Rachel. "You need the *chuckwagon*. And you're in luck, since our restaurant opens for lunch at high noon. That's very early to eat lunch in Spain but here we cater for tourists. Usually after lunch people like to have a siesta, so I'll sort out rooms in the Sheriff's Office. Would that be five *single* rooms?" she asked sweetly. "After being cooped up together for so long, sleeping alone might seem lonesome? Maybe the gals would like to share? And a couple of you boys?

I'm afraid we don't have a triple room free. Of course if you'd prefer to pair up differently…?"

"I'm happy to share with Barbara," Juno said quickly.

"And me," said Chuck, "with Jim." To me: "If you don't take that amiss."

WE ATE BURGERS and drank glasses of Sangría, which seemed like sweet fruit juice but packed a punch, as we discovered. Skip to outside the Sheriff's Office.

"This is a *jail*," protested Jim. "Bars on the windows."

Rachel laughed. "I assure you the rooms are much better than cells, and you do get your own keys."

I felt very woozy from the Sangría. So were we all. A siesta wasn't an option but a necessity. Nice-looking modern bed in my room, checked gingham curtains at the windows, some kind of stove for winter use, chest of drawers, a smoke or fume detector on the ceiling. I slept soundly till about five o'clock when banging on the door woke me, interrupting a dream of walking through the desert, the Spanish not the Martian. Just in case of a woman being outside, I wrapped a sheet round me. It was Jim, out in the corridor in his cowpoke gear.

"Our suits have *gone*. I woke up a bit ago, so I walked to that dressing-up building, and *no suits*. Rachel says Appleton went off with all the suits and Pablo. She says Pablo will be back here tomorrow bringing Appleton's money. I said we never agreed to sell! She made like she was astonished. All our cams and pads have gone missing too, unless Chuck kept his. He's still out cold after that Shangri-la stuff. We gotta make Rachel phone Pablo to say no deal and to bring our stuff back. I need your back-up."

"Jim," I said with perfect conviction, "the suits won't come back here now."

"I suppose this country has a police force!"

"Think, Jim, think. Policemen lock up guys with no ID. And then we have no control over our fate. None at all. At least here we can still walk around. We do have the keys to our cells."

"The police'll have to contact the US Embassy to check us out, even if they don't believe we're astronauts or that our Mars-suits have gone for a walk!"

"And what if Uncle Sam decides it's best for our nation if we never returned in a fucking flying saucer? Either we're dead on Mars or we've been on Earth all along with the collusion of NASA and Uncle Sam. Embarrassing, huh? Better swept under the nearest carpet? We just don't know enough to risk that. We *might* know enough after a few weeks, or a few months. Africa might still be the best bet."

"So you mean that for now we should negotiate with Rachel..."

"Even learn to ride horses. I dunno, we can be the Something Gang. With two wicked women members, one of them black to add extra colour. We'd better wake up Chuck and the ladies." This did really seem to me the best plan at the moment, and as mission commander I had a responsibility to my crew.

THE MAGNIFICENT, OR Malevolent, Five headed out to confront Rachel. Behind us, the adobe bank was being robbed for the benefit of onlookers. Up ahead two gunslingers were squaring off, shouting a dialogue of insults at each other in heavily accented English, while other costumed tourists looked on appreciatively. It was all go. One of those tourists, wearing a Marshall's badge, decided to uphold the law, advancing boldly with his six-shooter levelled at one of the gunslingers. Grinning evilly, the miscreant fired a couple of times: bang bang. Dramatically the tourist dropped his gun, clutched at his heart, then sank carefully to the ground while his wife and friends applauded.

Something fell out of my pocket and I scooped it up. Oh, that bit of food in its clingfilm. This time I noticed a tiny sticker, uncrumpled it, read: Gunther's Deli, Rachel NV.

NV for Nevada. No connection with Rachel the wardrobe mistress.

My old flying days came to mind. Rachel NV, a tiny tiny place near Nellis air force range close to Area 51. Famous in the world of UFO believers because of strange sightings along Highway, I forgot which number, but years ago the State of Nevada had officially designated that road *Extraterrestrial Highway*. A nice day-trip out from Las Vegas.

I'd stopped at Rachel once. Oddly its weather station monitored gamma radiation as well as the weather. Gunther's Deli was news to me. Maybe trade was picking up locally.

It couldn't be, could it, that the USAF, unknown to NASA, *did* have access to alien technology? They couldn't bear for us to die on Mars, but couldn't exactly reveal themselves either? Today had been pretty busy so far. I just couldn't digest this new fact.

We succeeded in passing the shoot-out without any blanks being fired at us.

YOU NEVER KNOW

PAT CADIGAN

*Pat Cadigan is a two-time winner of the Arthur C,
Clarke Award for her novels* Synners *and* Fools. *Her
work has appeared in over a dozen languages around
the world (and that's only counting the legal editions).
Born in Schenectady, New York, Pat grew up in New
England but now lives in Original England with her
husband, the Original Chris Fowler, and her son,
musician and composer Robert M. Fenner; all under the
watchful gaze of Miss Kitty Calgary, Queen of the Cats.*

STANDING IN THE doorway of the curio shop, Dov shook
his head. "Can't believe it."

Kitty looked up from the box of prints she'd been
flicking through for the past ten minutes, her dark
brown forehead wrinkling slightly. "Something to
disbelieve in this day and age? I'm shocked."

Dov jerked his grizzled chin at the record store across the
street. "They've hired another deckhand for the *Titanic*."

"I told you, Napster's no match for the combined
might of the music industry," Kitty said as she turned

to look. A young girl was at work on the record store's front window with a squeegee, sponge, and bucket while another employee on the other side of the glass clowned around, pointing at spots she had supposedly missed. The girl showily ignored him as she slopped soapy water onto the glass in wide arcs. "Oh, Kee-*rist!* What is she, *eight?*"

Dov chuckled. "Fourteen, give or take a few weeks."

"*Bull*shit. My new gynaecologist? *He's* fourteen. *She's* barely out of third grade."

"You say that about everyone," Dov said, laughing some more.

"Everyone but you." Kitty turned back to the prints. "And me." She started over at the first print and it seemed to Dov that she was looking at each one a bit longer this time. Kitty was the most regular of the regular customers. She came every day without fail – well, every day that he was there – to browse through the prints in the box on the trestle table outside under the awning. Dov could usually count on seeing her twice a day, occasionally three times, and once in a great while, four or more. She didn't always buy a print but in the two years Dov had been managing the store, he had never known her to buy anything else.

This was her first visit of the day, either a late break or an early lunch, and she had come over from St. Vincent's in such a hurry that she still had her stethoscope slung around her neck; not the most eye-catching accessory on the lower east side of Manhattan.

"Any sign of Big Brother?" she asked him.

"Not yet. The owners said sometime in the next two weeks. That could be any time between this afternoon and Labor Day."

Kitty flicked an amused glance at him. "Now, now – don't go wishing away the summer."

Dov didn't answer. After the Fourth of July holiday, time turned to amber. Then all at once, it was getting dark indecently early and there was a cold bite in the air, and December was slipping away like it had somewhere better to go and couldn't wait to get there.

The security system was supposed to be in by then. Maybe if he rewound the tapes, it would slow things up a little.

Which was probably the most absurd idea he'd had lately, he thought. Although not much more absurd than installing a camera surveillance system in a one-room junk shop. 'Curio shop' was the polite name and that was the term on his employee contract but Dov had yet to find anything he'd have called a curio. Most of the inventory came from estate sales and house removals, or from other stores that had gone out of business. Except for the stock of cheap souvenirs, and even those were leftovers, things that hadn't sold in previous years, junk the owners had picked up for next to nothing from vendors needing shelf space for the current junk. One third of a wall was given to, among other things, I Heart NYC snow globes (a perennial favourite), Empire State Building barometers and pencil sharpeners (also classics in fake bronze), Staten Island Ferry ballpoint pens with a tiny boat that slid back and forth through some oil in the top half of the barrel, Twin Towers coffee mugs, lighters, clocks, and shot glasses (For World-Class Doubles!). Very few items had dates so only a retailer would know they were close-outs. Or connoisseurs of tacky souvenirs. Dov didn't doubt such people existed but they had yet to find their way here. When they did, he'd probably find out he'd sold them something worth $50,000 for thirty cents and the owners would fire him.

Yeah. Right. His head was full of silly things today. A man in a slightly shredded straw hat paused to look through the old photos Dov had put out on the table. Unlike the prints, which were all matted, wrapped in cellophane, and numbered, the photos were loose in an old cardboard box, unordered and unidentified except for names or short notes on the back – *Dad at Sarah's house summer 1980; Hamptons Graduation Trip; Uncle Tony and Sally at 6 mos; May 1964.* They came with the second hand stock, stuffed into the packing like an afterthought, the last traces of the end of an era for someone somewhere. They were priced at a nickel apiece, fifty cents for a dozen but Dov usually let them go for less, sometimes even giving them away to some of the bigger spenders. He couldn't imagine why people would buy old photos of strangers and though he was tempted to ask, he never did.

"Huh," Kitty said. She had pulled up one of the prints and was studying it with serious eyes. After some unmeasured period of time, she showed it to Dov.

Number fifty-four, according to the small white sticker in the upper left corner, was a detailed drawing of the Manhattan skyline, with water-colour accents. As subject matter, it was unremarkable – Dov had seen the city rendered in more ways than he could count on paper, cloth, and skin, and sculpted in almost every medium from Play-Dough to chocolate. Here, however, the precise, hair-thin ink-line seemed to be one unbroken stroke, the artist not lifting the pen even for the unreadable scrawl of signature in the lower right corner.

By contrast, the water-colour was careless, pale daubs here and there. You had to study the thing for a while to see that the two tallest buildings were actually columns of empty space.

Or were they? Dov took a closer look, then held it at arm's length before remembering his reading glasses in his shirt pocket. They didn't help much. Finally, he handed it back to Kitty. "On the house."

Her eyebrows went up again. "Wow, thank you. I feel bad for asking for a bag."

He fetched one from under the counter inside, one of the white plastic sacks he saved specifically for her. "I wish I hadn't seen that," he said, holding it open for her.

She looped the bag over her wrist. "It's been there for quite some time, you must have seen it already."

"Oh, sure. But then you came along and showed it to me." His gaze drifted to the record store. The girl had finished the window and was now dumping the water carefully in the gutter. She straightened up to go back inside and then paused, her head cocked as though she were listening to something. Dov heard only the usual chorus of car and truck engines, the sigh and wheeze of buses, the jackhammers from a block over starting, stopping, starting again, a siren starting to wail and then cutting off abruptly, an alarm that sounded like a death-ray from a Sci-Fi movie, a passing car pumping out bass at a volume that suggested the driver was deaf.

The girl went inside and Dov saw that Kitty had been watching him watch her. "Something?" he asked. "Or did I already miss it?"

She made a see-saw motion with her free hand. "Sometimes you don't notice what you've noticed until you notice that you didn't notice at the time."

An enigma wrapped in a puzzle with a hole in the bottom; he smiled. "You never know, I guess."

"You never can tell," she corrected him and checked the watch pinned to her flowery scrubs. "Damn, I'm late."

Dov looked at his own watch. "Are you sure?"

"Excuse me, I *will have been* late. The domino effect." Instead of hurrying away, however, she turned to look at the record store.

"She'll come over, won't she." Dov cupped one elbow and rested his mouth briefly against his fist before he realised and propped his chin on it instead. "By herself, do you think?"

"That coin is still in the air, hon." Kitty looked at her watch again. "Damn, now I really do have to run."

Dov stared after her, allowing himself a few quiet moments in her wake before it subsided and the day resumed in whatever form it now had. That was as close as he came to getting his mind around the concept of wave functions collapsing. Kitty had actually tried to walk him through it once. He had understood each part in succession but all of it together, not so much.

A young mother pushing a stroller with a sleeping toddler paused to look in the window at something. Dov moved aside to let her ease the stroller over the threshold without waking the child. Boy? Girl? He hadn't looked closely enough. Maybe, he thought as he went back inside, he could avoid doing so.

Which, in keeping with the apparent theme for the day, was *really* silly. Kitty would have laughed and told him *that* wave function had collapsed elsewhere some time ago with no help from him. Then he would have asked her – again – about the difference between wave functions that hadn't collapsed and those he didn't know already had, but he wouldn't have understood the answer – again. He had been tempted to ask her if any of these wave functions, whatever they really were, could collapse if there was still someone somewhere who didn't know it had but it sounded too silly even just in his mind.

Considering how full of silly things his head was today, this might have been the right time to ask. He started to pick up the newspaper and then grabbed the novel he'd left next to the register instead. The paper was full of collapsed wave functions but not as far as he was concerned. Today he wouldn't collapse anything if he could possibly avoid it. At his age, the possibilities weren't endless so he might as well hang onto as many as he could.

Of course, that might be more difficult after the cameras were installed.

Now that was Olympic-class silly. He decided to distract himself by changing the window display. He hoped Kitty might make it back before he went home at six; no such luck. This week, a tall, skinny guy named McTeer had the evening shift. McTeer was one of a handful of people the owners had hired just to plug personnel gaps in their various interests. More than that, Dov had no idea – none of the people who took over for him was given to chitchat and McTeer was practically mute. *Hi* or *hello* was his limit, occasionally *hey*; other than that, he either shrugged or grunted, and never at the same time. He wasn't hostile, he simply wasn't very responsive, like a stranger in an elevator or a waiting room. Maybe that was how he saw his job, or at least this particular assignment, Dov thought, and wondered where McTeer was really going and what he'd be like when he got there. If he ever did. As Kitty had said in the course of an explanation Dov otherwise no longer remembered, all take-offs were optional, all landings were mandatory, and all destinations were guaranteed because everybody had to be somewhere.

'OnWatch – Security & Assurance' read the large, royal-blue letters on the side of the white van, in the kind of dignified typeface Dov associated more with a stationer or a printer than a security company. The woman who climbed out of the cab was dressed in an immaculate sky blue coverall that seemed to have been made for her. Maybe it had – the name 'Fabiola' was embroidered rather beautifully in dark blue thread over her left breast pocket.

"Not a big space to cover," she said in a light Spanish accent as she looked around. "But I'll be here a while. I'll have to run some wire, do a little drilling. But don't worry, that won't take long and I'll put down drop cloths to keep the dust off your stock."

"In this store, the dust is part of the purchase price," Dov said.

"Well, at least there's no food to worry about." She moved to the centre of the store and looked around again, more slowly this time, as if she were measuring by eye. Then she turned to him with a slight frown. "Are you the owner?"

"No, but I can sign any work orders or receipts."

Her frowned deepened as she gave him the same measuring look. "Funny, I could have sworn you were the owner."

"If you need to speak to them, I can get their number –" He started toward the office. He actually knew all four phone numbers by heart and there was a longer, more detailed contact list in the register but he wanted to get away from that stare.

"Nah, don't bother," she said cheerfully. "I must be thinking of another job. I'm pretty busy these days. Suddenly everybody wants cameras. Orders are through the roof."

"Really?" Dov was surprised. "And here's me thinking Big Brother was still the black sheep of the family. So to speak."

"That's a good one." The woman grinned at him. "It's an insurance thing. Burglar alarms aren't enough now for a lot of these carriers, they want a belt *and* suspenders. Besides, when's the last time you heard one of those go off and you *didn't* think it was a false alarm?"

"I should have known," Dov said with a small laugh. "I mean, this is a pretty good space but it's not ballroom size. There's not much I can't see from behind the counter."

"Well, the cameras'll catch all that and more, you included." She leaned toward him, lowering her voice slightly. "I always remind all the good working people I meet on a job that the moment I flip the on switch, the only privacy'll be in the facility. Word to the wise." She tapped the side of her nose and winked.

Dov became aware that he had his index finger pressed to his upper lip, covering the scar that was all but invisible now. Irritated with the old habit, he jammed his hand in his pants pocket. "Thank you. Is there anything I can do to help?"

"Not a thing," she said. "I've done this so many times, I can sleep through it. Just pretend I'm not here."

"Let me know if you change your mind," he called after her as she went out to the truck. His hand was already out of his pocket, going for his face again. He put it in his pocket again and went back to his stool behind the register.

He seldom saw that look of appraisal any more, not like when he was a kid with all the grown-ups staring at him and exclaiming how *good* he looked, that surgeon was an *artist*, you'd almost *never know*. Some days, he'd spend every waking hour hiding his mouth behind a book or a piece of paper or his hand. Till he was thirteen, when pretty Ruth Shapiro had saved him by giving him his first kiss and declaring he was the best kisser in Hebrew school (maybe the best in public school, too, but she only kissed the boys in Hebrew school). After that, his self-consciousness had faded right along with the scar.

Still, once in a great while, he would suddenly become aware of his finger resting against the area under his nose, hiding not only what was there – a scar he could barely see himself any more – but also what wasn't: the two little folds that ran vertically from the base of the nose to the flesh of the upper lip.

It was called the philtrum; he had looked it up. Most people didn't seem to know the term or care what it was, but they all had philtrums. They didn't seem to notice that he didn't, not even Ruth Shapiro, whose full, pouty lips made hers look especially pronounced to him. Apparently it was one of those things you only missed if you'd never had it.

Someone made a polite, throat-clearing noise and Dov came out of his reverie to see a young woman standing at the counter with a few dull metal bracelets and a set of salt-and-pepper shakers shaped like dancing goldfish. He rang them up for her, automatically glancing toward the table outside. Still no Kitty; past where she usually stood, he could see the OnWatch woman taking boxes out of the back of the truck and stacking them on a dolly. As she wheeled it into the store, the prints seemed to catch her eye and, for a moment, Dov thought she was actually going to stop for a look but she didn't.

Dov wondered what would have happened if she had and then Kitty had come along. He remembered something Kitty had told him about waves emphasising each other or cancelling each other out, depending on how they collided. Then there was another customer waiting to pay for something else and he put it out of his mind.

The afternoon stream of customers was a bit heavier than usual and just about all of them were in the mood to buy something, which kept him busy enough that he practically forgot about the OnWatch woman except when the sound of her drill reminded him. It was a small drill and the noise wasn't as loud or as grating as the average power tool. A genteel drill, Dov thought, watching the woman attach a bracket high up on the wall in the far corner, just below the ceiling. She sat astride the top of her step-ladder with casual ease, untroubled by the height. A well-balanced individual, Dov thought. Not to mention tidy – true to her word, she had covered everything immediately below her, although any dust she'd raised was invisible. The white drop cloths looked as immaculate as her coverall.

* * *

THE MONITOR TOOK up a lot of space on the desk in the office but that didn't bother him as much as the black computer tower on the floor underneath. It was just the right size and in the right place for him to bang his knee on it every time he sat down.

"Pretty clear picture, isn't it?" the woman said, urging him to be as pleased as she was.

He made himself nod. The display rotated every five seconds among four separate feeds, three in the store and one on the back wall of the office, just above the door to the tiny employee lav. If he hadn't known what he was seeing, he wouldn't have recognised it. He barely recognised himself when the office came up on the screen, but then the camera was positioned above and behind him. The woman looked pretty much the same, though. Some people, the camera loved. They were photogenic, or telegenic, whatever. Him, not so much, but he still couldn't see himself all that clearly –

He'd been staring at the screen for at least two minutes, he realised suddenly, maybe longer. Every time the display changed, it sort of blinked, like an eye. Store 1 2 3 4 5, store 2 2 3 4 5, store 3 2 3 4 5, office 1 2 3 4 5; store 1 2 3 4 5, store 2 2 3 4 5, store 3 2 3 4 5, office 1 2 3 4 5. The effect was both annoying and hypnotic. *Like real television – all it needs is a laugh-track*, he thought sourly.

"Is there something wrong?" the woman asked, concerned now.

"Oh, no, not at all," he said quickly. He was hiding his lip in the curve between his index finger and his thumb, as if he were thinking something over. With an effort, he pulled his hand away from his face to point at the tower. "Why not put that… thing, whatever it is, on the desk with the monitor?"

"This is a very sophisticated system, not in general use yet. We tell clients to keep it out of sight. Don't tempt fate, or individuals weak in character."

Dov gave a short laugh. "Yeah, I guess it would be embarrassing to have to report your security system stolen."

The woman's sidelong glance suggested to Dov that the word *jejune* was in her vocabulary. "People don't always steal. Sometimes they just smash stuff up."

"True," Dov admitted, trying not to feel chastened. "But that transmits everything to you, right?" The woman nodded. "So even if someone did smash it up, you'd have a record of everything up to the point where it stopped."

"Yeah. But then there's the cost of replacing the unit." The woman grabbed a takeout menu Dov had left lying on the desk, wrote a figure in the margin and showed it to him. "Will that be Visa, MasterCard, or Amex?"

Dov blinked, aghast. "*That* much? But it's just a computer. Isn't it?"

"Well…" The woman grimaced. "That's the simple description. I'd give you the full rundown but to be honest, I don't really understand it well enough. I mean, I understand it but –" She looked around quickly, pointed at the telephone next to the keyboard. "I understand that enough to use it but don't ask me to explain how it works. I'm installation – I plug in wires, I hook up cameras, I adjust the focus and set the time-stamp. I can show you how to re-wind so you can check what happened two hours ago or last night – it's not too hard. And here's the quick-start." She stood a small instruction pamphlet to one side, between the keyboard and the monitor. "It's got all the instructions you're gonna forget I told you."

Dov chuckled politely. "How far back does it go? I mean, how long will it record before it records over whatever it's already recorded?" He paused, replaying what he'd just said. "Did that make sense?"

The woman laughed. "Yeah, I gotcha. It's unlikely you'll ever need anything beyond the previous twenty-four hours. But if for some reason you ever do, we'll have it archived. But I gotta tell you, in all the time I've been doing this, I never heard of anyone having the cops ask them for 'surveillance footage' –" she made air quotes that Dov could almost see. "Except on a TV show."

She produced several forms for him to sign, gave him copies, and before he could ask her anything else, she was scurrying around, packing up her tools, collecting empty boxes, styrofoam inserts, and folding up drop cloths. He went to carry the ladder out to the truck for her but she waved him off with a firmness he didn't dare argue with, despite her cheerful smile.

So that was that. Perched on the stool behind the counter, Dov looked directly at each of the three cameras in the store – one in the far corner, one over the door to the office, and one on the wall directly opposite where he was sitting. And when he sat at the desk in the office, the fourth would be looking over his shoulder.

Abruptly, he realised he'd been looking from one camera to the other every five seconds. "Oh, *hell*," he muttered. Yesterday he'd been silly; today, head-bugs were eating his brain like Pac Man. The cameras hadn't

even been in for a day – not even for an *hour* – and he
already had some kind of bizarre OCD. He slipped off
the stool thinking he'd go back to the office and then
remembered the camera there. He'd forgotten to allow
for that one when he'd been doing his weird OCD thing
just now. Damn it, he couldn't even get *that* right.

Leaving the ring-for-service bell on the counter, he
went back to the office anyway, striding past the desk
without looking left or right to shut himself in the tiny
lavatory. Privacy at last. He flipped the light switch; the
bulb flashed and went out.

Now he had *real* privacy, even from himself. The
way he was going, by tomorrow this would seem like a
luxury. And still, he realised, he had a finger over his lip.

He opened the lav door intending to stride back out
to the store again still not looking at the monitor on the
desk, except it was the first thing he saw. The view of
the top of his head was just long enough to tell him that
he'd been in denial about how much he was thinning up
there. Then the screen blinked and he saw the girl from
the record store had come in. Blink: someone was at the
table outside looking through the box of prints and it
wasn't Kitty. He rushed into the store. The girl glanced
at him but he barely noticed. There was no one at all at
the table looking at anything.

Dov started toward the stool behind the counter but
some impulse made him turn around and go back to
look at the monitor. Two of the cameras had a view
of the table; the one in the far corner showed no one
standing there. The one over the office door, however,
said there was. The person was mostly hidden behind
the front door frame but Dov could see enough to
recognise the coverall. He could even see part of the

sign on the truck and that she had left the back doors open.

He went out to the store. No one was there; the truck was gone. Still, he went all the way out to the table and stared at it for some ridiculous length of time. Two teenaged girls who had been looking through a pile of old postcards stopped to give him a wary look. Dov flashed them a perfunctory smile and went back to the office.

The far corner camera showed him what he had just seen; the other was still watching the woman from OnWatch flipping through the prints.

And the camera across from the counter showed him sitting behind the counter, reading a paperback.

Dov and the display blinked together. He fidgeted through fifteen seconds before the screen showed there was no one behind the counter. Something flickered or twinkled in the lower lefthand corner of the monitor but it was too small to make out even with his reading glasses. He had to get the magnifying glass out of the drawer to see they were numbers, tiny little white numbers changing so quickly they were flashing. Would a time stamp have that many digits? Before he could see whether they were going backwards or forwards, they disappeared.

He straightened up, rubbing his lower back although he felt the ache only distantly.

The woman said they archived the recordings. Maybe they'd been re-running the feeds to synchronise them. Maybe the clock on that thing was out of step with the one at OnWatch.

Only then did he realise that the woman had never answered his question about how far back the recording went.

He heard a single, polite *ding*! from the bell on the counter. The screen showed the girl from the record store waiting at the register from three different angles and then his own back, as transfixed as a dog watching a light beam play over a wall.

"Sorry, sorry," he said, hurrying over to wait on her. She had two of the old restaurant-style creamers, one with a blurry pink floral pattern, the other with two thin austere green lines around the base.

"I see you've got them, too, now."

He paused with his fingers on the register buttons. "Pardon?"

She pointed at the camera behind her, nodded at the other two.

"For the insurance company," he said with a nervous laugh. "Don't ask me, I just work here. You know?"

"Yeah. I heard some places just have dummy cameras. They print up stickers with a company name that sounds authentic but it's fake."

"Good luck to them, I hope their insurance company never finds out." Dov wrapped each small pitcher in a sheet from the financial section, then discovered he was all out of bags, except for the ones he used for Kitty's prints. He hesitated, then searched the shelves under the counter more thoroughly. Still nothing, probably plenty back in the office –

The girl was eyeing the cameras with an odd, wary expression.

"They're all real," he told her. "Personally, I try to avoid looking directly at them."

Her eyebrows disappeared under her bangs. "You do?"

"Yeah. You know, like *Ghostbusters*. Don't look directly at the streams."

Her puzzlement intensified. "I thought it was don't *cross* the streams."

The idea bloomed all at once and fully-formed in his mind. "Maybe you're right and I'm thinking of something else," he said, and gave her an extra twenty-five cents with her change.

THE LADDER WAS old but solid; he used it hundreds of times to change lights, put up shelves and take them down again but he hadn't ever needed to do anything up near the ceiling before. And he didn't need to now, either, insisted the still, small voice of his common sense. Ignoring it was – dared he even think it? – fun. Weird, silly fun, which would probably end right sharpish when he got a call from OnWatch asking him why he was tampering with the cameras.

He could tell them he'd thought the angle looked wrong, like maybe they'd slipped a little.

Oh, good, claim Fabiola had done shoddy work, get the poor woman in trouble – was he a *mensch* or what?

He decided to compromise – he wouldn't touch the office camera or the one pointed at the counter, just the other two. If they'd even move – for all he knew, they were nailed, screwed, and glued in one position.

But they weren't. The range of movement was limited but just enough that he was sure each camera could see the other two. He adjusted them, readjusted them, paused to ring up a Coney Island plastic tumbler and a black and brown serving tray with an only slightly scratched bamboo pattern, and re-readjusted them before finally allowing himself to check the results on the monitor.

He stared for a while, then tried again, changing the positions as much as he could without tearing the cameras out of the brackets. Then he changed the third camera so it was pointed at the other two.

The result was the same. Which was to say, the displays were at less-than-optimum angles to view the store but showed the areas on the walls up near the ceiling perfectly. The feeds were as clear as ever and still changing every five seconds. They just didn't show any cameras. The cameras saw everything except each other.

Dov left them that way for an hour. OnWatch did not phone demanding to know what he was up to. Finally, he put them all back the way they had been, or as near to it as he could remember, checking the display for each one. When he was satisfied, he found an old sweater on a coat-hook and threw it over the monitor till McTeer came in.

It wasn't until he was almost home that he realised he hadn't seen Kitty even once.

SHE CAME THE next day before he had even opened, materialising on the sidewalk just as he put up the trestle table.

"Early for you, isn't it?" he said with a broad grin.

"You, too." Kitty looked at the watch pinned to her scrubs. Pale blue floral today, over darker blue trousers; they didn't quite match.

"I woke up at five-thirty and didn't feel like going back to sleep." He glanced at his wristwatch, did a double-take, and held it to his ear.

"A *ticking* watch?" Kitty's eyes twinkled with amusement. "How retro."

He saw she had the same time he did: 8:15. "I'm an old-fashioned boy. I like a watch I can wind." He gave the tiny knob an extra twist before he went in to get the prints. To his surprise, there were only about half as many in the box as there had been yesterday. There was always a little variation in the number of prints beyond what he sold but never anything this large.

Kitty had never mentioned coming back to buy prints when he wasn't there but he supposed she did, and if so, she was under no obligation to report in to him about it. Nor was it impossible that other people also bought them from McTeer or whoever took over for him at six. For all he knew, the store had a whole different life after he left, with regular customers unfamiliar to him buying inventory he wouldn't recognise. Maybe the night staff kept the place open past ten till two or three in the morning or held raves on Sundays when it was supposed to be closed. Then they cleaned up after themselves and by the time he came in the next morning, he saw only what he expected to see. There was no way of knowing –

Yes, there was.

He stood in the doorway with his arms folded, looking at each of the cameras in turn. Possibly for five seconds each but he wasn't counting.

Kitty's quiet voice broke his rhythm. "You seem very serious today."

Dov's smile was perfunctory. "Why didn't you come yesterday?"

"Busy day," she said, not looking up from the box. "The ER's part organised chaos, part systematic crisis, part random lightning strikes, running on coffee, adrenalin, and the triage nurse's last nerve." She paused at one of the prints, hesitated, then flipped past it. He waited for her to say something about there not being as many in the box as usual but she didn't seem to notice.

"What happens when the triage nurse's last nerve goes?" he asked.

Her eyes twinkled as she glanced up at him. "By then they've all grown back."

"That's amazing."

"It's a gift." She slipped two prints out of the box and held them out to him. "I'll take these."

Number 82 and number 11 were both black-and-white photographs. The former showed an enormous cloud of thick, dark smoke and, at the bottom in the centre, a lone firefighter seen from behind, spraying a stream of water into it. The latter showed a gigantic Ferris wheel caught either by the shutter or in fact at a forty-five degree angle between the white sky above and the city below. Dov fetched a bag for her, trying to remember the last time Kitty had bought even one photo and couldn't. If there'd been a camera out here, he'd be able to keep track.

As if she had caught a sense of his thoughts, Kitty said, "So can Big Brother see me from in there?"

"Only partly – the door jamb's in the way. Were you worried?"

"Just curious." She traded him a couple of crumpled bills for the bag.

"Well, for what it's worth, you haven't shown up on the monitor at all yet," he said, laughing a little. "Whereas I'm the star of the sh –" he cut off, remembering the glimpse he'd had of himself behind the counter. It had to have been a recording, of course. "Star of the show," he finished.

Instead of hurrying away, she lingered, watching him put out the photos and the postcards along with some novelty bookends and a tray of assorted picture frames. He was about to make a joke about her breaking routine and buying something other than a print when she said, "I bet the last thing Orwell ever imagined was that we'd make Big Brother into a game show."

He had to think for a moment. "Oh, right. Is that still on?"

"No one ever went broke underestimating etc, etc," Kitty said.

"Oh, I don't know," Dov said. "If that isn't rock bottom, it's close. The novelty's bound to wear off pretty soon."

"It's no-cost entertainment. All you need is a camera and pretty soon, you won't even need that because you'll always be in sight of at least one lens."

Dov's chuckle was uneasy. "Not getting paranoid on me now, are you? Or is it just that your nerves haven't grown back yet?"

She was silent for a moment. Then: "Do you remember when you asked me about the difference between wave functions that hadn't collapsed and those you didn't know had already collapsed?"

He nodded.

"I thought you would." And then she was hurrying away toward the hospital while he stared after her.

CUSTOMER TRAFFIC WAS brisk throughout the morning into the lunch-hour, with everyone apparently in the mood to spend money – retail therapy, they called it now – but the day went at a crawl. Dov stepped into the office whenever he could to check the monitor but there was no time for more than a quick glance. Sometimes he would have sworn that the system was actually looping the same ten minutes over and over again. It was just that he was busy, he thought. Plus, he was getting a double dose of the store now, with his own eyes and on the monitor, so of course he was coming down with a case of déjà-vu all over again.

He tried an assortment of busy-work to keep himself from haunting the office every few minutes, rearranging the window, rotating stock, even taking a quick-and-dirty inventory of the tacky souvenirs. There were half a dozen new snow-globes, albeit with glitter rather than fake snow. Most of the globes had glitter these days. Maybe the fake-snow globe was becoming an endangered species, he thought, as he picked up one of the larger ones and gave it a shake. Glitter swirled around an Empire State Building being scaled by a giant blonde woman in a pink evening gown, with a tiny gorilla tucked under one arm. He hadn't thought there'd be that much wit in the tacky souvenir industry. He stashed it under the counter and made a mental note to ask the owners where it had come from and if there were any more around.

But nothing he did would make the day pass any more quickly. It was hard to believe he had seen Kitty only that morning – he felt as if it had been at least a whole day. He told himself he ought to try to appreciate it, it was better than feeling as if time were pouring away like fast-running water.

In his mind's eye, he saw the photos Kitty bought, the firefighter and the Ferris wheel, then glanced at his watch: it was two minutes later than the last time he'd looked. Irritated, he took it off and put it in the register, in the always-empty slot meant for fifties and hundreds.

As ALWAYS, THE customers thinned out after lunchtime. He was serving the last few customers when a teenaged boy dropped off a brown paper bag containing lox on a bagel with a perfectly-applied schmear, an assortment of carrot and cucumber sticks, and a can of cream soda. The boy was long gone by the time Dov opened the bag. He was about to call the deli and tell them their delivery boy had made a mistake when he saw the note on the bag – *Nosh! xx Kitty*.

He spread a napkin out on the counter then paused, looking up at the camera. The owners probably wouldn't approve. Gathering everything up, he started toward the office, then stopped. The idea of eating while that eye blinked at him every five seconds threatened to kill his appetite. Knowing that every fifteen seconds, he'd be treated to the sight of himself eating lunch gave him indigestion before he'd even taken a bite. Or he could hide in the lav.

He sat at the register with the bag in his lap.

McTeer was a no-show at six. At six-thirty, the owners' secretary phoned to say he should close up and go home. She was cordial but offered no explanation. Apparently there was no one to plug this evening's personnel gap, Dov thought. Maybe McTeer had run off to the Bahamas, leaving them shorthanded. He started to turn off the lights and then, on impulse, called back and offered to stay on until ten.

The secretary's cordial tone had a hint of steel in it as she told him that wouldn't be necessary and he should have a good evening.

"Well, okay," he said to the phone receiver, although the woman had already hung up. "Don't ask me, I just work here. Till six." Again, he went to turn out the lights and then remembered the table was still outside.

He brought everything in, folded the table legs down and left it behind the display window where he always found it in the mornings and put the box of prints on the floor nearby. Then he went back to the office for a final look around to make sure everything was all right, even though he'd already done that at least half a dozen times already.

There was nothing to see on the monitor now, except for the office feed. Because he still had the light on. He flipped it off and watched the screen as it blinked through a series of vague shadows. It seemed like a big waste to keep them on all night when they had no night-vision utility.

Not his problem. He should go home and have a good evening, he thought as he sat down and pushed the keyboard aside so he could put his feet up on the desk.

HE HAD NO idea how long he'd actually heard the sharp sound of metal rapping on glass but he thought it must have been a while. Awareness flooded in accompanied by aches and pains in every part of his body. He lifted his head and gasped slightly at the flare of sharp pain in his neck. His shoulders and back chimed in as he straightened up.

The rapping sound went on, someone knocking urgently on the window with a coin or a key. He ignored it while he pushed himself to his feet, groaning as his knees cracked and popped. How the hell had he fallen asleep here? With his head on the desk, no less. Why hadn't he gone home? His head didn't want to turn. He'd probably have to put some chiropractor's kids through college before he'd be able to look both ways crossing the street.

The knocking was getting louder and more urgent now. Someone wasn't going to take no for an answer, although they'd have had to if he'd gone home instead of trying to cripple himself. He couldn't imagine who would have come knocking now anyway, nobody knew there was anyone in here –

His gaze fell on the monitor, blinking every five seconds. No, somebody knew. Somewhere somebody knew where he was and they knew that he had seen what the cameras had seen.

Rubbing his shoulder with one hand and his lower back with the other, he shuffled out to see who was scratching up the window.

Kitty's wide eyes met his. "Uh," he said. "What time is it?"

"Late," she said.

He looked at his watch then remembered it was in the register. "Uh," he said again and leaned his head against the jamb. "I did the stupidest thing." He was about to elaborate when his head exploded.

It might have been minutes later before his vision cleared and he realised he had both arms around Kitty in a clumsy hug, while she held him up. The sound of the explosion seemed to resound in his ears and he had the impression that the whole building and a good part of the street had shaken under him.

Horrified, he pulled away from her. "I did the stupidest thing," he said again. "I – I did the stupidest thing –" He tried to tell her the rest of it but his voice refused to come. For several moments, he floundered while every siren and alarm in Manhattan went off at once, almost drowning out the shriek of human voices. Overhead, there was something dark in the sky and the air brought the smell of oil and metal and other things burning.

"I didn't mean to know," he told Kitty desperately. "I didn't mean to!"

"I know," she said.

A man in a wrinkled grey suit ran past holding a cell phone to his ear shouting, "Holy fucking shit!" into it over and over. The street began to fill with people all talking at once, to cell phones, to each other, to anyone who could hear and everyone they saw.

The man in the grey suit came back, still holding the cell phone. "I swear to *Christ*," he told the cell phone. He stopped, looking around as if he didn't know where he was, then noticed Dov and Kitty. "I thought a gas main blew up or a gas truck. An airplane crashed into one of the Twin Towers. A fucking *plane*! I swear to Christ you never know in this city, you never fucking *know*!"

Kitty put a finger to Dov's lips; not really necessary since his voice had deserted him again. "And you never can tell."

The second explosion came a little over fifteen minutes later. Then she went back to St. Vincent's. When he couldn't find his way home he went there as well, although amid all the crowds and the noise and the panic, he couldn't find her either.

THE SECOND EXPLOSION came a little over fifteen minutes later. Kitty went back to St. Vincent's. Dov went back into the office and watched. Sometimes he saw Kitty looking through the prints. A few times he saw himself behind the counter, but he always saw himself in the office and, when he realised he always would, he locked up and went home.

YESTERMORROW

Richard Salter is the editor of the anthology Short Trips: Transmissions, *and the author of over a dozen short stories that have been published and plenty more that haven't been yet. 'Yestermorrow' was born from his love of all things time travel, from* Doctor Who *to* Slaughterhouse Five.

Monday June 5th, 2017

THE MAN RUNS because his life depends on it. He does not want to be late – the fate of the universe hangs on him being in the right place at the right time. Or rather the wrong place at the wrong time. The streets of Brighton are pretty much deserted at this time of night. The only vehicles that pass are taxis or buses. He dashes across the road, not waiting for the lights to change. He doesn't even bother looking as he runs – the accident doesn't happen here.

He is running up St James's Street now, away from the Steine and towards the point of no return. He feels oddly nervous. No matter; this is where he is meant to be.

The uphill sprint makes his lungs heave and his chest ache but he does not fear a heart attack. He pulls a tattered leaflet from his inside coat pocket, just to have it ready. 'Know Your Death Date!' is emblazoned across the cover.

At last he reaches Chapel Street. He glances at his mobile phone, notes that he still has five minutes. He collapses in a heap on the street corner, fighting for breath, not caring that he's getting dirt on his jeans. He checks the date and time stamped inside the leaflet yet again, sets his mobile down on the pavement by his side and forces his breathing to calm down. This is his final day – the last day he will live through. He has known this day was coming for four years now – the leaflet only confirmed what he already knew. There's no getting away from it. You can't cheat death.

His time is up. He stands and balances on the curb, his mobile forgotten on the ground. He places the leaflet reverentially back in his pocket and closes his eyes. He can hear the bus coming and knows what he must do. By his right foot, his mobile phone beeps an alarm. He takes a step forward.

A hand grabs his shoulder and yanks him back. He turns to face his saviour. "No, you don't understand," he says as the bus whizzes past him. The person who just saved his life has his face covered by a black hood. The masked rescuer drags the man onto Chapel Street, into the shadows. The man protests and struggles as he is thrown to the ground. He feels no pain as the blade slices through his chest, only surprise.

"This isn't how I'm supposed to –"

* * *

Tuesday June 6th, 2017

THE RAIN SPATTERS off the pebbles as my boots crunch across the beach. It's hard to walk with purpose when each step sinks and slides. At the bottom of the rocky incline, the gently lapping waves spread out between the rocks, the water searching out countless paths to follow in its push onto land. Here the pebbles are darker and glisten from the constant wash of the tide.

The body lies slumped on its side, the feet and legs still encircled and released by each ebb and flow. Its posture and pallor resemble the carcass of a beached whale – the flesh bloated and bleached white. I avert my gaze, scanning the promenade for police cruisers conspicuous by their absence. The APP should be all over this case like flies on a cow's arse, but instead they're stuffing their faces with egg McMuffins and cheap coffee.

Why should they hurry? They know this case will never be solved.

Maybe I can prove them wrong.

I crouch down and push aside the victim's shredded shirt with a gloved hand, examining the wounds. I've viewed the photos already, of course, but this is the earliest after death I will have a chance to see this. I reach into the inside pocket of the man's coat, pulling out a sodden pamphlet. I check the faded date, time and place stamped inside, barely readable now. 'June 5th, 2017 – 3:05AM – St James's Street and Chapel Street, Brighton – Suicide – stepping in front of a bus.'

One hour later the others show up. There is no crowd of gawkers to be dispersed – the murder is already old news. Jim Haggerty is making his overweight way down the sliding shingle slope towards me, coffee in one hand, the other outstretched to maintain his balance. He hasn't shaved, his hair is only vaguely combed and his tie hangs as limply as his dick probably does when his wife can be bothered to try and wake it up. I can't stand this guy, will never be able to tolerate his unsanitary appearance and shitty attitude.

"What's the rush?" he asks in that nasal whine of his. "Mr Parkhurst isn't going nowhere."

I ignore his butchering of basic grammar and turn to the body.

"Have you lived through the fifth yet?" I ask, while motioning for an APP photographer to approach.

"Yesterday? No."

"When you do, can you be on Chapel Street at 3.05am and catch this fucker?"

"You know that would be against the rules."

I turn on him angrily. "This guy doesn't give a shit about the rules, so why should we?"

Haggerty spreads his arms wide innocently, spilling a little of his coffee onto the pebbles. "We're the good guys," he explains. "The damage this fuckhead is doing to the timelines is nothing compared to the heap of shit we'll unleash if we try and stop him."

I mutter something under my breath. That's the problem with the Anti-Paradox Police – everything's got to be played according to established history. Sets an example, the government says. If everybody did anything they liked, the universe would explode. How I would love to put that theory to the test.

Back when we were real policemen, back before the Slip, we'd have put this killer away in no time flat. I already know all trace of his DNA has been washed off by the water but there's an obvious pattern to these murders that would be his undoing if only our hands weren't tied.

The other officers are bagging up the body now. None of them are taking a lot of care to preserve the evidence.

Screw that. I don't have a whole lot of days left. If the killer can change history then so can I.

I GET HOME late this evening and Laura is mad at me, which is kind of her default state anyway. Usually she spends her time coming up with new reasons to hate my guts. It's not like I don't provide a ton of justification.

"I'm sorry. I was working on the Parkhurst case."

"Why? Why waste time on a case you can't crack? I swear you're just looking for an excuse to stay away from home."

"I'm doing this so I'll have *more* time at home."

"Jason's asleep now, so that's another day you won't be spending with him. I know you don't want to be with me, but for fuck's sake, Craig, are you such a heartless bastard that you can't spend what time you have left with your son?"

I don't answer. She doesn't understand. She's like all the others, blindly doing what she's told, living every day according to how things are supposed to be. Exasperated, she announces she's off to bed and heads upstairs. After I hear the door to our bedroom close I creep into Jason's room and watch him sleeping. His body is four years old but I wonder how old his mind is. How many days in the future has he lived without me? If I'd spent any time with him today I might know by now. Am I robbing him of time with me by obsessing over my death?

As quietly as I can, I pull out a leaflet from my pocket. 'Know Your Death Date!' it says on the front. I don't have to look inside to know that fateful date and time, but I do anyway. I know it's right because I haven't lived through any days beyond Monday.

If time still flowed linearly, I'd be dead in six days.

Thursday January 15th 2015

I AWAKEN TO the sound of my alarm and immediately crack open my diary to find out what day it is. The leather bookmark indicates that today is January 15th. I read yesterday's entry, as I always do, where I've written some details about what's going on in my life right now. This helps me catch up quickly – everyone does this if they want to stand a chance of keeping track. Tonight before the Switch, I will enter details about what happened today. So far, all today's entry says is that the swearing in ceremony for all APP officers is this afternoon. I've been dreading this day for quite some time. It feels weird to be starting a job I've already been doing for a while. Everyone has to start somewhere.

All across the country during this time period, pre-Slip police forces are converting into APP units. Crimes don't require a whole lot of investigation these days. The future doesn't just tell us who the perp is, it also tells us how long they'll spend in jail.

I enter the station, careful to avoid the myriad folks setting up this afternoon's ceremony. On one side of the lobby a huddle of officers is trying to calm Haggerty down. He is pretty distraught.

"What's going on?" he wails. "I lost two years, two fucking years of my life. Don't you people understand? Was I in a coma? What the fuck?" The other officers attempt to explain it to him and he launches into another tirade. "What are you talking about? What's the Slip? You telling me I spent two years wearing some bird's nightie?"

"Different kind of Slip, Jim," Sarge says from behind the desk.

I wave to him as I walk by. "Noob day?" I ask, nodding my head towards Haggerty.

Sarge nods his head. "Happened to us all."

I can't help but laugh. Great day to get as his first after the Slip. He'll have to understand life in general before he can possibly grasp what his new job is. Last night in his own timeline, Haggerty went to bed on Tuesday February 19th 2013 – the day before the most important date in human history – with no concept of the Slip, no idea what happens at midnight every day, not an inkling of what it means to live your life out of order. I remember my first day post-Slip. I jumped straight to a warm summer day in 2015. It took me about twenty days bouncing around inside my own lifetime before I got to grips with the idea that time no longer works by lining up days in a reasonable order. Most people get used to it surprisingly quickly. Some never do. Some go mad waiting to live a day before that fateful Wednesday, but nobody jumps to a date pre-Slip. That's not how it works.

*   *   *

THAT AFTERNOON, THE ceremony goes without a hitch and everyone on the former police force becomes APP. "Stop the Paradox, Save the Universe!" – the slogan is bandied about carelessly throughout the festivities. To me it rings hollow.

Haggerty is laughing with his APP mates now. He seems to have grown accustomed to the idea pretty damn fast. He's one of the lucky ones. That'll help him a lot when he wakes up tomorrow and finds he's eighty-five years old, living in a nursing home and unable to pee all day until suddenly his bladder explodes. Okay, that's an exaggeration, I'm sure. Haggerty probably embellished the story. Still, lucky that wasn't his Noob day. Confused as hell and unable to pee – can you think of a worse way to start a new life?

Thursday June 8th, 2017

THIS COFFEE SUCKS! Why do I come here? Every fucking day I sit here in this café with Haggerty before we start work. Even on weekends. Haggerty's wife hates him more than Laura hates me. We hate each other, we hate this café and we hate the coffee. But it's familiar. It's routine. It's something we do automatically, regardless of what day this is. Routine is what stops us from going psycho. Everyone's the same – that's why I know every person in this place by name. Like *Groundhog Day*, except *everyone* feels as if they're living the same day again and again.

We all crave the same things: stability, order, meaning.

But this is June 8th. In four days (as the clock flies) I will be dead. My opportunities to catch the killer are running out.

"How many times has this guy killed?"

Haggerty grimaced as he sipped his coffee. "You still on this? Jeez, let it go."

"Indulge me, I don't have long to live."

"Bullshit. I bet you have a ton of days left to live before Monday."

To be honest, I'd lost track. Some people, Haggerty included, kept a memorized tally of how many days they'd lived through and could work out how many days they had left. I gave up doing that a while back – the numbers involved were too depressingly small.

"How many times?"

Haggerty sighs, which turns into a belch. "Fuck, whatever. Assuming it's the same guy, Ten. Or maybe eleven. Lessee, linearly speaking, three before Parkhurst. Seven follow him. Or is it five?"

"How many have you lived through?"

"All three of the ones in the past, two of the ones in the future. I think. I don't remember."

"You know why you don't remember?"

"No, why?"

"Because you're a dick."

"Funny."

"Seriously though, don't you think it's weird?"

Haggerty signals for the waitress. "We all know we never catch the guy so to be honest I don't lose a lot of sleep over it."

While my partner orders another coffee and a Danish, I ponder my options.

"WE'RE SUPPOSED TO be responding to a call!" Haggerty wheezes. I ignore him, climbing the steps to the

Brighton Archive two at a time. The converted 19th century building stands opposite the Royal Pavilion and once housed shops and apartments. Now, the entire complex is given over to a massive storage facility.

"Nuts to the call," I reply.

"His wife is convinced he's going to bottle out of topping himself at 11:20am. That's in thirty minutes. We've got to make sure he steps off the ledge. Carter, wait up!"

I'm not listening. Instead I wave my APP badge at the guards and they let me through to the security check. Haggerty is close behind; his breathing is annoying me. Getting him to quit smoking and lose some weight is impossible of course, since that's not what's going to kill him so why should he stop?

I stride up to the reception desk. "I need to see the Chief Librarian," I say to the diminutive lady polishing her nails.

"Would a 'please' kill you?" she asks, not looking up.

"I'm APP. The Librarian, *please*."

She looks me in the eye and straightens, putting down the little bottle and brush. One cool side effect of being an APP officer: people respect those who are technically allowed to change history, even if we rarely do.

"Certainly, Sir. I'll have him paged. And can I ask, Sir...?"

"What?"

She whispers conspiratorially, "Can you get me a job at the APP? Something in admin is fine. It's just that this place is so dull. Every day is exactly the same."

"Some people like that," Haggerty says, having finally caught his breath.

"Not me," she replies. "I want to do something with my life."

I stare at her. "Do you get a job at the APP?"

"Well, no. Not that I've seen yet."

"So you're asking me to change history for you?" My tone is slightly threatening.

She straightens some papers. "Of course not. What gave you that impression? Here he is!"

A tall, middle-aged gentleman dressed in scholar's robes and carrying a huge ledger under his arm descends the stairs to the lobby. He seems distracted, annoyed at the interruption. He approaches the front desk.

"What is it? I'm very busy, it had better be important."

"My colleague here has only lived a few days since the Slip so he's never seen your facilities before. I wonder if you'd be so good as to show us around."

Haggerty is about to protest so I flash him a look, silencing him.

"I'm far too busy for this interruption. Let me find someone junior –"

"We were rather hoping you would do the honours, since there's nobody more knowledgeable about the Archive."

He looks horrified at the prospect. "What? Me? Oh very well."

"You live here, at the Archive, right?"

"Yes, yes, what of it?"

I follow the Chief Librarian through a set of double doors into a room filled with desks and workers. There isn't a single computer in the room, just people and furniture and endless shelves heaped with stacks and stacks of diaries and pamphlets and ledgers.

"Nothing, just impressed at your dedication to the job," I tell him.

He turns on me. He's no spring chicken, but he's imposing nonetheless. "Job? This is not a job! It is my life! I keep records of everything. Without me, without this Archive, how would people know for sure when they are going to die? How will they know when to conceive their children or quit a job or break their leg? How can we be sure that history will run according to plan?"

"Well, quite. So where do you sleep?"

"Fourth floor," he replies. "And no I will not show you my apartment."

"Fifteen minutes to the suicide," Haggerty tells me in a stage whisper.

"And in here," the Librarian continues, soldiering on, "we have the most dedicated staff in the region. On this side of the room, workers memorize details of what has happened today, so the next time they live a day in the past they can record those details. On the other side of the room, our workers record their memories from the future so that pamphlets can be sent out in good time. The next room I'll show you is where we process the pamphlets."

"What's that book you're carrying?" I ask.

The Chief Librarian freezes in his tracks. "This? This is my personal ledger." He seems uncomfortable discussing it.

"And what's it for?"

"For? What's it for? Well, I record things of course."

"What, specifically?"

"Well, at a high level, every major event from each day that has been memorized from the future, and every major event that actually happens today. I use it to check and validate everything that is recorded and every pamphlet that is sent out. We must be sure our details are accurate."

"Absolutely. That's a lot of work, though?"

"Indeed. Which is why, gentlemen, I must ask you to leave now. I am a very busy man."

"Of course, we'll leave you alone. Thank you for the tour."

On our way out, I stop by the receptionist again.

"I'd like to send the Chief Librarian a token of my thanks. Any suggestions? Does he drink?"

The receptionist chuckles. "Like a fish," she says. "He's very partial to scotch. Single malt. Better make it a large bottle or else he'll finish it in one evening."

"And when should I have it delivered by?"

"As long as it gets here by 6pm you're golden."

"Thanks, Miss...?"

"Bridges. Helen Bridges."

"Thank you, Miss Bridges. I'll put in a good word for you at the APP."

"What was that about?" Haggerty asks once we're outside. "We've missed the suicide. I bloody hope he went through with it or we're in a shitload of trouble."

"That ledger – you always see him carrying it around when he's shown on the TV Reminder Reports. He's never shown anyone the contents."

"Why do you care?"

"Anyone with access to that ledger is potentially our killer," I explain.

"That doesn't make sense," Haggerty argues. "It doesn't take much effort to find out when someone is going to die."

"No, but to know precisely enough to step in at the last moment and kill them yourself. That takes a very detail-oriented mind."

"You think the Chief Librarian is the killer?"

"Think about it. Why is this guy never caught?"

"Because he just isn't. We... I'd remember it."

"It's more than that. It's because he knows exactly whom he can kill with impunity. He targets those who are going to die alone and he knows where they will be and at exactly what time. But he cares about history, don't you see?"

"Cares? Why do you say that?"

"Because he's only killing people who are going to die anyway."

"Surely that's just so he can cover his tracks."

"That's part of it, but I think he believes that if you're about to die, you're fair game."

Wednesday February 20th, 2013

TODAY IS DAY One and everyone is happy.

Breaking the habit of a lifetime, I skip the café and just go for a walk along Western Road. It feels like the day after a massive storm, like the power is out and nobody can get to work or even turn on a television. There's a sense of community, camaraderie, as if we're all in this together.

There's no panic, no rioting. Day One is like a national holiday. With the exception of those having the most confusing Noob Day imaginable, everyone else has already lived days beyond this one. They all know what the Slip was; they all know that at midnight, every night, the Switch will happen and it'll be some other day, a random day of their life.

But today is different. As I pass by, everyone smiles and says hello. Everyone knows the rules, but the rules haven't been put in place yet. Everyone knows that they will soon be getting pamphlets telling them when to fuck, when to buy a car, when to die. But not today. The Archive hasn't been set up yet. The APP doesn't exist. The government hasn't locked down Britain's borders, imposed martial law or abolished the election process yet. They did shut off access to the internet beyond Britain's borders though, that was done pretty fast. Nobody knew they *could* do that until it happened.

Still, today everyone feels free.

In reality, we're no freer today than any other day of our lives post-Slip. But it feels as if we are.

I'm tempted to get on a plane while I still can and head for Mexico. Rumours are that while North America, Europe and most of Asia go into lockdown just like Britain, some countries – especially in Latin America and Africa – just go with the flow. Whatever will be, will be. Kind of makes a mockery of the whole, "Don't change history or the universe will explode" concept.

It's a fair walk back to the Seven Dials and my house. Laura greets me at the door, Jason in her arms. I take him from her and kiss his head. I've heard it said that when your mind is that of an adult and you wake up one morning as a baby, you don't remember any of it.

I wouldn't know because I was already an adult when the Slip happened. I look into Jason's eyes and I see... something there. Will he remember me?

To my surprise, Laura leans over and kisses me so passionately I feel compelled to avert Jason's innocent eyes. He coos uncomprehendingly.

"What was that for?" I ask Laura.

"It's Day One," she says, as if that explains everything. Everyone seems in a good mood today.

I ask hopefully, "Is it time for his nap?"

AFTERWARDS, WE LIE together and enjoy the silence of the bedroom. Mercifully, Jason hasn't stirred in nearly an hour. We know we don't have long now before he wakes.

"Tell me about Jason," I say. "Will he be a doctor?"

"No. A musician."

"Really? Cool! Anyone I might know?"

"Heard of Pagan?"

"Yeah!" I sit bolt upright. "You're shitting me! Really? Wow. I heard people talking about this Pagan guy and wow, he's huge! Never put two and two together before."

"Jason plays bass in Pagan's band."

"Oh. Well, that's still pretty cool."

She sits up. Her body, trapped in linear time like everyone else's, displays the legacy of motherhood. Her breasts are swollen and her nipples are tender from feeding a voracious baby. Her once smooth stomach is now wrinkled with stretch marks and excess skin. Bags beneath her eyes betray the sleepless nights she has endured. She has never looked more beautiful to me.

"I do love you," I tell her. Right now it's the truth.

"I know. I hate what the Slip has done to us but I don't hate you."

I hold her tight. I know the baby will cry at any moment. He may well have lived two thousand days of his life already, but very soon he's going to need a feeding and a nappy change.

I promise Laura that in the days I live after this one, I will try to be nicer to her, and spend more time with Jason.

She holds me a little tighter.

"Bass player for Pagan? Really?"

She laughs. "I know. He's quite well off too, so you don't have to worry about the four of us after you're gone."

My blood runs cold. "Four?"

"I mean two. The two of us. Jason and me." Laura turns pale.

I stand up, not caring that I'm naked, not bothering to keep my voice down.

"You said four."

She stands up and starts to dress, her head bowed. "I didn't mean anything by it."

"That's why our marriage is a failure. That's why I always get the cold shoulder from you. That's why Jason looks at me oddly when he's old enough to wonder who I am. I kept waiting for the day when you'd tell me why our marriage is failing, but I wasn't going to find out, was I? You fucking whore!"

"You expect me to stay a widow for the rest of my life?"

"No! But... shit. Four? So you have another kid with him, right? Boy or girl?"

"Craig, please…"

"Boy or girl?" The baby is crying now.

"A girl," Laura whimpers.

"And what's his name?" I don't want to know; I *have* to know.

"David. I meet him a year after you die. I'm not unfaithful while you're alive!"

"Bullshit!" I'm screaming now. I'm flying out of control. I'm so mad I can barely see straight. I want to smash something. "Each day you're with me – the next day you're with him! Then you're back with me again, but I'm no *David*, am I? You can't wait to get through the days with me so you can be back with him. Am I right?" I yell the last question again. "Am I right?"

She is in tears now, wanting to tend to the baby but I'm standing between her and the door.

"So these years post-Slip you're living through with me before I croak – they're just an inconvenience. They're just something to burn through until you can be with my replacement and your two perfect kids and…" I tail off. "Dear God. Jason calls him Daddy."

Laura is shaking her head now, trembling.

"He calls that *fuck*, 'Daddy', doesn't he? I'm dead and gone, and that *fucker* knocks you up and moves in and steals *my* son!"

She stands, her fists clenched. "Listen to me. I have a lot more days to live than you do so cut me some slack, okay?"

But I'm not listening. Laura is already lost to me, has been since this crazy jumping in time shit started. Now at least I know why, I'm the stopgap in the way of the real love of her life. What really kills me, what eats at the very core of my being, is that my son doesn't know what to call me because he already has a dad. I can't believe how self-absorbed I've been that I never stopped to think about this before.

"How come I don't already know this?" I demand. "Why didn't anybody tell me?"

"I asked everyone you know not to tell you my future. I didn't think you'd be able to handle it."

"Too fucking right I can't handle it! My God, my wife is having a… a trans-temporal affair, and my kid doesn't think I'm his dad!"

Today was set to be the best day of my life since the Slip. Now it's the worst.

Wednesday June 7th, 2017

I'VE BEEN ITCHING to get back to this final week of my life for so long. I've lived what must be months in my own timeline subsequent to Day One. Since then I've not even been able to look Laura in the eye. Sometimes she knows why, sometimes she doesn't. I idly wonder if my attitude towards her since finding out about David is actually the cause of the divisions between us, but I dismiss those worries because she'll have known she ends up with David long before our marriage breaks down. It makes my head hurt thinking about it, so I don't. I have one goal now. Just one.

Waiting all day is agonizing. I join Haggerty on some APP calls but I'm barely there. I coast through our talk with a guy who refuses to give all his money to charity. In his hand is a pamphlet, 'Miscellaneous Actions' written on the front. Haggerty is telling him that, like it or not, on this day he will give his favourite charity all his money. It's always happened, it always will happen. When he still won't do it, Haggerty makes the transfer himself, ignoring the man's protests.

But I don't care.

Just one goal.

Darkness falls at last. I tell Haggerty I have to go home but instead I head for the Archive. Over the last few months in my own timeline, I've found every excuse to come down here and study the security layout of the building. The Archive is well protected but break-ins are so rare now that the guards almost never see action, and when they do they all know it's going to happen. Consequently they are bored, indifferent and easily avoided.

8pm. Right on cue, the guards change shift. As usual, the team clocking off congregates on the front steps, waiting for their replacements to arrive. I'm already on the other side of the building, crouching and staring at my watch. 8:10pm, the cutover occurs. That's when the new shift reactivates the alarm system in case any of the sensors need resetting. That means the whole system is down for thirty-five seconds. I use that time to smash a hole in a basement window with a well-wrapped arm and slide inside.

It doesn't take long to get up to the fourth floor. I know the motion sensors are down tonight because three weeks ago I used my APP override pass to book a remote maintenance upgrade for tonight. Strictly speaking, while APP officers are authorized to change history, it's only supposed to be a last resort. I say screw that.

I break into the Chief Librarian's apartment with ease. He's sleeping soundly because two weeks ago I arranged to have a large bottle of whisky sent to his rooms.

Expensive enough so that he wouldn't put off opening it; not so expensive he might save it for a special occasion. The bottle stands empty on a table and the snoring can be heard throughout the apartment.

I find the ledger on his bedside table. I consider for a moment looking for the murder weapon but he's unlikely to keep it here.

Instead, I open the ledger to the entries for this week. Each day has been allocated two facing pages, full of names, dates and details. The left-hand page bears the relevant day's date. Beyond today the details are a little sketchier but not by much.

I turn to June 5th. Sure enough, there's Parkhurst. Nothing about his entry stands out, but the Librarian wouldn't be stupid enough to circle and highlight his next victim. I spend some time reading the details for the days I have not yet lived through after June 5th. There's not much point in looking at days before that – I already know they contain no other victims. Frustratingly, I don't see any candidates. I'm looking for people who die alone, but there's nobody. Nobody until the 12th, anyway. I spot one likely candidate, details inked onto the right-hand page in perfect handwriting. With a sinking feeling, I realize that there's really only one potential victim before I die.

Me.

"WHAT THE HELL do you want?"

My boss doesn't sound happy. It's late now, 10:30pm. Mobile phone held to my ear, I'm crouched in a bathroom on the third floor of the Archive, hoping that nobody will hear me. I don't want to whisper because that may tip off my boss that I'm somewhere I shouldn't be. I mumble something about my kid being asleep and talk as loudly as I dare.

"Chief, listen to me. I think I can catch Parkhurst's killer."

"Jeez, are you still on this? We never catch him! Let it go."

"Sir, I don't have long to live, linearly speaking. Just indulge me."

There's a long suffering sigh on the other end of the line. "Fine, what do you want to do?"

"On the 12th of June, at the time that I die, I want a dozen APP officers watching me, in hiding."

"Uh uh, Carter. You die alone. I saw your pamphlet. Not even the APP can change that."

"I'm not asking you to change anything about how I die. I just want our people there in case… in case I'm the next victim."

"You think the killer would dare attack an APP?"

"Why should he care what my job is? All he cares about is that I die alone, early in the morning, in an exposed location. Doesn't matter if I'm APP, he knows we won't break the rules even for one of our own."

"It's out of the question, Carter. I'm sorry."

He hangs up. I sit with my back against the tiled wall beside a row of sinks, head in my hands, wondering what the hell I'm going to do. And then I know.

Sunday June 11th 2017

ACCORDING TO MY pamphlet, I'll be walking through Brunswick Square early on the morning of the 12th. 3am to be exact. It's nearly 3am now, but I'm here a day early. On the evening of the 10th, Laura had asked me why I set my alarm so early for the next day. I told her that the day before I die, I want to walk through the streets of Brighton and especially around the place where I'll die. I tell her it's my period of mourning for my own life. She doesn't understand but she doesn't argue.

So here I am. It's cold, colder than it should be in summer. I wonder if global warming is to blame – then I realize that I've never actually asked anyone who lives longer than I do if global warming turns out to be real or not. I make a mental note to do so before I reach the 12th and I've used up all my days. In fact, there's an awful lot of stuff about the future I've never asked anybody.

I sit down on a bench and watch a taxi drive around the perimeter of the square and exit onto Brunswick Terrace.

Hands grab me.

I struggle, fighting back as my attacker pulls me over the back of the bench. I land hard on the grass, knocking the wind out of my lungs. He's wearing a hood – I grasp at it to try and pull it free. A knife swings towards my gut but I twist out of its way, holding his arm and trying to wrest the weapon free. We roll over and over on the grass, both of us struggling to gain the upper hand.

Suddenly he is pulled off me. Strong hands lift me to my feet.

APP officers. Three of them are holding the struggling perp.

Haggerty takes off the hood.

The Chief Librarian.

"Got you."

He spits at Haggerty. "You're breaking the rules!" He cries. "You can't all be here at the time of his death."

I chuckle. "It isn't the time of my death," I say. "You're a day early."

He stares at me now, no longer struggling. "What?"

"It's not Monday, it's still Sunday. I tore a page out of your ledger, the left hand page for June 12th. I made the entries on the right-hand page for the 12th look like they occur on June 11th."

"What? When?"

"I broke into the Archive several days ago and found out I'd be your next victim, so I made you think I'd die tonight instead of tomorrow. That way all my friends here could accompany me without breaking any rules. Well, no major ones anyway. Barry here is supposed to be trying for a baby. How's that going, Barry?"

"It'll happen," says Barry, twisting the Librarian's arm a little higher behind his back. "I doubt being here this morning will change that."

"So there you go, Mr Chief Librarian. No harm done to the precious timelines. Although what catching you will do to history, I've no idea. Maybe the universe will explode."

"You have to let me go! I'm not supposed to be caught!"

"Nope, but in special circumstances, APP Officers are authorized to deviate from established history to serve the public interest. I don't know how many people you were going to kill after tonight, but I reckon if those people die the way they're supposed to it'll more than balance any damage done by throwing your sorry arse behind bars."

Haggerty steps forward. "Chief Librarian Thomas Hague, you are under arrest for gross-divergence from the established time line, at least three counts of murder and for assaulting an APP officer. You have the right to remain silent but anything you say today or at any time in the future may be used in court against you. Take him to the station, lads."

Cursing and spitting, the Librarian is dragged away, leaving Haggerty and me alone.

"Fuck me!" says Haggerty. "You did it."

Monday June 12th 2017

I SIT ALONE on the same bench I sat on yesterday – well not yesterday for me, but yesterday as the world turns – in Brunswick Square. It is warmer tonight, but a gentle breeze flows from the waterfront and cools the air. I remember very clearly the arrest of the Chief Librarian in this very spot yesterday. I feel absolutely fine, even though my time is nearly up. I will die alone and in the future a man called David will be called daddy by my son. Catching the Librarian has proved that the future can be changed – the media woke up to that revelation in a big way – but there's no escaping the aneurism that will take my life. I spent the day in hospital having more tests done, even though the law forbids a person from attempting to avert their own death. The doctors are less bothered by the rules these days. Things have changed, for everyone. They haven't all changed at the same rate, on the same days. It's been a gradual thing, but in the days I've lived since Sunday, I've noticed. Every day since then I've spent either in the hospital trying to find a way to cheat death, or with Laura and Jason. I've told them everything, I've tried to put David out of my mind, and I've managed to enjoy what little time I had left with my son.

Ultimately the doctors couldn't help. They couldn't do anything about the problem with my brain. It was worth a shot though.

"I hear you've been changing history again."

It's Haggerty. He shuffles over and sits down on the bench next to me, wheezing slightly. I can't help but smile.

"You're not supposed to be here," I say.

"Nobody should die alone."

"What's it like now? The future I mean?"

"Well you must have seen some of it in the past. It's uncertain, weird. I don't remember many details, too many things changing. I only remember the linear-past for certain. I suppose that's how it always used to be. Makes life more interesting, that's for damn sure. Nobody bothers with the pamphlets any more. The Archives have all been shut down. The Chief Librarian gets life, I know that for sure. Apparently he killed twenty people before the Slip. Afterwards he stopped for a while but then worked out a way he could carry on. An addiction, the psychiatrists call it. Fucking psycho if you ask me. We have to be careful that when he lives days before he got caught, he doesn't try to kill anybody again. He may be the first person to be retroactively arrested!"

He is quiet for a moment and then says, "I'm sorry you won't be at the trial."

I shrug my shoulders. "It's okay. I'm fine with it, really. I made a difference, what else can anybody hope for?"

"'S true."

"One thing I still want to change though…"

"Jesus, leave history alone already. What's it done to you?"

"No seriously, one more thing."

"What?"

"Next time you see me can you suggest we go somewhere with better coffee?"

Haggerty laughs. "Sure," he says. "I can do that."

"So I guess I'll see you yestermorrow," I tell him.

"Yestermorrow. I like that. Sure. See you then."

We sit in silence for a full minute.

My watch starts beeping.

Then, like a light switch, my brain turns off.

DREAMING TOWERS, SILENT MANSIONS

JAINE FENN

Jaine Fenn is the author of three novels to date – her Hidden Empire series, published by Gollancz, namely: Principles of Angels, Consorts of Heaven, and Guardians of Paradise. "Dreaming Towers, Silent Mansions" was inspired by a dream, though not one of hers...

<start transmission>

We're through.

Visual matches the probe data: we're on a wide ledge of green stone with steps going down, with structures – buildings – all around us. The air smells, uh, thick. Rich, even.

The portal's stable but featureless from this end, just as the footage showed. It looks like a funhouse mirror hanging in mid-air. I'm going round the back now... yep, it's identical from both sides.

Hassan is going to try throwing a small projectile back through the portal. He's using a stone he brought from Earth. He's going to throw it – now.

Right.

The stone bounced, as predicted. He's picking it up. It appears unchanged.

He's about to carry out the test on the other side of the portal. And...

Same result.

We'll repeat this exercise with any local objects we find, in case that makes any difference.

Until then... looks like the theories were right, Control. This is a one-way trip.

<end transmission>

Though she had reviewed the original footage more times than she cared to remember, nothing prepared Charli for the reality of being on another world. Her mind kept trying to make connections, to draw parallels. Speaking to control when they first came through, she had wanted to say "the air smells like it did when we were on honeymoon in Tahiti." She was glad she hadn't. An experienced explorer (if such people still existed in the 2020s), or someone with a military background, would never have come out with something so unprofessional. But then she wasn't trained for this. None of them were.

She still had no idea what the common factor was that defined their small, disparate, group. Over six thousand volunteers had come forward when the Foundation went public with its discovery; how come only five – and why these five – were found to be capable of passing through the portal? Everyone else had been repelled before they got within a metre of it. No one claimed the five of them were the brightest and best amongst the volunteers. The only thing they had in common was that none of them had close family, but that was a prerequisite of being accepted on the volunteer program. Only the lonely, as she keeps thinking; she knew that Rory would have laughed at that, and said something like "Don't romanticize self-selection, Charli."

A chance to train and bond together would have made her little team (as she couldn't help thinking of them) more comfortable with each other, but given the portal's limited lifespan, the decision-makers had kept the 'softer' aspects of the mission's preparation to a minimum.

She wondered if any of the others had noticed the scuff mark on the edge of the portal platform when they arrived. If they had, no one mentioned it.

<start transmission>

We've nearly finished building the garden enclosure. The waste composter's up and running, and Ranjit's revised the soil requirements downwards slightly. As he says, the less mass you send now, the more time we've got to ask for whatever we forgot. Rainfall and temperature remain constant; Shelley says we've got ideal growing conditions.

<end transmission>

NOW SHE HAD been here for a couple of weeks, Charli found herself faintly disappointed that Alpha-One appeared so normal. (She disliked that designation, with its arrogant implication that there would be other sites, that opening a portal into this impossible place wasn't a fluke.) The cloudy sky could have been anywhere on Earth, the air composition was normal (that initial whiff not withstanding) and the buildings were human-scale. As Rory had said when the first probe went through, the city looked like it was made for, and presumably by, human-sized entities with bilateral symmetry. As for who, or where they were now, that was anyone's guess.

The colours of the structures that spread out to the horizon ranged from sandy yellow to mid-green – again, ordinary enough - but the stone did have a disconcerting translucency. She kept thinking 'alabaster' – reaching for those comforting analogies again – but she was an administrator, not a geologist, and whatever the towers were made of, she doubted anyone back on Earth had a name for it.

She hated the silence though, and did her best to drown it out, either by playing her music or by talking to the others. At night, when the tears came, she turned her head into her pillow rather than have the sound of crying drift out of the open doorway. These people were her responsibility; such stupid weakness would damage the group.

<start transmission>

Good Morning, Control. Frivolous news first: the chickens have started laying. We're having an omelette for supper. Just the one so far; we'll have the share it.

The drone sweeps are almost complete; Andresh has created a detailed map extending out from the portal in a two kilometre radius. Hassan still hasn't found any evidence of life, at least nothing our instruments can detect; we're glad we don't have to worry about alien bugs, though Ranjit isn't sure how this Earth-like atmosphere is being maintained without an obvious ecosystem. Perhaps we'll find something further out.

Ranjit hasn't had much luck analysing the portal from this end. There's no loose material here to throw back, so he chipped off a sample from an internal wall. The result was the same as with the terrestrial stone: it simply bounced off.

<end transmission>

"WHY YOU LET him do it?"

Charli tried not to mentally correct Andresh's grammar. "Because we needed to know if local material could get back through the portal."

"Is sacrilege, Charlotte."

She knew Andresh used her full name out of respect; correcting him would be counter-productive. "I appreciate that you feel that way about the city, but no harm was done. And I'm sure you want to get home as much as the rest of us."

"Of course I want to leave. We should not be here at all." With that, the team's archaeologist-cum-architect stalked off to his room, leaving Charli alone in the echoing space they had designated as the team's 'common room'.

Andresh had initially voiced his opinion that their presence broke some profound law of the universe over supper the previous evening. Ranjit had humoured him and Hassan had stayed silent but Shelley had appeared to take his side. 'Appeared to' because Shelley was beginning to step up her play for the men's attentions; Charli knew her type and with three men and two women, Shelley needed to make sure she came out scoring on top in the relationship stakes. Unfortunately, so far none of the men had seen that as a priority.

Charli was tempted to tell her that she could have all three for all she cared, but she knew that wouldn't help.

<start transmission>

Control, we found the initial probe; the one that disappeared. Well, what was left of it. We think it malfunctioned and ran off the portal platform. It actually fell all the way to the ground. Interestingly, although the probe was smashed up completely, there was very little damage to the area where it came down. I suppose we should have expected as much given that the ground's made of the same material as the towers are.

<end transmission>

"I'M NOT SAYING someone actually *pushed* it!" This was the closest Charli had seen Ranjit come to losing his temper. She found herself increasingly empathising with him, possibly because he was the nearest they had to a scientist – to the role Rory should have had. But not that near: he was a physics teacher. He had only applied for the programme as a way to enthuse the kids in his class about science. Ranjit never expected to end up on another world.

"I'm sure that's not what Shelley's saying either," said Charli, keeping her tone calm and conciliatory. "I think what she's getting at is that my report back to Control included conclusions that aren't entirely," Charli smiled tightly, "foregone."

Shelley said, "We all saw those marks on the edge. The probe was pushed."

Charli continued, "I agree that that's what it looks like. But the later probes were monitoring the platform and immediate area constantly after that and they saw nothing. We've found no evidence to indicate we aren't alone here. So, until and unless we do, the only logical explanation is some sort of spontaneous mechanical fault. If anyone can suggest any other *plausible* explanation, then please, just say."

No one did. The meal continued in silence, until Hassan, opening his dessert package, smiled and said, in his gentle, lilting voice, "Hey, these peaches taste of peach. Finally the boffins are getting it right!"

"Oh," said Shelley, "that reminds me. We've got shoots!"

Andresh and Hassan, the non-native speakers, looked momentarily confused, until Shelley leaned forward slightly and said, "Lettuces! They've come up. In the garden."

Everyone smiled at the news that they were one step closer to the self-sufficiency necessary for long-term survival. Shelley basked in their appreciation of her gardening skills. Charli felt a certain sympathy for the other woman: she was the only team member whose main function here had only been her hobby, not her career, back on Earth.

It was – nominally – midweek, so no after dinner games were scheduled. With the evening rain shower having passed, Charli decided to go for a walk. Shelley was flirting furiously; perhaps when she got back one of the men would have succumbed to her wiles, and everyone else could relax a little. Not for the first time, Charli thanked their good luck that the male contingent of the party didn't contain any alpha-types who would feel the need to fight for what Shelley was happy to give freely.

She considered fetching her lamp from the roof, where it had been charging all day ready to light her room at night, but decided against it; there was still an hour before night fell, and she wasn't going to be long. Days here were just over twenty four hours, with eight hours of darkness, perfect for human circadian rhythms, something which Charli had initially found a little creepy but which she was now grateful for. A well-rested team was going to work better together.

She had several set walks, circular routes through the stairways and passages of the city, but this evening she just wandered. Not that she was covering new ground. All of them were intimately familiar with every room, every staircase, within easy walking distance of their camp.

She found the statuette in a dead-end room, just lying on the floor, as though someone had dropped it there. At first she thought she was imagining it; the room was lit by a single window, and the light wasn't good. But when she looked closer she found a human figurine, only about ten centimetres high, made of the same material as the city.

She crouched down beside the object. Closer, she saw that it had more of a glow to it than the surrounding rock, although that might have been a trick of the light.

She reached out to pick it up.

It disappeared.

It didn't crumble to dust, she didn't drop it, it just... went away.

At the same moment, everything around her became crisper, sharper. Afterwards, the rush reminded her of her long-ago forays into recreational drug use, back when she was studying for her psychology degree. At the time, it caught her up utterly.

The next time she was aware enough to check, she found that three hours had passed. She straightened slowly – she had ended up sitting on the floor – and looked around. The room was dark, but not as dark as it should have been given that night had fallen. She could still see enough to take in the perfect beauty of the room, the way every angle, every wall, was correctly, perfectly proportioned.

She took her time getting back to camp. Despite the lack of light she felt no fear, merely a mild disappointment that she could not appreciate the view fully at night.

Hassan was still up. "We were going to send out searchers soon," he said in his slow, calm way.

"Thanks, but I'm fine. Better than fine." She almost told him what she had found; Hassam was the most likely to understand, with his air of peace hard won from his past as a child of war. But she was not sure how to begin to describe her experience, and so she said nothing, and went to her room where she fell asleep at once.

She never normally remembered her dreams but this one was vivid: in it, Rory was calling out to her from some sort of tower, trying to warn her about something. She struggled to get closer, to hear his warning, but whatever doom it was engulfed her then, and she woke up sweating and terrified.

<start transmission>

Control, we have a medical emergency.

It's Andresh. When he didn't turn up for breakfast I went to his room and found him lying in bed just staring at the ceiling. We can't find any sign of injury or illness. He just appears to have fallen into a coma.

Hassan has put him on a drip. We're not sure what else we can do.

<end transmission>

EVERYONE WAS SCARED. Each of them responded in their own way: Shelly with wild theories and demands for attention, Hassan with solicitous calm, Ranjit with an increasingly desperate search for the logical explanation. Charli observed their reactions, knowing full well that she should bring everyone together, should provide support and guidance in this time of crisis, but somehow disinclined to do so.

The suffusing beauty she had felt on picking up the statuette remained with her, though now tinged with unease. More than once, she found herself thinking: *this place is too much for us.* Had she believed in God, she might even have used words like 'holy' or 'divine'.

Andresh died the next night. No one was with him, and when they checked in the morning he looked exactly as he had when they left him, only dead. Hassan, after examining his body as best he could, said sadly, "It is almost as if his life just ebbed away."

"That's crazy-talk, Hassan." Shelley's warm tone belied her words; Hassan was finally responding to her overtures. "But if that's how it is, it's our duty not to despair, isn't it?"

Hassan nodded solemnly, taking Shelley's last comment at face value.

There being no way of burying or cremating Andresh, they carried his body down to ground level and left him in one of the rooms there. Charli suggested each one of them spend a while alone in the room with him, to say their farewell. It was a manufactured ritual, and they all knew it. Shelley was in there for only a few seconds; Ranjit for slightly longer; Hassan longer still, no doubt praying for their comrade. When Charli's turn came she reached for the gold crucifix Andresh wore. As she put it outside his shirt she whispered, "I think you were right about this place." For all the good that did now.

Charli did not feel grief as such; she hadn't known Andresh well enough for that. She did feel a kind of unfocused fear, because losing one of the group brought home the gravity of their situation. At the same time, she found herself increasingly disconnected from their small, mortal, problems. Being amongst such alien beauty gave her a strength she never knew she had. To walk on stone crafted by a powerful unknown race, to breathe the rich air – and it was rich, in every breath now – to hear that silence, which was more like distilled peace than an absence of sound: this was what truly mattered. She had been too busy worrying about who was happy and who wasn't, and stressing about what would happen when the portal closed, to revel in the wonder of being here, in this amazing, impossible place.

She didn't mention the figurine to the others. The time wasn't right. They had enough to deal with.

Shelley and Hassan got together three days after Andresh's death. Charli was distantly relieved that Shelley was being kept distracted.

Ranjit's response to Andresh's death was to throw himself into his work. He spent most of his time up at the portal platform, trying to find a way to get them home.

<start transmission>

Ranjit's come up with an idea about modifying the portal from this end and we reckon it's worth a try. His theory is based on lasers, and will probably mean more to you than it does to the rest of us. I'm going to give him the headset now so he can describe what he needs...

<end transmission>

"WHAT DO YOU mean 'team shrink'?" Charli snapped.

"Just what I said," retorted Shelley. "That's your qualification, isn't it? Your key skill."

"Oh, and yours is...?" Charli would never have let Shelley goad her like this a few weeks ago, never have let their discussion move onto an argument and into a full-scale row. "Because I'm not sure what use a spin doctor is to us out here."

"PR exec," said Shelley, tightly. *Good*, thought Charli, *I've got to her. See how she likes it.* Then she added, "But you're meant to be our beloved leader, even if that was naked nepotism."

"Why yes," said Charli, "my position is connected to having been married to the project's chief scientist, I won't deny that. Because I lived with Rory I had – still have – a higher level of knowledge of the portal than the rest of you. And I'm also more qualified to manage people than anyone else. If you didn't like that, you shouldn't have volunteered for the project. Most people have slightly less drastic mid-life crises than trying to run away to another world."

"It's a pretty dysfunctional response to grief, too." Before Charli could defend herself Shelly continued, "What I was saying about your position is true though. Given that you are our leader, how come you're spending so much time wandering round the city? You're meant to be there for us, aren't you?"

"I am, if anyone wants me. They don't. And it's not like anything I – or any of us - can do is going to change things. We need to accept our situation."

"You're losing the fucking plot, Charli," said Shelley, and walked off.

The insult did not hurt as much as it should have.

<start transmission>

Control, I'm afraid that Ranjit hasn't succeeded. He also injured himself in the attempt. I think he threw himself at the portal. He's bruised, perhaps concussed. Hassan has sedated him. We'll report any further developments.

<end transmission>

CHARLI KNEW ABOUT denial; she had studied its mechanics, and had seen it in operation in the many teams she had managed throughout her administrative career. Part of her knew Shelley had a point; she was neglecting her duties. But why not? Ranjit had devoted himself to his work, Shelly and Hassan had each other. Why shouldn't she enjoy the city she was coming to love?

She only realised her ulterior motive when she found the next figurine.

Again, it was in a location that had been empty before, this time near ground level. Charli didn't hesitate: she sat down and reached out eagerly.

The rush this time was not quite the same. Less intense: more familiar. Almost as if something already inside her was being enhanced. And the afterglow was different: instead of the sense of reverence and beauty she felt an incredible peace, and a surety that she could bring harmony to those around her, if only she could get them to see the wonders they walked among. When she recovered enough to look around her, the colours of the city seemed brighter and her body felt more alive. And the silence sang to her.

She rushed back to the camp; this time she should tell them, and it would bring them together, and even if, as Charli had now come to suspect, there would never be a way back, it wouldn't matter.

There was no one there. Charli didn't panic: she was beyond panic. Ranjit would still be at the portal. Shelley and Hassan were probably out and about somewhere. They'd come back when they were ready.

<start transmission>

Control: Hassan's disappeared. The three of us are going to look for him now.

<end transmission>

"WHEN DID YOU last see him?" Charli had to force the concern into her voice, fighting the calm veil that had descended over her.

"This morning. He said he was going out for a walk. Like you keep doing, you know?"

"Charli! Shelley!"

They both turned at Ranjit's shout, drifting up from the platform outside the common room window.

"I've found him."

Charli wasn't surprised that Hassan was unconscious. He'd collapsed on a high platform, a step away from a steep slope.

Shelley stayed with him. The next day Hassan died, as Charli knew he would. Shelley insisted that she and Ranjit help her carry his body back to base camp. Ranjit looked to her for guidance, and after a moment's thought she agreed. The flesh was nothing, but she may as well humour Shelley.

It wasn't as though Charli spent much time at the camp anyway. She spent her days, and some nights, walking the city. She knew now that it had not been built in the same way humans build things. It had grown here. Or coalesced. There were no words in her limited human vocabulary to express the concepts nibbling at the edge of her consciousness. This was like waiting for an inevitable revelation, but the more she tried to analyse the feeling, to pin it down, the faster it receded. Which was why she needed to keep looking for the figurines.

She still tried to reconnect, when she remembered. She knew, intellectually, that Ranjit and Shelley were her responsibility.

She also knew that Andresh's and Hassan's deaths were her fault. The others had no idea. Shelley was panicking about alien diseases, but whatever killed Andresh and Hassan wasn't a disease. It was a condition twenty-first century science had no concept of, like dying of a broken heart. She had actually thought she might do that, when Rory went. She could barely remember that pain now.

She needed very little sleep these days, but whenever she did rest she dreamt constantly. Not about Rory again; the dreams almost felt as if they belonged to someone else, and they evaporated when she opened her eyes.

<start transmission>

Control, there's only me and Shelley left now.

Ranjit jumped off the portal platform. He left a note. It said, 'I'm so sorry I couldn't get us home.'

That's all.

<end transmission>

CHARLI DECIDED TO move up to the camp Ranjit had made at the portal. There was an element of guilt in her decision, she observed coolly: she knew she should have seen the signs in him, spotted that he was low enough to kill himself. That was her job. Had been her job.

When she told Shelley she was going to the portal, the other woman screamed at her. "You can't!"

"Are you worried about your garden? You can still tend it, if you like." Not that Charli was concerned with food much anymore.

"Sod the fucking garden. You see everything around you as puzzles to be solved, Charli, but we're *people*. Were people. Most of us are *dead* now. You don't care about anyone or anything, do you?"

"I cared about Rory."

"Really?"

"When he died," Charli paused, able now to look at the gap her husband's death had torn in her without feeling the pain, "my heart died too."

"So you're sure he's dead?"

"What do you mean?"

"I saw his file. I saw quite a lot of files, some of which I don't think you ever knew about."

"What? How?"

"Oh, the how was just... I persuaded someone. That's my talent."

"Your talent... yes. Yes it is. Whore."

"*What?*"

"Your archetype. You use affection, attention, and of course sex, to get what you want –"

"– why you –"

"– yes, because Andresh was an ascetic and spiritual seeker, Hassan was a healer and mediator. Ranjit was a logical explainer, a teacher; he despaired because nothing made sense and he had no one to explain it to anyway. Of course! That's it: archetypes. It's all about archetypes."

"I have no idea what you're on about, Charli."

Charli looked at Shelley, coming back to the present conversation. "It doesn't matter. Not to you. What did you find out about Rory?"

"The Foundation would never let him go through. He was too valuable. After all, he'd come up with the design in the first place. In a dream, apparently."

Charli thought back to her old life, so distant now. "He was concerned they might not let him go. But he said he'd persuade them. And then he disappeared. Killed himself." That betrayal, so unexpected, so complete; she'd nearly died of it too.

"Disappeared, yes. Killed himself, no. They found his car, his apparent suicide note, but not his body."

"I know that. The river was in flood –"

"I think he came here. He built the portal, so of course he could come through it, but because the powers that be thought he might be able to build another, he knew he would never be *allowed* to go through. And he cared about the portal more than he cared about you, Charli. So he faked his death and came through. When he got here, he trashed the probe that would have filmed him leaving the platform. It all fits."

"Yes," said Charli, slowly, "it does."

"What? You call me a whore then agree with my theory? What the hell have you become?"

"I'm not sure. You work it out, if it matters to you. I'm going back to the portal. I'm going to bring this back to everyone, this revelation." Because the alternative, the seductive, dangerous alternative was that she would just keep searching for the figurines, and never stop.

Shelley shouted after her, "*What* revelation?"

Charli ignored her.

SHE FIRED UP Ranjit's computer more out of curiosity than because she expected to find anything of use. Somewhat to her surprise she understood what he had been trying to do at once.

The key was light, or rather EM emissions. Solid objects couldn't pass back through the portal, but radio waves could. What she needed to do was convert herself to light.

It sounded crazy, but six months ago a portal to another world had sounded crazy.

But it had been beyond Ranjit's abilities. *Ah, so that had been the final straw, the reason he jumped.*

Was it beyond hers? Her mind was so much sharper, so much bigger, than it had been.

But she needed more. She needed to find and absorb another statuette.

Except there wasn't one to be found. She searched for the best part of a day, climbing the steepest steps, descending down to the shadowed ground, looking into every room she passed.

As she ascended the staircase back up to the portal platform, she heard something. A tiny sound, too faint to identify, but enough to disturb the perfect silence. She hurried up the last few steps.

Her camp had been destroyed. The modulating laser, Ranjit's laptop: all smashed.

As Charli stood there, staring at the devastation, Shelley stepped out from behind the warped mirror of the portal. She was holding the hand-gun the team had been issued in case they had, despite the evidence of the probe, found any hostiles. Charli had forgotten about the gun. They had all had basic training but, on Charli's recommendation, Hassan had been looking after the weapon. Thanks to his unpleasant childhood in Africa, Hassan both knew how to use a gun, and would be unwilling to do so lightly.

"I found one too," said Shelley, conversationally.

Charli flinched to hear the silence broken. "One what?" she made herself say.

"You know what. A statue."

Charli said nothing. Part of her, the part that had arrived here, felt vindicated; in occasional cold, logical moments, when she stopped to think, she had worried at the lack of corroborating evidence for her experiences. Save for the dead team members, she might have thought she was going mad.

Shelley advanced on her. "Stop pretending, Charli. You've obviously found more than one. You've changed so much. I want to know what you know, what you're planning."

"No."

"I'm the one with the gun, Charli."

"So you are." Charli rushed her. It wasn't a conscious decision, and her mind caught up a fraction of a second later, and was appalled.

The gun clicked.

Charli barged into Shelley. Neither of them knew how to fight. They were just grappling, wrestling. Then Charli managed to knock the gun out of Shelley's hand; Shelley's gaze followed it, just for a moment, then caught as the gun fell.

Everything seemed to slow down. Charli knew she was fated to push her, and that Shelley was fated to step back. Once. Again, because she was off-balance now. Then again.

And then there was nothing to step back onto.

She didn't make a sound as she fell. Charli experienced brief gratitude and respect towards her for that.

The gun must not have been loaded. Hassan had probably emptied it, when he saw how things were going.

Charli looked around. She was unsurprised to find a figurine lying in front of the portal. It hadn't been there earlier. She reached out for it.

This time, the rush knocked her unconscious instantly.

<start transmission>

Control, this is the last message you'll get from me. Don't bother to reply.

We shouldn't be here. I know that now. This city – what we perceive as a city – is not somewhere we are ever meant to see. Not while we're alive, anyway. That makes it sound like heaven, but that's not it. This isn't hell either. More like a dimension of the spirit. No, still too mystical. Though I keep thinking of that biblical quote: 'In my Father's house there are many mansions.'

Part of us lives here. Part of all of us. All humans. And I think it manifests, possibly in response to our physical presence, possibly spontaneously. It's about archetypes, you see. The five of us who came through were each the epitome of a given archetype. That didn't make us extraordinary people, just the ideal representative of a particular personality.

And sometimes those archetypes manifest here, in a reduced, symbolic form. I found some of those representations. I... took them on myself. The archetypes they corresponded to didn't survive. Just gave up life. I do wonder if those statuettes represented actual people, back on Earth, and whether those individuals died too. I think they probably did, in which case, I'm sorry.

The last statuette I found, I think that was 'mine'. My archetype, anyway. Certainly I've experienced an exponential increase in my mental capacity. I'm definitely more-than-human now. Food, sleep, bodily functions, these are no longer relevant. I dream all the time now. And the towers aren't silent anymore.

For the record, I did want to get back to Earth, at least before that final statuette. I had such wisdom to impart. But that's changed. We weren't meant to come here, but we did. And what I've – *we've* – become isn't something that should ever be allowed to return.

None of this is testable, of course. But I'm going to ask Rory, if I find him. He's been here far longer than me; he'll have taken more statuettes. Of course, if this city really is infinite, I'm unlikely to run across him. But I'll keep looking. After all, I've got all the time in the world.

<end transmission>

ETERNITY'S CHILDREN

KEITH BROOKE AND ERIC BROWN

Keith Brooke is the author of a dozen novels, including The Accord *(Solaris),* The Unlikely World of Faraway Frankie *(NewCon Press) and* alt.human *(due from Solaris in 2012). He lives in Essex, but please don't hold that against him. Eric Brown has published forty books which have been translated into sixteen languages, and more than a hundred short stories. He is a two-time winner of the BSFA Award for short fiction. Eric also writes a monthly SF review column for the* Guardian. *'Eternity's Children' is the latest of several collaborations between Eric and Keith, and a collection of their co-written work,* Parallax View, *is available from Immanion Press.*

LOFTUS SANK INTO the body-couch as the shuttle began the spiraldown towards the surface of Karenia, 31 Cygni VII. Far below, the colony world was a vast dappled meniscus arcing across the void; above, the supergiant binary system burned bright, 31 Cygni A and B almost joined in a single fiery mass.

Loftus had made the journey to Karenia three times over the past hundred and fifty years – visits always hedged with trepidation – but this trip would be the last.

"Ed? You 'kay?" Softly, the question came from the woman at his side.

He turned from the viewscreens.

The body-couch swaddled all but her tanned face, making Elana look like a baby in a papoose.

"I'm fine." He tried to keep the weariness from his tone and returned his contemplation to the view below. Seen from this altitude, as the shuttle sliced through the troposphere, the planet appeared wrapped in chiffon clouds of mauve, with glimpses of purple and blue land between the strands.

Minutes later, he glanced at Elana and saw that her eyes were closed, her face serene. She was one hundred and seventy years his junior. Sometimes this charmed him, her youthful enthusiasm, her often startling naiveté, spilling over, filling him with a renewed zest for life; sometimes it irked.

Now, he looked at his lover's peaceful, innocent features and he felt physically sick, assailed by guilt again.

Why had he asked her to accompany him to Karenia? Simply because it was easier to have her here, an emotional crutch, a distraction from other, more intense guilt?

One hour later they made touchdown.

"THIS MIGHT BE a little uncomfortable," Loftus murmured.

Elana nodded, her dark eyes tracking the movements of the medic in the sealed terminal obelisk as he withdrew the slug from its wrap and approached her.

"Open up."

She opened her mouth and accepted the clear bolus of gel. She swallowed hard, and pulled a face. "God..." she gagged. "It tastes awful. And..." She shook her head as the bolus coated her trachea and climbed her nasal passages, creating a seal which would act as a barrier against the poisonous spores of Karenia.

Loftus swallowed his own slug and closed his eyes. He would never get used to the sensation of the bolus at work in his head. It felt as if a mouthful of food had come to life and was trying to escape through his nostrils. He felt the membrane coating his eyeballs, and his vision temporarily blurred.

The medic passed them each a blister-pack containing two small pills. "Take the first when you're safely back aboard the shuttle, the second an hour later. They'll have dissolved the membrane by the time you reach the ship." Finally, the medic added, "And remember: the barrier will only last for four weeks max; after that it becomes too loaded with spore debris and you..."

"We suffocate," Loftus finished for him. He slipped the pills into his breast pocket. "Okay," he said. "Let's get out there."

THE AIRLOCK DOORS hissed open and Loftus heard Elana gasp.

"It's beautiful," she said.

Loftus nodded, and blamed the lump in his throat on the protective membrane.

The landing strip was a gash carved through jungle that twisted and tangled in gaudy purple knots as high as a Tokyo skyscraper. Whistles and buzzes filled the air, shifting in pitch and volume so that Loftus felt as if his ears were continually blocking and clearing. Looking to his right along the landing strip, he could see through the jungle to rolling hills, cultivated land, fields with grooved rows of kreen, all of it shading from blue-green through blue to purple.

A fine haze overlay everything, like gauze held up before the eyes. The pale lavender mist was the effect of the ubiquitous spores, a constant reminder that this planet, despite its idyllic first impression, was deadly.

It was, as Elana had said, quite beautiful, and Loftus was here to destroy the place.

He rolled his aching shoulders. Karenia was a planet like a dozen others, just another backwater colony world. He was here to do a job, no more.

His musing was disturbed by a gentle touch on his arm. "Can I go first?" asked Elana. "I need an establishing shot."

She stepped from the airlock and walked across the apron. At its lip she stood and swung her head in a wide arc, sweeping from the tangled wall of jungle to the nicely framed view of fields at the far end of the landing strip, the first buildings of Turballe.

Loftus left the airlock and came up behind her, listening to her commentary.

"Karenia, the world to which everyone in the Expansion owes so much. For it was here, three hundred years ago, that Omega-Gen researchers made the discovery that would change the destiny of our species..."

He wandered out of earshot of her clichés. Three other shuttles were parked to one side of the landing strip. Their cargo bays gaped wide as workers transferred hessian-swaddled bales of processed kreen from drays pulled by native draft animals resembling eight-legged rhinoceroses.

Work paused as the men and women caught sight of him. They stared, with something like wonder in their eyes. Even here at the port, off-worlders were an infrequent sight; despite Karenia's inherent beauty and historic significance, not many were willing to endure the protective bolus in order to visit. Everything about him, he knew, would appear strange to these workers, from his tight, bright apparel to his attenuated thinness. The colonists were short, dumpy, and garbed in loose dun jackets and pantaloons. Like something from Brueghel, he thought.

He raised a hand in a brief salute, and they smiled and waved in return, then resumed their work.

"Ed?" Elana called.

He turned. She was striding towards him, beaming. This was the start of an adventure, to her. She could think no further than her reports. Footage from this visit would be netted widely, used and re-used by anyone with an interest in the reclusive world that had allowed humankind to battle the tyranny of time. This trip would make her name.

"You're not still...?" he began.

"No. I caught you here, silhouetted against the sky. I'm glad you waved. It was a gesture both of greeting and almost of farewell." He stared at her and wondered if her radiant youth and beauty disguised an insight he had failed to apprehend, or if, perhaps, he was finally succumbing to her banalities.

Just then, a wheeled vehicle drew up in a cloud of dust. A short figure jumped out, flustered by his late arrival. He was grey-haired, rubicund in healthy old age.

"Mr Loftus!" the man called, approaching with his hands spread wide. "Mr Loftus, Ms Kryadies... Welcome to Karenia. We're honoured. I'm sorry I wasn't here to greet you..." The man gestured at his vehicle. "I had a breakdown." He spoke a formal bureaucrat's English and his accent was muddy, words running together in a thick rush of consonants. Loftus managed to follow, but he could see that Elana was struggling.

The man held out a stubby hand. "I'm Christopher. Christopher Dupré."

Loftus accepted the archaic gesture of the handshake, anticipating Christopher's grip and trying not to wince.

"Christopher." Loftus smiled. "You were..."

"I was five," Christopher said. "But I remember you. I still have the plastic horse you gave me back then."

Loftus recalled the tubby, red-faced boy from his last visit, and fought back the sadness that welled within him.

Christopher smiled. "Sixty years ago... who would believe it?" He looked Loftus up and down, taking in the visitor's unchanged appearance. "Come, I'll show you to the manse. I've already picked up your luggage."

"Everything is in place for the board meeting?" Loftus asked.

Christopher paused, and Loftus felt a moment's guilt for steering his host back to the business of his visit. The man nodded, said, "Yes, Mr Loftus, it's all prepared. We meet tomorrow."

They descended the steps and eased themselves into the car in testy silence.

Sixty years ago Loftus had been greeted by Alain Dupré, Christopher's father, then in his late thirties... He had last heard from Alain eighteen years ago, a brief message to say that his sister Helen had passed away. It would be too much to hope that the wry, philosophically-minded patriarch would still be alive.

"Alain...?" said Loftus, cursing Karenia's inwardness, the lack of information at his disposal.

Christopher smiled over his shoulder as he took a track through abruptly thinning jungle. "My father is looking forward to meeting you again," he said.

His initial surprise and delight that Alain was alive was soon followed, inevitably, by despair. What he had to tell the people of Karenia would be hard enough, but he had assumed he would be telling it to a world of strangers... In the few days he had spent on Karenia sixty years ago, Alain had become a friend.

"He's one hundred in a month," Christopher continued. "He wasn't up to making the journey, though he wanted to. He's been wheelchair-bound for a few years now. But," Christopher tapped his head, "he still has it up here."

They passed through fields of native herbs. Loftus stared at the tangled rows of kreen, the turquoise vegetation towering metres high.

To Elana, Christopher said, "We're honoured to have you here, Ms Kryadies. I hope you appreciate that you will have unprecedented access to Karenia. We are an insular people... We do not welcome the scrutiny of others. If it were not for Mr Loftus..." He paused, then went on, "We would hope that you do not take this access lightly, and that you will ask at all times before recording. My people are not all as outward-looking as I am."

"Of course," said Elana disingenuously. Loftus knew she would be filming this exchange already. "I am honoured by your welcome."

Loftus turned away and stared through the side window. He just wanted this to be over.

"WOOD..." ELANA SAID, in awe. She fingered the warped timbers of the balcony as if they were gold. To her future audience, she said, "Far from being proscribed as it is on Earth, here on Karenia timber is the staple building material. The manse is almost three hundred years old."

Loftus watched her. So young, with hundreds of years ahead of her. Could she truly apprehend the fact that she would still be alive, barring accidents, in a thousand years? What did that mean to her?

Could he, for that matter? At a hundred and seventy he felt old, weary, dragged down by the anomie of virtual immortality.

She swung to face him, bearing down with her invisible retinal-cams. "Edward Loftus, what's it like to be back on Karenia after so long?"

He raised a forbearing hand. "Please, Elana. Not now, okay?"

She touched her temple, stilled the cams, murmured, "Sorry, Ed."

He pulled her to him and they kissed, and again he felt a pang of guilt that he should so easily dismiss her and find comfort in her within a single breath. "It's okay," he said. "I'm tired. It was a long trip."

They stood side by side at the balcony rail and gazed out over the hazed land. Crops of kreen swept away across the rolling terrain. The two great suns hung in the sky, grossly swollen in comparison to Sol; the first, burnt orange, was going down over a range of mountains to the east. The second, smaller and redder, sat at its zenith. Midday at this latitude was hot on Karenia, eased only by the stiff southerly breeze.

In the distance, smudged, were the kiln houses where the crops were dried and the drug extracted. From there it would begin the long journey back to Earth, starting on a dray cart and finishing on a faster-than-light ship.

"Edward!" Loftus turned. "Edward, it's great to see you again!" The voice was strong, in contrast to the shrunken man who sat, wedged by cushions, in the wheelchair pushed by Christopher.

Alain Dupré smiled out of a sunken, lined face.

Loftus felt something constrict in his throat.

"Alain," he said, advancing and taking the man's frail hand. "It's good to be back. This is Elana. Elana Kryadies."

Elana was visibly shocked by the manifest ill-health of the man before her. Such physical infirmities were beyond her experience.

She rallied, smiled, and took his thin hand in a brief shake. "May I film?" she asked.

Alain gestured with a frail hand and nodded. "Come. Lunch is prepared. We'll eat downstairs on the veranda."

The patriarch descended the timber staircase on a stairlift, the others following slowly. Dupré grinned up at them. "Bet you thought you'd never see me again, eh, Edward?"

"Well, to be honest..."

Dupré laughed. "I'm surprised I'm here myself. I'm a hundred in just over four weeks. The medics give me another month, so I might just hit the century if I'm lucky."

Beside him, Loftus heard Elana draw a sharp breath.

Dupré went on, "Cancer. Brought on by the genetic engineering. How ironic! A two edged sword, eh, Edward?"

"Can't anything be done...?" Loftus began lamely, then cursed himself.

"What? Here on Karenia, at my age? Now maybe on Earth..." Dupré said, and winked.

Loftus felt a well of despair open within him.

"But I've had a hell of a long life, I'll take my destiny," the patriarch was saying as he rolled his chair from the stairlift and trundled across the polished timber floor to a sun-flooded veranda overlooking the fields.

A table was loaded with fresh food.

"Please, be seated." Dupré gestured to a cluster of chairs.

A woman came onto the veranda, bearing a jug of juice. Christopher Dupré made the introductions. "This is Catherine, my daughter-in-law. My son Jack – Catherine's husband – is busy with the kilns."

Catherine was tiny and dark, and could scarcely bring herself to meet the eyes of these long-lived strangers from Earth. When she did look at Loftus, he experienced a sudden shock and the memories flooded back, bitter-sweet.

Only when she bent, carefully, to place the jug on the table, did Loftus notice the bulge of her belly. He couldn't help but stare.

Elana touched her temple and looked at Loftus, recording his reaction.

Dupré pulled himself up to the table. "My great granddaughter is due in six weeks, Edward. It's my ambition to see her before I go."

Steeling himself, Loftus smiled and said, "And I'm sure you will, Alain. I'm sure you will."

They took their seats and ate a simple meal of bread, cheese and salad, and Loftus tried to banish all thoughts of Catherine and her child.

Loftus wondered if Alain Dupré had picked up, from his manner, that all was not right on this visit. The old man possessed an intelligence that Loftus found daunting, as well as a keen insight into the workings of the human heart.

"Life here is simple," he had told Loftus sixty years ago. "The rest of the Expansion might think us backward peasants, Edward, but the slow, rural way of life gives us time to dwell, to consider the way of things... We prefer to turn inwards. We are at one with our world in ways that more... *modern* societies have lost."

Elana spoke up, "Mr Dupré, I wonder if I might ask you a few questions? I would be interested in knowing more about your life."

The old man smiled. "A museum piece, eh? And don't call me Mr Dupré, okay? I'm Alain."

. "I'm sorry. Alain. I was wondering..."

Loftus busied himself spreading soft cheese on a piece of coarsely grained bread, mentally wincing at the thought of what crass inanity Elana might consider a legitimate question.

"I must admit, Alain, that I was expecting... I don't know – not so much hostility, but perhaps suspicion from the people of Karenia, despite the assurances

Edward gave me. Could you say something about how you regard us... the people of the Expansion?"

"Other than that you have lost touch with the universe, you mean?" Dupré laughed and waved a chunk of bread. "You know, we don't have long-lifers along that often–" He winked at Loftus. "So it's good to have the opportunity to talk."

"You don't resent us?"

Beside Dupré, his son smiled and shook his head. The patriarch matched the gesture. "Of course not, Elana," the old man said. "So we live eighty, ninety, a hundred years if we're lucky. While the rest of you out there – if you can afford the treatment! – live a thousand years and more... but you've got to understand that this is our choice. We live peaceful, quiet lives. We expect no more. In fact, I'm filled with horror at the thought of possibly living a thousand years."

"But you're not angered by the irony that it is the drug that you harvest which grants the rest of us...?"

"Angered? But our forefathers knew the deal when they chose to stay on here. And we're paid well in return for the drug – how would we be able to afford the genetic treatment for our children which makes them immune to the effects of the spores–?"

"Some critics of Omega-Gen accuse them of having it both ways," Elana went on. "They say that Omega-Gen is getting the anti-ageing drug, and you're paying for the genetic treatment that allows you to harvest it for them."

Dupré shook his head, almost sadly. "They pay us well, and that allows us to live here, in paradise. We are a part of this world, Ms Kryadies, just as it is a part of us."

Jesus Christ, Loftus thought, hanging his head. What will they think of Omega-Gen after what I have to say at the board meeting tomorrow? He glanced across at Catherine, the curve of her belly just visible over the table. What will they think?

"Edward?" It was Dupré, his tone solicitous.

Loftus quickly lifted his head. "I'm sorry. I'm fine. A little tired, that's all.".

"Well, don't stand on ceremony, Edward. Why not go take a siesta?" The patriarch smiled. "We have plenty of time to do the tour this afternoon."

"That's kind of you." Loftus rose from the table and left the veranda. At the foot of the stairs, Elana caught up with him. "Ed?"

"I really am tired, Elana. Give me an hour alone and I'll be fine, okay?"

Smiling uncertainly, she nodded and returned to the veranda – no doubt, Loftus thought, to continue her damned interrogation.

He found the bedroom, lay down and attempted unsuccessfully to sleep.

"WE'LL GO THROUGH the fields to the location of puffball prime, as I call it," Dupré said, and then for the benefit of Elana, "It's the nearest puffball to the manse. They go off twice a day, and it's quite spectacular. We should just be in time to catch the second eruption."

They rode on the flat-bed of a rickety tractor, bales of kreen doubling as stolid cushions. Christopher steered the tractor along the narrow lanes between the purple fields, Alain Dupré riding beside him in a jerry-rigged frame containing his wheelchair.

"I still like to get out and about," he explained. "And an eruption is one of the highlights of the day."

Cygni B had set, while Cygni A still rode high in the sky. Karenia was commencing its long, slow swing around its primary sun: the period of total daylight was coming to an end. Soon, in a matter of days, Karenia would move away from between the suns and around the back of Cygni A, and the planet would face the immense darkness of space every night. Then the people of the colony world would experience a period, lasting some ten days, of total darkness, sixteen hours out of thirty two. The colonists called this period True Night.

"It's a special time," the old man called over his shoulder to Elana, prompted by her question about True Night. "I suppose it's natural that we should come to see True Night as special, occurring as it does only every eighteen Terran months, but we take our lead from the Yanth. It's a kind of festival for us, and for them too: we share the same space along the river, mix freely... It's quite something."

Once, sixty years ago, Loftus had caught a fleeting glimpse of the planet's native, semi-sentient species immediately following a period of True Night. They were small, blue, upright lizards – or that was the approximation he made at the time – perhaps a metre tall and, like their Terran analogue, fleet of movement. They possessed a rudimentary language and for much of the time dwelled in great catacombs underground, emerging only during True Night and the periods of twilight on either side.

Dupré said, "They might look like lizards, but really they're much more like mammals. They have warm blood, they give birth to live young, not eggs, and have a kind of fur growing from the base of their body scales. They have a complex social structure, too. The most comprehensive xenological study done, way back, drew parallels with our australopithecines. Anyway, they celebrate True Night by flooding from their dwellings and consuming the fruit buds of the kreen crops."

Elana said, "And it's this consumption, when evacuated, which seeds the land for the next crop?"

Dupré smiled. "That's right. You've done your homework. So the cycle continues, and however unlikely it is, the people of the Expansion are in debt to these tiny, rarely seen troglodyte creatures. Or rather, indebted to the seeds they shit out." Dupré winked as he said this, and Loftus suppressed a smile.

They bumped along in silence for another fifteen minutes, before Dupré pointed and said, "Ah... there it is."

Loftus followed the direction of the patriarch's wavering finger. They had come over the crest of a small rise and before them spread a great purple plain dotted with kiln houses, all distorted and part-obscured by a diaphanous lavender haze. Half a kilometre ahead Loftus made out the hemispherical dome of a puffball, perhaps ten metres across, swelling from the surrounding fields like an ugly grey goitre.

"The eruption will be triggered by the rising heat of the afternoon," the old man said. "Once a certain internal temperature is reached, it's explosion time."

Dupré himself had taken Loftus to witness the eruption of a puffball sixty years ago, the day before he was due back aboard the mothership. He'd marvelled at the spectacular explosion, but had regretted missing True Night a few days later and the consequent alien ceremony.

This time he would witness everything, the eruption and the festivities at True Night – and the guilt that he would be bringing the colonists' way of life to an end would be compounded.

Dupré was saying, "The puffballs and the kreen exist in a symbiotic relationship. The spores of the puffball give nourishment to the kreen plants, and the kreen, in turn, rot back into the earth and compost the puffballs. Of course, we're careful to ensure that when we harvest the kreen, we return a percentage of it to the fields."

Christopher brought the tractor to a halt on the lane fifty metres from the domed puffball. No kreen grew in the vicinity, and they had a grandstand view of the swollen growth.

Loftus watched Elana. She was staring eagerly at the puffball, like a child anticipating fireworks.

They had discussed his mission to Karenia before light-out aboard the mothership, and Loftus had been angered by her simple acceptance of the inevitable. He wondered if it were her youth, her belief in the manifest destiny of the human race, which sanctioned her pragmatism: so a way of life on a colony world would come to an end, and families would be torn apart, but the colony had served its purpose in the scheme of things...

Paradoxically it was he, Loftus, the Omega-Gen company man, whose conscience was riddled with doubt and pre-emptive remorse.

The patriarch's excited commentary brought him back to the present.

"Listen. Hear that? It's the rind, splitting in the heat. Just seconds away from blowing."

Loftus turned his attention to the puffball. Under immense internal pressure, the grey skin of the dome was swelling, splitting. As they watched, a loud crack like the report of a rifle split the air and the apex of the puffball detonated, the flesh lacerating as a vast cloud of purple spores shot into the sky in a plume hundreds of metres high.

Laughing, they watched the spores spread and drift and rain down around them, like lilac confetti, glittering and flickering in the sunlight.

Dupré breathed deeply, and as Loftus watched him he thought he saw a revitalising glow bringing colour to the old man's cheeks.

Loftus pulled a wipe from his pocket and passed it to Elana. Already he could feel the membrane at work in his throat and nasal passages, expelling the powdery spores.

A thick, mauve gunk was running from Elana's nose, spreading along her top lip. She mopped up the mess, pulling a face. Feeling a tickle below his nose, Loftus put a finger to one nostril and blew hard, spraying the ground with purple snot, then repeated the process with the other side. He nodded to Elana, who was filming him, and said, "They call it the bushman's handkerchief."

Nearby, Dupré giggled at them. "It does have the effect of making one rather... light-headed," the patriarch said. "Even, I venture, euphoric."

Elana turned to him. "What did the first settlers here make of the puffballs?" she asked.

Dupré was watching the slowly falling spore mist with rheumy eyes. Loftus wondered whether that was an effect of the spores themselves or pity for those first settlers. He turned and smiled at Elana, at the millions of viewers who would watch her documentary in the years to come.

"The first colonists worked for an exploration company out of Mars," the old man said. "It was a second-rate, cost-cutting venture that sent out ill-equipped colony teams on the cheap." He shrugged. "They found Karenia and studied the biology. The chemists gave the place the all clear. The spores didn't seem anything other than a cause of the sniffles and a pretty optical effect. It was only forty, fifty years later that the effects of the spores began to manifest. Just as they eat away at the lining of the gut of the Yanth, they attack the moist membranes of our lungs and throat, leaching virus-like particles into our bloodstream."

"Colonists began dying," Elana supplied.

"They succumbed to a spectrum of gradual wasting diseases and neurological dysfunctions and died within six months of first presenting symptoms. Few lived beyond about forty years. The colony faced evacuation, but then some of the biochemical studies showed interesting results. Omega-Gen bought out the original exploration company and followed up the early, somewhat crude studies. They found that the kreen, or rather extracts from it, helped in the treatment of certain cancers. At the same time they found a gene tweak that allowed people to live here without full biohazard suits, so that each generation, when receiving the splice, had immunity from the deadly effects of the spores. What they couldn't do, of course, was prevent the colonists developing a biological dependency, one similar to the Yanth's; that dependency is genetic: just as the gene-splice protected us from the spores, it bound us to them."

And therein lay the irony of the situation, Loftus thought. The colonists were dependent on the spores, but the spores could not be synthesised, and they broke down within a day or two of release, so the colonists could never travel off-world. They were tied to Karenia.

Dupré was saying, for the benefit of the viewers who would one day watch Elana's documentary, "Not long after Omega-Gen began taking the kreen, one of their chemists chanced on a miraculous discovery: a variant of the chemical that stopped cancer cells multiplying and allowed normal body cells to divide beyond the telomere-shortening limit, so that subject primates tended to stay young and live beyond their normal span. It wasn't long before the drug was tested on humans, and so extended longevity was achieved."

A silence fell then, and Loftus considered what Dupré had left unspoken...

A SHORT TIME later they arrived at the kiln house. Christopher lifted his father from the tractor and propelled the wheelchair into the cavernous shadow of the building.

Loftus followed, taking in the heady aroma of dried kreen.

The kiln house was like a vast timber barn, packed with lines of funnel-shaped vats underneath each of which was an oil-fuelled heater. The heat was intense, and workers, naked to the waist, transferred tangled bundles of kreen from the back of tractors and pitch-forked them into the vats.

Dupré led Loftus and Elana through the open-ended barn and indicated a conveyor belt onto which the funnels discharged the desiccated remains of the kreen plant, a mounded mix of blue-green fibres and grey ash. He talked them through every stage of the plant's harvest and treatment, Elana switching between paying close attention and wandering off for establishing shots and different perspectives for the final edit.

Loftus moved away, heading for the sunlight. He emerged from the furnace heat of the kiln house, into the relative cool of the day, and leaned against the timber frame.

He wondered if it had been the sight of the kiln house workers and the knowledge that this scene would be multiplied a million-fold across the face of the planet that brought the reality of the situation into stark relief.

In a matter of months all this would cease to be; an entire way of life, a culture with its traditions and rituals built up over two centuries, would be no more.

And here he was, their Judas, welcomed into the home of an old friend only to tell them that all this was over.

He sensed movement beside him, and turned. Elana was watching him, with her documentary eyes: he wondered how long she had been filming him.

She walked away and swept her head in an arc, taking in the lie of the land, the turquoise crops of kreen overlaid with the gauzy mist of the puffball spores, and commenced a portentous voice-over.

"Tragedy compounds tragedy, here on Karenia. The colonists are tied to their planet by their dependency on the spores that cannot be synthesised. Also, they are doomed to live lives as did our forbears: four score and ten, on average. The tragic fact is this: the terrible price the colonists must pay for their dependency is that their metabolism is rendered immune to the effects of the anti-ageing drug, itself a derivative of the spore-kreen symbiosis."

Elana turned, suddenly, to face Loftus. She was perhaps five metres away, staring at him intently. "And as if that were not tragedy enough, this man must tell them that their way of life here on Karenia is coming to an end."

Despite a sudden flare of anger, Loftus played his part, an actor in a docu-drama that would enthral millions. Pained, he turned and walked slowly into the kiln house.

Dupré lifted his hand in a genial wave. "Ah, there you are, Edward. How about we get back and rest up before dinner this evening?"

Loftus smiled and agreed, unable to bring himself to look his host in the eye.

HE EXCUSED HIMSELF early from the table again that night and walked alone through the grounds of the Dupré manse. He stopped frequently to look at the patterns of whorls on the bark of a native tree, the fruiting bodies bulging sticky and pearl-white on a network of roots spread across the ground, the dusting of spores on the surface of a small pool... The buzzing and whistling of native wildlife filled his ears, swelling and cutting off to a pattern that wasn't quite a pattern.

He emerged on a trail that took him down towards the settlement of Turballe. The first building he encountered was a chapel, its wooden board-walls painted white, its tin roof patched orange with rust.

In the chapel grounds, each grave was marked with a small engraved slab set into the crusty turf.

He had passed this way before on previous visits, a landmark that indicated the edge of town.

The Dupré family had one corner of the cemetery to themselves. The slabs here were well-tended, the vegetation trimmed back, the surfaces scraped and swept clean. At first, Loftus did not find what he sought, but of course... she had married, changed her name to Carson.

Helen Carson.

He knelt, reached out, ran a finger along the grooves of her name on the stone's surface.

Three days. That was all it had been. All the Omega-Gen schedule had permitted before he was shuttled away from the planet. Three days.

So many what ifs, so many what might have beens.

He straightened, turned, and saw movement in the chapel doorway, a shadow, a shape.

Catherine, the wife of Christopher Dupré's son.

Loftus stared at her, and inevitably his eyes were drawn to the bulge of her belly.

He turned, took a stumbling step, and then was out of the graveyard, back on the trail past sticky fruiting bodies and purple-skinned pools, breathing heavily the air that was thick with heady scents and spores, gasping.

He turned and stared, but the chapel was lost to jungle, the trail behind him empty.

More slowly, he headed back up to the manse.

ELANA MUST HAVE been watching out for his return, for she soon joined him in their room. They closed the shutters on the semi-light of the false night and held each other.

Very soon Elana was breathing evenly, sleeping the sleep of the innocent. Loftus lay awake, unable to settle, beset by fear and dogged by thoughts of tomorrow's meeting with the colony's ruling elite.

His vision adjusted to the darkness, and he turned onto his side and regarded his lover, wondering why he had invited her along. He wondered at the motive of his old self, his self of six months ago. Had he really loved this woman enough to want to help her career by giving her the opportunity to accompany him?

Or did he have an ulterior motive, hidden even to himself at the time?

He wondered now if he wanted Elana to document not only the beginning of the end on Karenia, but also his part in it, so that the world would understand how he had suffered as the harbinger of dire tidings. Was the entire exercise nothing more than a consequence of his need for absolution, the desire to have his suffering witnessed by the watching millions?

He ran a finger along the declivity of her naked back, and felt a renewal of guilt at using her like this.

Some time later, a sound came from outside, a high-pitched chittering like that of a bird. He sat up, careful not to disturb Elana.

He swung himself out of bed, slipped into a pair of jeans, and crossed the room. Carefully he eased the shutters open slightly and peered out; the twilight was too bright for him to see anything at first. When his vision adjusted he saw the balcony rail, a twisted array of flowers growing up one pillar. He almost turned away, but then movement caught his eye, something beyond the rail, something out in the manse's grounds.

He edged the shutters open and stepped out onto the wooden decking of the balcony. Down where manicured garden segued into jungle there were three – now four

– squat blue figures, pushing and skipping like children in a school playground. Every so often, a chittering cry came from one of the creatures.

They were Yanth, the native semi-sentient species.

Loftus had seen them on previous visits, but only ever fleetingly, distantly. As he watched, they froze, as if one. For a second or two they were as statues, and then they melted into the undergrowth and were gone.

Loftus was aware of his increased heartbeat. His throat was dry.

What were they doing here, so close to human habitation?

He hesitated for only an instant, and then was heading down the steps, his bare feet crunching through spore-crusted grass.

The ground where the Yanth had been playing bore the impressions of their feet, dark imprints where the dusting of spores had been dislodged. Loftus stared at the edge of the jungle and saw a thinning, what might have been a way through.

He straightened, took a step, then another. With his third step, the jungle wrapped itself around him and the manse might have been nothing more than a distant memory.

The mauve twilight of half night, which had seemed so bright when he first opened the shutters, was but a murky gloom in the depths of the jungle. Frequently, Loftus headed for a thinning between the trees only to be pulled up by a web of crystalline fibres snagged across his face and body. He almost turned back after a few minutes of this, but then he heard the chittering again.

Soon he was unable to determine how far he may have come, his progress so full of false starts and doubling back. Eventually, the twilight grew brighter ahead and he knew he must be approaching some kind of clearing.

Aware of the noise of his progress, he slowed, easing his way towards the thinning, his heart pounding again.

A brow of rock cut through the jungle here, covered only by a thin layer of undergrowth. The mauve sky hung seamless overhead.

Loftus' eyes took a few seconds to adjust, and then he saw the Yanth, four of them, sitting cross-legged by a dark opening in the rock, their faces turned back towards him, apparently unperturbed by his clumsy pursuit.

All pretence of stealth abandoned, he stepped out into the open and brushed himself down, aware of the many scratches from the jungle fibres across his arms and torso.

Unsure what to do, or even what kind of danger he could face, he raised his hands palms outward, shrugged, and for want of anything better said, "My name is Ed Loftus. I'm a friend of the Duprés. A friend of the Yanth."

When Loftus took a step forward, the aliens remained where they were, watching him with no visible reaction.

He approached them slowly, marvelling at everything about the creatures: the soft, almost pastel, blue of their features, their half-scaled half-furred body-coverings, the midnight blue of their eyes.

Finally, within a few metres of them, he dropped into a crouch so that he was at their level. "Friend," he said again, feeling as if this was some kind of first contact while knowing that people had lived on Karenia for hundreds of years and this scene must have played itself out around True Night countless times before.

One of the aliens opened its thin lips and emitted a string of sound, individual words indistinguishable in the stream of bird-like chatter.

Loftus raised his hands helplessly, hoping to convey by sign his lack of comprehension.

This time, the alien dropped its head a little and spoke to him in a fractured bureaucrat's English.

Loftus rocked back on his heels, shocked. He had been unaware that the Yanth could speak anything but their own language.

But the alien had said, "Our destiny is yours."

Loftus shook his head. He felt tears on his cheeks, a strange rushing sensation in his ears, and briefly he wondered if his protective membranes had failed and this was the first onset of some kind of spore-induced psychosis.

The alien said, "No guilt, no pain, no fear."

And then all four turned and disappeared into the cave mouth.

Loftus, delirious, fell forward on his hands and knees and pressed himself into the opening, calling after the aliens, wanting to know more, begging the Yanth to return and bless him with their knowledge.

He fell to the earth, sobbing, and passed out.

He had no notion of how long he lay there. He came awake suddenly, recalling his confrontation with the Yanth. He pushed himself onto hands and knees and looked at the cave, and then back at the jungle.

He stood, uncertainly. He spotted the gap where he had emerged from the jungle. He knew he should not have followed the Yanth, that he should be back in his room with Elana. He must return and compose himself. The day ahead would be long and traumatic.

He found his way back to the manse's grounds and then up to the balcony, where he sat with his feet up, watching the patterns of the light on the jungle vegetation. He went over and over what the Yanth had said and wondered again if he had been affected by the spores, or if he were losing his mind.

Later, much later, Elana joined him without a word. She did not say anything about his absence, and he did not ask if she had noticed him gone. She knew what the coming day meant to him and now, in her silent companionship, he was selfishly grateful that she was with him and he was not alone.

THE BOARD MET in Turballe's town hall, a timber-panelled building almost as big as the Dupré manse. Loftus allowed Christopher Dupré to escort him through the building to a large second-floor meeting room, one entire wall of which was made of glass, looking out over the rooftops of the town clinging to the gentle incline down to the river. Beyond the settlement stretched fields of kreen, the neatly aligned rows broken occasionally by the bulge of a puffball. Loftus imagined the leathery surfaces of the puffballs tightening under the suns' growing warmth, ready to burst again later in the day and release their bounty of spores.

He turned away and took his seat at the long meeting table, his back to the view. Ranked along the table were about two dozen divisional directors of Omega-Gen's Karenian presence, Alain Dupré in his wheelchair towards the far end, smiling reassuringly at Loftus whenever he caught his eye.

Off to one side, not formally part of the meeting but here by consent of the board, Elana sat with her back to a wall, recording, always recording.

"Directors," Christopher Dupré said, as the last to arrive took her seat to the right of Loftus. "Welcome to this specially convened meeting of the OGK directorate, the fourth in the presence of Consul Edward Loftus." With that, he bowed his head in the direction of Loftus, who had at that moment, for some reason, a vivid flashback to the chubby boy who had once been so delighted to receive the gift of a small plastic horse. Loftus had needed to explain what a horse was.

Loftus nodded in greeting, and spoke a few words, conveying his gratitude for their hospitality and his great pleasure to be here again, among friends. As he spoke, he choked back on the guilt of his duplicity.

"Our production figures hold steady," said Alain, then. "We have a record of several decades of balance between productivity while maintaining the intricate feedback cycles between kreen, sporeballs and Yanth." He smiled at Loftus again, and added, "We have served Omega-Gen well, no?"

Loftus would not meet his old friend's look. He cleared his throat. "You have," he said. "You do. The corporation has no complaint." He paused, then raised his gaze to look around the gathered board. "I have not come here to review the figures," he continued. "I come as the messenger, one with news that will forever change the status of the colony world of Karenia."

He had their full attention now. Finally, he met Alain's look. "Eight months ago, the final trials were completed of a new, synthetic equivalent of kreenol. Omega-Gen can now manufacture in the laboratory that which could only previously be extracted from kreen grown on Karenia, in that delicate ecological balance that you describe."

He hesitated. He noticed Dupré and other members of the board exchanging looks.

Dupré said, quietly, "Which means?"

"Which means," Loftus said, "that over the next forty months kreen extraction on Karenia will be phased out." Now he looked down again, and, more softly, said, "I'm sorry."

In one short speech he had removed the single raison d'être for this colony world, with its elaborate mechanisms to protect its people. Their off-world income stream would vanish, and they would no longer be able to afford the gene-splicing that allowed them to live beyond forty or so years. And yet... those who had already been treated could never leave, because of their in-built bond with the spores.

"As part of the transition plan," he went on, "Omega-Gen offers to remove all new-born children from Karenia and fund their relocation on other colony worlds. Your children, at least, will be offered a fresh start before the spores can do them any harm. There will also be on-going support for those left on Karenia..."

When he looked up he expected to witness resentment, grief, hostility; in planning this presentation he had been advised to anticipate physical violence as a distinct possibility.

Instead... the last thing he had expected was sympathy.

Christopher Dupré was on his feet, approaching. He placed a hand gently on Loftus's arm.

"Come outside," he said. "Leave the board to their deliberations. Come along, Edward, my people need to talk."

Elena was already out in the ante-room, recording his emergence from the meeting.

He raised a hand to cut her filming.

"What's going on, Ed?" she asked, when Christopher Dupré had returned to the hall.

He shook his head, pouring himself a glass of water from an iced jug. "It's as if... they already knew."

"Word from Omega-Gen?" she asked.

"I don't know. I don't know what to think."

They took about ten minutes to reach a conclusion, and soon Loftus was back at his position at the head of the long meeting table, the purple-swathed panorama of Karenia at his shoulder.

"Directors," he said, "I have full details of the transitional support package here. I represent you before the Omega-Gen board and I have fought hard to secure as favourable a package as was possible. I –"

"Ed." Alain Dupré's voice cut through his floundering words. "Ed, we know that you have fought for our interests and we thank you for that. We accept the support of our parent company, but we will not be giving our babies away."

Loftus stared at his old friend. "But..." he said, "without the splice, your children will only have forty or fifty years at best!"

Dupré nodded. "A life lived on Karenia is a rich and wonderful thing," he said. "This is our world. We choose to stay."

Loftus thought then of the last deal the colonists of Karenia had accepted: be tied to the planet for a normal human lifetime, while the rest of humankind is granted near immortality. What was it about this world that made its people choose Karenia at almost any cost?

LOFTUS STOOD ON the sloping lawn of the Dupré manse, Alain Dupré slightly above him in his wheelchair so that they were almost on eye-level.

"You knew, didn't you?" he said. "You knew what I had come here to say."

It was Dupré's turn to avert his gaze. Loftus thought back to his earlier feelings of guilt and wondered just who was deceiving whom.

"It could never last," Dupré said. "The kreen extraction operates according to a delicate ecological balance on one rather dangerous and remote colony world. It could only ever be a matter of time before OG developed a more reliable alternative."

"But you knew..."

Alain nodded. He raised a hand and pointed towards the entangled wall of jungle. "Our friends the Yanth told us, Edward. They saw it in your... presence... last night."

"They read my mind?"

"They read who you are, what you are. Edward, they see the world in a different way to you or me. Where we see boundaries between self and other, they see continuity. Last night you were them and they were you, but you just didn't see it. You're not equipped to see it."

"And you are?"

"I'm trying."

"And this is why your people are staying here, why they'll accept that their children will only live forty years instead of forever?"

Dupré nodded again. "You really want to live forever, my friend?"

Loftus felt suddenly vertiginous, standing over the abyss of years. A hundred... a thousand... *ten* thousand?

"Stay here with us, Edward. Our destiny is yours, my friend. Stay with us."

THE DETAILS TOOK some sorting out, but it was only a matter of days, time for the regional directors to report back to their people and confirm that there was no dissent from the terms accepted. Nobody would be giving up their babies to Omega-Gen.

"You're really thinking of staying," said Elana.

She sat on the leaning bough of a fallen tree, picking at the flaky whorls of bark with long painted fingernails. They were in the Dupré garden, almost out of sight of the manse at the foot of a slope where water gathered in a run of dusty pools. This exchange was off-camera, just them.

"I don't know," said Loftus. "I really don't know." He couldn't work out how to put into words the thoughts and feelings that had occupied him for the last few days, while his brain had concentrated on the detail of the transitional planning.

"You should come with me," she said. "You have a whole life to look forward to."

If he stayed, he would have fifty years more, at best. If he went... forever.

"You have a whole future to look forward to, too," he said. He stepped towards her, held her head against his chest. "What you have seen and recorded here will open so many doors for you. You really can go on and do whatever you want."

Now, in this moment of separation – whether he left with her or not – he felt closer to Elana than he had ever felt before.

He stepped back, and saw her as if for the first time. Elana Kryadies was no naive young irritant only fit to comfort a self-obsessed old misanthrope like Loftus. She was strong, she had a whole life ahead of her; many lives.

She reached up and touched his cheek. "What we had... what we have – it means a lot to me, you know? I didn't come with you just because–"

He touched her lips, silencing her. "Elana, I know."

Elana would stay for nine more days on the planet of Karenia, but this was their real parting, their last true embrace, here in the garden of the Dupré manse, with half night dwindling and the chorusing of the jungle all around.

TRUE NIGHT DESCENDED, a darkness that was surprisingly swift to take hold.

The people of Turballe were out in force, elaborate picnics spread out along the parkland that fringed the river. The whole thing was lit by paper lanterns suspended from the trees.

Within minutes of darkness, the trees started to dust everything with spores that puffed out of the veins of what passed for leathery leaves. People sneezed and coughed; others caught the spores in jugs of drinks which they then mixed and poured into tall glasses loaded with split berries.

Loftus took a glass from Christopher's youngest daughter Mabelle. He sipped, and felt his protective membranes working overtime to filter out the poisonous spores. To one side, Elana looked on, recording everything.

Earlier, she had asked again what he was planning to do, and still he had been genuinely unable to answer.

Now, he pushed away through the crowds. He had seen Catherine heading off determinedly, and he had a feeling he knew where to find her.

As he walked up the main street of Turballe, he did the sums again in his head. Sixty years...

She was kneeling over Helen Carson's grave, rubbing at the stone with a piece of cloth. She looked up at his approach, as if she had known he would follow.

He crouched beside her, put his hand down to the stone, touched Helen's name again.

"I only knew her for a short time," he said. "She had a whole life after that."

Catherine smiled. "My grandmother..."

"Are you...? Was your mother...?"

"I don't know."

He thought then of the Yanth's words, repeated later by Alain Dupré. *Our destiny is yours*. Catherine may not know for certain the details of her ancestry, but the Yanth did. They saw things differently, more deeply, Alain had said.

Finally, he thought of immortality. He could leave with Elana, and live for as long as he wanted among the stars. But there were other forms of immortality.

He reached out, put a hand tenderly on Catherine's pregnant bulge, and almost immediately felt movement.

His destiny, his inheritance, here on Karenia.

* * *

DOWN BY THE river the party was in full swing. The spores in the drinks were clearly at least mildly intoxicating, and there was much music and laughter. People said that the Yanth were among them, but Loftus saw none as he rejoined the Dupré group.

"They are?" he said. "Where? I haven't seen them."

He found Elana, wrapped her in his embrace, and said, "The Yanth. You have to film the Yanth."

She laughed, and kissed him. Then, more sombrely, said, "I'm going in the morning, remember? There's still time for you to join me, Ed."

He stepped back from her and shook his head. "Are you filming?" he asked.

She was, and so he took the blister pack from his pocket and popped the first pill. It tasted of nothing.

He still had time to reach the shuttle before taking the next pill and shedding his immunity.

Instead he headed down to the river, looking for the Yanth, hoping to understand how it was that they saw things differently.

Soon he would take the second pill, and then he would breathe deep. His destiny was here. The Yanth had known.

And he was all too eager to find out just what that would mean.

FOR THE AGES

ALASTAIR REYNOLDS

Alastair Reynolds was born in South Wales, studied at Newcastle and St Andrews Universities and has a Ph.D. in astronomy. After a period working in the Netherlands as an astrophysicist for the European Space Agency, he returned to Wales and is now a full time writer. His first novel, Revelation Space, *appeared in 2000, since when he has been responsible for nine novels, two collections and several chapbooks. Alastair's next novel is set to be* Blue Remembered Earth, *first in the Poseidon's Children series.*

IT'S A TERRIBLE and beautiful thing I've done.

I suppose I already had it in mind, when the last uplink came in. Not that I'd come close to voicing the possibility to myself. If I'd been honest about the course I was on, I might well have requested immediate committal to stasis.

The right thing to do, in hindsight. And maybe we'd be on our way home now, back to the gratitude of a thousand worlds. Our house would have crumbled into the sea by the time we got back. But we could always have built a new one, a little further from the headland.

Let me tell you something about myself, while there's still time. These words are being recorded. Even as I speak, my suit's mouse-sized repair robot is engraving them onto the suit's exterior armour. Isolated in this cavern, the suit should be buffeted against the worst excesses of cosmic ray and micro-particle damage. Whether the inscriptions will remain legible, however, or whether in some sense *you've already read them*, I won't begin to speculate. There's been enough of that already, and I'm a little burned out by it all. Deep futurity, billions of years – the ultimate futility of any action, any deed, enduring for the smallest fraction of eternity – it's enough to shrivel the soul. Vashka could handle that kind of thing, but I'm made of less stern stuff.

I am – let's be honest, *was* – a human being, a woman named Nysa. I was born on Pellucid, a world of the Commonwealth. After a happy childhood I had dreams of being a dancer or choreographer. In my teens, however, I showed a striking aptitude for physics. Not many people have the right mental architecture to fully understand momentum trading, but I grasped the slippery fundamentals with a quick, intuitive ease. Rapidly it was made clear to me that I had a duty, an obligation, to the Commonwealth. The encouragement to study propulsion physics was fierce, and I duly submitted.

In truth, it wasn't a hard decision. I would have been one dancer among thousands, struggling for recognition. But as a physicist I was already a singular, bright-burning talent.

It was at the academy that I fell into Vashka's orbit, and eventually in love. Like me, she'd been plucked from obscurity on the basis of a talent. Vashka's brilliance lay in nothing so mundane as the mechanics of space travel, though. She was drawn to the grandest and oldest of the physical disciplines: the study of the origin, structure and destiny of our universe. This project, this entire mission – sponsored by the economies of hundreds of planets, across dozens of solar systems – was her brainchild.

I think of Vashka now, when her hate for me had reached its bitter zenith. We were in *Sculptor*'s conference room, all twelve of the vivified crew, debating the impact of the latest uplink. Through the upsweeping radiation-proof glass of the windows, the pulsar's optical pulses strobe-lit the glittering face of Pebble five times a second. Each pulse sapped angular momentum from the pulsar's rotation. In ten billion years, that little city-sized nugget of degenerate matter would have exhausted its capacity to pulse at all. But it would still be out here, a softly radiating neutron star. In a hundred billion years, much the same would still be true.

"It's not a question of whether we do this," Vashka said, looking at each of us in turn with that peculiar steely gaze of hers. "We have no choice in the matter. It's what we were sent out here to accomplish; what the entire Commonwealth is depending on us to get done. If we turn back now, we may as well not have bothered."

"Even allowing for this latest uplink," Captain Reusel said carefully, "the majority of the symbol chains won't need significant modification. There'll be a few mistakes, a few incorrect assertions. But the overall picture won't be drastically different." Reusel spoke with judicial equanimity, committing herself to neither side until she'd heard all the arguments and had time to weigh them.

"If we knowingly leave errors in the Pebble engravings," Vashka replied, "we'll be doing more harm than if we'd never started."

I coughed by way of interjection. "That's an exaggeration. Our cosmological descendants – the downstream aliens, whoever they are – will be at least as smart as us, if not more so. They'll be aware that we weren't infallible, and they'll be alert to mistakes. We don't have to get this absolutely, one-hundred per cent correct. We just have to give them a shove in the right direction."

Vashka couldn't mask her disgust. "Or they may be so inflexible in their thinking that they tie themselves in knots trying to reconcile our errors, or decide to throw Pebble away as a lost cause. The point is we don't have to take a chance either way. All we have to do is *get this right*, before we leave. Then we can go home with a clear conscience."

In the run-up to the decision about the latest draft the tension had opened a cleft neither of us was willing to bridge. Vashka, rightly, saw me as the one thing standing between her and the satisfactory completion of the project. In my instinct to caution, my willingness to accept compromise over perfection, I'd shifted from ally to adversary.

We'd stopped sleeping together, restricting our interactions to acrimonious exchanges in the conference room. Beyond that, we had nothing worth saying.

"You won't have a conscience to keep clear, if the cores go critical," I said.

Vashka shot back a look of unbridled spite. "Now who's exaggerating, Nysa?"

Reusel sighed. She hated bickering among her crew, and I knew ours caused her particular hurt. "Estimated time to engrave the new modifications, Loimaa?" The question was directed at the willowy senior technician in matters of planetary sculpture.

"Based on the last round of modifications," Loimaa said, glancing down at hidden numbers, "with both grasers at maximum output... thirty thousand orbits, give or take. Around a thousand days."

"Forget it," I said. "That'll take us much too far into the red. I'm already uncomfortable with the existing over-stay."

"Home wouldn't have uplinked the modifications if they didn't mean us to implement them," Vashka said.

"Home don't have realtime data on our engine stability," I countered. "If they did, they'd know that we can't delay our return much longer."

"Things are that critical?" Reusel asked, skepticism and suspicion mingling in her narrowed eyes. "If they were, I trust you'd have let me know by now..."

"Of course," I said. "And for the moment things are nominal. We're probably good for another hundred days. But a thousand... that's completely out of the question."

By accident or design, *Sculptor*'s starboard engine pod was visible through the conference room windows. I didn't have to ask any of the others to glance at it – their attention was drawn anyway. I imagined what they were thinking. The light spilling from the radiator grids – was it hotter, whiter, than it had been a week ago, a month?

Of course. It couldn't be otherwise, with the momentum debt we'd incurred reaching Pebble. A debt that the universe sought to claw back like a grubby-fingered pawnbroker.

It would, too: one way or the other.

"We could begin the resculpting," Loimaa proposed, looking hesitantly at Vashka for affirmation. "Stop it the moment Nysa gave the word. It wouldn't take more than a few days to clear up shop and begin our return home."

"A few days might still be too much, if the instabilities begin to mount," I said.

"Abandoning the work half-unfinished isn't an option either," Vashka declared. "The corrections are too complex and inter-dependent. We either implement them fully, or not at all."

"I see your point," Reusel said. "At the moment, the Pebble engravings embody errors, incorrect premises and false deductions. But at least there's a degree of internal consistency, however flawed it might be. The sense of an argument, with a beginning, middle and end."

Vashka's nod was cautious. "That's correct. It offends me that we might leave these errors in place, but it's still better than tearing up half the logic chains and leaving before we've restored a coherent narrative."

"Then it's simple," I said, trying hard not to let my satisfaction break through. "The lesser of two evils. Better to leave now, knowing we've left something self-consistent in place, than be forced to bail out halfway through the next draft."

The captain was thoughtful. Her heavy-lidded eyes suggested a fight against profound weariness. "But it would be unfortunate," she said, "to let our sponsors down, if there was a fighting chance of completing this work. Never mind the downstreamers." Alertness snapped into her again. Her attention was on me. "Nysa: I can't take this decision without a comprehensive overview of our engine status. I want to know how the real odds lie." She paused. "We all accepted risks when we volunteered for this mission. *Sculptor* has brought us thousands of light years from home, thousands of years of travel from the friends and loved ones we left behind on our homeworlds."

We nodded. We'd all heard this speech before – it was nothing we didn't know for ourselves – but sometimes the captain felt the need to drill it into us again. As if reminding herself of what we'd already sacrificed.

"Even if we were to commence our return mission now," she went on, "at this moment, it would be to homes, worlds, most of us won't recognise. Yes, they'll reward our return. Yes, they'll do all that they can to make us feel welcome and appreciated. But it will still be a kind of death, for most of us. And we knew that before we stepped aboard." She knitted her fingers together on the table's mirror-black surface. "What I mean to say is, we have already taken the hardest decision, and here we are, still alive, chasing a neutron star out of the galaxy, falling further from the Commonwealth with every passing second. Any decisions we make now must be seen in that light. And I think we must be ready to shoulder further risks."

"Then you've already made up your mind?" I asked, dismayed.

"No, I still want that report. But if the odds are no worse than ninety percent in our favour, we will stay.

We will stay and finish Vashka's work. And then we will go home with heads high, knowing we did not shirk this burden."

I nodded. She would have her report. And I hoped very much that the numbers would persuade her against staying.

THE NEIGHBOURHOOD OF a pulsar, a whirling magnetic neutron star, is no place for anything as fragile as a human being. We should have sent robots, I thought, as I went out for a visual inspection in one of our ridiculously armoured suits. Robots could have completed this work and then self-destructed, instead of worrying about getting back home again. But once Vashka had implanted the idea in their minds, the collective leaders of the Commonwealth had demanded that this grand gesture, this preposterous stab at posterity, be shaped under the guidance of human minds, in close proximity. Ultimately, the Pebble structures might be the last imprint that the human species left on the cosmos. The last forensic trace that we ever existed.

But even this wouldn't last forever.

Why had we come?

It was simple, really. We knew something, a single cosmic truth, one that we had discovered through patient scientific observation. It was one of the oldest pieces of information known to the species, something so elementary, so easily grasped, so familiar to any child, that it seemed self-evidential.

Before the Commonwealth, before our emergence into space, our ancestors had peered into the night sky. They mapped the starry whirlpools of other galaxies, at first mistaking them for nearby nebulae, formations of spiralling gas. Later, their instruments had shown them that galaxies were in fact very distant assemblages of stars, countless billions of them. And these galaxies were located far beyond our own Milky Way, out to the horizon of observations, out to the very edge of the visible universe. They were also receding. Their light was shifted into red, evidence of a universal cosmic expansion.

Backtracking this expansion, our ancestors deduced that the universe must have emerged from a single dimensionless point of spacetime, less than fourteen billion years ago. With a singular absence of poetry they labelled this birth event the Big Bang.

Quite a lot has happened since that discovery. We have settled interstellar space and spread our influence through a wide swathe of the galaxy. Our science is vastly more sophisticated. We don't think of the birth event as a 'bang' at all, or even an 'event' in the accepted sense. But we continue to preserve the notion that our universe was once infinitely small, infinitely dense, infinitely hot, and that there is no sense in which anything can be said to have happened 'before' this eyeblink epoch.

Our Earthbound ancestors made this discovery using telescopes of glass and metal, recording spectral light onto silvery plates activated by crude photochemistry. That they were able to do it at all is a kind of miracle. Of course, it's much, much simpler now. A child, with the right demands, could reveal this truth of cosmic expansion in a single lazy afternoon. The night sky is still aspray with galaxies, and each and every one of them still feels that tug of cosmic expansion.

There's a catch, though. The galaxies aren't just rushing away from each other, like the blasted fragments of a bomb. If they were, then their mutual self-gravity would eventually retard the expansion, perhaps even bring the galaxies crashing in on each other again.

Instead, they're speeding up. Eight billion years into the universe's life, something began to accelerate its expansion. Our ancestors called this influence 'dark energy'. They measured it long before they had even the sketchiest understanding of what might be motivating it. Our understanding of the underlying physics would be unrecognisable to them, but we still honour their name. And dark energy changes everything. It's the reason we came to this miserable and desolate point in space, around a dense dead star that will soon leave the galaxy altogether.

It's the reason we came to leave Vashka's message, engraved into the crust of a world made of star-fired diamonds.

I circled *Sculptor*, taking care to keep away from the banks of gamma-ray lasers that were even now etching Vashka's patterns. The ship's orange peel orbit brought it over every part of Pebble eventually, the lasers sweeping like spotlights, and when we were done there would be no part of the planet's surface that hadn't been touched. The lasers took the raw diamond of her crust, melting and incinerating it to leave elegant chains of symbolic reasoning, scribed from the sky in canyon-wide lines. The chains of argument formed a winding spiral, quite distinct from the surface track of our orbit. That spiral converged on a single spot on the planetary surface, the entry point to a cavern where the entire statement had been duplicated for safekeeping.

In truth we were finished; had been so for many orbital cycles. What *Sculptor* was doing now was completing the tidying-up exercise after another uplink from home. We were finishing off the ninth draft, and now home wanted us to begin again on the tenth.

We'd left the Commonwealth with what appeared to be a complete, self-consistent statement of physics and cosmology, encoded in terms that ought to be decipherable by any starfaring intelligence. But by the time *Sculptor* arrived, the eager minds back home had had second thoughts. A tweak here, an edit there. The first and second drafts had been simple enough, and there'd been no cause for concern. But by the time we were on the fifth and sixth edits, some of us were having qualms. The changes were progressively more sweeping. We'd had to begin almost completely from scratch – lasering the planet back to a blank canvas before starting over, changing our story. As fluent with physics as I was, the level of encoding had long ago slipped beyond my ready comprehension. I had to take Vashka's word that this was all worthwhile. She seemed to think it was.

But then she would, wouldn't she? This entire project was Vashka's idea. Always a perfectionist, she wasn't going to settle for second best.

The problem was that we couldn't stay here forever. Which was where my own narrow expertise came in.

For thousands of years we've been crossing interstellar space using momentum-exchange drives – long enough that it's easy to think that the technology is routine and safe. For the most part, that's exactly what it is. Give or take a few tens of kilometres per second, the stars and planets of the Commonwealth are all co-moving in the same spiral arm, travelling at the same speed with respect to the galactic core. Interstellar transits proceed without incident. We steal momentum from the universe, but we give it back before the universe gets irritated. The net momentum deficit between a ship starting its journey around one star, and the same ship ending its journey around another, is close enough to zero to make no difference. Momentum – and by extension kinetic energy – has neither been created nor destroyed.

But that's not true here. Because the Pebble and its pulsar are hurtling away from the galaxy at twelve thousand kilometres per second, we haven't actually *stopped*. We started off at zero relative to the Commonwealth, and we're still travelling at a good clip away from it.

Which means that a momentum debt is still waiting to be repaid.

The engines were a dull red when we arrived, but with each day that we *delay* paying that debt, they glow a little more intensely. That's the universe reminding us, in an accumulation of microscopic thermal fluctuations, that we owe it something.

Leave it long enough, and the antimomentum cores will undergo catastrophic implosion.

But that wasn't going to happen today, or tomorrow, or for months in the future. As much as I'd hoped to find some problem or trend that could be used to justify our early departure, nothing was amiss. The cores were progressing according to expectations. Loimaa's thousand days might be a stretch too far, but I had to admit that we were good for at least the next two or three hundred. And if and when the cores started deviating, I'd be able to give Captain Reusel plenty of warning.

That didn't mean I felt easy about it.

Yet I'd turned things over in my head long enough, and knew that twisting the facts, over-stressing the hazards, wasn't an option. Reusel would see through that in a flash.

As would Vashka.

My suit picked up a proximity signal. I used the thrusters to spin around, in time to see another suit looping out from behind *Sculptor*. Like mine, it was an upright armoured bottle with manipulators and steering gear. The ident tag told me exactly who it was.

"Come to talk me into lying?" I asked.

"Not at all. I know you better than that, Nysa. You'd never lie, or read anything into the data that wasn't really there. That would take…" Vashka seemed to trail off, as if her thoughts had carried her in a direction she now regretted.

"Imagination?"

"I was going to say, a streak of unprofessionalism that you don't have."

"Yes. I always was the diligent plodder, while you made the wild, intuitive leaps."

"I didn't mean it that way."

"But it's not too far off the mark. Oh, don't worry. I'm not offended. It's basically the truth, after all. I'm very good with fixing engines and making them work a bit better. That's a rare skill, one worth cherishing. But it can't be compared with what you've done, what you've brought into being. No one had ever thought of anything like this before you did, Vashka. It's all yours."

"It was a shared enterprise, Nysa."

"Which wouldn't have happened without your force of will, your imagination."

Vashka took her time in answering. "Until it's done, and we're on our way home, there are more important things to think about than credit and glory."

"Well, I've good news for you. My report will conclude that proceeding with the tenth draft is an acceptable risk. And you're right. It never occurred to me to bend the facts."

"I'm... happy," Vashka said, as if she feared a trap in my words.

"It won't be perfection," I added. "It'll be a step in that direction. But don't delude yourself that this is the end. As soon as we're back on Pellucid, you'll be wishing you changed this or deleted that. It's human nature. Or yours, anyway."

"Then perhaps I'll program my stasis berth so that I never wake up."

It was a flip response, something that – had it come from anyone else – I'd have been more than willing to dismiss as bravado. But with Vashka, I was prepared to believe quite the opposite. She would easily choose death over living with the knowledge of irreversible failure.

Always and forever.

"I'd best get back inside," I told her.

THE DAY SHE first explained it to me we were in our old house, the one we bought together during our time at the academy, the one that overlooked the bay, with the ground floor patio windows flung open to salt-tang sea breezes and hazy morning sunshine. I was doing dance exercises, going through the old motions of stretching and limbering, but still listening to what she said. I'd made the mistake of only half-listening before, nodding in the right places, but from bitter experience I knew that Vashka would always catch me out.

It wasn't that I didn't care. But I had my area of obsession and she had hers, and it was increasingly clear that the two only slightly intersected.

"Dark energy is the killer," she said. "Right now we hardly feel it. It's making all the galaxies accelerate away from each other, but the effect is small enough that people argued over it for a long time before convincing themselves it was real." Vashka was standing at the door, doing stretching exercises of her own. Whereas mine were in the service of art, hers served no higher purpose other than the toning of her body, a maintenance routine to keep the machine in working order.

I knew enough about cosmology to ask the easy questions. "The Milky Way's just one galaxy in the Local Group. Won't the gravitational pull of nearby galaxies always outweigh the repulsion caused by dark energy?"

Her nod was businesslike, as if this objection was no more than she'd anticipated. "That's true enough, and most galaxies are also bound into small groups and clusters. But the gravitational pull *between* groups and clusters is much too weak to resist dark energy over cosmological time. At the moment we can see galaxies and galaxy clusters all the way out to the redshift horizon, but dark energy will keep pushing them over that edge. They'll be redshifted out of our range of view. Nothing in physics can stop that, and there's nothing we can ever do to observe them, once they've passed over the horizon."

"Which won't happen for a hundred billion years."

"So what? That only seems like a long time if you're not thinking cosmologically. The universe is *already* thirteen billion years old, and there are stars now shining that will still be burning nuclear fuel in a hundred billion years."

"Not ours."

"We don't matter. What does is the message we leave to our descendants."

She didn't mean descendants of humanity. She meant the alien beings who would one day supplant us, in whatever remained of the galaxy that far downstream. Carriers of the flame of sentience, if that doesn't sound insufferably pompous.

"Fine," I said. "The dark energy pushes all those galaxies out of sight. But the local group galaxies are still bound."

"That's irrelevant. For a start, they can't be used to detect the expansion of the universe, for the same reason that dark energy doesn't disrupt them – their short range attraction predominates over long range cosmological effects. But it's worse than that. In six or seven billion years, the local group galaxies will have merged with each other, pulled together by gravity. There'll just be a single super-galaxy, where once there was the Milky Way, Andromeda, the Clouds of Magellan, all the other galaxies in our group. This isn't speculation. We've seen galactic mergers across all epochs. We know that this is our fate, and we know that the mixing process will erase the prior histories of all the involved galaxies."

"I accept this," I said. "But if aliens arise in that super-galaxy, tens of billions years from now, they'll have billions of years to consider their situation. Our technological science is a few thousand years old. Isn't it presumptuous of us to assume that they won't be capable of making the same discoveries, given time?"

"Physics says otherwise. There'll be no observable galaxies, other than the one they're inside. They may not even retain the *concept* of a galaxy. All they'll see around their own island universe will be a perfect starless black. And there won't be any easy way for them to measure the expansion of spacetime by other means. The cosmic microwave background will have been redshifted far into the radio frequency, and it'll be a trillion times fainter than it is now. They could send out probes to gauge the effects of expansion, if it even occurred to them, but it would take billions more years for those probes to get far enough out to feel measurable effects." Vashka paused in her workout. "An unpalatable truth, but truth is what it is. We happen to exist inside a window, a brief moment in the universe's history, in which intelligent creatures have the means to determine that the universe was born, that it has a finite age, that it is expanding. To not know these things is to not know the universe at all. And yet the downstreamers will be unable to determine these absolute fundamentals! That is why it is our duty, our moral imperative, to send a message from our epoch to theirs."

"This monument you've been talking about."

"I've submitted my ideas to the Legislation. And it'll have to be more than a monument. We can't leave a message on Pellucid, or any other planet orbiting a solar-type star: it'll be incinerated when the star goes red giant. And even if that didn't happen, the galactic merger event will play havoc with stellar dynamics. The best place would be around a star bound to the local group, but on an orbit that will take it far enough out to avoid the convulsions. A bystander. I think I might even have found a candidate."

"You're getting ahead of yourself, if you've only just submitted that proposal."

"There's no point counting on failure, Nysa. If I'm going to see this through to completion, I might as well start working on the details. It's a pulsar, with a planetary companion, on a high-velocity trajectory that will take it far from the Milky Way."

I hardly dared ask the next question. "If we were to go out there, how long would it take to get home again?"

Vashka looked out through the open patio windows, to the headland and the wide sweep of the bay. "If we left now? The fastest ship could get us home again in just under five thousand years. Four, if we could get a little closer to the speed of light. To do that, though – and to make rendezvous with such a fast moving object – we'd need a number of radical breakthroughs in engine design." She shrugged, now that she'd delivered her lure, the hook that would sink its way into me. "Whatever happens, this house will have crumbled into the sea by then. We'll just have to get a new one."

"We?" I asked.

"You'd come with me, Nysa." Vashka closed her eyes, resumed her stretching. "You know you would."

SCULPTOR SWUNG AROUND Pebble in its endless winding orange peel. Loimaa's gamma-ray lasers were scribing constantly. They scissored and whisked like knitting needles. From the inspection cupola we'd watch their furious industry, mesmerised as the landscape was reshaped to our latest whim. It wasn't simply a question of ablation, boiling diamond away in plumes of atomised carbon. Loimaa's methods were so skilled that she could literally *move mountains* – slicing chunks of diamond here, pushing them there – and then allowing their interlattice bonds to reform again. She could melt diamond and use shockwaves to compress it back to solidity in a dozen different allotropes. She was carving a world with light.

Days passed. *Sculptor* completed hundreds of orbits. The engines glowed a little hotter from day to day, but the thermal progression was entirely within expectations. To her credit, Captain Reusel still demanded a constant supply of updates, keeping a nervous eye on our status. The ritual was always the same. I'd tell her that nothing untoward had happened, but that I was still uncomfortable with the overstay.

"Objection duly noted," Reusel would say. "But until we've something better to go on than your natural tendency toward pessimism, Nysa, then we keep cutting. You have my word that we'll break orbit the moment things change."

"I hope we have sufficient warning, in that case."

"I'm sorry, Nysa. But we're doing this for the ages. We can't leave it as a botched job, not when there's a chance of getting it right. No one's going to come out here again and correct our mistakes."

I accepted this. I might have not liked it, but I wasn't so self-centred that I couldn't see things from Reusel's viewpoint. She'd been a good and kind-mannered captain and I knew she wasn't one to make snap decisions. In her shoes, I'd have done exactly the same thing.

Things thawed between me and Vashka.

Now that she'd got her way, Reusel on her side, she admitted that she'd always understood my position, sympathised with my professional concern for the engines, but felt she had an equally pressing duty to fight her corner over the engravings.

I feigned understanding and forgiveness. It was almost like old times.

"I didn't mean it to turn so bitter," Vashka told me, the last time we slept together. "But you know how it is. We've both given up so much to make it here. It's worth spilling some blood, if that's the difference between perfection and good enough."

"I just wish some of that blood hadn't been mine."

"You know I still love you." She stroked the side of my face with a tenderness that snapped me back to our first days together on Pellucid. "Besides, it's all water under the bridge now. We're well into the tenth draft. It'll be done before you know it."

"Unless another update arrives."

"They wouldn't dare." Vashka declared this with the flat certainty of a believer, not a scientist. "I've studied this iteration, and it really is beautifully self-consistent. There's no scope for improvement. If they sent another draft... I'd reject it."

I smiled, although I didn't really believe her.

"Daring of you."

"This one is right. I know it's right. I know when *I'm* right."

"It's always good to have self-belief. I wish I had more of it myself. Perhaps I should have stayed a dancer."

"As a dancer, you died a thousand years ago," Vashka said. "Forgotten and obscure, just another middlingly talented artist on a little blue planet in the Commonwealth. As you, as Nysa the engineer, you're still alive. Still out here. Doing something magnificent. Participating in an act of altruism that will endure across cosmological time."

At that moment I found Captain Reusel's choice of words springing to mind. "For the ages."

"Precisely," Vashka said, pulling me closer, as if everything was and always would be all right. "For the ages."

And for a while it was right, too. Until it hit me what I needed to do.

I'D BEEN OUTSIDE, making another engine inspection. After dispensing with my suit, I travelled through *Sculptor* to what we still referred to as the 'engine room', a name that conjured an archaic, sweating furnace of boilers and pistons, but which was in fact merely a cool, calm control node, isolated far from the fearsome, transgressive physics of the engines themselves. The room was empty when I arrived, as I had expected it to be.

My hands summoned the control interfaces. They sprang into obliging solidity under my touch. My fingers danced, caressing rainbow-coloured keys and sliders. Around me, status graphics swelled for attention. To anyone not schooled in momentum-trading, these squirming, intertwining, multi-dimensional figures would have seemed as strange and unfathomable as deep-sea organisms, engaged in courtship and combat. To my eyes, they signalled chains of branching probability, tangled meshes of counter-intuitive cause and effect.

Thermal-kinetic tradeoff matrices, momentum-event spinors, clustered braids of twistor-impulse covariance. Lucid to my eyes, but only just. It still took tremendous concentration to make sense of the entirety. That I could do it at all was the wonder.

Sweat prickled my skin, drying instantly in the room's cool. A necessary wrong was still a wrong. For a moment, I quailed. Perhaps Vashka really was right, and we should see this through.

But no.

There was a mode, a faculty, to push the engines out of their stable operating regime. It was a test function, nothing more. It was meant to be used only in those rare instances when we might want reassurance that the automated safety cut-ins were functioning normally.

The mode could be misused.

I meant only to nudge the engines, to push them a little more into the danger regime. Not enough to endanger us, but enough to be able to demonstrate the glitch to Reusel, to make her think that we were better off cutting our losses now. "Look at that spike," I might say, all plausibility and professional concern. "It's a warning sign. I thought we could hold back the debt longer than this, but the stochastic coupling's evidently running away from us. There was always a chance…"

"It's understood," she might say, with a regretful nod, trusting my professional judgement implicitly. "Prep *Sculptor* for immediate departure."

I'd echo the same grave nod. "It's a pity," I'd say, "that Vashka's work won't be finished."

"Vashka will just have to live with imperfection, like the rest of us."

That's not the way it happened, though.

I knew my error as soon as I'd made it. There are no simple mistakes in momentum-trading, but I'd come as close as possible to making one. A slip of inattention, a failure to consider all repercussions. We were in one stability mode, and I'd neglected to remember that the test function would, by default, assume a slightly different one. Much earlier, as part of another, entirely innocent test exercise, I had disabled the safety overrides that would have prevented this mismatch. I could have corrected matters, had I remembered, and still perpetrated my lie. But by the time I did, it was far too late to do anything about it.

Sculptor was going to die. It was going to give back to the universe all the energy it had stolen to get here. The antimomentum cores would surrender their debt in a lightless eruption of transient exotics, imparting a barely measurable kink into the local dark energy distribution. An obligation discharged.

But just as the inward collapse of a denegerate stellar core results in an outward pulse of energy and matter – a supernova – so the failure of the antimomentum cores would have a vastly more visible effect on the rest of *Sculptor* and its contents.

When panic hit me, it was as novel and unanticipated as the kiss from a new lover. All the exercises, all the simulations, had failed to prepare me for this moment. My routines deserted me. As much as it shames me to admit it, I had no instinct other than my immediate self-preservation.

I still had enough presence of mind to warn the crew. "Engine overload!" I shouted, pushing my voice throughout *Sculptor*, using emergency privilege to override any other business, even that of the captain. "Repeat, engine overload! Abandon ship! This is not a drill!"

Even as I knew it wouldn't do any of them the slightest good.

It was different for me. I'd just come back in from outside, and I didn't have far to go to reach the suit I'd only recently vacated. The suit was still warm, and it welcomed me back into its armoured embrace.

Then I left.

With the suit's thrusters on maximum power, I aimed myself at Pebble. With the criticality event in progress, *Sculptor* had automatically shut down its scribing operations, so I didn't have to worry about falling into the path of the gamma-ray lasers. Not, of course, that that would have been a bad way to go. Instantaneous annihilation, as painless as non-existence. A kiss from eternity, then nothing.

But then I wouldn't be here, thinking these thoughts, leaving this testimony.

To survive the death of *Sculptor* – the momentary energy pulse would exceed the neutron star's emissions by a factor of a thousand – I'd need a lot of shielding between me and the ship. There wasn't time to get around the other side of Pebble, to use the planet itself as cover. But there was time to reach the cavern.

I knew even then it wasn't to save me – just buy me enough time for self-reflection. The panic didn't care, though. All that mattered to the panic was the next five minutes.

I followed the spiralling logic-chain to its dark epicentre. With a tap of thruster controls I fell into the hole in the world's crust. Down through the glittering, symbol-lined throat, until the shaft widened and

I could finally bring the suit to rest. I aligned myself with the local vertical, and settled down to the floor, taking care that my arrival should not damage any of our finely graven inscriptions. This was our backup policy: a reiteration of the entire external statement, on a much smaller scale. If some unforeseen cosmic process scrubbed Pebble's crust back to a blank canvas, there was still a chance that the engravings in this chamber might endure. Here, in duplicate, was Vashka's cosmological statement. It began near the top of the cavern and wound its way around and down in gorgeous glittering intricacy. Squandering suit power, I drenched it in artificial radiance.

I had to admit that it was quite an achievement. And it would last, too. I didn't doubt that. Whether anyone would ever find it... well, that was a different question.

Sometimes, though, you just had to take a gamble.

I'VE SAID NEARLY all that needs to be said, I think. I've been truthful with you, or as truthful as I can be with myself. We came here to do something glorious, and it would be unfair to say that we failed. The ninth draft is complete, after all. You, whoever you might be – however far downstream you may be from us, a hundred or a thousand billion years – will, I'm confident, be able to make absolute sense of our primitive cave-wall scribblings. Because (I'm certain) you'll have been around for a very, very long time, and by the time you stumble on this little diamond cinder, spinning through the dark galactic void, you'll be infinitely cleverer than us. The mistakes we fret about, the errors and inconsistencies, won't trip you up at all. You'll have the wisdom to grasp the shining truth behind our fumblings, and in doing so you'll look on us with a sublime combination of gratitude and pity. Gratitude that we committed this deed, in order to reveal unto you this one cosmological truth that lies forever beyond the reach of even your science.

Pity because you'll see us for what we truly were. Dragonflies who lived and died in the first few heartbeats of creation, leaving no more than a scratch on time.

Vashka's gone now, along with everyone else. But I think she can rest easy. As much as it would have pained her to think that we left the project riddled with mistakes, it was still sufficient for its intended purpose. Vashka was just too close to her work. She always had been, from the moment we met. Always reaching for the unattainable. Me, I'm much more of a pragmatist.

That doesn't mean I'm not open to possibilities, though.

This suit was never designed to keep me alive this long, so I can't be sure that what I'm about to say isn't the result of some gradual neurodegenerative breakdown, caused by the starvation of oxygen to my brain. But the mere fact that I'm able to frame that doubt... doesn't that speak to my higher faculties still being more or less intact?

I don't know.

But I can be certain of this much: since I've been in this place, in the chamber, surrounded by Vashka's symbols, I've felt something. Not all the time. Just occasionally. Like a searchlight sweeping through me. A sense of presence, of the numinous. I don't believe in God, so that's not the answer. But I'm prepared to believe in you.

Downstream, however many billions of years that might be, you find this place. You find this cavern, and you find what's left of me, bottled in my suit. A creature you don't recognise, dead so long that generations of stars have come and gone since my demise. I doubt that there's much of me left. Unlike diamond, I'm prone to decay.

On the other hand, I'll be in vacuum, in the cold between the galaxies. So who knows?

These moments of presence, these numinous interludes... a skin-crawling sensation of being watched, studied, scrutinised... could it really be *you*, at the end of time? Running some kind of scan, for want of a better word, on the relics you find? And the effects of that scan, rippling back in time to me, here, in my suit?

And how do you feel about me, exactly?

I can't imagine that you'll have had much difficulty unravelling the symbols scribed on my suit, and then stitching them into language you understand. Allowing for the gulf of species and time separating us, I'm certain you'll have been able to comprehend the shape of my account. Why we came here, what happened when we arrived. The sordid outline of my crime.

I hope you won't judge me too harshly. I acted out of fear, not malice. I had our best intentions at heart. I just got things slightly wrong, that's all.

The point is, if I'm the only one of us you ever find, please don't taint us all with the flaws that were mine alone. I'll take responsibility for what I was, what I did.

But then the thought occurs.

Why would you need to know at all? These markings aren't indelible. My little mouse-sized robot still has power, and while I'm under no illusions that I'll be dead soon enough, for now I still have some air and life-support, and presumably sufficient intact brain cells to maintain some kind of lucidity.

I wonder if there's time to change my story?

THE RETURN OF THE MUTANT WORMS

PETER F. HAMILTON

Peter F. Hamilton is one of the best-selling authors in British science fiction. He had his first book, Mindstar Rising, *published in 1993, and his seventeenth novel,* Great North Road, *is due out late summer 2012. Although known for writing big space opera he is now starting a children's book project for David Fickling Books. He continues to live in Rutland UK, with his wife and two children.*

THE WRITER TOOK breakfast out on the penthouse apartment's balcony overlooking the Thames. His housekeeper had prepared his usual of eggs benedict and freshly squeezed orange juice, with a napkin over the toast so it would stay warm.

He sat down facing the river, with the warm summer sunlight striking the glass and chrome buildings of Chelsea opposite. It was a late breakfast because it had been another late night; Clarissea had been so delighted about winning her new contract with DiVinaci lingerie she'd been keen to party. Friends and fellow celebs had come over to congratulate her – and him. They hadn't left the club until after four. And there had still been several paps hanging round outside, snapping pictures of them together. Those images of them, his bow tie undone rather like George Clooney, should make *Tatler*, or at least *Hello*, rebooting his profile. After all, he hadn't been on Radio 4 for a couple of months now, which had started to trouble him. His agent said not to worry, after all, the new book wasn't out for another six weeks, they'd start rebuilding his public profile soon in a big (publisher financed) build up to the Booker nomination season. Clarissea would be a big help in that department.

Sipping the orange he glanced at the morning's post, which the housekeeper had placed on the tray. Usual rubbish: bills, charities, foreign publishers (nothing from Hollywood – again, damn it) redirected fanmail, and a grey blue envelope with a logo he hadn't seen in a decade. He blinked in surprise at the rocketship and star which even today still managed to look faintly Soviet. There had been a time, twenty years ago, when an envelope baring that logo popping through the letterbox would have made his whole week. *Singularity Crystal* was the UK's premier SF magazine, the launch pad for so many genre careers. He'd even managed to have a couple of stories accepted himself in his early twenties.

The writer frowned at the envelope, slightly puzzled as to how the magazine had got his address. He supposed it would be a begging letter, he was vaguely aware that *Singularity Crystal* had slipped to a quarterly schedule a few years back, with a move to online issues imminent. Short story SF was a dwindling market these days.

Puzzlement turned to outright bewilderment as he opened it and read the contract inside. It was a notification that *Singularity Crystal* was to publish his story 'Mutant Worms Of Kranakin' in their next issue, there was a transfer authority code for £73.40.

He picked up his mobile and scanned in the number on the letterhead.

The editor's voice hadn't changed, still the old-school growl of a forty-a-day man. But then he'd always been a 'character' best avoided after ten o'clock at conventions – more than one poor waitress had found out the hard way how dangerous a beanie cap could be on the wrong head. "My dear boy, haven't seen you for years. We must've been going to different conventions."

"Yes," said the writer, who'd stopped going to all of them twelve years ago – how was he to know another fan girl was wearing the same masquerade costume. "There seems to be a slight mistake. You've sent me a contract for a short story."

"That's right, your 'Mutant Worms'. So glad I could finally get round to publishing it. Our schedule has been very busy."

"You must have got my name mixed up with someone else, I haven't sent you a story for a little while."

"Humm, yes, I've got your file up on the screen now; your subscription seems to have lapsed as well. It's a shame, we are about the last paying outlet for new talent left in the country. We need all the support we can get from the arts community."

The writer tried to ignore the slight flush that was colouring his cheeks. "Ah, sorry about that. My PA must have forgotten to renew it. I'll get her to sort that out today."

"You have a PA? Congratulations my boy, you are doing well for yourself now, aren't you. From humble beginnings like my little old magazine, eh?"

"Quite. About the story…"

"Yes, I'm really proud to have your name in the magazine again. In fact our next issue should be out at the same time as your new book is published. I'm hopeful the two will complement each other. I might take an advert out in *Publishers Weekly*."

"I haven't sent you a story."

"You did. Time was when you sent me two a week. Around the office we used to call you the best known name on the slush pile. Course, there's no office any more, just me now."

"Really, I'm a novelist now, I haven't even written a short story for years."

"That's right; 'Mutant Worms' was submitted twenty-one years ago."

"Twenty-one years!"

"Yes. I sent you an acceptance form which you signed and returned; and a deposit cheque for £8.00, which you cashed."

"You can't be serious. You can't hold me to a twenty-one year old contract.

"Perfectly legal," the editor assured him. "Especially as you cashed the cheque."

"But I couldn't even write twenty-one years ago."

"It is a little rough and ready, I admit. I'll do some editing and send you the proof script, of course. Let's face it, you're not the first SF writer I helped knock into shape now, are you? Out of all *Singularity Crystal*'s discoveries, you were always my favourite. So don't worry."

"No. No no. This is totally unacceptable. I have a literary book coming out. This would be a... distraction."

"People will enjoy the contrast, I'm sure. About time we saw some decent SF from you again."

"I don't write sci-fi anymore."

"That's such a shame. I always found it odd that your backlist isn't available, almost as if you're ashamed of it. Perhaps this will trigger a demand for older stuff that your publisher can cash in on. After all, we all loved that enormous weird alien sex trilogy of yours."

The writer felt his jaw muscles tense up. "The Day's Twilight trilogy was not about alien sex!"

"Really? That's strange, I certainly remember there being pages and pages of it. I was thinking we might publicise your new story as a sort of prequel."

"I've never written anything else in the Day's Twilight universe."

"No, but thematically it's similar isn't it?"

The writer took a deep breath, trying not to smash the phone. "I don't recall the story."

"Well let's see: our heroine is Abele Maspar who crashlands on Kranakin one dark and stormy night…"

The writer stopped listening. *Now* he remembered, after all, nobody ever forgot their first true love. He'd been eighteen, and Adele Mason had gone to the same sixth form college. He'd really, really, fancied her. And when she delivered that final no he'd expressed the soul-crushing rejection in the only way an eighteen-year-old literary geek could, by writing a… "Oh crap," the writer whispered.

"So you see," the editor continued cheerfully. "What Abele makes that poor worm do really does qualify for the alien sex category, wouldn't you agree?"

"You can't publish it. You simply can't. Tell you what; I'll write you a completely new story. No, two new short literary sci-f– *SF* stories. And I won't even ask for payment. You're quite right, *Singularity Crystal* deserves all the support I can give it. I'll even mention it on Radio 4 next time I'm presenting."

"I haven't heard you on that arts show for ages, I thought they'd dumped you."

"No, I'm just resting. So, how about that for a deal?

I'm going on a huge publicity tour, I can cross-promote the magazine."

"Well, I'd like to, but we're already at the typesetting stage, that's expensive."

"I can pay for the new stories to be typeset instead. It would be my pleasure."

"That's a very kind offer. I'm happy to see you thinking that way. You see, I regard the effort I put in to young authors as an investment in the future. Specifically, my future. You don't really think I want to spend my best years reading through endless clichés about aliens and wormholes and vampire robots and brass bikinis because I'm some kind of demented masochist. No, like I say, this is an investment for me. Ninety per cent of that investment comes to nothing, but the other ten per cent… ah now that's what makes it all so worthwhile. Especially in retirement."

"What are you saying?"

"I'm saying – and this is not one of your metaphors – that I own 'Mutant Worms'. I paid a huge personal price for it and all the other dross I've read, and there's twenty-one years of interest accumulated."

The writer shuddered, but there really was no way out. He couldn't bear to think what the TLS would say, and as for the *Guardian*… No! It couldn't be allowed to happen. "I would be delighted to buy back the 'Mutant Worms of Kranakin'," he said faintly. "Did you have a price in mind?"

"Why my dear boy, that's so generous of you. Think of a figure…"

"Yes?"

"Then go quantum on it."